THE UGLY STEPSISTER

MEGAN VAN DYKE

THE UGLY STEPSISTER

MEGAN VAN DYKE

CITY OWL
PRESS

THE UGLY STEPSISTER
Reimagined Fairy Tales, Book 2

CITY OWL PRESS
www.cityowlpress.com

Cover Design by MiblArt. All stock photos licensed appropriately.

Edited by Heather McCorkle.

For information on subsidiary rights, please contact the publisher at info@cityowlpress.com.

Hardback Edition ISBN: 978-1-64898-191-3
Paperback Edition ISBN: 978-1-64898-190-6
Digital Edition ISBN: 978-1-64898-189-0

Printed in the United States of America

PRAISE FOR MEGAN VAN DYKE

"Van Dyke puts an imaginative spin on "Cinderella" in her second Reimagined Fairy Tales romance, The Ugly Stepsister, which takes place after the traditional tale's happy ever after. Van Dyke keeps readers guessing with a clever, twisty plot that proves stories are always filtered through the point of view of their tellers. The hero and heroine make a swoon-worthy pair, and supporting characters add color, especially rebel Mina and her brothers. This adult fairy tale will captivate fans of fantasy romance." — *Publisher's Weekly*

"A fun, sexy, swashbuckling read. Hook is a swoony, caring, protective surprise of a hero, and he meets his match in the dauntless and sassy Tink, who'll go toe-to-toe with a pirate any day. Magical creatures, seafaring adventures, plot twists and turns, steamy kisses (and more!) await in this exciting, reimagined version of the story of Captain Hook and Tinker Bell." — *Amanda Bouchet, USA Today Bestselling author of The Kingmaker Chronicles*

"A seductive reimagined Neverland fairytale dusted with magic, passion, and adventure that will hook readers from page one!" — *InD'Tale Magazine*

"Such a wonderful retelling. Fast paced, well plotted, full of glorious pirate action and a great enemies to lovers romance at the heart of it." – *The SFFRomCast Podcast*

"Van Dyke's action-packed debut puts a sexy, adult spin on Tinker Bell and Captain Hook. On this daring adventure, mermaids become the least of their problems, as Hook and Tink come under threat from their mutual enemy, Blackbeard. As they spend time together, they learn the complicated truth behind each others' storied pasts—Van Dyke does a good job making Hook and his crew sympathetic—and a fiery passion grows. The steamy scenes, explosive battles, and adventurous treasure hunt make for a gripping tale." — *Publisher's Weekly*

"Packed with steamy romance, adventure, and an unforgettable cast of characters, Megan Van Dyke's clever reimagining of Peter Pan, centering Tinker Bell and Captain Hook, is an absolute treasure. The writing is effortless and draws you in immediately, leaving you fully immersed in a fantastical world that feels both familiar and fresh." — *Paulette Kennedy, International Best-selling Author of Parting The Veil*

"Keep your hands and feet inside the ride at all times. Ladies and Gentlemen we are going to Neverland. But not the Neverland you remember from your childhood. Hook and Tink are amazing in this new twist on a classic." — *Melody Caraballo, author of Unhinged Witch*

"Megan Van Dyke's story resets the balance of Neverland, turning an imaginary playland into a world that lives and breathes through every scene. Highly recommend!" — *K.J. Harrowick, author of Bloodflower*

"A delightful, sexy romp set in a fresh, yet familiar fantasy world. Perfect for anyone who has shipped Tinker Bell and Captain Hook!" — *Jeffe Kennedy, award-winning author of Dark Wizard and The Forgotten Empires*

"A fun read that hooks you from chapter one with vivid characters and a smooth, fluid writing style." — *Desirée Niccoli, author of Called to the Deep*

"Megan Van Dyke just became a one-click author for me." — *Ashley King, Author of Painting the Lines and Forever After*

"A fun and sassy retelling that's impossible to put down." — *Kat Turner, author of Hex, Love, & Rock and Roll*

To Reed
Thank you for loving me for who I am.

The kingdom rejoiced when the prince chose Ella to be his bride. A commoner, one of their own, plucked from the misery of her life to live in the castle as his one true love.

It was the thing of songs. Of stories told to children.

The people's affection only grew as Cinderella shared the terrors of her recent years. The wicked stepmother and stepsisters who'd bullied her, torn her gowns, forced her to work the fields, and called her names. They even made her sleep next to the fireplace and called her "Cinderella" for the soot that clung to her face and hair when she woke.

And because she was young, and beautiful, and the prince loved her, the people believed every single one of her lies.

1

*T*reason was a tedious affair. Anna peeked through the bushes, watching the guards take their sweet time setting up camp. She'd already been waiting there for hours before they showed up and was truly desperate to move something, anything. The few bugs creeping along her clothing had almost become friends. Almost.

After these last few months scrounging a living working the fields of generous farmers, ones happy for the extra hands and who didn't look too closely, she should be used to dirt and grime. Still, too many years of reasonably comfortable living were hard to shake, even if that life was gone. The loneliness was worse. She still woke every morning expecting to see her sister Charlotte at her side, only to have reality punch her in the chest.

Tingling numbness burned in her leg. How she longed to move it, to reposition her body just a bit. *Too risky.* If those guards managed to nab her, she'd be done. There'd be no help coming for her sister and mother, and definitely none for her. Anna watched the guards move in the dimming sunset slanting through the trees. The biggest one had already taken up his post by the supply wagon while the others got a fire crackling nearby and laid out bedrolls on the packed ground.

They seemed to favor this spot on the trek north to the fairy godmother's workhouse, almost always stopping here for a night of rest for both men and horses before continuing on. Anna wrinkled her nose, the only movement she'd allow herself. Stupid, that's what they were, forming such a regular pattern that she'd been able to figure out after only a few weeks of watching the road.

Or maybe they'd already grown so confident as not to worry about robbers or dissenters. After all, everyone in the city was *so* enamored with their new queen, the graceful, beautiful, and all-around charming Cinderella. Anna choked back a snort. If only they knew.

Though she had been like them too—once.

Soon the guards would be so distracted by food, they'd let their attention drift. *Hopefully. Maybe.* If not, she'd have to wait and see if the guard on watch slipped up and nodded off or went to relieve himself in the woods. She leaned forward, pressing her face ever so slightly into the branches for a better view. No matter what, she couldn't let them catch her. They might kill her outright if they figured out who she really was. Worse, they might take her to the queen—her wicked stepsister.

Cinderella. Cinderella. The people praised the beautiful commoner-turned-queen. It was enough to make Anna's blood boil.

Their *poor* queen. She'd only been married to the prince for such a short time before he and his father, the king, fell ill. The king went quick. A royal wedding and a funeral in the same season. Such terrible luck. The prince ascended the throne and declared Cinderella his queen. A month later and he was gone too. Anna rolled her eyes. As if a mysterious illness would touch the royal family and a few of their close supporters but leave most of the city unharmed. But then, the people seemed to believe all Cinderella's lies thanks to her faithful fairy godmother. *Tricky witch.*

The whole kingdom knew the stories about the horrible treatment Cinderella received at the hands of her stepmother and stepsisters before Prince Nikolaus whisked her away to become his bride. But no one knew the truth—Anna's truth. Those evil deeds were true, but it was Ella, with the help of her fairy godmother, who wrought them upon her family.

Savory scents of food roasting over the fire made her mouth flood with saliva. Her stomach let out a little rumble that set her teeth on edge. How long since she'd had a proper meal? Anna glanced at her arms.

Though she could barely see them in the darkening shadows, it didn't take sight to know the toll hunger had taken on her body, carving down her curves until she was tall and thin like the gangly young man she pretended to be.

Anna fought the urge to reach for her hair and run her fingertips along the short, brittle ends. It'd been her pride and joy once, even with its dull brown color. Muddy and plain, Ella always said, and Anna was ugly as a pig wallowing in it. She hunched ever so slightly, the old words still powerful after so long. Though Ella had mocked her hair—her everything in the end—Anna had loved the way it cascaded over her shoulders and down her back.

No more though. Like so much else, it had had to go.

Laughter and conversation rose up around the campfire. The trek north was always more relaxed, more lighthearted for the delivery boys. After all, the wagons had already delivered their goods. Hopefully, they weren't too empty, or it wouldn't be worth the risk to sneak in.

Every week, a new shipment of potions was carted down from the fairy godmother's workhouse to the castle. And food and goods for the people, of course, elsewise what would they lace the potions into? Everyone loved gifts, especially free food, and that was what the queen counted on. A few drops here, a little there, and she controlled much of the population. Walking around the city, it was easy to see which people accepted the tainted gifts and spot the skeptical few who avoided them.

Would the guard's food be tainted? Could she steal some? A little morsel wouldn't appear amiss. *Maybe just a crust of bread or a small chunk of meat.* Her stomach rumbled again. It'd been so long since she had anything decent. Long gone were the days when she and Charlotte would make little cakes together. Anna pressed her lips closed and swallowed down the saliva building in her mouth. Even Ella had joined in once their parents married—at least, before Ella's father died and everything became darker than the deepest of hells.

You've got bigger things to worry about, she reprimanded herself.

Her pulse quickened as the guard near the wagons wandered over to join the others by the fire. This was it, her chance. The distraction of the food and the din of conversation might be the best cover she'd get. Not to mention the sun had slipped below the horizon, painting the world in shadow. Burning tingles raced up her legs as she finally moved them.

She nearly groaned in mixed pain and relief, rubbing her leg to get the feeling back into it. No sense trying to sneak in on a leg not fully working. And running away when the time came? *Hah!*

Slowly, far too slowly for her fraying nerves, feeling returned. *Should have done this sooner.* She gritted her teeth over the error as she edged out from her hiding place.

The guards were eating yet. There was still time.

Anna froze as something large, human-sized, dropped from a tree off to the right. Every inch of her went still as death. Her heart leaped into her throat. She couldn't breathe and didn't dare turn her head.

But the guards didn't react. Nor did they rush to arrest her. The form —a man?—didn't notice her either, just moved like a fleeting shadow to the side of one wagon away from the fire.

Anna blinked in disbelief. *Hells. Are they planning to rob the guards too?* If there was anything useful in there—notes for the fairy godmother, a spare uniform, leftover potion, something that would get her a step closer to freeing her family or taking down her wicked stepsister—it was hers. *Damn it.*

A rational person would run. Even as she slipped the hidden dagger from her boot, she battled the desire to turn and sprint through the trees before anyone could notice her.

But this chance wouldn't come again. Whether this idiot got caught or not was anyone's guess, but the chances of the guards noticing something amiss, or missing later, was high. Once they did, her opportunity would be gone. They'd change up their routine, have more men on watch, or take a new route. All her days of watching, waiting, and plotting would be for nothing.

She couldn't have that, not with her mother and sister held prisoner for falsified crimes against the queen. It should have been Anna too. Her fingers flexed on the dagger. The guards meant to capture them all. They would have if Charlotte hadn't distracted them long enough for her to run. *Charlotte.* Regret twisted through her, threatening to tie her up where she stood. She'd never forget her sister shoving her away, screaming at her to run. Her anguished cry and that of their mother were a constant dull echo in the quiet. That and shame at being the one who ran rather than the one who sacrificed herself for her sister's sake.

Anna pushed down the terrifying emotions that had crippled her for weeks. No more.

The man edged around to the back of the wagon, keeping behind the wheels as best he could. She held her breath as she watched him pull open the flap at the back. One quick peek, then he shimmied inside far easier than he should for someone his size.

No way was he getting first pick. Anna sped through the night to the wagon's side, dancing on her toes and dodging leaves and sticks that might give her away. Not for the first time she wished to be a magical creature—maybe one of the pixies, with their lithe forms and wings. That would make it easier to sneak around, possibly give her an advantage. But no, she was just a clumsy human like pretty much everyone else in the kingdom. Once she reached the wagon, Anna stepped into the shadow of the wheel, as the man had done, and pressed her ear against the wooden side. Between her pounding heart and the guards laughing at something one of them said, she couldn't hear a darn thing inside.

Somewhere nearby, a bird twittered.

Anna scooted one small step at a time to the corner. Just before she reached it, another birdcall answered, this one so close it made her hair stand on end.

Stupid bird. If one of the guards had looked for it, they could have seen her. She'd have to wait. Soon the other thief would come out of there. She'd stop him and—

Shit. And what? She could smack herself. He looked bigger than her. Probably armed and up to no good.

"Hey!" one of the guards snapped.

Anna sucked in a breath, willing herself to fade into the shadows.

"Quiet," the guard ordered. "You see that?"

Oh no. Her heart plummeted. The hilt of the dagger pressed into her skin. She adjusted her stance, ready to flee.

"What?" someone else asked.

"Something in the woods."

The woods?

"Scared a' some old wolves?" another mocked, letting out a shrill howl as his companions laughed.

A loud smack sounded just before the laughing man roared, "Hey!"

"Shut it," a commanding voice snapped. "All of you."

Anna leaned on her toes, stretching until she could just see around the edge of the wagon. Her pulse hammered in her throat as she took in the men sitting and standing around the fire, all stiff-backed and on alert. The smallest sound would set them off.

"I swear, man," the first spoke again, pacing back and forth near the flickering flames. "Something's out there." He gestured to the woods opposite the wagons. But still, how long until they turned her way?

Any darn minute.

Anna slipped back behind the wagon, prepared to flee, when a hand clamped over her mouth.

2

"*D*on't say a word," Will hissed in the stranger's ear. The last thing they needed was this idiot giving them away and ruining everything.

He'd reached for his bow and knocked an arrow the moment he saw the form slip from the bushes and move toward the wagons. A threat, that's what he'd seen. Too many of those these days, and any one could be his undoing. He'd aimed at the stranger, ready to fire. One deep breath in, release on the out—except something had stayed his hand. What, he couldn't quite say. Maybe that the person was too small and lean to be a guard on patrol. Not to mention a guard would have alerted the others, not slunk through the shadows. One whistle, and a guard could have had the wagon surrounded before his friend had any clue he'd been seen.

The guards spoke again, a few venturing toward the thick trees by the sound of things. Good, at least the direction they planned was working.

Will pulled the stranger tight against his chest. They didn't resist, didn't even move, as if frozen in fright. With his other hand, he angled his dagger toward their throat. "One sound, and I slit your throat. Hear me?"

The words tasted bitter on his tongue. Threatening others would never sit right with him. The old him would have balked at the idea, but so much had changed over the past year. He barely knew the person he was anymore.

The stranger gave the slightest nod as they shivered. It wasn't due to the weather on this unseasonably warm night. They were terrified.

They should be.

Something pricked his stomach, causing him to suck in a sharp breath.

"Hurt me, and I gut you," the stranger whispered.

He ground his teeth together. *Damn it.* He hadn't seen the blade. Even Koen's skill with medical herbs might not save him if this thief struck true. And that assumed Koen got out of the wagon before the guards noticed him. The stranger was slight in form but not in height. Short hair, from what he could see. No whiskers tickled his skin. A boy?

Probably an orphan or a runaway trying to steal a little gold. Who else would be so stupid as to approach a caravan belonging to the queen? Still, Will couldn't let him mess this up. He and his companions had one chance. Once word got out about a caravan being robbed, they'd up the guard. It'd be harder, if not impossible, to steal potions. Koen wagered if he could get his hands on the stuff, he might be able to figure out how it worked, or at least how to fight it. And they needed every advantage they could get. It was the best plan he and his companions had.

It'd taken weeks as it was to convince their man on the inside to slip one box of the stuff aside on delivery day. The old man wouldn't smuggle it out to them. That was too risky. The guards checked every worker who came in and out of the castle, and to risk the queen's ire was to risk being sent to the fairy godmother's workhouse up north. *Once you went there...* His fist tightened on the dagger in his hand. No one came back.

The best the old man would do for them was make sure the box got added to the return trip, its contents intact. From there, he didn't want to know how they got it, if they did, and they sure weren't about to tell him. Their deal was done. Best they never saw each other again.

Shouts rang out near the campfire.

The stranger flinched, the tip of his dagger retreating just enough for Will to breathe.

"I told you!" one guard shouted. Boots thumped across the ground.

Will held his breath. *This better work.* If not, they were in for one mess of a fight, assuming this kid didn't try to end him before it even began. Will had argued to be the one to sneak in, but Koen, always the level-headed one, had a point. If their plan went awry, Will was the only one skilled enough with bow and blade to save their asses.

Metal scraped against leather as guards drew their swords.

"What's that?" a guard asked.

"Smoke?" another guard said.

The barest hint of it caught in the firelight between the wagons.

Will had to try to salvage this. "If I drop my dagger, will you lower yours?" he whispered.

The stranger gave a jerking nod. Will swallowed the tightness in his throat. *Good enough.*

In one quick move, he shoved the dagger into its sheath and pushed the boy away from him.

"Cover your mouth with your shirt." Will jerked the kerchief around his neck up until the sweaty cloth covered his mouth and nose.

"What?" the boy asked in a whisper.

"Do it, kid." He grabbed his bow. There wasn't time to worry about him.

"I'm not a kid." The boy's hands balled on his hips.

Fine. Will grunted as he pulled an arrow from the quiver across his back. The young man could pass out with the guards. What did it matter? Guilt stabbed through him hot and sharp. Except it did matter. He couldn't leave an innocent out here. The guards would kill him, or worse, send him to the fairy godmother. He twisted on his heel toward the stranger. "Cover your—"

In the faint light, he could just make out the shirt covering the young man's mouth and nose. Would it be thick enough? The back of his neck heated. *Damn it.* He reached in his pocket and pulled out a spare kerchief. *Always carry a spare. Always be prepared. Never let the beast catch you unawares.* The old hunting lessons chimed through his head, but they worked in this situation too.

"Use this." He shoved it at the young man. "Do it."

He didn't wait to see if he obeyed. If he was wise, he'd run off into the woods and never look back. One quick glance around the side of the wagon showed men on the ground, unmoving. His arm flexed, arrow pulled back and at the ready.

Deep breath. In. Out. Slow. Careful. Just like hunting deer.

Except it wasn't.

He couldn't forget that first life he took months ago. First human life anyway. It haunted him. But it was kill or be killed, and he couldn't die yet, not until he avenged his family.

Never look your prey in the eyes, he'd been told as a boy, just before his first hunt. *If you do, you won't be able to send your arrow straight and sure. A bad shot that wounds the poor beast but doesn't kill? Well, son, that's a terrible sin.*

Will exhaled a heavy breath as he finished counting the bodies. He wouldn't need to send his arrows straight and true. Not today.

The strange concoction Koen developed worked just as they'd planned and knocked out all the guards. Will used the toe of his boot to roll one man away from the fire. How long it'd last, they weren't sure.

"Clear," he called, just loud enough to be heard by his companions still in hiding.

The wagon groaned as Koen hopped from the back, a cloth secured over his mouth and nose. How the tall man had managed to be so careful and quiet sneaking in there was beyond him. Will was dubious of his abilities, at best. Koen could be precise when he cared to be, though Will had only seen that side of him seated at his workbench. At least he was quieter than Koen's brother, Brandt, who thundered his way through the underbrush like a bull.

Will nearly groaned as he turned to find the stout younger brother shoving low-hanging branches out of his way. His muscled form and thick beard could intimidate almost any man in a back alley, but a troop of the queen's guard? He snorted. *Hardly.*

"Got what we came for?" Will whispered to Koen, ignoring Brandt as he leaned over a downed guard to search him.

Koen wiped at the spectacles he'd pulled from his pocket before placing them on his nose. Will shook his head in impatience. These siblings were going to drive him mad before they were done. Only then did Koen reach back into the wagon and pull out a small box. "Yep. This should do."

Good. With any luck, no one would notice the missing box of potions that shouldn't have been there to begin with and they would assume it a robbery, nothing more. He knelt beside a guard. His nose wrinkled at the stench of sweat and grime wafting off the body as he searched for anything of value. Will swallowed the acidic taste at the back of his throat. The guards had never been so foul during the old king's reign. He'd have remembered.

"You're stealing potions?"

The stranger's voice hit him like a punch to the chest. He hunched in on himself before raising his head to take in the young man who stood way too close to Koen for anyone's good.

"Who in the blazes—" Brandt pulled his sword and advanced on the newcomer. All the excitement of distracting the guards and tossing the knockout smoke their way still had him on edge—his shoulders set, aggression in every heavy step he took toward the skinny stranger.

"Hells." Koen jumped back, nearly dropping the precious box.

Will's hand tightened around the small bag of coins he plucked off the guard. He assumed the young man would have run off. An error. A terrible one. "Get out of here, kid."

"I'm not a— Yowch!" The stranger jumped, twisting around to the lithe form behind him.

Mina. Will smacked a hand against his forehead before dragging it down his weary face. Could no one ever listen to him?

"You were supposed to stay hidden," Koen said to his sister.

Mina adjusted her stance, her arm wobbling, as she pointed her little blade toward the young man. "I'm helping." He didn't need light to see the deep blush creeping across her face.

Mina had spent most of her fourteen-odd years as Koen's assistant, never using a blade other than to chop herbs or cook a meal. Or so her older brothers said. They'd given her a dagger for protection as a last resort, nothing more.

The stranger had her in height and likely in muscle too. Even if he weren't skilled with a blade, he could probably take her in a fight. Not all of them though.

"Drop it," Mina hissed, glaring at the young man's dagger.

Wisely, the stranger raised his hands and let the blade fall to the ground.

"What'll we do with 'im?" Brandt asked, tapping the flat of his blade against his palm.

Will cut him a hard look from the corner of his eye. Brandt would be lucky not to cut a finger off doing that. Strength and brawn he had plenty of. Skill with a blade? Not so much. Clumsy as Brandt was, Will had half a mind to rip the pommel from his hand before he hurt someone.

The young man looked between them all, stiff and wide-eyed in the flickering light of the fire. His clothes hung loose. His arms might have some strength, the kind gained from laboring in the fields, but not the brawn of anyone used to wielding a sword or heavy tools.

His eyes, though... Even with the distance separating them, it was hard to look away. Knowledge and awareness flickered there. Maturity. Determination. And something else...something deeper.

"Should I teach 'im a lesson?" Brandt continued.

Will shook his head and held up his hand toward his companion. "What do you want, boy? Gold?" He jangled the little bag he'd acquired off a guard. It wasn't much, but it'd keep the stranger fed a little while.

"I—"

"Spit it out," Koen said.

The young man backed away, his hands up, until he hit a wagon. The slight touch had him leaping forward as if set upon from behind again. *A jumpy one. Definitely not an experienced thief.*

"You snuck up to the wagons," Will said. "What were you after?"

"I—" He looked between them all again, swallowed. "I hoped to steal a uniform. Maybe some information, potions..." His gaze darted, unwilling to meet Will's as he neared.

"They don't carry extra uniforms." Wherever this stranger was from, he knew nothing about the way things were done in the castle or any part of the king's—his lips pressed thin—the *queen's* military. Probably a poor farmer's kid, but he should be after food then. Or money. "Why do you need one?"

The young man's eyes snapped to his, all fire and fury hiding behind his glaze of fear. Will's brows rose as his chin notched higher. "They imprisoned my family. I plan to free them."

Brandt let out a deep guffaw.

"Shh," Koen bit out.

"That's very brave," Mina whispered, just loud enough to be heard. She'd lowered her weapon. Will bit back a sigh and shook his head. She had much to learn, but a deeper part of him couldn't help but agree with her observation. There was something admirable in the young man's foolishness that called to his own stubborn heart.

"Brave but foolish," Koen said. "He's seen us." Koen's level gaze settled on Will.

And therein lay the problem. Even with cloth pulled up over half their faces, they were a unique group, enough to get their descriptions plastered on Wanted posters all over the kingdom. That was a complication they couldn't have. Will's chest burned, and he fought the urge to rub at it.

"I won't tell," the young man said, perhaps sensing his thoughts.

This was no kid as he'd initially thought. Now that Will looked closer, he was sure *young man* was a more apt description, even if he lacked whiskers and his voice wasn't that deep. Neither was Koen's, and he was older than all of them. Maybe it was the way he held himself, or the determined set of his jaw.

"You're against the queen? So am I," the young man said. "We're on the same side."

Sides? There were none. Only the queen, Cinderella, those who followed her, those she enchanted to follow her, and the few, like them, who slipped through the shadows like rats pretending to follow her.

None of that would change until they could take her down, and one young man wasn't going to mess that up.

"I can help." The stranger straightened, a poor attempt to make himself more intimidating. "Let me prove it."

Will's fingers slipped over the hilt of the dagger at his side. The young man locked gazes with him once again. Something twisted in his chest, and he gritted his teeth at the battle raging there.

He'd seen his eyes, his determination, his fear, and something that reminded him far too much of himself.

A low groan cracked through the air behind him, raising every hair on his body.

Shit. Already?

Brandt's gruff expression faded into one of still terror. "Should I—" He glanced at his blade.

No. He wouldn't ask that of his friend, of the man who saved his life. And killing a defenseless man, a queen's man who was probably poisoned with magic like so many of the kingdom into believing her lies? He wouldn't. He couldn't.

"We run."

Mina made a small sound and bolted for the woods. Koen grabbed the box and was quick on her heels. Brandt's gaze shifted to the young man who stooped to pick up his dagger and slide it back in his boot—the most unthreatening act possible.

Damn it all.

"He's coming with us."

Before the stranger could argue, Will grabbed his hand and hauled him toward the waiting tree line.

3

*a*nna's lungs burned like she'd swallowed fire.

Of all the ways she'd seen this night play out in her head, this possibility had never developed. Someone else robbing the wagon train the same night as her? Getting dragged into their flight from the guards?

She'd have laughed if she had any breath left.

Her cheek stung as another branch clawed at her face. They'd been moving at a steady jog or run, depending on terrain, for ages. Though she hated to admit it, all of them were in better shape than her. There hadn't been much occasion to run growing up—at least, not in recent years. It wasn't something well-bred women did, or so her mother said. Such reckless pastimes of running down the docks and playing in the sea, hoping to spy the merfolk, vanished when her mother remarried a well-to-do merchant years after her father died. Mother insisted her daughters become proper ladies and trained them in more practical skills: cooking, cleaning, sewing, tending a garden, music, painting. The things her mother tutored her, Charlotte, and even Ella in never ended. She insisted they were qualities necessary to attract a good husband. One like the prince. Not that the addle-headed pretty boy wanted anything more than a lovely face. He made that clear enough at the royal ball, fawning all over Ella like a dog in heat.

Sometimes, Anna almost felt like he deserved his bride and the death she almost certainly had bestowed upon him.

Almost.

A man like that wasn't the kind she dreamed about anyway. Back when the future seemed to have endless possibilities, especially after Ella and the terror she wrought left their home, she dreamed about a charming man who'd see her not for the beauty she lacked but the woman within.

Maybe one like the man who'd dragged her into the forest. Her chest swelled at the thought. He said not a word to her—none of them spoke—but he'd hauled her through the creek when she thought the water might wash her away over a boulder-strewn ledge and helped her up each time she slipped on old, rotting leaves or tree roots.

Every time their hands touched, a little thrill rushed under her skin. It was enough that the embarrassment from her poor skill navigating the woods was a worthy price to pay to earn his assistance.

He acted like a gentleman, even if he didn't look like one with his too-long brown hair and the rambling beard covering his lower face. He was a far cry from the clean-shaven faces and trimmed, styled locks the nobles preferred. Well, except for the whole threatening to slit her throat thing. That she could have done without. Though had the situation been reversed, she'd have probably done the same. Judging by his reactions afterward, he wouldn't have done it if it came to it. That was one reason she'd asked them to bring her along. They were against the queen, same as her. If she helped them, maybe they'd return the favor. The Mother knew she needed any help she could get.

They ought to help after ruining her one plan, however laughable they thought it.

Heat rushed to her face for the millionth time as she stole a glance at the man at her side. Of course, he thought she was a boy. She shook her head. That was fine. Romance was off the table, a heaping helping of revenge and saving her family in its place. Nothing else mattered. Not really. At least her disguise worked. She'd never had much womanly figure anyway, so it was easy to pull off. Remembering to lower her voice a bit was the tricky part. But she'd never had a high, musical voice like Ella. Yet another thing her stepsister teased her over.

Finally, they slowed.

Anna nearly cried in relief. Sweat slicked her skin, sticking the baggy clothes to her in ways too risky for her guise. She wore bindings over her small chest to conceal the little bit of womanly shape she had, but still the loose clothing helped. The less people saw, the better.

"You all right?" the man finally asked.

She couldn't manage words. Not while sucking in one deep breath after another, so she nodded instead.

At least he hadn't called her "kid" again. Her teeth clamped together. If he did that again, he'd have another thing coming. Bigger than her or not, her fist would tell him exactly how she felt about that title. *I am a grown woman, for goodness' sake!* She was almost a year older than her stepsister, the queen. *Okay, I dress like a young man, yes, but "kid"?* It had to be because it was dark. She pursed her lips. That's the reason he called her that. Romance might be off the table given her situation, but it didn't stop her foolish heart from wanting. He was handsome, in a rugged, unkempt sort of way, and she was still a woman no matter what she played at.

"We'll rest here tonight," he said.

Anna took in their surroundings and the small, flat expanse of ground near the rocky cliffside where they'd stopped. Her pack, which she'd managed to snag from its hiding place at the start of their flight, slid down her shoulders to plop into the dirt.

"No fire," he continued. "Too risky. We'll set out at first light."

"And where are we going?" she asked.

Four heads snapped her way as if they'd only just remembered they'd dragged her along with them.

"Ye're going home," the shorter, gruff one said as he folded his muscled arms in front of his chest.

Anna fought the urge to reach for her braid, which no longer existed. "I don't have a home to go back to."

The admission still stung, hollowing out her chest and leaving her raw and aching in a way that had nothing to do with the flight through the forest. Though her words were only partially true. The home where she'd lived after her mother married Ella's father still existed, but she could never go back there. She'd snuck back only once since the guards came to arrest them shortly after the king's death. It'd been a huge risk, slipping in unseen with the watchman posted in the woods, just waiting to see if she'd be foolish enough to return.

She didn't linger long, just a few moments to grab a few clothes and a sack full of food to sate her gnawing hunger and take one last look at the little painting of her birth father, whose memory had grown blurry around the edges in the years since he passed.

"He needs us," the girl, at least a handful of years younger than her, if not more, implored, pulling her back to the present.

Her appearance was similar to the heavily bearded, gruff one—dark brown, almost black hair, tanned skin. *A brother, perhaps?* If there was sympathy to be gained, it'd be from her. It didn't hurt that she reminded Anna of her younger self, quiet and shy compared to her sister Charlotte with her loud voice and occasional gruff words, nor was she outgoing and in constant need of attention like Ella.

"You said you were trying to get your family back?" Her long, braided hair, so like how Anna's used to be, slipped over one shoulder as she cocked her head to the side. "We are too. The queen took our—"

"Mina," the spectacled one snapped, shushing her. He adjusted his glasses and turned his attention to Anna. Moonlight highlighted the grey near his temples. "You said you can help. How so?"

Anna shifted her gaze back to Mina, relaxing her features into what she hoped begged sympathy. "I used to work in the fields at the home where the queen grew up."

A soft gasp slipped from the girl's parted lips.

It was true, though maybe not the way they perceived it. Anna had loved tending the plants and helping bring in the harvests. Her stepsister Ella had loved to mock the dirt under her fingernails and smeared on her clothes, but no amount of eye rolls or barbed comments could keep Anna away from getting her hands dirty working with living things. She loved it, dirt and all. It was probably why her flower garden was one of the first things Ella destroyed.

"I know her a bit," she continued. If anyone could truly know her stepsister's wicked heart. "It may help."

"Hah." The girl's brother spat on the ground at his feet. "Knew this one was trouble. Probably spying on us. Gonna run right back to the queen."

"No!" Anna raised her hands in the air, slightly cursing the way her voice rose in pitch. *Heavens and hells, that isn't it at all.* "She was horrible. The things she did to her stepsisters, to others." The transgressions started small—the pulled-up flowers, dirt sprinkled on cakes, outbursts. She was just a poor young woman in mourning. It would pass, many said. But it only got worse. Few knew about Mother's *stumble* from the ladder that broke her arm. Then there was what happened to Charlotte's precious cat...

The gruff thief made to speak again, but the taller one, the one who stirred the desires she tried to force away and who'd yet to speak since he asked if she was all right, waved him off and stepped in front of her.

"It's said the queen's sisters were the ones who were cruel to *her*." He leaned in, looking her up and down, seeing way too much. "Abused her. Called her names. Forced her to sleep in the ashen fire to stay warm at night. Isn't that where she got the name Cinderella?"

Each accusation had her nails digging harder into her palms, nearly drawing blood. Heat raced under her skin until she could no longer meet his gaze and had to look away. She'd heard the stories. *Oh yes.* They'd spread from the moment Cinderella wed Prince Nikolaus. Every horrible thing Ella ever did to them she told everyone about—except she said Anna and Charlotte were responsible for the misdeeds. Or her kind mother, who'd never hurt a soul and had cared for Ella like one of her own, especially after her husband passed and left the young woman in her care. That was the worst of all. Her mother might be a bit soft in the head sometimes, prone to bouts of daydreaming, but could she intentionally harm someone? Never. Ella even took the name Cinderella, painting herself a sympathetic victim for all the kingdom.

The days after the wedding had been some of the worst and best of Anna's life. On the one hand, everyone thought her a villain. But on the other, they were finally free. Ella was gone, out of the house, off to her castle. The lies would fade in time, they always did, and every day wouldn't be spent walking on eggshells and trying to guard her heart and her family. Inside the walls of their home, it was peaceful, happy. For a short time.

Until news arrived of the king's untimely death a few, short months later. Then, everything changed.

Anna took a chance, a leap of faith that these people might see her side, even if they didn't know who she was. "Cinderella was the horrible one. The things she said her family did to her…" Anna shook her head, trying to block out the memories screaming in her mind. "*She* did those things to *them*. Some on her own, some with the help of her fairy godmother and her magic. They couldn't speak out against her. They didn't dare, especially not once she married the prince."

The man looked away, his mouth wrinkling in distaste—for her or the queen?

"Surely, if the queen took your family, you understand how terrible she can be," Anna pushed on, looking from one to another. Everything in her screamed in silence. *Believe me. Someone.*

It'd be so much easier if she could tell them who she was, but the price on her head was the highest in the kingdom. There was nothing the queen wouldn't pay to have her "horrible, ugly stepsister" brought to justice. Anna, the one who got away, the one who knew the truth, whose face was on posters around the city. It was why she'd chopped off her hair, dressed like a man, and never took the time to scrub all the dirt off her face. Even if they disliked the queen, a reward like that was too much for most people to ignore.

The shorter man sat down on a rock, his arms still crossed. "Sounds about right. You c'n just look at the queen's haughty, pointed nose and tell that."

Finally. Thank you! She wanted to scream. Of all the places she expected support, he was the last, but she'd take whatever she could get.

"What do you think, huntsman?" the oldest one asked, turning to the man inching ever closer to her from the shadows.

Anna stiffened as he drew near, still looking her up and down as if he could see past her disguise. *"Huntsman," they called him.* With his ragged, wild looks and the bow still strapped across his back, he looked the part. Not to mention that he'd managed to hide in the forest and sneak up on her back at the wagons. His experience navigating the woods supported that title too. She craned her neck, staring him down in challenge—and if she were honest, in admiration. Wild though his appearance might be, it enticed her too. She'd never favored the pampered, perfumed men that Ella fawned over. A man of the woods though? Anna found that infinitely more attractive.

"What's your name?" he asked.

"An—" *Shit.* She snapped off her words. She'd been so distracted by her thoughts—by him—she'd nearly spilled the truth. "Ansel. It's Ansel." She swallowed at the taste of her birth father's name on her tongue. No one had known him here. They hadn't come to live near the castle until a few years after his death when her mother remarried the traveling merchant, Ella's father.

"Well, Ansel, you better be as helpful as you claim."

Anna let out a breath and rocked back onto her heels. They wouldn't turn her over to the queen or cast her out into the night—wherever exactly they were.

Mina rushed forward and then stopped a few feet short before dropping her gaze to the ground. Not even the night could hide the blush that crept across her cheeks. "I'm Mina," she said, as if Anna hadn't already picked up on that.

The girl twisted her hands behind her back. "These are my brothers Koen..." She pointed to the one with glasses. "...and Brandt." The stocky one nodded her way.

A family. Siblings, like the one she'd lost. Anna swallowed down the tightness in her throat.

"Not him?" Anna asked with a quick glance at the man who'd backed off a few paces. *Thank goodness.* Her heart finally slowed its rhythm now that she was out from under his close inspection. He saw too much, and something about him made her far too clumsy.

"Nah," Brandt said before Mina could gather herself. "Found that one half-dead in the woods. Took him home, and he stayed like a lost pup."

The huntsman cut him a hard look. "Who's kept meat on the table these past months?"

"Guess ya haven't been totally useless."

Anna mimicked the man's actions from earlier. Every step she took closer to him, he drew up taut like the strings on his bow. With all her focus on him, it was easy to ignore the cramps in her legs from their hasty retreat. He was used to being the predator, the huntsman of the forest. He wasn't prepared for the *boy* he called "kid" to put him on his heels. A delicious thrill ran though her with every step, just as strong and alluring as when they touched during the trek.

"And what's your name, Huntsman?"

His throat bobbed. "Will."

She forced a half-smile, hoping for one in return. What would he look like without a scowl on his face? Unfortunately, his grimace didn't budge.

Unable to hold the carefree ruse, Anna turned away and retreated to the shelter of the rocks. Mina gave her a shy wave and gestured to a space next to her, which she gratefully accepted.

"Enough chat," Will mumbled. "You'll give us away."

Anna's nose wrinkled. She wasn't the loud one.

"We move at dawn."

4

*H*e'd sat in still silence for the better part of an hour. The birds no longer squawked in alarm. Small creatures skittered nearby, oblivious to his presence. With the afternoon sun slanting through the trees and casting its dappled light upon the forest floor, Will could be staring at one of the serene paintings he'd admired in his youth.

The gnawing pit in his stomach was an all too constant reminder that those days were long gone. They hadn't bothered with more than minimal supplies. Best to travel fast and light. Besides, they needed space in their packs for the precious potions.

Koen had unpacked the glass vials at their rocky resting point the night before. He took his time, turning them this way and that in the moonlight, before wrapping them up in old cloths and tucking them into their packs. They spread them out, a few for each of them, except the new man, in case something should happen. If they could get just a few back intact, he could work his experiments and find a cure to the strange spells Cinderella poisoned the people with to coerce their obedience.

It'd been months since he'd figured out what was happening—why sometimes he saw a beautiful queen and other times a cruel witch—and avoided the tainted food. Even so, he could still taste the sweetness at the back of his throat. Anyone who didn't willingly obey was arrested—or worse. He grimaced at the haunting memories that assailed him. He still had the scars to prove it.

Lost in thought, Will missed the approaching buck until it snapped a twig not twenty paces from him.

The barest smile twitched on his lips. It was a small breed of deer, not the large stags of the mountains, but they'd eat more than old crackers tonight.

Without a moment's hesitation, he pulled back the bowstring and let the arrow fly true.

*B*randt rose from his place near the fire as soon as Will came into sight of their little camp. "Mhmm mm, we're eating well tonight," he bellowed with a deep laugh.

Will shook his head. The easy way the man shed his cares was admirable, if not a little too reckless for his taste.

Since noon, they'd veered closer to the main road. Koen whistled a lively tune. Brandt told bawdy stories that made Mina and Ansel blush. They followed the lessons he'd learned in his early days of hunting—blend in, become one with your surroundings. If they looked like a family out hunting and gathering herbs, that's what people would see.

With Brandt's help, he unrolled the hide near the fire they'd started in his absence to reveal the choicest parts of the meat. There was plenty they could stuff their bellies with for the night and more they'd dry to carry with them. The rest he'd left in the woods. Better the wolves have an easy share than come after their dinner.

From the way Ansel's eyes widened as he sat on a log next to Mina, one would think Will had unrolled a sack of gold coins. He *was* skinny for a young man. A little muscle clung to his arms, but not enough. There wasn't much hair on his bare forearms for that matter either. One might think him a tall youth until they looked into those deep, brown eyes. They weren't the eyes of a boy, no matter what he'd called him the night before. Worse, they beckoned like the old wishing well he'd tossed rocks into as kid, always tempting him for one more look or to lean in a little too close. He'd have probably drowned himself in its depths if he hadn't had a friend nearby to jerk him back from the edge. Will had to be his own anchor now.

"Ya just gonna sit around?" Brandt snapped.

Ansel and Mina both jumped to their feet and gathered up the pointed sticks resting near the fire. At least they were prepared.

His stomach rumbled as the first skewer of meat was propped near the flames. To think he'd once taken a solid meal for granted.

Will side-eyed Koen as he grabbed a flaming stick from the fire and used it to light his pipe. For all their plans to be quick and discreet, the man just had to bring his pipe with him.

"What?" Koen arched a brow as he took a pull. His eyes closed in a shiver of pleasure before he blew out a puff of smoke.

"Couldn't wait?"

Koen shrugged. "It's medicinal."

Right. Will rolled his eyes. Koen *was* a genius when it came to herbs and how to use them, but sometimes he tended to enjoy certain selections a little too much. When he'd suggested they relax, act natural, he hadn't meant *that* relaxed.

Ansel adjusted a skewer of meat near the fire and then froze. His eyes went wide, hand lingering close to the flames until he snapped it back. He'd seen hares chased by hounds less spooked.

"Wh—" But then he heard it.

Hoofbeats. The crunch and thump of someone—multiple someones— moving off the path and heading their way.

"Calm." His harsh whisper grabbed Ansel's attention.

He blinked and shook himself, but anyone could tell he was still on edge. Mina wasn't much better. A flush colored her cheeks as she hunched her shoulders, letting her long hair she'd let loose from her braid fall around her face.

Mina covered Ansel's hand with hers, and Will swore the young man blushed just as bright.

"Let us do the talking," Will said, looking between the two.

A quick glance to Brandt, and the man touched the hilt of a sword carefully tucked behind him. Koen blew out another puff of smoke and gave the smallest nod.

Good.

Will inhaled a steadying breath as he rose and turned toward the sound.

Riders appeared between the trees. At least three of them trotted their way. Enough light still filtered through the canopy for him to clearly make out the grey coats of the queen's guard, her new pink rose insignia replacing the king's old coat of arms.

Everything in him screamed to grab his bow from where it was propped against a tree or slip his dagger from its sheath. It took effort to pull his lips up in a cordial smile and call out a friendly greeting to the advancing riders. "Ho there."

The leader of the trio broke into their clearing and pulled his mount to a stop. The hard lines of his face crinkled as he took in their little campsite.

"How can we help you this eve?" Will asked.

"What are you doing out here?" The man's eyes darted from one of them to the next as the other two men drew up behind him.

"Hunting and gathering some herbs." Will gestured to the meat crackling on the fire and the plants they'd bound into bundles and left out just in case this situation arose.

"Hrmph." The man wrinkled his nose and adjusted the reins.

Stubborn and skeptical. He'd bet his bow this man was loyal to the queen without the help of the fairy godmother's magic.

Will bent to the fire and retrieved a skewer of meat. "Fresh venison. Shot it myself this afternoon." He hoisted the skewer toward the guard.

If the lead guard was interested in his offering, he did a good job of hiding it. One of the men behind him, though, perked up immediately, shifting in his saddle and staring at the meat with greedy eyes. Will grinned and passed the offering to the man. "Always happy to share with the queen's men."

The guard groaned as the meat touched his tongue. "It's good."

The lead guard cut him a hard look. The younger man winced but kept eating.

"Care for a smoke instead?" Koen pipped up behind him. "Got some fresh herbs 'ere. My own personal blend."

"Have you seen anyone else around these parts?" the lead guard asked, ignoring Koen.

Will wrinkled up his brows and tapped a dirty finger against his bearded cheek. "Saw a few merchant carts on the main road this morn."

"Girl," the third guard, by far the oldest, snapped toward Mina.

Will stiffened, his grin vanishing as he turned to the two sitting near the fire.

To his surprise, Ansel raised his head and stared the man down as if he'd called him kid. "I'm a man."

"Not you, boy."

Ansel snarled, white teeth flashing in his mouth. He really didn't like being called a boy.

"That girl."

Mina flinched as she was called out again, but she brushed back her hair and stared at the man out of the corner of her eye.

"You're scaring my sister," Ansel said, wrapping his arm around the girl and pulling her close.

Will raised one brow. *Nice work.* The young man was a better actor than he expected. Looking at them, he could almost believe they were siblings rather than two people who'd just met a day ago, even if their coloring was different. But families didn't always look alike.

"These your brothers?" the guard asked.

"Of course, they are. Who else?" Mina's face flushed as if he implied something improper in his question.

"Ah, come on, Walt, these ain' them," said the guard before tugging another mouthful of meat off the skewer.

The hair on the back of Will's neck prickled. So they were searching for someone, almost certainly them. The guards they knocked out and robbed must have woken quick and raced back to the castle.

"Have you seen anyone else?" the main guard asked Mina.

"Just the merchants my brother mentioned."

Will stiffened as the lead guard wrinkled his nose in thought. This was it—doom or freedom.

The guard turned his mount.

Will nearly sighed in relief, his fingertips slipping from the hilt of his dagger.

"Good day," the man said over his shoulder before trotting off into the trees.

The older man waited until the others trotted into the tree line before drawing his mount near. Will drew up straighter. From the corner of his eye, he saw Brandt start to rise. "There're ruffians about. Best take the younger ones home."

Will nodded, not trusting himself to speak as the old man trotted off. He waited there, still and silent, until the hoofbeats faded and the bird calls returned overhead.

"Nice work," he said to Ansel. He'd told the young man not to speak, yet in the end it'd probably helped.

Ansel shrugged and poked at the fire. "People see what they want to see."

That they do. Mina poked Ansel's side, giving him a smile and making some silly comment about being her hero. Watching him smile back, Will couldn't help but wonder what lay beyond the poor young farmer he wanted them to see.

5

*T*he worst sight imaginable came into view as they crested the hill. Anna's stomach whirled, all the venison she'd gorged on the night before turning leaden in her stomach.

The castle. Her stepsister's grand new home.

Anna's legs locked up, refusing to move another inch. White spires stretched toward the cloudy sky from the hillside the castle dominated, overlooking the city sprawled out across the valley. Trees blocked most of it from view, but here and there she could just make out rooflines and tendrils of smoke wafting into the sky.

"Keep a move on." Brandt gave her a hard shove, nearly sending her tumbling down the hillside.

She scowled at him, but it was mostly for show. The stalky man liked to act tough and spew barbed comments, but he was all bark and no bite. Though how he'd managed to keep a leash on his temper with the guards yesterday, she still wasn't sure. She'd seen him reach behind for the blade he'd tucked away more than once. She'd been ready too—weight shifted to the balls of her feet in case she needed to spring up and run away.

No way were the queen's men getting her. Even though it'd be a shame to leave this crew behind. They were nice enough, and oh, how her soul longed for companionship. She hadn't realized it until she woke up at their camp after that first night and took comfort in having others nearby. It was the first time that waking up without Charlotte didn't threaten to choke her. They'd shared a bed their whole lives, first out of necessity when they were young and living above their father's shop, then later out of habit.

Will came to a stop next to her and stared off at the same sight that had tripped her up. His jaw stiffened, and he looked like he might spit something foul out of his mouth at any minute.

He didn't say much. Frankly, other than Brandt, none of them did. That was just as well since she had little to share with strangers. Just having others around was a comfort. Over the past few months, she'd been wary of getting too close to the farmers whose fields she worked in, terrified of being found out. The way the huntsman looked at her, like he could see past her disguise, set her teeth on edge.

Or like he was interested in her. Maybe he liked men? Who knew?

To make matters worse, part of her wanted him to look, to see her. Pushing that foolish wish away was harder than she cared to admit to herself. Perhaps trusting them was a mistake after all, but she needed them.

Still, it didn't help that each time she caught his gaze during their trek, all she could think about was the way she'd been pressed up against his body that first night. The threat of the blade had nothing on the hard muscle of his chest, the woodsy smell that invaded her nose, or the way his warm hand felt against her skin.

Men wouldn't dare touch her growing up. First for propriety's sake, and by the time she was old enough to warrant and want male attention, there was Ella gobbling all of it up. The few men who looked her way quickly heard lies from Ella's lips that turned them away—back to her. Except that once... A knot lodged in her throat. She'd thought finally a man wanted her, and he did, but only so he could tell his friends how ugly she was under her clothes too. He'd been Ella's favorite for a few weeks after that, until she discarded him like all the rest.

A soft touch on her arm brought her back to the present. Will was staring at her—again. Her lips pursed as she looked up at him.

"We should keep moving."

Right. Off to their home, wherever that was. No one had properly told her what they planned to do once they got there or how they'd use the potions they stole, and she knew better than to ask. They'd tell her when they were ready. If their plan was stupid, she could always cut and run—go off on her own as she'd done for a while now. Despite the fact they had robbed the guards—or more accurately, because of it—she was pretty sure they weren't going to just poison her, steal what little she had, and leave her for dead in a gulley somewhere.

"So where's this home of yours?" she asked no one in particular.

Please say this side of the city, please—

"Other side of the city," Brandt replied.

Dang it.

"So we go around?" It'd add to their trip, but what were a few more hours of walking?

"Through," Koen said, never breaking his stride.

Anna froze for the second time in as many minutes. "Through?" she squeaked, her voice entirely too high for the ruse she played.

The rest of them stopped and looked back at her.

Through the city? That close to the castle? Her body locked up. *No. No way.* She hadn't been there in months. The last time she'd dared to go near, she'd seen the posters with her face on them. They'd painted her with hair still long, nose a little too big, and the word *Wanted* scrawled across the top. The picture wasn't a great representation of her—it accentuated all the horrible details Ella liked to taunt her about, but they'd gotten one bit right, the distinctive mole near her right eye.

Will leaned in close, sending her rocking back on her heels. "It'll be fine. If the guards yesterday didn't figure us out, no one in the city will. Plus, they'll be looking out here." He gestured to the surrounding forest. "They won't expect the thieves to go to the city, especially not so close to the castle."

This close, his scent of leather and pine sent her head swimming. "H-how do you know?" Without thinking, she leaned closer, staring into his warm, brown eyes.

His gaze cut away. "I spent enough years around those guards to know how they think."

What? The comment popped the bubble of her curiosity, and she edged away from him.

He glanced back at her and gave a half-smile that stirred up more feelings than such a simple thing should do. "The king liked his meat fresh, and the guards never wanted the duty of hauling it into the castle."

He had to be the king's huntsman, or one of them. *That's right.* Some of the tension slipped from her shoulders, causing her pack to sag. It wasn't just a nickname, his skills the day before proved that well enough.

"You don't worry about them recognizing you?" she asked.

He stiffened, halting midstride where he'd started to follow the others.

"You being one of the former king's huntsmen and all? Surely some of the guards knew you."

Will turned to her slowly, his head cocking to the side as he stared at her with that gaze that saw too much. Instant regret slid through her. Anna bit her tongue, wishing she could take back the words if only so he wouldn't look at her that way. Still, she couldn't help but wonder about him. She wanted more—so much more.

Ahead of them, Mina stopped, bouncing on her toes as she stared at them. Brandt grabbed her arm and urged her along.

The silence told her everything. This man would give her nothing. She shook her head and turned to follow the others. "Never mind. Sorry I asked."

"People see what they want to see." His comment was so quiet it could have been a rustle of leaves as the breeze drifted through the trees.

The sorrow laced into each word tugged at her, begged her to stop. She did, closing her eyes against the echoes of pain she could never quite escape. Slowly, she glanced back over her shoulder. Will's eyes were downcast, his shoulders hunched inward. *Oh hells, you'd think I'd called him ugly or something.*

"I dissented the queen's claim to the throne. Guards chased me as I fled the castle. One stuck me with an arrow." He rubbed a spot on his chest as his focus dipped.

Anna sucked in a breath. *Goodness, he must have said or done something outrageous.* Perhaps she wasn't the only one with a price on her head.

"I fell into the river. Pretty sure they thought I was a goner."

Or perhaps he wasn't a wanted man if they truly believed him dead.

"Then Brandt found you," she whispered, filling in the little bit of his story she'd heard.

He nodded.

Her chest clenched tight. "Thank you for telling me."

Seeing the emotions he tried to hide rush across his face made her want to spill everything to him, let him know that he wasn't the only one who'd suffered—he wasn't the only one the queen wanted wiped out or hidden away. At least his face wasn't stuck on posters.

But telling anyone was too risky, especially someone she barely knew. Anna adjusted her pack, prepared to march on, when he spoke again.

"You're worried about someone recognizing you."

Her breath caught in her throat. Her hands locked onto the pack straps. She glanced at Will from the corner of her eye. "Of course not. I'm no one."

It was the worst lie she'd ever told. It burned through her with the knowledge that it was true in too many ways. For the first time in months, she wanted to be someone again. She turned her back on him without waiting to see if he accepted her words. Only when his footfalls sounded behind her, calm and even, did she let herself breathe again.

6

$\mathcal{T}$he city looked entirely the same as she remembered and completely different all at once.

People and horse carts meandered down the cobblestone streets. Vendors shouted their wares from stalls and storefronts. Children ran about chasing one another and probably pocketing a few coins from anyone foolish enough not to watch their belongings. Signs of the season sprung up as colorful late-blooming flowers in little window boxes—not that the fragrant blooms did much to disguise the tang of human waste that always clung about.

All that was the same as it'd always been—at least, as long as she'd lived in their little manor home outside the city.

If that had been all she'd seen, Anna might have been able to delude herself that not much had changed. The central square, however, erased all of that.

"What in all the heavens and hells is that?" Anna sputtered, absolutely baffled by the monstrosity occupying the far side of the square.

A large mirror, at least three full-grown men in height and gilt in gold, occupied a raised wooden stage. With its size and positioning, people would be able to see it from any part of the wide, open space. Even the fountain gurgling in its center couldn't completely block the view.

Brandt grumbled, looking this way and that.

Okay, I definitely spoke too loud, but seriously, someone should have warned me. She glanced around too, but thankfully no one paid them any mind.

"You truly don't know?" Mina asked, dark brows drawn together in question.

Will clapped an arm around her shoulders. "Seems our friend here has spent too long in the countryside," he said, a little louder than normal.

Her cheeks heated. True, but she should have known better than to speak up about something that'd make them all look out of place.

"That," he said, lowering his voice to a whisper and leaning in close, "is the queen's mirror. She uses it to talk to the people without leaving the *safety* of the castle."

With his arm around her, tucking her against his solid form, it was hard to focus on the words he said, on anything other than the strange, tingly feeling running through her.

"Wouldn't want anything to happen to our *dear queen* after the sudden illness that struck down the king. Or *kings*, rather."

Figures the haughty Ella wouldn't trifle with the very people she was supposed to lead. Only months into her reign, and already she erected more barriers between the commoners and nobility.

Ella hadn't always been that way. She'd been kind at first, a bright and giggling ray of sunshine. Anna still remembered the first time they visited the square, the way Ella giggled while clutching her hand and practically dragging her to her favorite shops. They were friends...for a time, before Ella's father passed. That bond of friendship made Ella's later abuse so much worse. If she were honest, it might be the reason she endured it so long. She hadn't wanted to give up hope that young woman would return.

But she never did.

Will released Anna, finally freeing her from his distracting presence. Her gaze dipped from the mirror—empty and reflecting only the surrounding square—to the multiple carts and wagons just below it. Guards in the queen's uniform handed out bread and vegetables to the long line of waiting peasants.

Now *that* she'd heard about. The queen's offering, a way to show her generosity to the people—and poison them with the fairy godmother's magic. People ate the magically tainted food, and their loyalty to the queen grew. It didn't matter that she demanded more goods and gold from farmers, tradesmen, and nobility alike as part of the royal tax. The food wasn't truly free, no matter what she said.

The effects of the potion were obvious if one knew what to look for: faces a little too bright, smiles too broad, laughter too loud. It was the eyes that gave them away most of all—that slight sheen and glazed look. It wasn't natural the way it made people behave, as if everything was bright and cheery all the time.

Anna snorted.

The false façade was the very opposite of how her life had been, especially recently.

A man in an elaborate costume with puffy pants and sleeves practically danced through the square. "Who is the fairest of them all? The fairest in the land?" he said in a sing-song voice.

Anna rolled her eyes. *Let me guess, the queen?*

"Come on," Koen urged them on. "We still have a few stops to make."

Ah yes. They had to extend her agony by visiting a few stores before continuing on their way. She ground her teeth a bit, wondering why they couldn't just save their shopping for another day when she wasn't with them.

"You, my dear!" The man in the costume skipped toward Mina, taking her hands in his even as she squeaked in alarm. "Could you be the fairest? You might! You might!" He danced around, tugging her with him.

Koen stood frozen in shock, probably worried about his precious potions.

"Let go 'a my sister!" Brandt charged the man, already rolling up his sleeves.

Oh no. No fights. Anna rushed into the fray and snatched Mina's hand from the dancing man as Will blocked Brandt's approach.

"I'd ask you to leave my sister be," Anna said, pulling the girl into the safety of her arms. Mina leaned her flushed face against Anna's collarbone, sinking into her embrace as if she were a real sister. *Or a lover?* Anna's own cheeks flushed at the thought.

"Of course, of course, but the queen seeks the fairest in the land." The man gave a dramatic bow and held out a paper that she swore hadn't been in his hand a moment ago.

Anna took the notice, willing him not to see the slight tremor of her fingers.

"Your sister might be a lovely addition to the queen's court. Don't forget to dress your best," he chirped before dancing off across the square, likely in search of other maidens.

The paper crinkled in her hand as she watched him go. Ella sought the fairest in the land? She'd already given herself that title, so what was she playing at?

"What was that about?" Brandt grumbled, staring daggers at the man who dared touch his little sister. She knew that look, had seen it in Charlotte's eyes a number of times.

Mina lifted her head. "Ansel's my hero, that's what." Her eyes held utter adoration. The soft sigh the girl let out caused Anna's chest to burn. *Uh oh.*

When she'd decided to be a man, it was for her own safety. A clever disguise she had thought. She never expected to attract romantic attention. How could she? Nose too big. Hair drab and cut short around her ears. Features as plain as they came. Or so Ella liked to tease her, especially in those last months before she wed the prince. Her stomach churned as she fought to give the girl a small smile.

She'd have to tell her. It might break her heart—better to do it quick before the feelings grew. But could she trust this lot? Anna glanced between the men. Will already looked too closely. If she revealed her true sex, it'd lead to questions, maybe too many.

Koen took the page from her hand, adjusting his glasses as he read it over. "This could be promising."

"What?" Anna balked, echoed by Brandt.

"Each lady may have one escort and should arrive at the main castle gate at dawn," Koen read from the page before lowering his voice. "It's only a few days from now. Might be our chance to get inside."

Inside? Anna stiffened, glancing around, though no one lingered close enough to hear them. *What could they possibly hope to achieve?*

"Ain' putting Mina at risk," Brandt said.

Mina stiffened, pulling away from Anna to stand on her own. "I can do it."

"Nuh uh." His arms bulged as he crossed them. "If I go in and get caught, whose getting you out?"

"I am," Will said, crossing his arms as well before glancing to Anna. "We are."

She stepped back. "We?"

The hint of a grin twitched on his lips, and Anna's stomach dropped. "Oh no. No way."

Koen rubbed his chin. "If we got a wig, the right dress…"

"No. I can't." Anna waved her hands in front of herself. She could *not* be a woman again. *Too damn risky.*

"You said you'd be useful, right?" Will cocked one dark brow. The smirk pulling at his lips stirred up way too many conflicting feelings.

Oh hells. She'd meant to be helpful with information, telling them about the queen. Maybe then they'd help her too. But this? It was too much.

The smirk broke into a wide grin that spread across his face as mirth twinkled in his eyes. "Time to prove it."

7

*S*unset colored the sky in bright hues of pink and orange by the time they neared the siblings' cottage. The wig in her pack, light as it was, weighed her down like a bag full of stones. Heavens and hells, they really expected her to dress like a woman and enter the queen's contest.

It made sense. Having more of them on the inside couldn't hurt—whatever their plan was. They still refused to tell her. Too risky to talk about in the city they'd said. *Fair.*

Anna glared at Will's back as he walked ahead of her. He just *had* to volunteer her, to call her on her offer to help. She groaned and adjusted the pack. At least they'd settled on a wig of shoulder-length coppery red. Will had wanted a plain, medium brown, more common and less likely to attract attention. But being so close to her hair color, she couldn't risk it.

Mina had a few dresses in mind that she thought would work for her. Though the girl was a few inches shorter than Anna's above-average height, the dresses would probably do, and she had a few days to make small adjustments. It wouldn't be the first time she'd altered a dress. Her birth father had been a tailor after all. She'd had a needle in her hand as long as she could remember, and her dresses used to be the envy of all the girls in the seaside town where she grew up.

"There she is." From the affection in Brandt's voice, one might think he'd just spotted a lover.

But no, stretching out in a clearing just ahead was a wooden cottage. The size of it—Anna whistled—two stories and fairly wide at that. When they'd mentioned a cottage in the woods, she'd assumed it would be small and cozy. Cozy this place might be, but small it certainly was not.

"*That* is your home?"

"Yep." Mina turned to her with a bright grin.

Anna, distracted by the sight before her, stumbled over a tree root. Her arms flailed in the fading light.

Will grabbed her arm before she could fall. "Steady on," he said.

Even with gloves on, his touch sent a little tingle through her. She pursed her lips. Traitorous little heart. There was no time for that, no matter that she couldn't get the attention of a man like him even when she was a proper lady.

"It's just—" she stammered, trying to cover the heat rising to her cheeks.

"Big?" Will asked.

Her gaze dipped to his trousers. She might as well have lit herself on fire for all the warmth coursing through her. *Hells.* What was she thinking? Immediately she snapped her attention back to the cabin. "Y-yeah."

"Well, with seven kids," Koen said, breaking into the conversation, "Dad had to keep adding on to make room for us all."

"Seven!" she squeaked. Her teeth rattled as she clamped her mouth shut, praying they didn't notice the way her voice rose an octave. "The family members you wanted to save..." She looked between the three of them.

To her surprise, it was Mina who spoke, even as her bright smile vanished and her head tilted downward. "I have four more older brothers."

"Your parents?"

"Passed a few years ago," Koen said. "It's just us now."

Anna swallowed the tight knot in her throat. Such a big family dwindled down to three. She'd lost her mother and Charlotte, and her father long ago—how much more would it hurt if she'd lost even more people she loved?

"What—" She cut herself off before hurrying ahead to catch up to Koen. "Can I ask what happened to them? Your siblings?"

He cut a glance to Brandt.

"Might as well tell him," Brandt said.

Koen let out a deep sigh, his sights set on their destination. "Most of the family worked the mines up in the hills, all except Mina and I."

"Ma wa'n't about to let her first born follow in his daddy's footsteps," Brandt laughed and gave his brother a little shove.

Koen rolled his eyes before cutting Brandt a hard look. "Then you came along, and she couldn't send you there soon enough."

Brandt grumbled something under his breath.

"Anyhow, the others were part of the group that protested the queen's increased demands. She wanted more gems that could only be found in the risky tunnels that had been sealed off years ago." He wrinkled his nose. "She couldn't understand why no one wanted to go there. It was the last place our dad ever went."

Her heart constricted at his words.

"Then, the guards showed up, trying to enforce her demands. The people who refused, our brothers included, were arrested. Taken east."

To the fairy godmother's workhouse. Her stomach turned to a mess of wiggling worms. That was where her mom and sister were—Ella wouldn't have wanted them close—but the place was a fortress, harder to get into than the castle, if what rumors said were true.

Finally, they reached the front door, and Koen dropped his pack to fish out the key.

"I should a' been there." Brandt scowled at the forest, refusing to look at anyone.

"Best you weren't," Will said. "What good would that have done?"

"I'd have—" He balled his hands into a fist. "I could a' showed them. Maybe given the others time to run."

Her throat tightened. *Just like Charlotte had done for me.* The guilt still gnawed at her every day. How much worse must Brandt feel about losing four brothers?

"Or gotten yourself killed," Mina muttered. She'd pulled her hair from its braid, letting it fall around her face.

"It's yer fault, you know," Brandt grumbled at Will. "If I hadn't wrecked my good arm dragging your half-dead ass back here—"

"Hush, all of you," Koen said in a harsh whisper.

The fine hairs on the back of Anna's neck stood on end.

"I hear something." Koen leaned into the door.

The forest was suddenly too quiet. Anna rubbed her hands up and down her arms as she listened.

A rustling came from the second floor. Soft, but loud enough to know the house wasn't as empty as it was supposed to be. Could the guards have figured out who they were? Did they wait inside, ready to arrest them all?

Koen looked between Brandt and Will, having some silent conversation Anna was oblivious to. Whatever the subtle looks and movements said, the two nodded in confirmation.

Slowly, inch by dangerous inch, Koen opened the door.

Anna held her breath. On instinct, she shifted her weight to the balls of her feet, ready to run.

Koen and Brandt slipped inside. Will stayed outside with her and Mina, his gaze sharp as a fresh blade. The forest was mostly still, its residents slipping into slumber with the loss of the sun. Anna squinted at each shadow, each ruffle of the breeze through the trees, but nothing seemed out of the ordinary.

A loud bang upstairs made her heart leap into her throat. A heavy thump and muffled exclamation followed. *Shit.*

Will bolted inside with Anna close on his heels. She dipped into a crouch, slipping the hidden dagger from her boot. Quick, light thumps raced across the second story, multiple sets by the sound of it. Anna adjusted her stance, blade in hand, but she could barely make out a thing in the dark home.

The skitter of nails on wood made her brows draw together. Several, but too quiet for anything large.

"What the—" Will exclaimed. He jumped back, bumping into Anna.

She squealed, unsteady on her feet as a trio of creatures raced by. Her foot slipped. "Oh!"

Will whirled toward her. "Ansel." He grabbed her arm, tugging her into his chest. The dagger slipped from her grip to clatter on the floor. The move unbalanced them, sending Will stumbling back a step and into something waiting in the dark.

And then he was falling, taking her down with him.

Anna yelped as she crashed down onto Will's chest. The impact knocked her teeth together and the breath from her lungs. In this dark, strange place, she could hardly tell which way was up.

A muffled curse came from Will as she squirmed on top of him, trying and failing to stand. *Hells, he is hard.* She'd be lying to herself if she said the muscular body under hers wasn't the reason why she couldn't make her limbs work properly. Pressed up against him—all of him... Heat spread through her chest and raced up her neck.

Will's strong hand slid up her thigh, cupping her backside.

"What are you—" she sputtered, her voice far higher than she intended.

Heavy steps thumped down the stairs.

It had to be her imagination, but she was almost certain his hand stilled, fingers flexing on the soft curve of her rear before sliding higher.

"What are you two doing?" Brandt's deep voice thundered through the shadows. Leave it to him to see just fine.

Will found her hip, pushing her up and off him. "Can't get up with you on me," he said to her, ignoring Brandt.

Anna pursed her lips. "You bumped into me." Her palm found the floor and gave her leverage to find her footing.

"Apologies," he groaned as her boot knocked into...something.

Will gained his feet as Mina lit a lantern, illuminating the room.

"What was that?" Anna asked, looking toward the staircase where Koen descended, glasses slightly askew.

"Raccoons," Brandt replied. "Greedy little bastards."

Raccoons. Right. Just forest creatures. Anna made to smooth her hair back behind her ears, only to touch the short ends. Old habits died hard.

"How'd they get in?" Will asked.

"That's what I'd like to know." Koen shot Brandt a flat gaze.

"Wasn't my fault," he protested.

"We'll see. Bring the lantern." Koen gestured to Mina. "We need to check the house."

"They looked hungry before we left…" Mina said, avoiding everyone's gaze.

The brothers stared at their sister before shaking their heads as if they should have guessed. A hint of a smile bloomed on Anna's face. The girl had a soft spot for animals, just like Charlotte. One more reason to like her.

"Raccoons always act hungry." Koen sighed. "Better make sure nothing else got in."

Will followed Koen. *Thank goodness.* She couldn't even manage to look at him. Her whole body flushed, and it had nothing to do with surprise woodland creatures. Perhaps joining this lot was a terrible idea after all.

heir search last night hadn't turned up anything more nefarious than the raccoons, thank the Mother in her high heavens. Will had sunk into a bed not long after and didn't waken until the sun was well into the sky. It'd been ages since he slept so hard. Might have had something to do with his dream. His gaze slid to Ansel. He respected men, admired them, loved them in ways familiar and friendly, but last night was the first time he dreamed of kissing one.

"So let me get this straight." Ansel paced around the main room of the cabin, arms waving through the air as he talked. "You plan to kill the queen?"

Will kicked up his boots onto a nearby stool. "That's right."

One would think they'd asked him to stalk into the castle naked the way he protested dressing up as a woman and entering the queen's contest. He'd have done it himself if he thought it likely to work. Will's lips quirked. Trying to fit himself into a dress would be a nightmare, and no way would anyone consider him the fairest in the land, not with his tall height, muscled arms, and body hair. Ansel was the smarter choice. The only choice. He might be a man, at least he claimed so, but he'd yet to sprout a single whisker in the days they'd been together. With his lean build and delicate facial bone structure, Ansel could certainly pass for a woman, and with four of them inside, they'd have a much better chance to get their plan to work.

"Ugh." Ansel ran his hands down his face. "It's so risky."

"Thought you had family that needed savin' too?" Brandt asked before finishing off the last of his breakfast and shoving the plate aside.

"I do." Ansel halted and plopped heavily into a chair.

In Will's dream, Ansel had the same spark of fire he showed now, freely talking about treason. Delicate lips had parted, so soft and inviting, Will could almost taste them. Even Ansel's voice had caressed him in a way no one had in months. It didn't help that Ansel's backside had a certain softness to it that he couldn't quite get out of his head.

He shook his head. What was he thinking? There was no time for anything of that sort. Not to mention he had nothing to offer someone—woman or man—anymore.

"You have a better plan then?" Brandt talked with his mouth full, a few bits of food crumbling into his beard.

Ansel's lips—a delicious shade of pink—pulled back in disgust. "I'd planned to steal a uniform, if I could get one." He glanced away. "Maybe sneak into the fairy godmother's workhouse and try to get my family out."

"Terrible idea," Koen said, never looking away from the vials and dishes in front of him. He'd been up before any of them, trying to dissect the potions they'd stolen. He hoped—they all did—he'd be able to figure out what they were made of or how to counteract them. Cutting off the supply of potions was too difficult, but if they could find a cure, perhaps they could lure more people to their side, maybe get the guards to wake up, or at least turn a blind eye long enough to take out the queen.

If they could get close to the queen during the upcoming contest, though, Koen's efforts might be unnecessary.

"And yours is better?" Ansel scoffed. "How exactly do you plan to kill her? Assuming they even let us inside the castle or anywhere near the bitch queen."

Will had voted for a sharp dagger to the heart. Maybe a well-placed arrow. Koen and Brandt had balked at his idea, and he didn't dare tell Mina. The poor girl might faint. The brothers had people to live for. They needed to kill the queen and escape. He, on the other hand, had no plans to flee. Even if it cost him his life, he would stay until the job was done.

"The guards work in pairs at the castle," Will said, picking some wayward dirt out from under his nails. "Can't say for sure, but I'd assume they do something similar at the fairy godmother's place. Got a friend who was going to help you?" He glanced at Ansel.

Ansel stared back at him, lips pressed thin.

"Thought not." Will shifted his focus back to his nails. So much grime. He really could do with a bath. "Most of the uniforms are tailored to the guards too. Think they'd notice if yours didn't fit."

"My father was a tailor. He…" Ansel swallowed. "He died years ago, but I remember some. I could fit it to me."

Poor fella. Must have been nice to have a father who cared—or seemed to, from the emotion written all over Ansel's face. He could never say the same about his own. The old man managed to find fault in everything. Nothing he'd done was ever right or good enough. Will hadn't even managed to give him the grandchild he'd always wanted before he died. Though that was probably best. One less person for his father to be disappointed in.

"Say you could blend in and make it inside," Will continued. "How would you get out again? And with your family?"

He glanced at Ansel from under his eyelashes, but the young man no longer looked at him. Instead, he scowled out the window. "I can't just do nothing."

Indeed.

"That's why we're taking out the queen." Brandt wiped his mouth with his arm and shoved up from the table. "If she ain't in charge, shouldn't have a reason to hold those who spoke out against her. Now this…" He wandered over to the edge of Koen's worktable. "…is my baby."

"Spilling all our secrets now?" Will cocked his head to the side as Brandt raised the powder, one he'd worked on for days, in the air.

Ansel scowled at Will. He nearly smiled in return. He couldn't say why, but getting under his skin a little here and there sparked pleasure in him like little had lately.

Brandt just shrugged. "He already knows enough to get us all arrested."

That much was certainly true. If Ansel was in league with the queen, they were doomed, but something told him that wasn't the case—far from it. He was scared, desperate, just as they were, and maybe even more determined. Will waved a hand in the air. *What could it hurt?*

"It's powdered apple seeds." Brandt broke out in a wide smile, so proud of his idea. Brandt had a habit of getting stuck on one idea and thinking it brilliant no matter how foolish it may be. Koen had gotten all the brains and left none for his younger brother. He'd barely gotten to know the others. *Heavens help them if they're more like Brandt and less like Koen and Mina.*

Ansel just blinked at him.

"They're poisonous," he continued. Disappointment colored his words, as if he shouldn't have to explain himself. "In concentrated doses. Thought we might bake a cake or something, give it to her as a gift."

"She doesn't like cake."

Will suddenly had something much more interesting to stare at than his nails.

"How would you know?" Brandt scoffed.

Even from across the room, Will noticed the way Ansel shifted on his feet, the slight increase in color to his cheeks.

"Have you seen her? She's so skinny. Perfect skin too. There's no way someone can love cake enough to eat one from a stranger and stay that thin." Ansel rambled on. "It's just not possible."

Brandt heaved a heavy sigh. "The wine then. We just have to get it in her wine."

"All that grit? She'd choke on it."

Koen leaned back in his chair and glared at them. "I have better poisons, don't worry."

"I still like the apples," Brandt grumbled. "Stole a whole cart of them that they'd planned to hand out to the people. Thought to give her a taste of her own medicine."

"Another reason we'll be using Koen's poison," Will said, settling the nonargument. *Or a dagger to the heart.* He toyed with the hilt of the one strapped to his thigh.

Awkward silence settled over the room, so full of unspoken words he almost regretted shutting down the debate. Will busied himself by opening an old box containing a game board and setting up the pieces. He rolled one of the carved castle towers between his fingers, savoring the craftsmanship. The siblings' father had crafted it long ago. Several of the colorful wooden pieces were faded and chipped—well-loved—from heavy use.

"What's that?"

Will nearly dropped the piece as his head snapped up. Ansel stood with his hands on the back of a chair across the table. He'd missed his approach.

"Ah, castles!" Brandt exclaimed, thundering across the room toward them.

"A game of strategy and conquest," Will said to Ansel. He quirked one brow at the younger man. "Care to play?"

Ansel slid into the chair opposite him, even as he replied, "I don't know how."

"I can teach ya," Brandt said, dragging another chair toward them.

"Ansel might be better taking advice from someone else." Will finished arranging the pieces on the board.

Brandt snorted but held his tongue. The man loved a good game, even if he often lost.

They set to it with gusto and even greater teasing. Ansel picked up the game quick. Only a few moves in, and he was already tweaking Brandt's advice and making moves on his own—good ones.

Will's brows arched as Ansel made an advanced move, pinning one of his castles in a corner. He glanced up, catching the younger man's grin that stirred up a gentle burn in his chest. *Damn.* If he was going to keep his winning streak intact, he needed to distract him.

"So your father was a tailor," Will began. "Anyone we'd know?" Not that he knew many tailors, but it was worth a shot. He knew too little about Ansel, and more than caution for their mission drove his curiosity.

Will dropped his gaze to the board, considering his next move.

"Not likely," Ansel said at last. "He was good, but we lived far from here. Muritz, on the Cerulean Sea."

Ah. The far western edge of the kingdom. He couldn't claim to know many people there, but the port city received many foreign imports, including the silks the nobility loved. It made sense a tailor would live where he could more easily get his hands on a variety of fabrics.

He made a move, earning an appraising whistle from Brandt. Ansel scowled, and Will couldn't help but admire the way he stared down the board like a foe to be slain.

"And your family moved here for a change of scenery? Better opportunity?"

Ansel's face fell completely, his gaze drifting from the board. His throat bobbed. Perhaps Will had pushed it too far.

"My mother married a man who lived near here a few years after my father died."

A common enough thing.

"Ah, sorry, lad." Brandt clapped him on the shoulder, sending Ansel jumping in his seat.

"It was a long time ago," Ansel said, but the way he hunched in on himself showed how much that loss still hurt.

Will couldn't say the same about his own father. They hadn't been close. And his mother? He could barely remember her. From his reaction, Ansel must have been close with his family, still mourning his lost father and trying to save whatever family members he had left. Will's gaze shifted to Brandt. The siblings, too, fought for their family. They were probably all better people than him.

"So what family are you trying to save?" Will asked. "Your mother? New father?"

"My mother and sister," Ansel replied at once, then snapped his mouth shut as if he'd said too much.

Will's brow scrunched together, a question rising to the tip of his tongue, when Mina stepped off the last stair in the corner of his vision. She'd been quiet as a mouse—he hadn't even heard her coming. The girl could make a great spy, but he wouldn't risk her safety. In the short months, she'd become like a little sister to him too. Besides, it might be nice if one of them could survive this without blood on their hands. The bashful girl had suffered too much already with so many family members arrested.

"I think this one will do." She held a dress of pale blue over her skinny arms. "I have some extra cloth we can add to the hem to make it long enough for you."

Ansel practically jumped from the chair and crossed the room to her. He ran his fingers across the dress, almost as if he had experience in the matter of women's clothing. "Yes, I should be able to sew onto the hem easily with this pattern."

Mina's mouth formed a perfect O. "You sew, Ansel?"

"A little," Ansel replied, matter of fact. "But I should make sure this fits first."

"And we should make sure Ansel can pass for a woman," Koen said, looking up from his work.

A huff of air caught in his throat. As if there were any doubt.

"Well then, show us," Brandt said.

"I can help you change," Mina offered, her voice as bright as the blush on her cheeks.

"I—uh—"

Mina didn't give him the chance to argue before she hauled him toward the stairs. *Too bad.* Their game would have to wait. Will dropped his gaze to the board, studying the pieces. Perhaps he could figure out a good strategy while Ansel was gone.

A few minutes after Mina and Ansel vacated the room, the tread of hoofbeats rang through the open window, accompanied by a high whinny.

Will stiffened in his seat and reached for his dagger. One quick look between Brandt and Koen answered the question ringing in his head. No, they weren't expecting anyone.

In the blink of an eye, Koen went from calm and studious scholar to a man on alert. Herbs were swept aside without care. Bottles shoved back into boxes at record speed. Brandt grabbed a cloth and tossed it messily onto the table. A box followed. In moments, the workstation had become a home of odds and ends, nothing more.

Meanwhile, Will leaned against the wall near the window, listening as men dismounted their horses. *Three, four, maybe more?*

Koen straightened his glasses and brushed off his shirt as he strode to the door with a calm any traveling player would envy. It was the very opposite of the pulse hammering in Will's own throat and the tingling anticipation coursing through his veins.

The eldest brother threw open the door before anyone could knock. "Hello there," he called. "How may I help you?"

Will inched toward the door, ready to strike.

"Sir," the man replied. Though out of sight, Will could picture the accompanying bow. He'd seen it a number of times from the king's—now the queen's—herald. "Our gracious queen is hosting a contest to find the fairest maiden in all the land to be her stout companion. As she herself arose from more humble means in the countryside, she ordered that we make sure all young women were invited to attend in two days' time."

The moment should have set him at ease. The queen's men weren't there to arrest them, only to inform them of an event they'd already learned of. But why try so hard to inform every maiden? His jaw shifted, his eyes squinting at nothing on the floor. Worse, he knew that voice. Would the herald recognize him?

"Do you have any young women in your household?" the man continued.

As if on cue, Ansel and Mina chose that moment to reappear on the stairs.

"Ah, I see that you do," the man said.

Mina jumped back with a little squeak. She stumbled a half-step and clamped onto the railing as Ansel stepped in front of her.

Words passed between Koen and the guard at the door, but Will barely heard a word. With quick long strides, he crossed the room to the stairs. Standing there, in a flowing blue dress that fell to mid-calf and a red wig, was Ansel. His wide-eyed gaze and parted red lips weren't for him though, but the man who'd stepped through the door without invitation.

"Oh yes, your sisters certainly must attend."

Will's legs locked up as he warred with indecision. Modest as the dress was, thanks to belonging to Mina, it didn't show any cleavage—or lack thereof, and the simple cut hid the lack of curves. A good ruse, but still just that. Turn and risk the man seeing him, or hazard letting him discover Ansel was a man? Not that he looked like one in that dress.

Both would demand questions, but only one might damn them.

He sucked in a breath and held out his hands to the pair on the stairs as if that's what he'd been planning this whole time. "Sisters," he bit out, a slight breathlessness to his voice that he couldn't hide.

Ansel recovered with far more ease and grace than he did, descending the stairs to take his hand. He tried everything he could not to think about the light callouses on Ansel's otherwise soft skin or the way his hand swallowed up the young man's.

"Sir." Ansel dipped into a perfect curtsy, lowering his head and flaring out the skirts of his dress as if he were a proper lady. It was almost too good, especially for a family of miners living in the woods.

Ansel stepped to the side and made room for Mina, who copied his curtsy, albeit with a wobble to her steps and a cascade of dark hair hiding much of whatever expression crossed her face.

"Positively splendid." The man clapped his hands in appreciation. "You must promise to bring them to the castle day after tomorrow. They're certainly two of the fairest maidens in this land."

Just leave already. Will swallowed, keeping his face partially turned away from the room.

"We would be proud to," Koen replied, wearing the mantle of head of the house with an ease any father would envy.

"Of course, sir," Ansel answered at almost the same time, his voice higher than before. Strangely, the tone fit him well, almost as if he'd practiced before coming downstairs. Maybe he had? Something nagged at Will about it.

The man's boots clicked on the floor as he turned. "Excellent. We must be off."

Will let out a heavy breath, his shoulders sagging as Koen led the man back to his escorts waiting outside.

No one spoke, barely anyone moved, until Koen returned and locked the door behind him and hoofbeats faded from earshot.

"Well." Ansel raised his chin, regarding each of them like the high-born lady he pretended to be. "I think we can agree I'll be helpful after all."

With that, he turned on his heel and stomped back up the stairs.

9

*W*armth tinged the night air despite the fading of the season. It wouldn't be long before the trees shed their leaves and the horrid snows of winter turned the ground white. A terrible time to be homeless.

Anna sighed as she pulled her shirt over her head and set it aside. Night breeze tickled her bare skin, and she savored the gooseflesh as it rose in a shiver over her body. It'd been too long since she'd bathed, a fact Brandt made sure to remind her of over dinner.

"Ya might look like a woman in that dress, but the queen ain't gonna be wantin' someone with your stench," he'd said.

She sniffed at her arms for the millionth time since then, and just like every time before, her nostrils wrinkled with distaste.

It wasn't the worst she'd smelled. She owed that to the time Ella stuffed a cow pie down her dress. However, she really could do with a good cleaning. No sense ruining all their plans by getting them turned away at the gate because of her stench.

Mina had given her some soap, and Anna claimed she'd wash up in her borrowed room, but the risk of being walked in on was too high. Not to mention the promise of sinking down into the clear river near the house

—no matter how cold—was too delightful to miss out on. Who knew when she'd have the chance again?

Tomorrow they'd journey back to the city and stay in an inn. Anna protested, said it was too risky—not to mention being in even closer quarters with people who thought she was a man. Koen had a good point though—they had to be at the castle in the early morning, and trekking through the woods in a dress wasn't something a lady would do. Plus, it was terribly difficult. One advantage of dressing like a man was wearing trousers. If she ever went back to being a woman, she'd be hard-pressed to give up male fashions for their simplicity and movement, if nothing else.

Nothing men wore was half so painful and restricting as a corset. Mina had agreed. Perhaps an advantage of living in the woods with a bunch of brothers was the ability to turn one's nose up at the restrictive garments and dress as one pleased. Mina certainly enjoyed a mix of trousers and modest dresses, favoring them to the low necklines and tight waists the nobles adored.

Anna discarded the rest of her clothes and crouched nude by the riverbank. She'd waited until the house was quiet, everyone asleep in their beds, until she slipped from her borrowed room, down the stairs, and out into the night.

With only the stars and hooting owls as her companions, she walked into the water, one careful step at a time. *Freaking freezing!* Still, clean water never felt so good. The stones under her feet, polished smooth by the current, were the perfect cushion as she edged into the deeper water, her soap in tow.

She'd loved the water when she lived by the sea as a girl. Even the scent of fish that always clung to the docks couldn't put her off wading into the surf to search for clams or pretty shells or fixing her eyes to the waves in the hopes of spotting one of the merfolk. But all that changed the night Captain Blackbeard raided the port. Her father had gone to the docks with a number of other men, ready to fight off the invaders and save the fabrics he needed for his business. He never returned, neither did her love for the sea. In fact, she was happy to see the back of it when her mother remarried one of her father's widowed business partners a few years later. It was a new start, a new life, free of the nightmares of pirate raids. Plus, she would be getting a little sister almost her own age. Never had she thought that future would be worse than the past she left behind.

Maybe it was the chilly embrace of the water or the painful shards of memory pricking her senses, but Anna didn't hear the sound of someone approaching or undressing until they splashed into the water just down the river.

Her heart leaped into her throat as she sank down into the current up to her neck.

A male groan shuddered through the night and settled warm and heavy in her core.

Oh, all the heavens and hells, this is a disaster. Friend or foe, it didn't matter. No one could know she was a woman and—she glanced down at the water—she was *not* letting anyone see her like this.

Moonlight illuminated a strong arm just around the bend. Thick shrubs blocked the rest of him from view.

Anna eyed her clothes where they lay on the bank a few steps away. Could she emerge and don them in time? She bit her lip, weighing her options. Running through the night in the nude lacked a certain appeal.

Before she could make her choice, the man edged further into the river. Anna's mouth went dry. The pale light illuminated a sculpted backside more chiseled than the statues outside the castle. A wave of heat rushed through her as she forced her gaze up inch by inch, taking in his narrow waist, muscular back, strong arms.

A soft gasp caught in her throat and had her sinking even deeper into the water.

Will.

Heavens and hells, it's Will.

She'd known the huntsman was strong the moment he'd pulled her against him outside the supply wagon, but seeing his form in all its glory...

Sweet saints.

She *had* to get out of there.

Something slick and scaled brushed by her leg.

A screech slipped out before she could clamp her jaws together or her hand over her mouth.

"Who's there?" Will lunged out of sight, likely going for his blade.

Damn it. Anna squeezed her eyes closed, willing herself to disappear. Water splashed ahead, and her eyes flew open as Will charged back into the river, dagger in hand and still completely nude. Worse, he faced her way.

Like an arrow to the target, she stared at that shadowy area between his legs. Warm, wet heat rushed to her core, and she considered sinking below the water. Nothing could ever wipe the memory of that part of him from her head, especially not as he stumbled her way through the water, the appendage between his legs becoming even clearer.

Too late to run. Nowhere to hide.

"Stop!" Anna squeaked.

Will froze in water just deep enough to hide the most damning parts of him.

"Ansel?" He leaned forward, his dagger dipping toward the water. "I heard a scream. What are you doing?"

"Bathing," she dropped her voice extra low. "What did you think?" *Idiot.*

"Ah." He rubbed at his bearded chin, suddenly quiet. His gaze wandered far away from her, off to the far bank. *Thank goodness.*

She barely sucked in a breath before he glanced back to her, making every muscle in her body go rigid beneath the water.

"You don't mind that I join you?"

J-join? Her mouth gaped. A swell of the river had her coughing and choking on crisp water.

He wandered to the bank, rising out the water. *Returning the dagger?*

This time, she was smart enough to look away.

"Y-yes, yes I mind," she sputtered. "I prefer to bathe alone, thank you very much."

"Oh?" He wandered back out from behind the bushes. "We're both men, aren't we?"

The suspicion in his tone, the hint of a tease, made her blood run cold.

"You think I haven't seen a naked man before?" he continued with a light chuckle.

She could boil the water with the way his words burned her up inside, both with worry and something she tried very, very hard to ignore no matter the melting feeling deep within.

"I could wash your back. It can be quite hard on one's own."

Insufferable man. He would choose that moment of all of them to suddenly have more than a few words for her. Mostly because she couldn't keep looking at him without turning scarlet, she turned said back to him, hugging her arms around her chest under the flowing water. "I fared quite well on my own, I'll have you know."

Water sloshed far behind her, but it could have been next to her for the way it made her stomach toss and turn. "Fancy words for an orphan farm boy. Though I guess you weren't always one, huh?"

The river freezing over would have chilled her less. *Oh, all the heavens and hells.* She'd been so worried about him figuring out she was a girl she hadn't thought about her words at all—or what she'd told him of her past. At least she hadn't told him her mother remarried a merchant of some standing and trained her daughters to be ladies worthy of it.

Anna bit her lip, nearly drawing blood, until the answer came to her. "I'm to pretend to be a lady worthy of a companion to the queen, am I not?" She let her voice rise to its natural tone, dripped in the elegance her mother would be proud of. "It won't do us any good if I get turned away at the gates. I promised to be helpful, and I will."

Silence lingered so long she'd almost convinced herself he'd left. But one sly, slow glance over her shoulder disavowed that thought in an instant.

He stood, still as a statue in the river, watching her. Moonlight caught on the muscular planes of his chest and highlighted the dark beard clinging to his jaw. It could use a little trim but did nothing to distract from his appearance. If anything, it gave him a bit of a rough edge she savored. Saints help her. If they'd met only a year sooner, she'd have done anything to catch his eye, Ella and her tricks be damned.

As it was, she needed to get away from him quick.

"You could do with some practice yourself," she snapped. "Would you treat your sister this way? If I were Mina, would you dare spy on her?"

A deep grumble rolled across the water. "Of course not."

Water splashed. She dared another glance behind her in time to see Will's shoulders hunch and his eyes glance away.

"I shall give you the privacy you desire, my lady," he responded in a mocking tone. After a deep bow, he stalked back around the bend.

Only after Anna had slipped from the river, donned her clothes, and trekked halfway back to the cottage did his words strike her. *My lady.* He was just playing along, right? For a moment in that river, she was certain he'd figured her out.

She shook her head and trudged toward the house looming in the darkness. In two days, they'd enter the queen's contest. With any luck, they'd put their poison to use, and she could free her mother and sister in the ensuing aftermath.

She swallowed down the bile burning the base of her throat. Ella had done horrible things, but she was still her stepsister. But if it meant freedom for her mother and sister...well... Anna shivered. Whether success or failure, Will and his strange behavior didn't matter, only freeing her family did. Soon he'd be nothing more than a moment in her past.

10

*W*ill had made a terrible mistake. What had he been thinking that night, trying and failing to get closer to Ansel in the river? It'd be a lie to say his offer was purely friendly. He'd been curious and gotten a good mental smack for that curiosity.

Will scowled into his whiskey. Probably a poor choice of drink at the edge of dawn, but it was the only thing that calmed his thoughts. *And oh, do I have thoughts.* Ansel had barely looked at him over the last two days. The whole trek to the city, Ansel had chatted with Mina, Brandt, and even Koen. But to him? Not a word.

He'd probably turned him off. That was fair. But the young man's fight and fire sparked a yearning for something between them, if even just friendship. Seeing him in a dress again...

He shook his head. It'd be too easy to delude himself to believing Ansel was a woman, a bright, headstrong one not afraid to get her hands dirty. The kind he'd longed for what felt like ages ago, back when he thought he had a choice in the matter, a future. For a moment at the river, he'd been certain Ansel was his dream come to life like a magical being to torment him. The shriek was high enough, but maybe he imagined that too? Heard what he wanted? He couldn't be sure anymore. And the more time passed, the less Ansel's identity mattered.

How foolish he'd been in so many things. He swirled his glass, watching the last of the amber liquid roll around in the bottom. The common room of the inn was still empty other than him. Not even the innkeeper was awake before dawn.

Only recently had the kitchen maid started working on breakfast, the savory scents of baking bread slipping out into the room. Will had poured the whiskey himself, leaving a generous payment tucked behind the counter. Soon the others should be up, Mina and Ansel dressing in their finest, powdering their faces with rouge—Mina to make her look older and not like the child she still was, and Ansel to further his disguise, not that he needed help.

The stairs creaked and groaned as Brandt and Koen descended. Brandt stifled a yawn, nearly tripping down the last three steps.

Koen dipped him a nod and tugged at the collar of his shirt. The formal attire fit him well, not just its cut, but his air. Between his serious nature, the spectacles perched upon his nose, and the grey spotting his combed and trimmed hair, he could pass for a man of society.

Will rubbed at his own beard. Perhaps he should have trimmed it up, made some attempt at looking the gentleman himself. He downed the rest of the whiskey, savoring the burn. *No, too risky.* It was better this way. The queen was looking for a fair maiden, not a male companion. A somewhat unkempt man at his side certainly wouldn't harm Ansel's chances.

"Are the *ladies* getting ready?" Gravelly notes colored his words, showing his lack of sleep. Trying to rest comfortably all crammed together in their shared room was impossible, especially with what they faced today.

"As should we." Koen flashed the vial clutched in his palm. They'd each have one tucked away on their person—except Brandt, who'd take up a post somewhere outside the castle and await their return. He'd argued about it half the trek here, but on that topic, he'd been sorely outnumbered, four against one. Brandt had many skills but subtlety wasn't one of them. The chances of him exposing their plot or getting them kicked out by accident were too high to risk.

Will took the vial and slipped it in an inner pocket of his coat. One moment, that's all they needed to find—a few seconds to drip the poison into the queen's wine, food she might eat, anything. There would likely be a spread of food—little pastries, fruits, small savories. There usually was at events in the castle, or there had been during the kings' reigns. Surely the queen wouldn't expect the young women to be famished all day. *Though who knows what that witch thinks.*

Poisoning others though—he swallowed the tightness in his throat—was best avoided, but if that was the only chance, he'd take it, damn the consequences. Everyone in the kingdom would be better off if the queen was dead, which meant it was worth the risks. But their new queen wasn't the only guilty party. Chancellor Stephan Friedrich, the old king's former advisor who lingered by her side, had just as much to answer for, maybe more. He slammed his glass on the table, causing the brothers to jump.

"Apologies. Didn't sleep well."

"How could ya on those lumpy, narrow beds?" Brandt asked, far too loud. He glanced toward the kitchens and gave a shrug when no one appeared to scold him.

Some time later, the innkeeper appeared with breakfast. Mina made her way down the stairs. Pride bloomed in Will's heart as he took in the girl, her hem held up in one hand, her other trailing down the railing like a proper lady.

"Now where'd ya learn that?" Brandt asked in awe.

She flushed and dipped a deep curtsy at the bottom of the stairs. "Ansel taught me." She glanced away, something he couldn't read in her usually obvious features. "We practiced for hours yesterday."

So that's what they'd been doing. Had it been anyone but Ansel, he'd have worried for Mina. Too many young men he'd known would try to take advantage in such a situation, especially with Mina's obvious infatuation. From the very first day, though, it was clear that Ansel wasn't that type. He treated Mina like his own sister. Perhaps she reminded him of the one he said he'd lost—imprisoned by the queen. Still, something was off with Mina this morning.

"Sure knows how to curtsy," Brandt mumbled around a mouth of bread.

No kidding.

"An—" Mina cut herself off with a quick glance at the innkeeper. She visibly swallowed. "My *sister* should be down soon." A weak smile flickered and died on her lips.

A name. They couldn't very well call him Ansel when presenting him to the queen. Of all the things to overlook.

Koen straightened and coughed into his palm. He glared at Brandt and Will over his hand. Apparently, none of them had considered this predicament.

Mina took an open seat at the table, prim and proper as any lady. Someone, perhaps Ansel, had swept back her hair and pinned it behind her head. She reached for it, trying to pull it across her face, before dropping her hand back to twist in her lap. They were all out of their element today.

He stirred in his seat, pondering all the ways the day could go wrong, and possible names for the young man, until Brandt dropped his spoon with a clatter. "Damn. Now that's a sight."

"Wha—" The words died on Will's lips as he turned his head toward the stairs. Ansel was a vision in the flowing dress of blue and white, a dream from long ago that turned to dust in the light of reality. Not even the deep scowl across his features, as fiery as the red of his wig, could detract from the air of grace and nobility he'd donned with the clothes.

"Siblings." Ansel dropped a low curtsy of his own, his voice still low and edged.

"Well, now." Koen grinned. "Quite useful indeed. You have the *perfume* I left for you?"

"Of course, shall we go?"

Where Ansel managed to hide the vial of poison, Will had no idea.

"There's one matter to discuss first." Will let his gaze scan the siblings before gesturing to the stairs.

Ansel rolled his eyes. "Seriously? In these heels?" He pulled up the hem of the skirt, showing off dainty, stocking-clad legs. It was a minor miracle that he and Mina wore the same size shoe. With a sigh of frustration, he turned and stomped up the creaking stairs with entirely too much ease for a man in heels. Will followed, the others not far behind.

"You need a name," Will said the moment he closed the door to their rented room. "A woman's name."

Ansel's chest rose and fell even as his face paled. Had he truly been a lady he met in the city, Will might think her about to swoon.

"Ansel..." Koen said, drawing out the letters. "Perhaps, Ann?"

"No!" Ansel snapped.

Will straightened, his head cocking to the side.

"Why not?" It was a common enough name.

"No." Ansel's hand opened and closed at his side. "Wasn't that one of the queen's sister's names? Or close to it?"

"You know—" Brandt rubbed at his beard. "I think you're right. The ugly one? One that got away. Had her face on those posters."

Will didn't miss the way Ansel's fist tightened. "Right, that one," he snapped. "Wouldn't do us any favors if the queen turned me away for a fake name."

Will pursed his lips. *No favors indeed.* His gaze raked Ansel's form as he debated other names with the siblings. He possessed such a lithe form. Even the curve of his neck was soft, along with the way the blue ribbon accented his skin. The bob of his throat as he swallowed, so flat and even—

Will blinked. Once. Twice. His heart gave a little misstep.

Surely not.

"Rosa," Mina said.

Everyone looked to her, even Will. The girl smiled shyly toward Ansel, her hands twisting in her lap. "I had a doll once..." Her gaze dipped toward the ground, but then she righted herself, straightening and looking at him straight on. When she continued, her voice had strengthened too. "It had red hair like your wig. It might be the perfect name, if you like it. And you can use our family name. We're no one. They'll never know."

"Rosa." Will rolled it around on his tongue.

With a quick glance toward the lightening window, Koen jumped to his feet. "It'll have to do. Let's go."

The walk to the castle was one of the longest of his life, despite being far shorter than most treks he'd made lately. Ansel had his arm looped through his like a proper lady, but the young man was strung up tighter than a bowstring. Rather than Ansel's arm resting on his, he might as well have been trying to balance a board. And though the young man—if that's what he truly was, and Will had his doubts now—expertly maneuvered the cobblestones in his heeled shoes, the scowl stuck on his features gave away his discomfort.

Will wasn't much better. Being this close to the intriguing young man, or woman, or whatever he was, fleeing the brush of his skirts against his side, was enough to excite even the most stalwart of men. He couldn't see Ansel this morning, just a lovely young woman, and that unnerved him as much as anything else. Though, if he were truly honest, he might favor Ansel's short hair and unpainted face.

"Relax," Will whispered as they turned down the last block.

The arm looped through his stiffened impossibly more. "This is a mistake," Ansel whispered in return. "No one will believe we're siblings."

Not if he couldn't get his act together, that was for sure. He rolled his shoulder. "We might if you'd let us buy the brown wig."

The young man groaned.

"Different fathers?"

Ansel scowled up at him. "I should be with Koen instead."

Will glanced at the pair keeping step at their side.

Koen shook his head. "It's a stretch for me to pass as Mina's father already." They'd considered sticking with the truth, but that might be less believable with Mina favoring their mother in looks and Koen their father, or so the siblings said.

Brandt hung back at a careful distance, not to be confused with the pairs of ladies and escorts headed to the castle road. His presence did a good job of keeping others a fair distance back from them. Ahead, a gaggle of pairs already gathered at the gates leading up the castle road.

If not a brother, they'd need to present a different relationship. He rolled some ideas across his tongue before whispering, "Fiancée then."

"What!" Ansel flinched. The young man jerked him to stop, staring up at him with that fierce scowl. "You can't be serious."

"I am." Not to mention it gave him another reason to stay close. "The queen might be moved by a man willing to relinquish his dear fiancée into the queen's service. She's quite..." He tapped a finger on his chin, searching for the right word.

"Vain? Full of herself?" Ansel spewed, paying no care for the volume of his voice.

Will pulled him closer and gave a meaningful look down the road. Engaged as the women were chatting with one another, based on the high giggle and excited words reaching his ears, they probably didn't notice. Still, they couldn't be too careful.

"Fine," he sighed. "Whatever." Ansel turned back to the women, this time pulling him along.

A knot built in Will's throat with every step back toward the castle. It was his first time back since...

His fist tightened. This had been a welcoming place...once. Now it fueled his nightmares. Its pale towers rose to the sky with high walls connecting them, and sculpted hedges guarded the road. The dark shadow shrouding his soul came out in force, rearing its ugly head to demand vengeance.

The daggers hidden on his form gave him strength. The poison in his inner pocket settled warm and comforting against his chest.

Today he'd end this, for better or worse.

But the slightest thread of regret sewed its way around his neck, tightening, tugging his gaze to the right, where Ansel stared up at the castle with a burning in his eyes bright and hot as his own.

A new and completely unexpected regret washed over him. If they failed, he might never get the chance to truly know this stranger who'd bewitched him.

11

iancée. Fiancée! The nerve of him. Anna scowled up at the castle.

If she didn't know better, Anna would think he knew her secret and was trying everything he could to provoke her into revealing it. She should be focused on her wicked stepsister and how exactly she was going to get close enough to poison her. Or just bracing herself to see her again.

Anna blew out a deep sigh and glanced around at the other women and their escorts gathering at the gates. A few were quiet and reserved like Mina, clinging to their companions and shifting nervously near the edge of the crowd. Most, however, seemed as giddy as the women before the prince's ball a year past.

It'd be hard to forget that night. A sudden heaviness filled her chest, threatening to drag her down onto the cobblestones. Without Will's strong arm looped through hers, it might have.

The prince had failed to choose a bride, and the king was impatient the matter be settled, or so people around the city said. So the king hosted a ball and invited every eligible maiden, noble and common alike, to attend.

It was Anna's chance, a way to free her family from Ella's abuse. She'd taken time with her appearance, however plain it was. That kernel of hope burned so brightly, she was certain it'd get the prince's attention. He would see the beauty within her and not be swayed by her sister's poisonous words like every other man she met.

But she never got the chance. Ella stepped in front of her to greet the prince first, and once he saw her, he never saw anyone else. When the prince passed by Anna, he didn't even turn his cold, brown eyes and strong jaw her way.

Now, Anna's stomach dropped, and she whispered a small prayer to the Mother and all her saints for letting her miss breakfast. It wouldn't do any of them good if she lost her meal all over the street.

Excited murmurs shifted and rose around them. Anna stretched on her toes, trying to see above the crowd as they shoved toward the gates.

"Carriages are coming," Will said.

She scowled at him. Of course, he was tall enough to see just fine. She was taller than most women, but between the ridiculous hairdos and hats most wore, it was difficult to see.

"Ladies and gentlemen," a booming voice rolled through the crowd, demanding silence. "Thank you all for coming. Our dear queen will be most pleased."

Anna rolled her eyes. *Dear indeed.*

"Though we appreciate each and every one of you, there are far more than we can escort to the castle."

Will stiffened at her side. Anna forced herself to look around. There were a lot of people here. She stretched on her toes and glanced over one shoulder. More still arrived.

Pairs began to press forward, scooting and nudging one another to get close to the front. Anna reached for Koen, taking his free hand in hers and forming a little wall lest they get separated.

"Be still, ladies," the man called, his raised hands just visible beyond the feathered hairpiece blocking much of her view. That woman clearly didn't know Ella's distaste for animals.

Anna's stomach turned over at the sudden memory of Charlotte's cat. How anyone could hate that sweet, fluffy boy, she didn't understand. But one day, Anna had found him stiff and cold in the garden. Poisoned probably. Anna never could tell Charlotte the truth, that she buried her beloved boy in the roses. Instead, she let her sister believe he ran off. *Good riddance*, Ella had said with a smirk. That's all she needed to know who was responsible, not that there had been much doubt.

"Your order will not matter," the man continued. "We shall see each and every one of you in turn."

High-pitched sighs surrounded them as the shoving stopped.

"Though only the fairest of you shall go to the castle and be presented before Her Majesty."

Oh, heavens and hells. Mina leaned around Koen, staring at her with wide-eyed dismay. The girl had been even quieter than normal this morning. Her fault probably, but there was no helping it now.

If they couldn't get to the castle, their plan would be ruined. All four would be best, but if even one pair of them could advance, that would be a chance. It would be better than going back to the cabin and relying on Koen to decipher the potion and its cure—*if* he could. And that was only step one of their ridiculous backup plan.

Anna flashed the girl what she hoped was a reassuring smile. She was lovely, if young. The queen would be a fool to turn her away.

Unless she wasn't looking for the fairest maiden...

She stiffened, feeling ill once again.

Will patted her arm. "You'll do fine."

She nearly snorted. Beautiful, she was not. But worse than being turned away for her lack of beauty, what if this was some grand trap? A way for her stepsister to root out the woman who'd escaped her guards? *Me.*

Anna pursed her lips. Her stepsister couldn't really think her that stupid. If not for these fools, she'd be far away from this place. Sometimes their mother had been a bit aloof, prone to bouts of forgetfulness and daydreaming, but that trait passed both Anna and Charlotte by. They had their father's sharp wit instead.

"Form a line please, ladies. Your escorts may stand with you," the man continued, his booming voice carrying over the assembled crowd. They moved to comply.

She trusted Mina. The girl would keep her secrets. Koen and Brandt struck her as honest too—the story about their siblings and the empty beds in their home were evidence to their cause. Only one of their number had any connection to the castle other than her.

Anna glanced up at Will. Something dark loomed behind his eyes. Though a thick beard cloaked his lower face, she could still make out the hard set of his jaw and the stiffness in his shoulders.

He was nervous in a way he hadn't been robbing the wagons, addressing the guards who'd come upon them, or any other time they'd been together.

Will had been the one to drag her along with them. The one to suggest she stay and to agree she could be helpful. And he was the only one who dared look at her like she might be a woman and not the young man she pretended to be.

The toe of her boot caught a cobblestone, and she pitched forward. Will moved with surprising speed to catch her before she could tumble onto the stones and muss her dress. That would surely get her eliminated. At the moment, that outcome felt preferable.

She leaned against his chest, trying to gather her racing thoughts as much as herself.

"Are you all right?" A strong hand ran down her back, stirring up a shiver even through the layers of cloth.

Anna breathed heavily. His gaze caught hers and held. All the jagged ice of moments ago was gone, replaced by genuine concern. Or so it seemed. Still…

She pushed off him and smoothed out her dress. "Yes, yes, of course." Anna forced a smile, as if all were right in the world and she truly couldn't wait to meet the queen. Thankfully, the vial pressed between her breasts hadn't become dislodged in her stumble.

A quick glance this way and that confirmed no one noticed her momentary slip. They were all too busy forming into lines to await the man's inspection. Koen raised one brow but said nothing. Beyond him, Mina stared straight ahead, her mouth opening and closing as much as her chest rose and fell. If anyone were to suddenly faint or fall ill, it'd more likely be her.

The queen's man, who looked vaguely familiar now that she could see him properly—*the herald from the royal ball perhaps?*—began his inspection of the women. He was quick, wasting no time on the feelings of the ladies he sent on their way with a wrinkle of his nose and wave of his hand.

Many more were turned away than sent on to the carriages. Some women managed it with grace, their heads held high. A few shed tears. One threatened him, saying his poor taste was an offense to the queen.

The guards ushering her away said otherwise. Her gap-toothed sneer likely didn't help matters.

With every pronouncement, the air grew thinner. Anna's dress was too tight, the weather too warm despite being pleasantly cool earlier that morning.

The herald started down their row. Will tugged down his brimmed hat and slipped his arm from hers before she realized what he was doing.

Anna swayed on her feet, suddenly adrift. "What are you—" But there was no time to ask as the man stepped in front of Mina and raked his inquisitive gaze across her.

To Mina's credit, she did an excellent job holding a serene smile and forcing herself not to look away.

"Yes, very well, on to the castle with you."

Mina squealed and beamed at Koen, whether in true delight or not, who could say?

Anna barely had time to let out the breath she'd been holding and pull in a new one before he stepped in front of her. Between the powder on his face and the pale, curled wig he donned, the man was a ghost of a person. The grey and white livery of the queen's staff didn't help matters. If not for his rich brown eyes, he'd look like a portrait that someone forgot to add color to.

"Such bold hair." He sucked on his teeth with a little popping sound. The look on his face wasn't exactly approving.

Maybe she really shouldn't have picked this wig after all. Anna stretched her smile a little brighter and dared meet the man's shrewd gaze. He was the first to look away.

"Suppose it could be seen as lovely," he mused, glancing past her—*at Will?* The man's brows wrinkled. He gave a subtle shake of his head, and the look was gone. "To the castle. Shoo, shoo."

Anna nearly swooned when he finally continued down the line to the next woman, whom he promptly declared too skinny and sent away.

Will caught up to her in three steps and looped his arm again through hers, causing Anna to skip a half-step and nearly trip over her hem.

"Stop sneaking up on me like that," Anna grumbled in a whisper, conscious of the queen's guards lining the road to the carriages waiting just ahead. "You shouldn't have left me to begin with."

He coughed into his free hand. "Thought you might shine better on your own. Seems I was right."

She rolled her eyes and scowled up at him. More like he didn't want to be noticed if the queen's herald remembered a former huntsman.

"Let me help you into the carriage," he whispered, as if she didn't know how to behave like a lady.

She swallowed her retort. Because, after all, she wasn't really supposed to know. "Of course, sweetheart," she purred in the most lilting voice she could manage. *Infuriating man.*

He took two more steps, stiffened, and glanced her way. His lips parted. An incredulous look shone in his eyes.

Anna just smiled. If nothing else came of today, at least she made him as uncomfortable as he did her.

12

*E*very bounce of the carriage set his nerves further on edge. Will would be lucky not to crack a tooth the way he kept grinding them together without realizing until his jaw stiffened and ached.

The herald almost noticed him.

He'd sucked in a breath, ready to push through the gaggle of couples and flee at the slightest movement from the man. Even now, his fingers kept brushing over a hidden dagger, the only thing keeping him sane on the short ride that stretched impossibly long like a hard winter.

And they weren't even inside yet. *Fucking saints, I am in trouble.*

At his side, Ansel kept pressing on the sides of his bodice as if he were a woman with a corset strung up too tight.

"What are you doing?" he ground out.

Ansel scowled at him before whispering, "The vial slipped."

"You put it where?" Will gaped as Ansel pushed on his chest, causing his breasts—*stuffing, right, just the padding he'd used*—to shift ever so slightly.

"In my bodice, where else did you expect me to keep it?"

Across from him, Koen shrugged as if to agree. Mina absolutely refused to meet his gaze, even as her cheeks deepened in color.

Ansel folded his hands in his lap again when the carriage rocked to a halt. A liveried footman opened the door.

Will sucked in a sharp breath. They were truly doing this.

The castle looked just as he remembered—from the outside. But once they stepped through the grand double doors, all of that changed. He wasn't the only one to draw to a sudden halt. Those in front of them gaped at the splendor of it all, commenting on the gilded molding on the walls or the fresco on the ceiling rumored to have taken the artist years to complete.

Those things were familiar to Will. He'd seen them before. What he gawked at were the changes that had overtaken the castle these last months. Gone were the navy carpets running the length of the hall and the tapestries bearing the king's crest. In their stead was the most horrendous shade of pale pink he'd ever beheld. It hung everywhere, clashing with the grace and beauty of the building.

His teeth clenched so hard his jaw popped. *Pink*. Not even a bright shade that might look lovely on a woman's form, but this pale color looked more like a skinned deer than—

A strong jerk on his arm pulled him back to the moment. Ansel beamed up at him with a saccharine smile he could almost believe was real.

"Coming, darling?" His companion drawled out the endearment.

Will's gaze darted around, taking in the pairs trailing down the hall flanked by castle guards.

"It is such a lovely castle," Ansel said, his voice soft and lilting as the lady he pretended to be. By the Mother, that voice tugged at him. "But we're needed this way." Another firm tug emphasized his words.

Will gave himself an inner shake.

It took effort to put one foot in front of the other and escort his *lady* through the hall. Will kept his gaze firmly ahead, planted on Koen's back, lest he accidentally make eye contact with anyone who might recognize him. Not to mention that it took everything he had to ignore the feel of Ansel's dress swishing against his breeches and the warmth of his arm looped through his own.

He couldn't like him, couldn't become involved with anyone, not yet anyway. It risked too much, far too much. The added danger wasn't fair to Ansel. He'd dragged them into this mess enough already, willing or not. Again, he ground his teeth together. He should have left him in the woods, given him some food, and sent him on his way the night they met.

If anything happened to Ansel...

Everything in him flexed and tensed.

"Darling?" Ansel looked up at him, batting his too-long eyelashes. If he was nervous, he did a damn good job of hiding it.

Will cleared his throat and patted "her" arm in a fake show of calm assurance.

The hallway emptied into the grand ballroom. It'd seen less change than the hall, still sporting the gilded wall of windows that spilled light across the black-and-white-checked marble floor. Tables draped with lace—the expensive stuff, imported from across the Cerulean Sea—dotted the space. The couples who had arrived before them already clustered around the tables in little groups, sampling delicate fare from silver platters.

"Mmmm." Ansel let out a groan that was anything but manly. "Lemon cakes. I can smell them from here."

The way he tugged his bottom lip between his teeth as he stared toward a heaping display was more enticing than any sweet. He had to be doing it on purpose. Messing with him, trying hard to convince everyone, including Will, he was a woman. *Damn, if he isn't a good actor. An act*, Will reminded himself, *that's all it is.* He was not the woman he dressed as. *He's not interested in me.*

Still, he couldn't quite make himself believe it.

"Wouldn't want to upset your stomach before meeting the queen, sweetheart." Will forced a smile, his eyes hooding as the last syllables left his lips. He'd bet his right hand everything in the room was laced with some concoction or other from the fairy godmother.

Color raced across Ansel's cheeks, brighter than the rouge he'd painted on them. His red lips parted before he regained his composure and tugged his arm free. "Yes, well." He smoothed a lock of long hair behind his ear, as if he'd done it a million times, and glanced away. "Wouldn't want that."

Effortless, despite the heeled shoes, Ansel strode across the room to join Koen and Mina near one of the tall windows. Will's hunter instincts took over as he watched him move.

He'd bedded more than a few women before all went to shit, knew the swish of their hips, the gentle slope of their necks. *Well, some of them.* What if his companion wasn't a man after all, but a woman? Despite how he'd looked when they met, it was possible. *But why?*

Will rubbed at the sudden ache of confusion burning in his chest. A trap? Some kind of ruse to lure them in here and get them captured?

It couldn't be. Not Ansel. He'd seen the fire in his eyes, the determination. And Ansel hadn't known a wit about them when they met, or even when he asked to join their merry little band.

Get it together, man, he scolded himself for the millionth time.

Koen caught his gaze across the room, the man's raised brows asking a question as clear as if he'd spoken. *What are you doing?*

Being a fool. He answered with a shift of his jaw, not that Koen likely knew what he tried to say.

The urge to grab a drink off a passing tray and down it in one gulp nearly won over the little voice reminding him that everything was likely tainted.

Get. It. Together.

Of all the places to question his sexuality or his companion's gender preferences, this was not it. One wrong move and they'd all be in the dungeons...or worse.

Koen pulled him into an embrace, like two friends connecting after a time away, as he joined their little circle. His friend slapped him on the back—hard. "Too many ghosts?" he whispered.

"Something like that," Will responded. *Or not enough ghosts.* He thought that would be the worst of it. He'd prepared for it, shut down that part of himself so that it couldn't bother him to see the familiar faces and lack thereof.

That *should* have been what bothered him.

"Looks like we're to wait here for now," Ansel said, scanning the room.

Will fought against the frown pulling at his lips. They wouldn't accomplish anything standing around here. They couldn't very well poison all these people on the off chance that the queen might decide to sample the buffet. Would they have the chance once she arrived or once they were taken to her? His gaze slid across the guards positioned around the room—they were alert, watchful. They weren't taking liberties with the queen's safety.

"Maybe. We need to find out what comes next," Koen said.

"Well," Ansel lifted the hem of his skirts. "I'll go ask."

Will stiffened. "Wait—"

He reached for her—him—but he was already striding across the floor toward the nearest guard. Will sped after him, his long-legged stride catching up to Ansel with ease, but not before he waved at one of the guards to catch his attention. "Oh, sir."

A mumbled curse slipped passed his lips at the vaguely familiar face. He couldn't get too close, couldn't risk it. Like a dutiful chaperone, he hung back, watching after his charge as Ansel spoke to the man with an air of class and confidence he doubted any other farm boy—or girl—could muster.

"Sir," Ansel said again, smoothing out his dress and giving a quick curtsy. "Do you know when we'll meet the queen?"

The guard's gaze dropped from Ansel's face, dipping to his chest. Will's fist tightened at his side.

Ansel gave a shy giggle, drawing the man's gaze back to his face. "You see, I've always wanted to meet her, and I'm so excited. If I could be the first to go...well, it'd be a dream." He covered his mouth with his hand, feigning embarrassment.

"Sorry, miss." He looked Ansel up and down again. "But you're to stay here for now and enjoy the queen's hospitality. His Grace, Chancellor Friedrich, will determine who sees the queen first."

Blood roared in his ears. Nails bit into his palms.

He'd kill the chancellor, that traitorous bastard. He'd had as much of a hand in the coup as the queen herself. Will had seen the scheming look in the man's eyes for years, the way he whispered to the old king and tried to control his actions with courtly words and strong suggestions. It had never been enough for him, being the king's trusted friend and advisor.

Ansel's laugh pierced the darkness that had descended on him. He poked at the guard, flirting like a professional, before sauntering back toward Will and casting a wink over his shoulder at his new friend.

Will's nose wrinkled.

"Oh my, you are the perfect picture of a jealous fiancé," Ansel whispered as he passed, just loud enough for him to hear.

Saints above. He turned on his heel and fell into step next to him. "Stop that," he all but hissed.

"What?" Ansel blinked up at him, the portrait of innocence.

Will leaned in so close that his wig tickled his cheek. He swore Ansel gasped, going still a few paces from their companions. "Taunting me. Distracting me."

The innocence fell from his face like a dropped curtain. "I'm not the one who looked like he was going to kill someone. He's just a guard, for goodness' sake. Not like he was going to figure us out," he said with a sharp nod toward the man in question.

A huff of laughter slipped from his lips as they rejoined their allies. If only that was the source of his fury. Will leaned in and dropped his voice to a bare whisper. "I need to get out of here. Find the queen."

"What?" Mina squeaked, a hand flying to her mouth.

"Too risky," Koen said.

Ansel nodded in agreement.

No doubt, but waiting around and missing their chance would be worse. And if the chancellor recognized him despite his attire and the beard and hair he'd let grow too long, they'd be doomed. He shifted his jaw. "You all stay, follow the plan. But I have to try."

"There are guards everywhere," Ansel hissed.

"Need a distraction." Will eyed the tables. Maybe he could trip into one. But they'd probably just send in some maids to clean. He couldn't start a fight. That'd draw the wrong kind of attention.

"I'll swoon."

They all turned to glance at Mina where she stood with her back to the windows. She pulled at her bottom lip with her teeth before straightening her shoulders and looking up at him. "I'll swoon," she said again. "It will draw attention, but not be too unexpected...circumstances and all."

"You're sure?" he asked, brows rising. It wasn't like the girl to put herself in the spotlight.

Mina's gaze cut to Ansel before a soft blush colored her cheeks. "Yes, I want to help."

She was smitten. Poor thing.

"Center of the room. Near that table." Koen gave the briefest tilt of his head toward the space in question. "I'll catch you."

"Now?" Mina asked.

Voices and laughter carried down the hall, another group on the way to the ballroom. "Good a time as any," Koen said.

Will nodded. Who knew how many more women and girls they'd send up to the castle, and if they waited too long, they'd miss this chance.

Saints be with us.

Will turned on his heel before he could doubt the plan and moved toward the far doors. A few other pairs filled the space, clamoring around the food-laden tables, though only one or two touched the delectable fare. *Probably too nervous to eat. Can't blame them for that.*

Heels clacked across the marble. A flash of red entered his periphery.

He sucked in a sharp breath. "What are you doing?"

"Staying near my chaperone like the proper lady I am," Ansel replied, far too sweetly for his liking.

"You have to stay here. Wait for what comes next."

"Do I?"

"Yes," he snapped. A few heads turned his way. *Shit.* Will twisted away from the onlookers.

As he did, gasps rolled through the crowd, silencing conversation. Heels clicked and thumped, accompanying the swish of material and whispered words as people hurried toward Mina's feigned swoon.

With a quick glance, he caught sight of Koen kneeling on the ground and guards hurrying over. He flicked his attention to the doors nearby, a silent prayer to the Mother on his lips. The two guards who'd been posted at the doors rushed past.

No time to waste.

Will bolted for the door, pulse hammering in his throat. He had seconds at best, no time to be cautious. He grabbed the brass handle, twisted it, pushed, and slid out into the hallway.

He skidded to a stop a few paces outside the door, twisting his head side to side as he scanned for movement, activity, life.

Nothing. But it won't last. Never did in this castle.

The door clicked shut behind him, raising the hackles on his neck. Without thinking, he pulled his hidden dagger, twisted toward the threat, and stopped an inch shy of a startled face.

Fuck.

Ansel's wide-eyed gaze focused on the silver blade.

13

*H*eavens and hells, he nearly killed me.

    Every sight and thought narrowed to the blade steady and lethal just before her eyes. She leaned away, her back sliding up the door. Each gilded accent pressed against her spine through the dress.

"Will," she hissed in a whisper.

His chest rose and fell. The dagger wavered, a match for the fury in his piercing gaze, all aimed her way. He'd said not to follow, but she wasn't letting him out of her sight. If he was some traitor, planning to tell her identity to the queen and gain her offered reward, she would do whatever she could to stop him. Better the guards catch them in the hall than Ella unravel her disguise.

"Idiot," he grunted before lowering the blade and sliding it back into its hiding place.

It was too late to go back, and a miracle they hadn't been seen already. *This is a stupid plan. Impulsive. Disastrous.* What had he been thinking? Maybe he'd just gotten jumpy and wasn't working for the queen, but she couldn't be sure yet.

"I'll follow you," she whispered.

He rolled his eyes and flicked his fingers in a motion to follow.

Anna trailed behind with careful steps, keeping her weight on the balls of her feet to stop her heels from clicking against the marble floors. *Darn things.* She wondered if she should kick them off. Her lips twitched as she imagined a guard finding a lone pair of shoes in the hall.

She had to give it to Will, his ability to move without making a sound was impressive. He was a skilled hunter even outside the woods. If they survived this, she'd have to ask him to teach her. Her heart leaped into her throat as he stilled just ahead.

Assuming, of course, that he wasn't about to sell her out.

Anna's brows pinched together as Will pulled back the side of a tapestry and slid behind it. As if the pale pink fabric, the same shade as the flowers she used to grow in her little garden, could hide them in this hallway. *No chance.* He stood out even more behind that thing.

But then, a soft click sounded. Will went eerily still, peering down the hall behind her as if waiting for something. It set Anna's teeth on edge and her pulse thudding harder—until the wall under his palm moved.

Her mouth dropped open as a gaping, shadowed entry appeared from nowhere.

Will waved her over with urgency. His whispered "Quick" barely audible.

Into the wall? The shadowy, dark place? The fine hairs on her arms stood on end. The perfect place to lead someone if Will wanted to make them disappear...or hand them over to their horrible stepsister.

She shouldn't have come. Her body grew stiff as a board.

Down the long hall, something crashed, like a door being thrown open. Voices raced into the quiet.

"Ansel!" Will hissed, waving frantically from the edge of the tapestry.

Oh, hells.

Anna bit her lip and lunged toward the tapestry, not stopping until Will grabbed her arm and hauled her into the shadows. The stones whispered as Will closed the hidden entrance, sealing them in absolute darkness.

"Where in all the heavens are we?" Even her barest whisper rang like a bell through the space. Anna twisted this way and that, searching for Will, for anything, but she couldn't make out a darn thing. Panic crept up her spine, the horror of being trapped in this tomb of a place accentuating it.

"Old servants' corridor."

The deep voice just behind her sent Anna almost jumping out of her skin. She tipped back on her heels, wobbling—

Will wrapped a strong arm around her middle as she fell back against his solid chest, earning a soft grunt. Warm breath caressed her cheek. All her focus narrowed to the feel of his wide palm against her stomach, separated only by the layers of fabric that suddenly felt infinitesimal as spider webbing. She barely breathed, couldn't think, as his fingers splayed wide.

His breath hitched. Will's chest shook ever so slightly against her back as he slid his hand across the expanse of cloth to grasp her hip. Strong fingers dug in—not enough to hurt, but enough to stir up a hundred treacherous thoughts about all the places she wanted those fingers to explore. Preferably without her clothes in the way.

If only he knew, if only he could see her as a woman. Not Anna, not Ella's stepsister, but just...her. Anna leaned back, savoring the feel of him behind her, this stolen moment where darkness cloaked all her thoughts and actions. Even if he turned out to be an enemy, she would never regret this moment.

Will cleared his throat. Her shoulders dropped as he settled her back onto her feet.

"Watch your step." The thickness in his voice slid straight down into her core, stealing the last of her rational thoughts.

Thank goodness for the darkness that shielded her blush.

Unerringly, despite the dark, he found her hand and threaded his fingers through hers. Lightning zipped up her arm.

"This way."

His hand in hers was her only guide. One careful step after another, they trod through the darkness.

"Where are we going?" Anna shivered as something, possibly a rat, skittered through the darkness.

"It connects to some halls and private rooms. If we're lucky, we'll find the queen."

Anna's stomach turned over. "T-to poison her. Right?"

"Shh," he hissed, as if someone might hear.

But who?

Spiderwebs snatched at her hair. She barely choked down a scream. Dread turned her skin clammy. "How do you know this place? These halls?"

"No time to explain."

Anna dug in her heels and jerked her hand free, every horrible possibility suddenly a certainty.

"Ansel." Will reached for her, finding her arm and clutching tight. "We have to move. Quick."

"Y-you, you're—"

"Snap out of it," he said, loud as anything he'd uttered since the ballroom. "You're braver than this."

"How do I know you're not going to hand me over to the queen?" The worry spilled out, quavering and laced with all her insecurity.

Will tugged her closer, until she could practically feel his warmth. "You came after me, remember? I could ask you the same thing. Besides..." She could almost see him, or perhaps her mind conjured an image of him. Tilted head, pinched brows, narrowed eyes. "Why would the queen want you?"

Oh, saints. Stupid, Anna, just stupid.

It was Ella's fault she couldn't fully trust anyone—*always assuming the worst*—no matter how their actions convinced her otherwise.

"Didn't you ever poke around where you weren't supposed to?" he asked, his voice suddenly soft.

Yes, a few times, but—

"The old king didn't like servants slipping around in the walls, so he outlawed the use of these but didn't seal them all. I was friends with Nikolaus—the last king—before his marriage."

Anna nearly gasped. He was friends with that arrogant asshole? Thinking of him as king still felt wrong, even if he was for however brief a time. He'd always be the prince in her mind.

"He showed me these when we were boys. Look, stay here if you must, otherwise…" His hand slid down her arm until it clasped with hers once more. "…we climb."

"Climb?" She couldn't make it up a ladder in a dress, much less in the dark.

"The royal apartments are up the stairs."

She huffed. "Fine." Stairs she could do, especially if it gave her a shot at revenge.

Will seemed to know just where to go, navigating through the dark with ease.

"Quiet now. Not a word," he whispered.

Stone groaned, so much louder than before. Though everything was loud in this hollow space. Light spilled in. Anna shut her eyes, throwing an arm in front of her face before letting her eyes adjust to the intrusion.

Will edged near the light, peeking out into whatever lay beyond.

Each heartbeat felt like a lifetime. Anna held her breath, waiting for something, anything.

Voices carried from down the hall. One? Many? The whisper of sound was too distant to make out. Will heard it too, straining toward the light. Then all at once, he slipped back inside and shut the stone door.

"Quick, this way." He grabbed her hand and hauled her further down the hall.

She could hear something, a soft scrape and whisper of sound. Perhaps his fingers trailing along the wall. They stopped again, and this time he didn't need to order her quiet. She was ready for the light, for whatever lay beyond.

The stone moved. Sound and light slipped in, though less than before, a heavy tapestry blocking much of the secret pathway.

"You're sure about this?" A high voice called from beyond.

Anna's heart skipped a beat.

She thought she was ready, was prepared for anything—except hearing Ella's voice.

Will went still as a statue, his eyes wide. He hadn't expected this luck either.

Ella heaved a loud sigh. Anna could imagine her stepsister rolling her eyes and tossing her blonde hair over one shoulder. "What if none of them are the right one?"

Anna scooted closer, trying to see around the edge of the tapestry to discover who Ella was speaking to. If only they could find a way to dispense their poison or...

Her fingers trailed along her boot as she crouched in the darkness. A well-placed dagger could work just fine. Though whether she had the courage to wield it was the bigger question.

Will held a finger to his lips.

Anna all but ignored him as she crept closer, straining her ears to hear.

"Then try again."

Anna's hair stood on end.

"Invite more girls to the castle. You're sure to find the right one eventually." The sweet voice held more bitter poison than any she'd heard. It was the stuff of nightmares.

For the longest time, Anna hadn't understood how Ella pulled off her terrible pranks or worked her claws into the hearts of everyone she met. Until that horrible night she'd first heard that voice coming from her sister's mirror.

Fairy godmother, Ella called her—as did the entire kingdom now. They thought her a blessing, sharing her magic with the people. But oh, how it corrupted, how it controlled in the worst ways. A person wouldn't even be fully aware that the godmother's magic manipulated their actions, thoughts, or emotions, subtle as it could be. Anna shuddered and glanced at Will.

He knew. The truth of it was written all over his face. Somehow, he knew that voice too.

More girls... They were looking for someone among them. The fairest in the land? *But why?*

"What if she doesn't wear it long enough? What if we miss her?"

Anna couldn't see her stepsister nor the fairy godmother, not unless she moved into the hall. Will gave the briefest shake of his head. *Not yet.*

The fairy godmother's cackle grated like a knife on stone. "You'll know. Just a moment should do, but longer will make the magic work faster."

"I've already sent you several women, even my *dearest* stepmother and one of her little brats."

Anna tugged the hidden dagger free before she knew what she was doing. All at once, she was rising to her feet, pushing toward the tapestry, fury burning like wildfire through her veins.

Will threw his arms around her, hauling her back against his chest. Her heels scrapped and clacked on the stone.

"No," he whispered, his lips brushing her ear.

Anna barely heard him over her pulse thundering in her ears.

"Can I expect more requests like this?" Ella demanded. "Already we send you all the things you ask for, people to labor for you, and permit... whatever it is you do."

"Magic, dearie," the godmother snapped, her voice sharp as glass. "Don't you forget it. Who's helped you these last years? Who's made all your dreams come true?"

Ella huffed, and Anna could picture the pout accompanying that sound. "Fine, fine. I'll do as you ask."

Footsteps echoed from down the hall, stomping in time with her racing heart. Will's arms tightened around her.

"Good. Just bring me the one that—" The fairy godmother's words were muffled by the scrape of boots. "The fairest in the land." Her echoing cackle cut off abruptly, but no doors slammed, at least none they could hear.

Will went utterly still, his breath hitching as the footsteps padded by the tapestry and the figure came to a stop. The silver and gold stitching on the newcomer's jacket would be enough to mark his rank, but though Anna had only seen him a few times, it would be hard to forget the sharp angles of his powerful face. The chancellor crossed his arms and glared at the direction from which the sound had come. Sunlight glinted off the silver in his beard and close-trimmed hair as he tapped his foot—whether impatience, habit, or to grab attention, she could only guess.

Will eased her off him. His strong hands about her waist snared all her focus, and she let her body move to his command.

"Ugh." Ella let out a dramatic sigh. Heels clicked, drawing close. "Creepy old bat."

"Careful. She might hear you."

The hem of wide, blue skirts swished into view. Anna's blood chilled. *So close.* Her fingertips ached to grab her dagger. In a mere moment, she could have the blade in hand, lunge through the tapestry, and stab that wicked woman. But...nerves drew her throat tight. They'd grown up together, been true sisters for a time. Before Ella's father died, they were a family. It was hesitant, awkward, but the threads of something more were there. Then he died suddenly, and Ella was never the same. She'd thought time would help, but in the end, Anna had mourned the loss of the young woman who had been her younger stepsister as much as she did her new father.

Things had certainly changed, but still. Anna wanted her gone, not dead.

And there might be no salvation for her mother and sister if she were caught killing the queen. She couldn't risk their future. *Never.*

"The mirror was back to normal again." A delicate, gloved hand waved in the narrow space between the chancellor and queen. A bracelet of glittering white gems dangled from the queen's wrist. "Besides, she needs me. Without me she was just a weird old woman peddling her potions to travelers. She wouldn't have her manor, her workers, or any of the things she's always asking for."

"And you..." The chancellor stepped closer and tipped her face up toward his. "...were just a pretty face without her." His lips curled, his eyes hooded, almost like...

Like...

Her throat went dry.

Like a lover. But the man was at least twice her age.

Ella shrugged him off. "Careful, Stephan."

"Of course, my queen." He took her hand, raised it to his lips, and placed a kiss on its back. "You did get what you wanted."

"What *we* wanted."

The sweetness of the words turned Anna's stomach.

"Indeed." Anna could hear the smile in his expression, even as he turned away from them.

Ella's golden hair trailed down her back in artful waves and curls decorated with ornate pins as she laced her arm through the chancellor's and leaned into his shoulder. "Let's get this over with."

Anna peered out of the opening, stretching on her toes to watch her evil stepsister as she rounded the corner with the man who had undoubtedly helped her snare the crown. He'd want one of his own—a king to his queen—she'd no doubt of that. He was probably just waiting until the appropriate time of mourning after Ella's *true love* had passed. Though she looked the opposite of a heartbroken queen. Anna's lips drew thin. She'd bet her last coin Ella hadn't bothered to don a mourning gown once after the private funeral.

She stared at the wall after they turned the corner. Waiting, hoping for...she didn't know.

"You there," Ella said, her voice sharp as ever. Whomever she spoke to was out of sight, around the corner. Even so, Anna's hair stood on end like she'd been caught. "Have the maids clean while we're gone. I'd like a bath the moment I return, and it better be hot this time. Not warm. Hot. Understood?"

"Y-yes, my queen," came the male response. *A guard?*

Anna stretched closer, listening for anything else. As she did, her gaze landed on the portrait on the wall. Nikolaus Kaiser stood in his full royal regalia, a cape sweeping down over his back, jewels and medals in abundance—though he'd never done a thing to earn them that she knew of. They'd captured his arrogance perfectly, as well as the cold, hard look in his eyes, almost as if he'd frowned at the artist through the entire sitting. It must have been the last one painted before his coronation and subsequent death. Or one of the last, for the artist had captured a man, not a boy, but he still wore his prince's coronet.

Fingers clamped around her arm, and a screech climbed up her throat. She barely stifled it when she whirled about and saw it was Will. For the briefest moment, he wore the same hard look as the prince. Anna shook her head, and it was gone. Just shadows. Or perhaps everyone in this dreadful place had mastered the look of misery and disgust. He'd said they were friends after all.

"We have to go," he said in an urgent whisper.

Anna gave herself a shake. Ella and the chancellor would be on their way to the women. They had to get back, not just to avoid getting caught or stuck in the castle, but to warn the others. Her stomach knotted itself. This stupid contest wasn't just to find the queen a pretty lady-in-waiting. Whatever the fairy godmother planned for the winner, it couldn't be good.

14

*W*ill's blood boiled. He'd missed his chance—their chance.

When the chancellor appeared, all thoughts of their plan fled his mind, replaced instead by the fire of vengeance. If not for Ansel pressed against him, he'd have jumped through the opening and slain the man on the spot—or tried to.

No matter that it'd probably get him killed and the queen would still reign over her stolen throne. To take out both of them before the guards stormed the hall? *Unlikely.*

He'd hoped to poison them both, a little detail he hadn't shared with his friends. They wanted the queen gone and didn't know the lengths of the chancellor's blood-soaked hands in this mess.

Ansel must have been thinking the same thing, because he glanced down at the bodice of his dress before whispering, "The poison."

Will gave a sharp shake of his head. "The maids."

If they were coming to clean, they'd take away any lingering food or drinks. They might consume some themselves, and then there'd be more unnecessary death. He wanted to avoid that—if he could.

If not…

He swallowed.

"But—"

He gave another sharp shake of his head. "We'll have another chance."

Saints, we'd better. If not, he'd have to find a way back into the forgotten tunnels, by himself this time. If he came back here...he'd have his revenge or die trying. They'd pay for the lives they stole—his family, his friends.

It was the closest he'd come, the best chance he had, and he couldn't lose it. Waiting weeks, months for Koen to figure out the potion—he couldn't. He was done waiting. Doing nothing had already cost him way too much.

Ansel didn't argue as he led him back through the tunnels. *Thank all the saints.* The feel of his dainty fingers twined through Will's nearly undid him. Between that and the chancellor's distraction, he nearly cracked a tooth grinding his teeth together. Trying to focus on the little marks and grooves on the wall that guided the way through the darkness proved nearly impossible.

If it were only a year earlier, Will wouldn't hesitate to linger with Ansel in the dark, if he'd have him. Man or woman, he wanted Ansel. But life took that choice away, along with so much else.

In no time at all, they reached the hidden door they'd used to slip into the space. Will held his breath, sparing no seconds on worry as he slid the stones to open the passage. Each scrape and sound set his nerves on edge. He dropped Ansel's hand, instead savoring the feel of the dagger hilt against his palm.

If the guards saw them, perhaps he could engage them long enough for Ansel to get away. He'd have to try. He wouldn't let him get caught up in his downfall any more than he already was.

The soft, grating slide of the stone stopped. Full silence filled the hall. No guards paced the marble floors, but that didn't mean none were standing watch, just waiting to shout an alarm the moment they stepped from behind the tapestry.

Will pulled Ansel back into the darkness and drew him close. It was just to whisper in his ear, to avoid being heard, or so he told himself. But it'd be a lie to say he didn't savor that moment—perhaps their last.

"If the guards see me, run."

He didn't wait for a response, even as Ansel tugged at his sleeve. With his muscles strung tight as bowstrings, he edged out from behind the tapestry, moving it as little as possible, which was still enough that the damn thing looked like a flag waving in the breeze.

Blood rushed to his head as he shifted his gaze this way and that, searching for the inevitable danger, bracing for that shout or stern question that would signal his end.

His pulse thundered so loud he couldn't hear anything else.

Will stepped from behind the tapestry and waited.

Thump.

Thump. Thump.

Holy heavens and hells.

He let out a breath and waved to Ansel. No sooner was he out than Will slid the door shut, every scrape drawing him up tighter. It was too much to hope they'd make it back here, but he had to hide his secret, just in case.

Together, they crossed the hall to the doors they'd left what felt like hours ago. Even if they got caught, he had to warn the women—shout it at the top of his lungs and let them know the queen's plan. Sending an innocent to the fairy godmother was out of the question. It might cost his life, but he couldn't let it happen. If these women knew, if the people knew, maybe they'd finally see the horror the queen and her witch wrought.

But to do that, they needed through these doors, needed them open.

He leaned against the wood, trying to make out anything amid the muffled sound on the other side. The guards would be back in their post near the doors within the ballroom. He and Koen should have worked out some kind of signal, another distraction for them to get back in, but it was too late for that now.

From the whisper of casual chatter slipping through the wood, the women hadn't been called before the queen yet. Once they were, it'd be even harder to rejoin the group.

With Ansel on the far side of the double doors and him near their center, Will whispered a prayer and tugged the brass handle down, pulling the door open the barest crack. A cacophony of sound rushed out into the hall.

More couples filled the room, blocking out most of the guards lingering around the other doors. They'd only have to deal with the closest ones. As he scanned what he could see of the space, he caught sight of a familiar figure waiting at the closest table. Relief surged through him.

Mina.

Koen would be close by. *Smart.* He rolled his shoulders, the hint of a smile creeping to his lips. He should have known they'd be waiting to help. *Now to catch her eye.*

As if the girl read his thoughts, she glanced toward the door, straightening ever so slightly as she caught sight of him. Without pause, Mina swayed on her feet, bringing the back of her hand to her forehead as if she might swoon again.

For all her shy nature, she could play the fabulous actress.

Then, Koen was there, putting his arm around Mina to support her and waving to the guards for attention.

Will glanced across the door to Ansel. Warmth swelled in his heart as a grin stretched across his face. They'd made it.

Ansel returned the grin, glancing to the ceiling and whispering what could only be a prayer to the Mother and all her saints.

He ushered Ansel close, ready to push the door wide and let him slip inside.

"You there!"

The call hit like a blow to the chest, knocking the wind from his lungs and sending his eyes flying wide.

They'd been seen. So close and yet—

"Kiss me."

Ansel's words snapped him from his panicked stupor. The young man stared at him wide-eyed and pleading. Ansel latched on to his hand, jerking it from the handle. "Kiss me," he implored again.

"You!" the guard called again, louder this time. Now he could make out the hurried steps headed their way behind him. "What are you doing?"

Without waiting for a response, Ansel took Will's face between his palms and pulled him into a crushing kiss.

Every single thought fled at the hurried press of Ansel's lips against his.

He forgot about the guard headed their way, the people lingering just beyond the cracked doors, his desire for revenge, and the queen's plot to fulfill the fairy godmother's insidious request.

Everything.

Except Ansel.

It was the kiss of his dreams from days ago, only this time the strange beauty wearing Ansel's face claimed his lips in a passionate embrace. His arms wrapped around him of their own accord, tugging his body close. Ansel gasped, his lips freezing even as Will ached to deepen their kiss. But then, like ice cracking over a frozen lake, the young man melted against him. The feel of Ansel against him was pure bliss and desire.

"What are—" The guard's angry outburst cut off as Ansel jerked away from him.

"Oh!" Ansel's hands flew to his flushed face in feigned—or real?—embarrassment. "I didn't know anyone was out here."

Will glared at the guard from the corner of his eyes. The man coughed and averted his gaze. He shifted on his feet, giving away his discomfort.

"I just...we just wanted a moment," Ansel rattled on, his voice soft and rich as cake. "I was so nervous about meeting the queen, you see." He reached a hand toward the guard as if it was the most natural thing, but the man flinched back. Ansel snapped his arm back in turn, twisting his hands together in front of his dress and shifting around as if they'd just been caught doing something far more intimate. "My fiancé was just trying to calm me down. Help me relax."

"I've got the measure of it." The guard spared barely a glance between them. "Back in there with you."

"Yes, yes, of course." Ansel gave a little bow before shoving Will toward the doors. "I'm so sorry."

Will nearly tripped into the room, so thrown off by the ruse.

Clever, clever man.

A huff of laughter shook his chest as he spied the guards seeing to Mina. All eyes were on the girl who might swoon again at any minute. No one paid them any mind as they slipped back through the doors and into the ballroom.

Will glanced over his shoulder in time to see Ansel close the door and brush away a smear of dust from his dress. A deep blush still colored his cheeks. The young man's attention flicked to him and then promptly away.

Embarrassed?

Ansel raised his chin and stared toward Mina and Koen. The girl thanked the guards for seeing to her so dutifully and assured them she was fine.

"You can thank me later," Ansel mumbled before striding off to join the others.

Myriad emotions flooded through him—ecstatic relief, admiration. He watched the subtle swish of Ansel's hips as he crossed the marble. Desire.

He scrubbed a hand down his face. That kiss might have saved them, but it would haunt him forever after.

At that moment, the doors on the far side of the room opened. The herald who'd sorted the women out front of the castle strode in without preamble.

"Ladies, ladies." He waved his hands in the air, stretching to be seen by the full sea of people.

Immediately, a hush descended over the room.

The guards returned to their posts, and Will took the moment to join the others.

Koen merely raised his brows in question.

At the slight shake of Will's head, he frowned. The quick, involuntary reaction had Will's chest tightening with an ache he yearned to rub away. His friend didn't even know the worst of it.

"Thank you all for gathering today." The herald's voice carried through the massive room, barely a whisper to contest him. "Let us hope that one among you will be a fair companion for our dear queen. Or maybe two or three?" He gave a little chuckle. Demure giggles echoed throughout the room.

But the fairy godmother had only asked for one. The fairest in the land. Unless they thought to send backups. His lips pulled thin. Based on the man's humor, he likely didn't know the real reason why the queen sought a companion. He'd seen him often enough in the past. He was frivolous and prone to drinking too much, but not cruel.

The man doled out more compliments to the ladies, breaking up some of the tension in the air. He'd wasted no time on the women's mood or vanity outside, but he did now. Will took advantage of the moment to whisper to Koen the most critical details of what they'd learned.

"The godmother, not the queen, wants a woman, the fairest in the land."

Koen's gaze turned dark, nearly unreadable as he visibly swallowed the news. "Can't let that happen," he whispered back.

They were of the same mind. Whatever the witch planned, it would be bad for them and even worse for whatever poor woman the queen chose.

Will crossed his arms and rocked back on his heels as he filtered through ideas for a way to stop this selection, not a one of them good.

"Now then," the herald boomed. "Let me introduce His Grace, Chancellor Friedrich."

Will's fingernails bit into his biceps as though they could strangle the man where he stood. He couldn't catch sight of him or hear his name without becoming blinded by rage.

For years he'd watched the man slink around the castle, a dangerous glint in his eye that somehow the king and others close to him failed to notice. Instead, the old king called him a friend, his advisor, his closest companion. He'd even spent more time with that snake than his own son.

Once, Will had gathered the courage to say something, to share his worries. The king had flown into such a rage, Will could still see the way his neck had purpled. The king had sent him off into the forest for days to rethink his actions, to become a better man.

Bitterness raced across his tongue, begging to be spit upon the marble.

Who knew when Cinderella caught the chancellor's eye, before she came to the castle or after, he couldn't say, but they were two of a feather now, and both would pay for their treason. They'd killed people he loved and had tried to kill him when he refused to bend the knee. His teeth ground together. They'd pay. Both of them.

Ansel cleared his throat and brushed against Will's arm. He glanced down in time to see the young man raise his brows and look meaningfully toward the chancellor, who received swooning praise from the women nearest him.

He rolled his neck and relaxed his arms, letting them fall slack at his side. Wishing for vengeance wouldn't do a damn thing if he lost his cool now.

"Thank you, ladies, thank you. You are all *quite* lovely."

Will rolled his eyes. *Oh, by the Mother.* The man's arrogance seeped from every word. He didn't even need to see the chancellor's smirking face. Will glanced around at the gathered people. Were they really so clueless as to only see whatever Chancellor Friedrich wanted them to?

"Now then, shortly you will be before Her Majesty, Queen Cinderella."

Women and their companions cheered. Several nudged forward, fanned themselves, or stared down their competition. All but Ansel, who stood absolutely still, the same look of barely controlled rage bubbling just beneath the tight smile on his face.

Toward the chancellor? Or the queen? The young man had nearly sprung into the hall when they'd overheard the queen talking to the fairy godmother. Ansel had murder and vengeance clinging to him like a second skin—he'd know.

The queen earned Ansel's ire then? Will cocked his head, examining the young man in his periphery. Ansel had said his family had been imprisoned, which was reason enough for fury, though the look in his eyes somehow felt deeper, more personal.

"One at a time, I'll call you forward to meet the queen." The chancellor paced as he spoke, that salt-and-pepper head visible beyond the crowd, towering over most everyone in the room. "Remember to present your best self. Curtsy. Address her as 'Majesty' or 'Queen Cinderella.'"

Ansel grabbed his arm. "We should get to the front," he said. "We want to be first to meet the queen, don't we?" Ansel leaned around him, catching the attention of Mina and Koen. "Would be a shame if she chose the fairest in the land without seeing either of us."

Damn it. He was right. If the queen picked early, they might not find a way to lay their poison, much less save whatever poor soul she chose. They'd have to stop her from choosing, but how could they do that without getting themselves arrested?

Unless...

He glanced at Ansel. "Do whatever you can to get picked."

His eyes widened. His lips parted.

If Ansel were chosen, he might have a chance to get close enough to poison the queen. Will slipped his hand into Ansel's and gave it a squeeze as he leaned in. "I'll get you out. You won't go to *her*. I promise." He meant it with every fiber of his being. No matter what he had to do, he would get Ansel out, even if it meant sacrificing himself to see that promise through.

15

*A*nna barely heard the words Will said. The touch of his fingers against hers brought up all the memories from moments ago. They'd kissed. She'd kissed him.

And holy saints, if he hadn't kissed her back. Sweat blossomed on her chest, and she desperately wished for one of the ornate folding fans several of the women carried.

It was just a ruse, just him playing along to distract the guard. *Yes. Of course. That's it.*

She gave his hand a squeeze. "I'll try."

Fairest in the land? Me? Not a chance. The opposite, if anything. But the fact that he thought she had a shot swelled her heart more than he could ever know.

"Let's go," she said to her companions.

They couldn't risk being at the end of the line to greet the queen if she wanted any chance of getting chosen—and by doing so, stopping her stepsister in whatever she plotted.

Anna didn't wait to see if they followed as she made her way to the side of the room where the doors they'd entered when they first arrived were, the same ones the chancellor had entered through. Everyone was so enraptured in his ridiculous speech, they hardly noticed as Anna squeezed by with murmured apologies.

Fairest in the land. She shook her head as she passed a stunning brunette, perfectly proportioned, immaculately dressed, and with a smile that made even her cold heart warm. Will didn't even know she was a girl. He was just being nice and building her confidence.

She hadn't quite made it to the front by the time the chancellor announced they were to proceed to the throne room. Still, it was better than being at the back.

Will appeared at her side, and she slipped her arm through his. More like stuffed it through. He was stiff as a board, his jaw set, his gaze unreadable. *Nervous?* Being so close to him, his form pressing her wide skirts tighter around her, was enough to stir up all the butterflies in her stomach.

In clustered pairs, they were led down the long hall once more. Guards flanked them on both sides, spaced just a few feet apart. There would be no sneaking off on this walk. Every step she took had her muscles drawing tighter, her breaths thinning. The fake smile that caused her cheeks to ache slipped off entirely. They spilled into the throne room. The sight of Ella sitting on the raised dais at the end of the room knocked the wind from her lungs and caused her to stumble a half-step.

Ella wore her crown like she was born to it, nose upturned, face serene, hair and attire even more flawless than the diamonds sparkling from the gaudy necklace draped around her neck that had to be terribly uncomfortable to wear.

Soft gasps from the other women teased Anna's ears. She understood, she really did. Ella had always been beautiful, flawless. If only what lay beneath the surface were half as lovely, they could have been the best of sisters.

An odd ache snared her, that other life tempting her with wishes that could never be.

Instead, Anna's beloved sister Charlotte, the one who'd used her own fire to counter the worst of what Cinderella could dish out, was imprisoned and their mother with her. All her mom had ever tried to do was love—her daughters, her new husband, his daughter.

It wasn't enough for Ella.

Nothing was.

And for once, Anna felt a twinge of pity, because beyond the veil of silk, jewels, and gleaming golden hair, Ella was a statue. Beautiful and cold, but not happy. No joy shone from her face, though she had everything she'd ever wanted.

The gilded trim on the walls and the scenes painted on the ceiling couldn't compete with the queen for the attention of those gathered. She was why they'd come after all. Anna scanned their faces, nearly choking on the hope etched there. Maybe if she didn't know Ella, she would be the same way, longing for life in the castle, but she doubted that days of wearing fanciful dresses and tending the queen's whims were what awaited whoever was chosen. Not after hearing the fairy godmother's voice in Ella's room through that horrid magic mirror.

She shivered despite the layers of fabric and the sweat beading beneath her breasts. Will pulled her closer, and she savored his presence, his warmth, as if he were a real fiancé who loved her and would shelter her from the ills of the world.

Guards lined the walls in the throne room too. They took no chances with the safety of their queen, not today. *Blast it all.*

But... Anna stretched on her toes, trying to see beyond the man in front of her. *Yes.* A sparkling crystal glass sat on the arm of the throne filled with a pale golden substance, probably wine. Long before their mother deemed it appropriate, Ella would sneak bottles of wine into her room. That glass might have been the sun for the way it glimmered with hope.

Pairs nudged and shoved, trying to get nearest the front, as if somehow that would help their chances. Lavender flooded her nose as one woman brushed against her, sending her stumbling back a step despite Will's arm through hers and the fierce glare he aimed at the offender. She either didn't see him or was pretending he didn't exist. All the perfume she'd bathed in probably addled her senses.

Being one of the earliest into the room hadn't helped, not at all. It was a constant shoving match as the rest of the women and their escorts filled the space. It was too much, too many people too close. Anna shifted on her feet, glancing this way and that for a pocket of open space that didn't exist. She stilled, her eyes going wide. Behind a row of guards was a giant mirror in a shining golden frame.

How she'd missed it, being tall as two men, she couldn't say. Maybe because she'd been so focused on Ella. But now that she'd seen it, it loomed like a great northern bear ready to eat her alive.

It wasn't any normal mirror. This was the twin of the one in the main square, the one that Cinderella used to speak to the people. It had to be. Something like thick fog swirled near the edges of the glass on the other side, like a living thing trapped within.

"Horrifying," Will whispered in her ear.

The tickle of his warm breath against her skin sent a shiver down her spine. She turned, a scowl pressing her lips thin, to whack him on the arm for startling her, but the chancellor chose that moment to call for silence.

Seemingly at random, he picked a woman from the crowd and led her to stand before the queen. Anna stretched on her toes to watch as Ella descended from the dais, her wine glass in hand—thank the heavens. She asked the chosen woman a few questions—her name, if she liked the sweet treats that Ella had selected herself.

Anna rolled her eyes at that. Ella didn't even like sweets. She probably had no idea what was served in the ballroom.

"Thank you," Ella said after less than a minute. With a wave of her hand, she sent the girl back to her companion. Though several pairs separated them, Anna still heard the dramatic sniffle as the girl's companion—likely her mother or an aunt—petted her hair and shoved a handkerchief her way.

Already the chancellor had another woman selected and striding to meet the queen. He wasted no time wandering through the crowd and deciding who to choose.

Anna pushed on the bottom of her bodice, trying to ease the vial of poison within reach. To anyone looking, she might appear crass, trying to lift her breasts to best advantage, but that was better than the truth. She waited one agonizing minute, as another girl was quickly interviewed and dismissed, before reaching down her bodice and slipping the vial into her palm.

At her side, Will cleared his throat and looked away. A faint blush colored his cheeks.

Ridiculous man. You'd think he knows I have breasts, small as they are. Her back stiffened as she glared at the profile of his stiff jaw. The dress was too modest to show any cleavage, a small blessing from the Mother. He couldn't know, could he?

"Lovely, but no," the queen proclaimed of another woman.

Anna tugged on Will's sleeve before whispering. "We have to get closer." That and they'd gotten separated from Mina and Koen.

More than one scowl and a declaration of "Well, I never" bounced off her as she and Will meandered to Mina and Koen, who'd managed a spot near the front. It was risky, getting close enough for Ella to possibly recognize her, but then, maybe that'd be a good backup plan. The queen would never choose the stepsister she'd once described as uglier than a pig, even in a disguise.

A hard knot twisted in her stomach. But if she revealed her identity, Ella would certainly take notice. Maybe she could get close enough to force the poison down her throat. It'd be better than sending some other poor woman off to the fairy godmother and letting Ella's reign continue.

Anna leaned in closer to Will, pressing her side against his even as he stiffened up like a board. She tugged his arm until he dipped his head close enough for her to whisper in his ear. "If anything happens to me, save my mother and sister."

Will wrapped an arm around her, pulling tight as if giving her a reassuring hug, but his touch was almost crushing. "What are you—"

"Please," she said, cutting him off. "Promise me."

He looked at her then, those brown eyes reaching into her soul and feeling her out. For once, she didn't look away. His lips were so close, barely parted, and oh so tempting. Their taste, all woodsy and masculine, still lingered on her tongue. He'd probably hate her if he knew the truth of who she was. He certainly wouldn't trust her. He would either believe her in league with Ella or believe all the horrid lies Ella spun about her. If only he could just know her as Ansel—as Anna—without the taint of her relations. But if she blew her cover, the boy Ansel would die a swift death. He'd never see her for who she was, if he ever saw her again at all.

"I don't know who they are," he whispered.

But he would if she told him who she was. A sad smile touched her lips. She couldn't. Not yet.

His jaw shifted as he weighed her silence. "Fine." He glanced away and then back. "I promise."

Warmth blossomed, spreading like a windblown flame through her body. In that moment, all she wanted to do was pull his face down to hers and kiss him again. He'd promised, and the sincerity painted all over his face said he'd keep it. That look alone lifted a weight from her chest she hadn't realized had been pressing on her for so long. If she had to reveal herself to get the queen's attention, her family might still have a chance.

Mom, Charlotte, you'll be free one day. I promise.

Anna jumped as Mina slid her dainty hand through hers. She tore her gaze from Will and took in the girl's shy smile. Mina gave her a little squeeze, a show of support, as if Anna were trembling the same way the poor girl's hand was.

Anna gave her a squeeze in return and stepped away from Will. He'd be fine, he was a huntsman after all, used to testing his wits and skills. Mina, however, was so far out of her element Anna was amazed she'd kept it together. She stepped closer to the girl until their arms brushed one another. Only then did Mina's hand stop trembling.

"You'll be fine," Anna promised, and she meant it. "You've done so well already."

Mina glanced at her from the corner of her eyes and gave a wobbly smile. With her dark hair pulled back, she couldn't hide behind it. How much courage it took for a girl who preferred the shadows to feign a swoon, not once but twice, Anna could only imagine.

"I'd like you to try this on," Ella said to the thin, blonde woman standing in front of her who, Anna felt, could almost pass for her twin if she were a few inches shorter. The new command from the queen pulled attention where little else had.

Anna leaned around the couple in front of her, watching as the queen slipped off her shoes. She hadn't seen them before, hidden both by the fall of Ella's dress and the crowds between them, but now that she did, they were striking—clear crystal, or so they appeared.

Anna's toes wiggled. Her shoes were less than comfortable as it was, but glass? That'd be torture. No wonder Ella looked so unhappy. No amount of fashion and finery was worth being that uncomfortable.

"Y-your shoes, Your Majesty?"

"Yes," Ella told her. "If you're to be my companion, the fairest in the land, you should be able to step into my shoes. Perhaps literally. If you please." She gestured to the shimmering heels.

Flustered, the woman dropped to one knee, fumbling with her own shoes in an effort to remove them.

Will's hand brushed hers, stirring up those butterflies again. But it was no accidental graze. When she glanced up at him, his brows rose, his gaze flicking toward the woman slipping off her heels.

The shoes. Anna swallowed against the sudden dryness in her throat. Could they be poisoned? Enchanted?

The interest flickering in Ella's eyes spoke volumes. This woman had potential in her, and the shoes were some kind of test to prove if she was the fairest of them all.

If so…

A cold sweat broke out on the back of Anna's neck. She'd have to do it —reveal herself. She couldn't let another innocent be taken away.

Anna held her breath as the woman slipped on the glass shoes. Her stepsister paced around her victim, her lips pursed, staring at the shoes, waiting for the Mother only knew what.

"Hm," she mused, tapping one manicured finger against her painted, pink lips. "Not quite perfect, I'm afraid." The queen heaved a sigh and shooed the poor woman away with a flick of her hand.

The blonde gave a quivering curtsy before twisting away to hide her teary eyes.

"Halt!" Ella called, snapping her focus back to the woman.

Anna drew in a sharp breath. The fine hairs on her arms stood on end.

"The shoes." Her sneer dipped to the objects in question.

A torrent of apologies spilled forth as the woman removed the queen's shoes. The chancellor had slipped from the crowd and took his time gracing Ella's feet with the odd footwear, not even bothering to clean them first.

It wasn't like Ella to tolerate such a thing. Dirt and sweat were from the deepest of hells, she'd once proclaimed. The shoes were definitely important.

Two more women were brought before the queen and sent away, not a one trying on the shoes, before the chancellor wandered in their direction. Will turned and vanished into the crowd without a word or sign to her. Anna fought the urge to look for him as the chancellor drew near, looking her over with a piercing gaze that made her skin crawl.

He didn't know her, but the way he narrowed his gaze and raked it over every inch of her made her pulse flutter like a caged bird.

This was it. She'd go before the queen, maybe stumble into her or something so she could slip the poison from her sweaty palm into her drink. Her thumb worked at the little stopper, about to pop it free, when his gaze shifted, landing squarely on Mina.

The corners of his lips drew up in a smile that sent chills racing across her skin. The chancellor held out his hand to Mina, and she gasped, her hand flying to cover her mouth. The poor girl swayed on her feet as Koen went stiff at her side.

"You're next, my dear." The chancellor flicked his fingers and stretched out his arm even further.

Mina. Anna yearned to call out to her, to tell her it was fine. *Go before the queen. Bow. Answer her questions. Come back. Don't try to poison her.*

With her nerves the way they were, Mina would never manage it. And if she got caught? Anna's nails dug into her palms. She'd never let it happen. Better she be arrested than Mina suffer that fate.

Mina took the chancellor's hand and was led before the queen. Ella's bored expression lit with interest, her gaze growing sharp as a cat's claws.

"You really are quite lovely, Miss..."

"Mina, Your Majesty." She gave a grand curtsy, managing only to shake just a bit. "Mina...Ansel."

Anna's cheeks flushed. Of all the fake names to use. And Mina hadn't even planned to use a fake one.

"You are quite lovely." She circled around Mina, her fingers grazing her long, dark hair where it fell over one shoulder. "Hair like a raven's wing. Perfect proportions. Such a lovely color to your skin. And your eyes." She stopped just in front Mina, grabbed her chin, and forced it up until Mina dared to look her in the face. Ella grinned. "Like the finest gems."

Anna glanced over one shoulder, then the other, scanning the rapt crowd. *Where in all the heavens and hells is Will?*

16

*W*ill shifted behind the tall man in front of him as the chancellor wandered the crowd. The moment his gaze landed on the man, everything in him locked up and felt like it burst into flame at once. In a different place, a different time, he'd have sprung on him, pulled his hidden dagger, and plunged it into the chancellor's throat. Will's hand clenched and unclenched as he watched him move from the corner of his eye.

And then he stopped, glancing back toward the queen. A murmur raced through the crowd. He stepped out from behind the tall man, craning his neck to see—

Oh, fuck all.

Mina.

When the chancellor headed their way, he was so certain he'd pick Ansel. One look in those rich, brown eyes and a glimpse of the kind intelligence within them and any man would be a goner. The chancellor couldn't know Ansel was a man, not in that disguise. *Hells, I keep forgetting myself.*

But Mina... She had to be shaking like a leaf. There was no way she could poison the queen, even with her standing so close, circling her like a cat.

Glass clicked on the floor. What was she—

He shoved past the couple pressed together in front of him, earning a sharp reprimand that he barely heard. The shoes. Mina was going to try on the shoes.

As he pushed by, aiming for a better view, a woman swatted him with a fan. Between the people ahead, he caught sight of Mina as she slipped her stocking-clad legs from her heels and slid one foot into the queen's glass shoe.

"The other one too?" Cinderella arched one blonde brow before staring at the shoes.

"I—" Mina's voice shook. Her hand flexed around something.

Breath caught in his throat. *She couldn't...* Movement out of the corner of his eye snared his attention.

Will turned and froze.

The chancellor stared at him. His eyes widened ever so slightly.

Fuck.

Out. He had to get out right now, shove past the guards, jump out a window, something. Acid burned the back of his throat. Running away again like a coward. He snorted air through his nose. His father would be *so* proud. But he couldn't die before he got his revenge.

He pretended to muffle a cough and turned toward the back of the room, pushing past the woman who'd whacked him only moments ago. But she paid him no mind, not as the queen barked in outrage.

Will twisted his head around in time to see Mina leap back from the queen, muttering a torrent of apologies.

"Clumsy girl!" Cinderella sneered, holding her wine glass aloft and scowling down at her dress.

His throat grew tight as guards left their posts near the walls and aimed for Mina. A quick glance showed the chancellor still heading his way. His fingertips found his hidden blade, wrapping around the hilt, ready to pull it free and fight his way out.

"How dare—" Cinderella's sneer broke off into a gape. Gasps rippled through the crowd. Even the chancellor turned toward the spectacle.

And then he saw it. A soft glow radiating from Mina's feet.

Gooseflesh broke out across his skin.

Mina turned to the crowd, staring wide-eyed toward Koen and Ansel, who'd reached the edge of the circle of onlookers.

"You," Cinderella sputtered. "You're the one."

"Ansel." Mina clapped a hand over her mouth, but no one seemed to notice her slipup. No one but Ansel, who stepped near the girl, heedless of the guards closing in.

He ground his teeth. It was the perfect distraction. The one chance he'd have to flee, but leaving them, possibly both of them in the hands of the queen...

"You." The familiar voice struck him like a slap to the face as Chancellor Stephan Friedrich grabbed his arm. "Who are—"

The chancellor's question broke off as Will turned to face him, staring him down with all the barely leashed fury raging through him.

The older man's eyes widened. "Impossible."

Will's lips drew into a smirk. "Seen a ghost, Stephan?"

He jerked his hidden dagger free and slammed it into the chancellor's side. The older man roared in outrage. Will pulled the dagger free. The chancellor stumbled back, releasing Will to grab at the wound in his side.

Chaos erupted.

Women screamed. People turned and fled, knocking into one another, some falling to the ground. Shouts rang out.

It wasn't enough. Not nearly enough. Will stepped closer, bloodlust urging him to strike again, to leap upon the older man like downed prey.

Beyond the mass of fleeing people, guards closed in, pushing through the gathered women and their escorts without care for their well-being.

He caught a flash of red hair as Ansel ran for Mina. Guards had already surrounded the queen with blinding speed.

Fuck. Will's fist tightened around the hilt as he turned toward the doors and ran.

"Stop!"

"Halt!"

The cries of the guards chased him from all directions like hounds closing in on a wounded stag.

A guard leaped over a fallen woman scrambling on the marble and drew his weapon.

Will's lips twitched. Dagger versus sword. Bad odds. But he'd trained too long and hard all his years to cower.

The guard lunged. Will dodged.

Another lunge. Too aggressive, too far. Will spun to the side with practiced ease and slammed the hilt of his dagger against the man's head.

He crumbled to the floor.

The man's eyes were glazed, a sure sign he was under the effects of the fairy godmother's magic—a strong dose at that. He wouldn't kill a man in that state.

Droplets of blood marred the polished marble not far away, but the chancellor was nowhere to be seen.

Will sprinted toward the cluster of people trying to cram through the doors when another guard separated from the blur of bodies and angled his blade toward his face.

"You're mine," he said.

This one had clear eyes.

So be it. No mercy.

This guard wasn't quick to strike. He paced back and forth, sword at the ready, as if he waited for something. The hair on the back of Will's neck stood on end.

Movement in the large mirror to his right caught his attention as the chancellor crept up behind him, bloodied but raising his own sword to strike.

Will whirled. Blades crashed. The sharp edge of the sword hovered inches from his face. His muscles barked in pain from the impact. Will gritted his teeth and shoved with his blade, hard, sending the chancellor stumbling back.

Blood spread in a crimson stain across his side. Wild fury burned in the chancellor's eyes, but damn it all, he held his ground, determined to fight. Will might admire it if he didn't hate the man.

More guards shoved against the tide of the panicked crowd. They'd be on him in moments.

Cold sweat broke out across his skin as Will turned away from the chancellor to face the guard advancing behind him, blade reared back and ready to strike.

Will rushed him, sliding low to avoid the wide swing and slicing his dagger along the man's side. The guard roared in pain. He grasped his side, failing to turn before Will planted a solid kick to his back and sent him stumbling toward the chancellor.

"Get him!" Chancellor Friedrich roared. "Stop him now!"

Beyond him, guards swarmed the queen, ushering her away toward the back despite her high-pitched screeches of protest. Ansel, Mina, and Koen were gone.

Safe or—

He shook his head and whirled toward the doors. *Safe, they have to be safe.* There was no time to look for them, not as more guards pushed through the remnants of the scattered crowd in his direction.

He had to get to the hall. *Now.*

Will sprinted toward the oncoming guards, shoving his blade back in its sheath. Just before he reached them, he lunged to the right, skidding across the marble toward his target—the towering candelabra.

"Fuck," he groaned, hefting it from the ground and swinging it toward his opponents.

Hot wax splattered. Flames fluttered and went out. A few candles tumbled off onto the floor, but none of that mattered. Will faced off against the guards, backing toward his destination. He had his defense, something that could hold up to their blades.

A young man, barely into his whiskers, lunged at him, his sword striking the candlestick with a clang that rang through the room. Will deflected the blow and swung, catching the man's shoulder and sending him stumbling back with a howl of pain. He'd be lucky to use that arm again anytime soon.

The chancellor still yelled, commanding the men, but he didn't advance. His hunched form and the blood seeping through his fingers where he clutched his side swelled something sinister inside Will that he didn't bother to tamp down. *Let him bleed out slow. Let him suffer.*

Revenge consumed him, distracting his focus, and he didn't see the man slinking near until too late. Will sucked in a breath, every bit of him going suddenly rigid. He swung the candelabra with all his strength, catching the guard's blade, but not before it sliced across his shoulder, leaving a trail of burning pain in its wake.

His arm gave out.

The candelabra dropped with a clatter to the marble.

Fuck all. He ripped his dagger from its sheath, angling at the advancing men.

He wouldn't go down this way. He couldn't.

Will took a step back. Sweat dripped down his neck as he snarled at the advancing men—who clearly didn't recognize him.

Idiots.

He could tell them. But it wouldn't save him—it might only seal his death faster.

He took another step back.

His heel caught something—hard.

Then he was falling, arms flailing, unable to right himself. He braced for impact, to crash against the glass of the mirror at his back.

It didn't come.

Instead, a cool, thick fog wrapped him in its embrace, suspending him in the air as sound faded to a murmur. Time slowed. The guards gaped at him. Their swords dipped. They didn't advance.

The mirror. A shiver wracked his form. He was in the mirror.

Tendrils of white fog wrapped around him like an embrace, sucking him in. He was swimming in it, his feet brushing spongy, insubstantial ground. Not only that, but his shoulder no longer burned, his muscles didn't ache, and even his thirst had vanished.

This was somewhere else. A place all its own.

Voices spoke in the ballroom, but he barely heard them. More fog invaded his view, blocking the sights beyond the shimmer of the mirror's surface.

Panic zipped under his skin as he roared and scrambled for freedom, to no avail.

All at once, the mirror spat him out.

Will fell to the ground, his head slamming against wood. He groaned as he forced himself to sit, to steady his grip on his blade, the only thing preventing the guards from—

But the guards were gone. The mirror loomed in front of him, reflecting his wide-eyed stare and bloodied shoulder. Behind him, the city square and cloudy skies loomed overhead. Somehow, he'd fallen into the mirror within the castle and out of the one in the square. The pain in his shoulder returned, roaring to life with the ache in his skull, his back, pretty much everywhere.

"What in all the heavens and hells?" Wood bit into his palm as he pushed to his feet.

Townsfolk had stopped in their tracks, gaping and whispering to one another at his sudden appearance. A woman pointed to his bloodied shoulder and nearly swooned into the young man at her side. Children squealed in excitement.

It felt like a dream, an illusion. But he knew the square well, the brown cobblestones, the familiar storefronts.

Tentatively, he reached a hand to the mirror. Only cold, smooth glass touched his skin.

His reflection blinked at him. It was a doorway of some sort, not just a means for Cinderella to speak to the people without having to dirty the hem of her gowns. And if he could go through—

He snapped his hand back and raced for the edge of the platform, ignoring the blood dripping down his arm and the ache as he tried to hold the light dagger.

The people who'd neared the stage floundered backward as he bolted by. There was no time for apologies, for politeness, not if others could pass through as he had.

Will reached the edge of the square as a chorus of gasps rose behind him, followed by shouts and exclamations. The back of his neck burned. *Damn it all, they're already here.* It was too much to hope that the strange magic of the mirror would dissuade their pursuit. The guards had little hesitation following him through the mirror and would be on his heels if he gave them the chance. He didn't bother to look back as he ran down the street and turned into the first alleyway.

Sweat drenched his clothes by the time he finally let himself stop and rest in the shade outside a blacksmith's shop on the edge of town. The acrid stench of forged metal nearly choked him, but the steady, muted clank of the man's hammer against whatever he worked on helped to calm his racing heart. His head thumped against the stone wall. What he wouldn't give to let his body slide down it into the muck of the alley, to close his eyes and rest.

But the guards wouldn't give up their search so easily, even if he had lost them a while ago. The chancellor, if he lived, would have every man he could spare scouring the city, the countryside—

Fuck.

He slammed a fist against the wall, savoring the pain. At least it distracted from his shoulder, if only for a moment.

The castle would be guarded as heavily as ever. The chancellor would expect him to return, to try and finish what he started. The bastard knew too much, and damn if he hadn't been the king's advisor for a reason.

The Mother help them. If Koen and Ansel hadn't gotten Mina out, they might be held captive, and it was his fault.

He'd been spotted. It'd been a risk going to the castle, but he couldn't let the opportunity slip through his fingers.

"Should have aimed for the neck," he muttered to himself before pushing off the wall.

All his aches made themselves known. And his arm—he pulled back the sliced fabric and grimaced at the deep wound. Bile singed the back of his throat. The arm needed to be cleaned and sewn. But he didn't have a damn thing on him that would help.

Months ago, he'd have stopped in any one of the houses he passed and asked for help. But that world could have been a lifetime ago for how things had changed. Now, he couldn't risk it.

Will forced himself to get up and walk the end of the alleyway. The farms outside the city were a better option with plenty of barns to hide in. He shook his head. How far he'd fallen.

As he made to round the building, the toe of his boot caught on a stray stone. He stumbled, his injured shoulder knocking into the building's façade. Teeth bit into his lip as he held back a roar of pain. Spots danced before his eyes.

"Fucking hells."

His fingertips dug into the wall as he tried to steady himself. Old papers crinkled under his hand where they'd been nailed to the side of the building. Will leaned his forehead against the stone and closed his eyes against the pain.

Deep breaths. Calm the fuck down.

When he opened his eyes, a drawing of a woman's face stared back, the word "Wanted" written in bold letters above it.

The artist hadn't been kind to the woman. Or perhaps the Mother hadn't. Bushy eyebrows, thicker than any man's, graced dull eyes. The bent, hooked nose didn't help either. And that mole near her right eye…

A vision of Ansel flashed before his eyes. The red wig. Warm, brown eyes. And that mole near his right eye.

He blinked and the vision was gone, but he couldn't quite shake it. The tips of his fingers trailed down the worn and faded parchment.

Anna Schneider.

Cinderella's stepsister.

Surely not…

He'd heard firsthand Cinderella's tales about the ills she suffered at the hands of her stepsisters. *By the Mother, it couldn't be…* Shame burned in his chest. He'd believed them. Every word.

At least at first, before he understood the fairy godmother's magic and how it swayed people toward the princess. Before the bitch had started the coup that nearly got him killed. He'd heard that one of her stepsisters evaded arrest. No one had seen the woman since, despite the hefty reward Cinderella offered.

Will traced his hand along the woman's jaw in the portrait, trailing his fingers back up to that freckle.

"Anna." He tasted her name. Savored the way it rolled across his tongue. Had he met her before the horrors of the past year? Blast it all. He couldn't remember.

"Are you Ansel?" he asked the portrait.

A surge of energy burst through him. If Ansel was the queen's stepsister and she'd had to face her today, if she'd put herself at such a risk for them…

Will twisted away from the portrait. He had to know. And there was only one way to find out. Guards be damned, he had to find Ansel.

17

*T*he cart bounced along the dirt path, rattling Anna's teeth.

"We should ditch it. Walk the rest of the way," Koen said.

Brandt snapped the reins, urging the stolen horse faster. "But Mina—"

"I'm fine," she said weakly, barely audible over the crunch of the wheels.

Anna swallowed the tightness in her throat. Mina was anything but fine. Everything had taken a turn from bad to the deepest, darkest of hells the moment Mina put on those ridiculous glass slippers. Anna's spirit had screamed out in horrifying silence the moment that eerie glow seeped like an ill-fated fog from the shoes and curled up into the air around Mina and her stepsister.

Even if the glow hadn't been enough of a hint, the triumph in Ella's eyes said everything. Mina was the fairest in the land, the girl the fairy godmother sought for some ill purpose. Anna couldn't let it happen. She wouldn't let Ella take another woman away like she had her sister, especially not someone as sweet and innocent as Mina.

Anna brushed the hair back from Mina's face where she lay with her head in her lap in the flat, open bed of the wooden cart. Her thick lashes fluttered closed.

"Mina?"

Koen lurched forward from his side of the cart, taking her hand in his.

An agonizing moment later, Mina opened her eyes. "I'm just so…so tired."

Koen stared at Anna over Mina's limp form. His eyes filled concern. Mina hadn't eaten anything at the castle, of that much they were sure. She'd been fine until she put those damn shoes on.

Ella. Anna's fist tightened at her side. She'd been ready to rush her sister, to jump between her and Mina and reveal her identity. *But Will! Will stabbed the chancellor!*

Her stomach turned over when she thought about the horror she'd seen the moment she twisted around and spotted Will with that bloody dagger in his hand. That eerie, gilded mirror stood like a specter behind him as the guards closed in.

She bit her lip, holding back the cry of anguish trying to break out. She didn't even know what happened to him. He must have done it as a distraction, a way for them to get out. He sacrificed himself for the rest of them. *If he is dead—* She shook her head, shutting down that thought. Will was a huntsman, used to relying on his wits and wiles to survive and hunt his prey. He could survive this too.

The moment chaos had erupted in the throne room, Anna had sprinted for Mina. The girl was stiff as a statue, staring wide-eyed at Ella, who'd backed away with a dainty ring-clad hand over her mouth. Guards swarmed in faster than she ever imagined, encircling their queen and practically dragging her from the room.

Without the distraction, they certainly wouldn't have gotten to Mina in time. Ella's screeched commands still echoed in her ears. "Get her! The fairest in the land! Don't let her go!"

The high-pitched torrent didn't stop until Anna had stepped in front of Mina and stared down Ella, her arms stretched wide, blocking all view of the girl.

Ella's words had choked off mid-sentence. Her too-perfect pink lips had parted.

She'd recognized her.

Maybe.

But that pause was all it took for the guards to usher her away and for

Koen to scoop Mina into his arms and bolt toward the door. The glass shoes fell from her feet the moment he'd lifted her into the air. Anna had kicked them away, praying they'd shatter, but the damn things hadn't.

Then she'd turned and found Will facing off with the chancellor, an island in the middle of the panic. Chills raced across her skin, then and now. She'd ached to go to him, to help, but Mina had called out for her. And then she'd remembered—she couldn't save her mother and sister from the inside of a dungeon.

And so, she'd run too, no matter that guilt still gnawed at her insides and the tears kept creeping to the corners of her eyes.

They'd joined the swarm of women and their companions fleeing the castle. The guards didn't even try to stop them. Actually, they'd helped, urging people away from the queen so they could handle the threat.

Koen had carried Mina all the way down the cobbled path to the city, where Brandt waited, red-faced and panicked.

"You did it?" he'd asked.

The hope in his eyes nearly gutted her. The deep bellow he roared at the shake of Koen's head reverberated with all the barely leashed emotion she held locked inside.

Mina had wobbled the moment Koen set her on her stockinged feet— light-headed, she'd claimed. Maybe it was from shock due to the events in the throne room—but they'd needed away from there and fast. So Brandt stole a cart as if it was something he did every week.

It had been a good thing too. Mina's condition only worsened with every passing minute. Carrying her all the way to their cabin in the woods would have been impossible.

The cart jostled, and Mina's eyes flashed open. "I tried."

"Tried what?" Anna asked.

The barest hint of a smile curved her lips. "To poison the queen."

Anna sucked in a breath and shot a look to Koen, but he barely noticed. "Did you touch it?" he asked. "When you stumbled into her, did some get on you?"

Anna's heart leaped into her throat. If Mina had been poisoned—

"No." The smallest shake of her head accompanied the word.

"I thought one had to consume it?" Anna said.

"They do." Koen pushed his glasses back up his nose where they'd slid down. "They should. But..." He swallowed.

But something was terribly wrong with Mina.

"We ditching this thing?" Brandt called over one shoulder as he drove the cart onward into the woods.

Eventually, someone would come looking for it—or them. Probably both.

Koen looked to Anna, and she nodded. She'd walk to the sea in these ridiculous heels if it'd keep them all safe.

"I'll drive this back toward town, then double back to you," Brandt said the moment they were on the ground, Mina curled in Koen's arms.

By the time he returned, Mina had completely passed out.

"Can't wake her?" Brandt implored. "What does that mean?"

Koen tugged at his hair, pacing beside Mina where they'd laid her on the ground. He'd been calm as a tranquil lake in the castle, but now nothing could ease him, not with his precious sister like this.

"It has to be magic," Anna said, brushing her hand across the girl's forehead. Her chest still rose and fell in steady breaths. She had no fever, no other ailments they could discern. To all the world, she looked asleep in the autumn-touched meadow.

"We have to get her back," Koen said, as much to himself as to the rest of them. "My potions might help. They have to."

"They going to come looking for us?" Brandt asked.

Koen stilled, turning on his brother like a snake about to strike. "We can't leave her like this!"

Anna flinched at the uncharacteristic outburst, but Brandt only crossed his arms and stared down his brother. "We ain't. But getting caught by the queen's guards won't help her."

"Then let's get there quick," Anna said. "Try the potions, then find somewhere else to hide."

"And where will we go?" Koen started pacing again.

He wasn't mad at her, not really, but the raised voice and frantic looks brought old memories creeping back to the surface. They pressed on her shoulders, hunched her back.

But he had a point. If they left their home, they needed somewhere to go.

There was one place the queen wouldn't look, not for the fairest maiden in the land. Anna's stomach turned over as she considered the idea. It would be safe for Mina, if not the rest of them. But could she go back there? Anna chewed on her bottom lip. Even suggesting it would raise too many questions, but she might not have a choice.

"We'll...we'll figure it out," Anna said. *Coward*, she scolded herself. "But first, the potions."

18

*N*ight fell along with their hopes. They'd made it back to the cabin, tried every potion and tonic that Koen thought could help, and still Mina slept. He'd been determined to stay beside her all the same, try a few more things as the night wore on, and see if they had any effect.

But every minute that passed, Anna's stomach dropped further. She could barely look at Mina without her eyes welling with tears.

The whole painful flight to the cabin, she'd assured herself that Koen would have a solution. He'd be able to save her. It had been a fool's wish.

Anna sunk into a chair in the main room, her head in her hands. If Mina didn't improve, she'd have to do something. *The shoes.* It had to be something with Ella's shoes. Were they meant to put the chosen woman to sleep?

If Ella's glass slippers caused Mina's illness, then Ella would know the solution. *Maybe.* But it was the fairy godmother who'd requested the fairest in the land, and it was undoubtedly her magic at work. If anyone were to have a cure, it'd be her.

"You don't know what happened to Will?" Brandt asked.

Anna jumped. She hadn't even heard him descend the stairs, and he was never quiet.

Will. Her chest clenched tight. How had he come to mean so much to her in so little time? She'd never thought their plan would fail this poorly. Maybe she'd get captured, maybe they'd go home without any success whatsoever, but failing and losing Mina and Will?

A tear slipped down her cheek. "No." She tugged off the wig and threw it across the table in frustration. "He was fighting some of the guards when we fled with Mina."

Brandt simply nodded and looked at the cold hearth.

Anna wrung her hands in her lap, waiting for him to leave, to go back upstairs, or worse, to berate her for leaving him behind. It was the right choice. The smart choice. And she hated it. That memory of him facing off against the chancellor would be burned into her mind as long as she lived. If he didn't lecture her on that, he was bound to ask about her identity. In the panicked flight she hadn't exactly been careful to lower her voice. She wasn't ready for that conversation yet either. Telling them she was a woman? *Fine. I should. But the rest?* Her stomach turned over at the mere thought of it. She liked them, trusted them, but not that much.

He turned, and she covered her face with her hands, content to sink back to her misery alone if only he'd let her be.

"He's a fighter, that one."

Anna looked up in time to see Brandt stroke at his beard.

"Thought he was dead when I found him." He dropped his hand, and his features hardened. "Wasn't the first body I found in that river." Brandt shook his head as if chasing away old, painful memories. It was a look she knew well, had worn often herself. "If he can live through being shot with an arrow and half-drowned, I'd say a few guards wouldn't do him in."

If only she could believe that. "I shouldn't have left him."

"And gotten yourself captured, or worse?" He looked her up and down. "Ye're not a fighter, 'specially not in that getup."

No, she wasn't, no matter how she tried to be. It seemed she wasn't meant to be good at anything.

"I—" He stepped near and then thought better of it. "I think he'd a' wanted you to run." Brandt rubbed the back of his neck and looked away, a hint of color rising to his face. "Ya know, I thought we made a mistake, bringing you on. But Will, he wouldn't hear it. Said we could trust ya, though he didn't know why himself."

She couldn't blame him for his doubts. Would she have let a stranger join them in a reverse position? With the quest to free her family on the line? *No way.* But Will...he'd done that for her, not even knowing her. She swallowed against the dryness in her throat. If not for them taking her in, she'd probably still be camping out in the woods, trying to find some weakness, some hint of how to free her mother and sister from the fairy godmother's clutches.

Brandt crossed the space between them and clapped a scarred and weathered hand on her shoulder. "Glad I listened to 'im. Ye're a good lad."

Heat raced to her cheeks. "Thanks."

"I mean it. I've seen the way Mina looks at you too. Once she's better..."

An odd fluttering filled her gut. *Oh heavens, we aren't having this conversation.* It was time to tell him the truth about being a woman.

But Brandt went still, glancing toward the front of the cabin.

"Wha—"

Then she heard it too, horses approaching, several of them. Light flickered outside the windows. Her body tensed, the urge to flee surging through her veins.

When things got tough, she ran. Ella's torments often sent her running to the fields and woods outside their home. She ran when Charlotte told her to the day the guards came to arrest them. She snuck away every time she thought someone might possibly figure out who she was. And today, she'd fled when Will needed her.

Her nails bit into her palms. She wouldn't run, not anymore.

Brandt cursed, his hands patting his sides, searching for blades that weren't there. He crossed the room toward the fireplace and the tools lingering there as Anna said, "Let me answer it."

His head snapped around so fast Anna could swear his neck popped.

"You said you trusted me," she rushed on in an urgent whisper. "Let me deal with this."

She could practically see his teeth grinding together even though his beard covered the whole bottom half of his face. Indecision flickered in his eyes as he grabbed the iron poker. "Fine, but they make one false move —" He slapped the iron rod against his palm.

Anna simply nodded, her mind already working out a plan as she quickly tucked her discarded wig away and crossed to the door. Still clad in the dress she'd worn that day, the hem still soaked with mud and dirt from their trek, she threw open the door. The lead rider dismounted, another three following suit behind him.

Her spine stiffened, but Anna forced a smile to her face and made her voice light as she said, "Visitors so late?"

"Apologies, miss." The lead guard gave a stiff nod as he approached, his helmet tucked under one arm. "An urgent request from Her Majesty, the queen."

"Oh heavens." A hand flew to her mouth in mock dismay. "Is it something to do with that terrible brawl that erupted earlier today?"

From the corner of her eye, she caught Brandt stiffen, but she ignored him. Better to be forthright, to pretend nothing was amiss. It'd worked for her for months, and she could only hope it would again.

The guard came up short, stiffening as he looked her over from head to toe. "You were there?"

Anna nodded. "Her Majesty did ask for young women to come. I hoped to be her companion, but alas, the queen was displeased with my hair." She touched the short ends. "So I cut it off."

"Y-you cut it off?" His brows furrowed.

"Strange woman," another man muttered. "No wonder."

She forced her smile wider, fighting the urge to roll her eyes. Some men really had no clue at all.

"Well." The guard shook his head. "No matter. Her Majesty, Queen Cinderella, requests we have each young woman try on a shoe to find the one whom it responded to earlier today—the queen's perfect companion, she said." He waved forward a young man who carried a box.

The glass shoes. Her skin turned clammy as she thought of Mina trapped in a magical sleep upstairs. Would the same fate await her?

"Please come in." Anna managed to keep the tremor out of her voice.

"Quickly," the lead guard urged on his companion. No doubt they had many homes to visit, but that they were already here spoke volumes. They must have some idea Mina wasn't from the city or they'd still be testing women there. It wouldn't take too long before they realized their error and doubled back.

"My fiancé," Anna gestured toward Brandt, who glowered near the empty hearth. Wisely, he'd replaced the poker, though he stood only inches away.

"Ah, yes," the man coughed, his discomfort clear. "We'll just be a moment."

"Good." He crossed his arms. "Was just about to show my *fiancée* how much I like her new hair. Should feel good under my fingers when she's between my legs."

Holy Mother.

The young man nearly dropped the box, fumbling it back and forth before steadying his grip.

Anna didn't have to fake the fiery blush heating her face or her wide-eyed glare.

Brandt broke into a thunderous laugh, slapping a palm on his thigh. "Come on, it's a joke."

Right... The small chuckle that slipped from her held anything but amusement.

Distracting the guards and making them uncomfortable, great idea. Being crude and memorable? Terrible.

"The shoe?" Anna asked. She took the closest seat and displayed a stockinged foot.

"Yes, right now." The guard flicked his fingers at the younger man.

The boy nearly dropped the box again while opening the lid. Inside lay the glass shoe on a silken cushion.

Anna inhaled a shaky breath as he knelt and placed it on her foot. It was a little small. Her heel couldn't quite slip down into the sole of the shoe. Though she expected something hard as stone with sharp edges that might cut at her feet, the shoe felt strangely comfortable. Perhaps Ella hadn't been in pain wearing them after all.

She held her breath, waiting and watching. Everyone in the room did. Not a word was spoken as seconds ticked by, muffled sounds of men and horses outside warred with the quick thump of her heart for dominance.

"Sorry, miss, I don't believe you're the one."

The sigh that escaped wasn't faked. But the frown that she forced afterward was. "I know." She touched her hair again for emphasis.

"Let's be off." He made another flick of his fingers toward the boy.

Anna made herself smile at him. Poor kid probably had no idea who he served. He smiled back. "Such a nice house for just the two of you." The lid closed with a thunk, and he hefted the box in his thin arms, completely unaware that the guard at his side had gone completely still.

Panic roared through her head. Her fingers curled into the fabric of her dress. *Think.*

"Indeed," the older man said, finding his words. "Are there other women here? Sisters perhaps?"

Because she couldn't think and feared whatever utter nonsense Brandt might say, she spoke the truth, or a version of it they might appreciate. "They were traitors, one and all. We're well rid of them."

The guard blinked at her, perhaps shocked at her honesty. "Right, well, good night then."

It wasn't until the door closed behind them that she let herself breathe again, gasping in one panicked breath after another. Her legs shook until she sat with a heavy thump, letting her head fall into her open palms.

Brandt said nothing until the sound of horses retreated outside. Then, "All clear."

Anna assumed he spoke to her until Koen's reply came from the top of the stairs. "Good."

Her head snapped toward Brandt, a question in her wide eyes. He nodded. Koen had been there the whole time and had heard every word. He probably had a weapon at the ready too.

"Go get some sleep. We all should." Brandt looked toward the stairs, but no reply came. Koen had quite some skill to walk through the house without being heard, she'd give him that.

At length, Anna pushed herself up from the chair.

"You're a good liar," Brandt said.

You have no idea. The words lingered on the tip of her tongue, but instead she said, "You're disgusting. There's a reason you're not married." Anna glared at him before she stomped up the stairs.

"Or maybe I'm so good with women I can't pick just one. You should try it."

Anna drew to a halt, spinning around so he could see her dramatic eye roll. "You really have no idea." *About so many things.*

He chuckled to himself as she rounded the bend in the stairs and strode to her borrowed room.

*a*nna couldn't get out of her dress fast enough. Finally alone, all the horrors of the day tried to strangle her in the laces of the dress—the fairy grandmother's cackle, Ella and all her arrogance and indifference, the guards' quest for some poor girl, Mina, her fainting spell and whatever magic kept her in slumber.

And then there was Will. Just the thought cut off her air and sent her head swimming. If the dress had been her own, not Mina's, she'd have ripped it off herself, reason be damned.

Will.

She didn't bother to stop the tears as they welled and slid down the make-up on her cheeks. That had to go too.

Off, off, off.

The dress caught on her feet as she slid it free, and Anna kicked it away with a cry of frustration.

Suddenly, even the nearly dark room was too small, too cloistered. She needed to run, to sprint through the woods until all her worries and sorrows were far, far away. Instead, she threw open the windowpanes, uncaring of the thin chemise hiding her unbound breasts. The owls wouldn't care, and she needed every breath of cool night air she could drag into her lungs.

She sucked in one after another until her heart rate slowed. Finally able to focus, she crossed to the pitcher of water, dampened a rag, and began to scrub away Mina's work from that morning. Tears slid down her face.

What a failure. She couldn't stop her stepsister from harming another, not even when she was so close. She couldn't save Will, couldn't do any of the things they'd planned on.

Is he chained up in the dungeons below the castle? Already in a cart on the way to the fairy godmother's workhouse? Maybe Charlotte would find him. Her sister had always been the braver, bolder one. She scrubbed harder, the cloth grating against her skin like tree bark. Maybe she could save them both—someday, somehow, her mother too. All the people she had left behind.

But what if he's already de—

"No." She slammed the cloth down, shutting her eyes against the pain that stabbed into her chest. "He can't be dead," she whispered.

"Who can't be dead?"

19

*T*he unholy scream that ripped from Ansel's lungs could have raised the dead.

Will lunged from the window, nearly tripping over his own feet before he grabbed Ansel and slapped a hand over his mouth to silence his screams.

He jerked the young man to his chest. "Shh, damn it. The guards could hear that screech miles away."

But he didn't need the reprimand. The young man had gone utterly still, his countenance paling in the dim light of the room. The pain in Will's arm flared from the sudden movement, but he barely felt it. His awareness took stock of the lithe form in his arms—and of the soft globes of flesh that brushed the top of the arm wrapped around Ansel's chest.

Holy fucking saints.

His stomach bottomed out. Molten fire poured through his veins, churning against the chills racing over his skin.

The pieces all clicked into place, his suspicion confirmed. The high-pitched scream, the way he—no, she—carried herself in a dress and heels, the Wanted poster.

Will's mouth went dry. Their kiss.

His hand fell limply away from her mouth, those soft lips he'd once dreamed about.

"Y-you're..." He couldn't form the words, couldn't pluck them from the multitude racing through his mind.

Her head dropped as if in shame.

"You're—" He tried again.

The bedroom door slammed open.

Will leaped back, bumping into a chair and sending it sprawling as Brandt and Koen charged into the room, blades bared.

Ansel—Anna?—squeaked, pulling her arms over her chest like a blushing maid.

Fuck. Heat burned up his neck. By sneaking in her window, he'd exposed her secret to them all.

"Will," Koen said, recovering first. His blade lowered as he blinked in surprise. The man's eyes were red, dark circles lingering under them.

Brandt half-snarled, scanning him head to toe, until Will's name sunk in and the tension in his form eased.

"Fucking hells. Thought you were—" He drew the dagger through the air in front of his throat.

"I'm not." He glanced at his wound. *Fucking hells is right.* Climbing had been a terrible mistake. "Not yet anyway."

"We're glad," Koen said.

At the same time, Brandt said, "Could have used the damn door."

He tried. They'd been bolted shut. He'd even knocked. Shouting might have worked, but it might have alerted the guards he'd seen leave. He'd almost considered it when Ansel threw open his—her—window. The nearby tree, one that half-hung over the house and that he'd recommended cutting down numerous times, bore thick branches. It had been an easy climb, even in his sorry state.

"Get out!" Ansel reached for the bed linens, trying and failing to tug them free and cover herself. Her wide-eyed, furious stare pinned them each in turn.

Brandt gaped. Koen merely blinked.

The deepest level of hell contained less fury than her. "Get. Out!"

That last command trigger-snapped something in all of them. Will sprinted to the door. Koen turned on his heel so fast he nearly fell. Brandt turned a shade of purple before he, too, ran for the door.

The door rattled on its hinges as he pulled it tight behind him, leaving Ansel alone in the room. He waited, one heartbeat after the next, his back against the wood. No sound came—no cries of fury or frustration, no tearful sobs. Not a damn thing.

Hells, we are in for it now.

"That—" Brandt snapped his gaze between them, his face a mottle of colors behind his beard. "Did he—he's a—"

"He's a she," Koen said with a level of calm that only he could muster, almost like he'd already guessed.

They saw. They knew. That damn chemise, threadbare, wrinkled, and damp with sweat, couldn't hide enough. *Hells.* He scrubbed a hand down his face. It didn't hide much at all.

No wonder he'd—she'd—been so flustered that night in the river.

Naked. Heavens and hells. She'd been naked in the river just a few feet away from him.

His traitorous cock twitched, and he fought down the desire those memories brought churning to the surface.

"I—" Brandt looked this way and that, like a deer ready to flee. "Fuck."

That really did sum it up.

"Did you know?" Brandt asked.

Will shook his head. "Not for sure." He'd wondered, guessed at it.

"You two are ridiculous," Koen said.

"You knew?" Brandt accused.

Koen shrugged. "I suspected."

Mina would be devastated to learn her crush wasn't the young man she believed. He cast his gaze around, searching for her familiar face.

Her absence hit him like a punch to the gut. A gaping chasm opened in his chest. "Where's Mina?" Horror rang in each syllable. His question sucked all the air from the room and the color from the men's faces.

She should be here. She would have heard the scream and come to investigate.

The sorrow in their gazes stabbed through him. She'd fled with them.

She had to have. The girl wasn't in the throne room at the end. He hadn't seen the guards take her away.

"Come with me." Koen didn't so much as look at him as he led the way down the hall.

Mina lay on her bed, hands clasped over her chest, still in the gown she'd worn to the castle. Her face was serene, as if she slept peacefully, but no one could sleep through the ruckus they'd made in the other room. Her lips were pulled up in the slight curve of a demure smile, like she might open her eyes at any moment.

"We haven't been able to wake her." Koen sat on the rumpled coverings at the edge of the bed—a place he must have occupied earlier—and swept a hand across her brow. "No fever. No discoloration. My medicines have had no effect."

A chill cold as death—cold as the spill in that river that nearly ended him—gripped his chest. "Magic."

Koen nodded.

Will glanced to the small table in the room. Vials, bowls, and powders covered its surface. One dish still smoked where it sat over a small oil flame. Koen's special glasses, a pair he'd designed to help him see things more closely, were cast off to the side.

"I'm trying," his voice cracked. "But I have no basis for this. I haven't seen it. Don't know what caused her slumber."

Nails bit into his palm, a welcome distraction from the pain still pulsing through his shoulder and his legs from the long run and trek here. "Those shoes."

"Yes, but how?" Koen's brows wrinkled.

"Ansel tried them on." Brandt's coarse voice at his back made him jump in his boots.

Will whirled on him, his mouth open in question. But his gaze hung on the figure who appeared in the doorway, a blanket wrapped around her shoulders, hiding her form.

Brandt turned as well, just as Ansel spoke. "Seems the guards are going door to door trying to find Mina." Her voice cracked over the girl's name. "They had me try on the shoe, but nothing happened."

Heaviness settled over them all until Brandt shattered it. "You, you're really a—" He gaped, stumbling over the word as if it was the hardest thing he'd ever said. "A g-g..." An old stutter Will hadn't heard since his early days with the siblings crept to the surface.

"A *woman*." Her gaze flicked to Will, so brief and fleeting, yet it stirred up a mess of emotions within him. "Yes."

"But I—" Brandt tugged at his hair. "I pissed in front of ya. Cursed. Made that joke about you sucking my cock."

Rage erupted from nowhere. "You what?" Will all but snarled.

Brandt flinched away, his gaze shooting back and forth between Will and Ansel. The hard glare she shot Brandt's way could have flayed a man.

"I didn't know." He held his hands up in front of him. "Fuck, I didn't—" He snapped his mouth shut, his face flushing dark red, almost purple at his neck.

"Why didn't you tell us?" Leave it to Koen to be the calm voice of reason.

Will had an idea on that score. He couldn't shake what he'd seen on that poster. Yet that image had been hideous, and Ansel was anything but. She might not be what others considered the portrait of beauty, but there was a deep steadiness and burning intelligence in her eyes that bewitched him. Even now, he couldn't tear his eyes from her, from that mole on her cheek, though she steadfastly refused to look his way.

"It was safer to be a man."

Because she worried about being a lone woman in the woods, or because someone could claim the bounty on her if they figured out her identity? The sum Cinderella offered would tempt anyone with a brain. No doubt a number of people had forced someone to pretend to be her just to try and claim the prize money. But he'd have heard if she'd been found. The city would never keep that gossip quiet—nor the queen.

It was tempting, oh so tempting. Not just the money, he didn't need that. But the opportunity held a sweetness he could barely ignore. She could be his ticket to get back in the castle, to get near the chancellor and the queen and finish what he'd started today. The thought taunted the worst parts of him, offering up a solution on a silver platter. Ansel, Anna —if that's who she truly was—could be the key to everything.

But risking her? Betraying her after she'd tried to help them at great risk to herself? The mere idea made his skin crawl. He'd meant what he told her at the castle—he wouldn't let the queen have her.

"Surely you know we wouldn't hurt you. You wouldn't be the only woman under our care," Koen said, gesturing to Mina.

Ansel gave a weak smile. "I..." Her shoulders heaved in a sigh, and she looked at the floor. "I wanted to tell you."

Lie. He could almost taste it in the air. She'd have kept that secret forever if she could. That warm, brown gaze drifted over him. Her sharp intake of breath tugged something low in his gut.

"Your arm." A soft hand flew to cover her mouth.

Though concern shone in her eyes, he'd bet that wasn't her only reason for mentioning it, especially as the brothers looked to him instead of her. *Clever.*

Will pulled away the torn fabric, baring the wound. Bile burned the back of his throat. *Damn thing looks worse than I remember.*

"Hells," Koen muttered, shoving to his feet. "I should have—" He took one step and swayed before steadying himself and shuffling toward the desk.

The man was tired, burned through. It'd be a lie to say his own legs didn't tremble. Only pain kept his senses sharp.

"I—we...we worried you might be dead." This time, her concern was genuine, so soft and tender it hurt worse than his wounds.

"What happened, man?" Brandt asked.

He grimaced at the wound. Telling them why he'd attacked the chancellor was out of the question. He'd known that the moment he decided to come back here. Instead, he said, "You all needed a distraction. A way out."

"You stabbed the chancellor," Ansel sputtered.

Will shrugged, then winced as Koen touched his arm, inspecting the wound. "Bastard had it coming." That much was certainly true.

Koen dropped Will's arm and began sorting through the vials on his makeshift desk.

"But how'd ya get out?" Brandt asked.

Dumb luck, really. "I fell through the mirror."

Koen jolted, knocking over a vial, and cursed. The others just blinked at him.

"*The* mirror?" Brandt's eyes bulged.

He'd have struggled to believe it himself. "Landed on the platform in the square. The guards seemed surprised." He could still remember them gaping as he fell through that thick mist, through that place—for it certainly wasn't of this world. "But they were able to come through too. Chased me through half the city before I lost them."

"You went through the mirror," Ansel echoed. She swayed on her feet, grabbing the foot of Mina's bed for support. "A doorway," she whispered, her gaze far away. "I never knew. She never—" She cut herself off, blinking.

A tingle ran down his skin. She never knew her stepsister's mirror was a doorway she could pass through? Or anyone else, apparently. Thought it was one-way. *Smart. A way to flee the castle but not enter it, as if Cinderella thought she might need an escape, or...* His teeth ground together. The fairy godmother had some other wicked plan up her sleeve, some monstrosity waiting to be unleashed on the unsuspecting.

Something burned and sizzled against his wound. Will hissed through gritted teeth.

"Hold still," Koen ordered. He was fully focused on the task at hand, a man consumed with his work. A usual state for him. It was either work or the plants he smoked. From the redness in his eyes, he'd probably already indulged this evening. Will couldn't blame him, with all that had happened. Especially with Mina as she was. Will's gaze slid over the sleeping girl.

"It needs to be stitched." Will cut his gaze to where Koen dabbed at the wound. The man's hand already shook. From exhaustion, fear, his smoked herbs? He didn't know, but he sure wasn't going to let Koen wield a needle on him in that state.

"I'll do it myself." His jaw slammed shut in anticipation of the pain to come. All cleaned up, it looked even worse. No wonder the damn thing hurt so bad.

Koen swallowed hard but nodded. "I have a paste that'll numb it some."

Some, but not all. Even Koen wasn't that skilled. No one was but death himself.

It'd be better than nothing though.

"I'll do it." Ansel pressed her lips together, sucking them into her mouth before she met his gaze. "That angle and the state you're in…" She shook her head. "I can sew. I'm good at it."

That was right. She was the tailor's daughter. Though was that story even true? He knew little about the queen's stepsisters, nothing more than their names.

"Sewing a dress is far different than stitching a man's skin," he said.

Her throat bobbed, and she adjusted the blanket around her shoulders, but to her credit she didn't look away. "I know."

"Do it quick, then rest." Koen passed the paste off to Ansel. "In the morning, we need to find help for Mina. Somewhere safer until we can heal her."

"Not here?" Will raised a brow. The city wouldn't be any better. And who could they trust? *No one.*

"I have a thought for that too," Ansel said. "There's a convent…" Her focus slipped to Mina, her features softening. "They helped me. They'll help her too, at least until we can find a cure."

A convent. He'd never considered it. Honestly, he'd almost forgotten about the women who lived apart from society at the base of the mountains. They dedicated their lives to the Mother and had often come to the city to give food to the needy—at least before Cinderella's reign. Once she started giving out her tainted food, the women were no longer welcome, turned away by the guards and shunned by the very people they'd once helped.

"The queen won't think to look there?" Brandt asked, stroking his beard.

"No," Ansel said far too quickly. "She thinks they're ridiculous." She pulled the blanket tighter. "Or that's what I gathered while I stayed there," she added in a hurry.

Or that's what she told you once. The thought hung on his tongue, unspoken.

But one way or another, he'd get the answer.

20

*I*t had been a terrible idea, offering to stitch his wound. Just the thought of driving a needle through his flesh over and over had bile burning the base of her throat and climbing higher.

The Mother help her, could she even do it?

She had to try. Koen was in no state to do it. Brandt? She nearly snorted. Brandt with a needle would be something to see, but Will would curse them all if he tried to stitch him up. And letting him do it himself? It just felt wrong somehow.

Will had fought a room of guards for them to escape. He'd nearly gotten himself captured or worse. The least she could do was tend his wound, even if the idiot had outed her gender to the rest of the group. Honestly, the fact that they hadn't figured it out sooner had started to grate. She'd never been the beauty, nor was she so well-endowed as Charlotte and her mother. Passing for a young man wasn't hard.

But still…it hurt. It chafed at everything inside her, especially where Will was concerned. Of all of them, she wanted him to see her, not just as a friend, an ally, but maybe, just possibly, something more?

A foolish wish. He'd barely looked at her since finding out she was a woman. He probably thought her as hideous as every other man had, especially once Ella dug her claws into them. Why would they ever look at her when Ella outshone her like the sun? Her stepsister had even said as much, and though so many of her jabs were lies aimed to cut and bruise, that one had struck deep as only truth could.

After she slipped into a shirt and pants, Anna found Will sitting on the edge of his bed, shirtless.

Heavens and hells. Her throat went dry. All thoughts fled. He was stunning. She'd seen him without his shirt once before, bathed in moonlight in the river not far from the cottage. But here in the clear lamplight, sitting on a bed no less...

He was beautiful, perfect in a way she never would be.

Fine, dark hair covered his sculpted chest, trailing down to a faint dusting over the defined muscles on his abdomen. Even the near-naked statues outside the castle hadn't been so glorious, so perfectly balanced and defined. A little trail of hair ran down the center of his lower stomach muscles, dipping down into the waistband of his pants and leading toward a place she dared not think about. She forced her gaze higher, admiring his arms. Even the fierce gash and lingering stain of blood couldn't distract from his appearance. Those arms... When they'd wrapped around her in the secret passageway of the castle, she'd wondered at their strength, relished the feel of them. She no longer had to. No wonder he could pull a bowstring with ease and wield a sword as if it weighed little. He was able to climb into her bedroom—

Will coughed, and her attention snapped to his face. The hint of a smile twitched at the corner of his lips.

Oh...oh no. Heat burst through her chest. It crawled up her neck to splash across her cheeks. She wanted nothing more than to turn and run from the room, but that wouldn't erase the last few moments where she'd literally gawked at him in unabashed admiration.

"I'd ask if you've ever seen a shirtless man, but I do believe you have." Mischief twinkled in his eyes.

Oh, to sink through the floor. To hide forever and never have to face him again.

"Indeed." That one word took the effort of ten.

His humor vanished in a heartbeat. "I'm sorry about that night, at the river." A hint of color rose above his beard to his cheeks. "Inviting you to join me, offering to—" He shook his head. "It was inappropriate of me."

Inappropriate, or he regretted it? She couldn't look at him, couldn't bear to see the regret in his eyes. Instead, she focused on the items in her hand—a bone needle already strung through with tough thread, a cloth, and a bowl of water. That she hadn't dropped it when she'd walked in the room and seen him was a miracle. "It's okay. You didn't know."

Silence lingered as she prepared her meager tools.

Will grimaced as he slid his fingers over and around his wound, smearing more of the paste that Koen had given him. It'd better work, for both their sakes. The needle she'd found was wider than she'd have liked, not ideal for what she needed to attempt. But leaving his wound to fester was a terrible idea.

Anna's heart leaped into her throat as she crossed the short distance between them and sat on the edge of the bed. Mere inches separated them. She could smell his woodsy scent, the hint of sweat still clinging to him. She had to touch him, had to guide the needle. But his face was turned toward her, those lips she'd kissed so close. Had that really been only hours ago?

If she closed her eyes, she could still feel their softness offset against the scratch of his beard. She recalled how his shock had melted away into something that had to be an act. It *had* to have been. Her eyes flashed open, and she sucked in a steadying breath.

"Don't be nervous." His voice drifted across her skin, stirring up goosebumps.

If only the needle in her hand was the thing distracting her thoughts.

"I…" She shook her head. "Can you look away?"

The sight was horrible, nauseating. But worse would be the feel. The puncture of flesh. The pull of thread. "Talk to me," she said.

"About?" Pain laced his words, but she'd wager it was far less than without the paste.

"Anything."

He huffed air through his nose, moving his arm just as she closed in with the needle.

Anna smacked him. "Don't move, idiot."

"Fine." Though she'd asked him to look away, he turned his head ever so slightly toward her. "Shouldn't you be the one distracting me?"

"I'm the one working here." She drove the needle through for emphasis, earning a soft hiss of pain.

"And I'm the injured one. Ever sewn a wound before?"

"No." Another stitch. She blew out the breath she'd been holding. "And I might never again after this."

"You'll want to keep the stitches straight and tight."

She rolled her eyes. "Worried about the scar? Wouldn't want my poor handiwork marring your perfect form."

He stiffened ever so slightly under her touch. "Perfect?"

Oh hells. She bit her tongue. She couldn't do anything right this evening. Confirming the comment was out of the question. Instead, she focused on his arm. One stitch down. Another started.

"You really think I'm perfect, Anna?"

She fought the urge to smack him again. "Stop trying to make me uncomfortable. I'm the one with the needle here."

"Oh, no payback for earlier today? What did you call me? Darling?" The word rolled off his tongue, thick and rich. If his arm still pained him, he did a good job of covering it up. "Or what about that kiss?"

She stabbed a little deeper on purpose and jerked the thread as she closed the last stitch and knotted it off. "You deserved that you—" The needle nearly slipped from her grip. "What did you call me?"

One heartbeat passed. She let out one shallow breath, then another.

He didn't answer.

When she could stand the silence no more, she forced her gaze away from his wound, crawling inch by tiny inch over his shoulder, up his neck, across his beard, to intense brown eyes that saw far, far too much.

His chest rose and fell. "Anna."

Her name. He knew her name. The way he said it, full of something she dared not guess at, sank deep into her soul. She closed her eyes, fighting against the traitorous feeling that bloomed in her.

It was over.

If he knew, if he truly knew, she'd have to run, flee before the others could catch up. No one would turn down the queen's reward. They'd be a fool.

She dropped the needle and leaped from the bed, from him.

"Anna, wait."

No. Out, out, out.

She didn't make it three steps before his hand clasped around her wrist, jerking her to a stop.

"Let me go." She turned to hit him, to stab him with the damn needle she'd stupidly dropped.

Will grabbed her other arm, grimacing in pain as she tried to jerk free. "Stop, please."

Panic roared through her, urging her to run, to flee. "No! Let go!"

"You'll wake the others."

"I—" She jerked in his arms. *Can't wake them. Must run.*

"Anna," he grated.

Her boots slid on the floor. *No. He can't have me. Can't turn me over.* "Sto—"

He lunged forward, knocking her off-balance and sending her stumbling as he released her. But he didn't back away. He pursued—fast. So fast. His good arm wrapped around her waist and drew her close.

And then his lips crashed against hers.

The world shattered.

Every thought, every fear, everything vanished, except the press of his lips against her own.

Her knees went weak, and if not for his arm around her, she surely would have fallen.

The coarse hair of his beard scraped against her skin, but she didn't care. She barely felt it over the surge of emotion tingling down her spine. Especially as he slanted his head, deepening the kiss as he pulled her tighter.

Her name didn't matter. She forgot her name. There was only Will. His arm around her, his lips on hers. Their first kiss had been nothing like this. It had been a ruse, a game, done in a panic to distract the guards. She'd loved the taste of him, the press of his lips on hers, but there'd been no choice. It had been a brief, selfish moment in their quest.

But this…

His fingers flexed on her side. Will pulled back, slowly, gently, until his heated breath tickled her face and sent a mess of warmth pooling low in her gut, drifting lower still.

"Anna."

Her name was her undoing, but instead of fear, it elicited something even more terrifying.

"Look at me, Anna."

She hadn't. She couldn't. She'd closed her eyes the moment his lips touched hers and dropped them the moment he pulled away. She couldn't ruin the moment, couldn't see all the horrible things she was sure she would glimpse in his eyes. He regretted the river. Probably their first kiss too, even with the farce it was. And now he'd kissed her again to silence her. Nothing more.

Strong fingers trailed up the base of her neck, along her jaw, leaving tingling shivers in their wake. Will took her chin and lifted it until she was forced to gaze up into those cold eyes.

But they weren't cold. The emotion simmering there wasn't regret. No shame shone in them, no judgment or condemnation for who she was.

Breath caught in her throat.

Instead, she saw something unbelievable, something so rare and elusive she couldn't place it at first—desire. Pure, simple want.

For her.

"Will." Something in her cracked and burst. Anna threw her arms around his neck, dragging his face back to hers. And he came to her, met her kiss like he was a drowning man who'd found a source of air. His arms wrapped around her, tugging her close until she was pressed against him, until they were one. His breath filled her lungs. The warmth of his chest seeped through her clothes. The flick of his tongue drove her to madness.

Anna groaned against him. Her hands weaved through his hair. They tugged and slid as if she could meld them together forever. Every bit of her turned warm and melty, like she might dissolve into a puddle of need and slide down his solid chest. And solid it was, so hard yet comforting.

His hand slid down her back, and all her senses focused on those strong fingers and the shiver of pleasure they elicited. Down they went, lower still, until he cupped her backside. No one had ever been so forward, not even the man who'd seduced her to get nearer her stepsister, but she loved Will's touch, craved it, never wanted his hands off her.

Those deft fingers flexed, tugging her impossibly closer. And then she felt it, the hard bulge of him pressing into her lower stomach. Her knees shook. Wetness blossomed between her legs.

"Will," she moaned against his lips.

His only response was a soft groan low in his throat as he flexed his hand around the globe of her backside.

Someone cleared their throat.

Anna froze. The cage of desire she'd been locked in swung open, and she ripped her lips from Will's. He spun them, twisting Anna away from the intruder before she could even spot who it was.

"I—"

Koen.

Her lips pressed thin. Locked in the kiss as she had been, she'd never heard the door open, much less someone enter. Anna stretched on her toes to see around Will, who'd turned his head to scowl at the other man.

"I forgot to give you this." He held up a jar, his gaze averted.

"Better be worth it," Will said, his voice low and hoarse. If looks could kill, he'd have slain his friend where he stood.

Her body flamed even hotter.

"It's to cover the wound. Prevent infection. I'll just…" He set it on the table, never quite looking at them, and fled.

Anna waited, frozen, unsure of what to say or do. Will's bare chest rose and fell under her palm. The smattering of dark hair there tickled her skin, and she fought the urge to tangle her fingers through it and slide them along those muscular planes.

The moment was gone. She should pull away and leave him be, but no one had ever held her like that and kissed her until the world disappeared. No one.

"You were afraid when I said your name."

She barely heard him. All her senses narrowed to the feel of his thumb as it made lazy, possessive strokes up and down her side.

"I…I understand why you hid yourself, your name, your identity."

At last, she looked back up into those eyes she could happily drown in. What she saw there echoed everything he'd said. She supposed he would understand. He'd been hunted by the queen too. Only, she believed him dead. Breath caught as dawning horror spread through her. "Today. In the castle. Did they know who you were?"

His throat bobbed as he swallowed. She knew before he ever said yes. Someone had seen. Someone had known.

"Will they come after you?" she asked.

A humorless smile twisted at the corner of his lips. "Didn't they already?"

Right, they'd chased him through the mirror, but they would have gone after anyone who attacked the chancellor.

"Yes." He grimaced, his lips pulling thin. "I put you all at risk even being here. I should—"

Anna placed her fingers over his lips. "Don't you dare say 'go.' We need you. I—" Her throat tried to close up, but she forced out the words. "I need you."

He took her fingers in his, curling them until he could place a kiss on the back of her hand like some noble at court. That act, that simple touch, had her squeezing her thighs together, fighting against her unquenched desire.

"You need rest," he said, his breath ghosting across her skin.

So true, but it was the very last thing she wanted. "Just tell me one thing. How did you know?"

His chest expanded with a swallowed huff of laughter as he released her hand. "I saw an old Wanted poster in the city."

Oh. Oh no. Shame consumed her, and she looked away. The posters were terrible, and he'd—

"A horrible rendition." He tilted her face back up. "They failed to capture your beauty, and you are lovely, Anna, inside and out, never doubt that."

Pretty words. She wanted to believe them, wanted so hard, but she couldn't make herself accept the compliment.

"But..." He ran his finger along her cheek, over that mole that marked her face. "There is one thing they got right."

My mole?

"This—" She gestured to it. "—was enough to identify me?"

His lips twitched. "Call it luck?"

She nearly snorted. Her birth father used to call it a lucky mark, but she'd never shared the sentiment.

"Do the others know?" she glanced toward the door.

He shook his head. "And they won't. Unless you want them to."

Would they turn her in, claim the reward money? *No.* The answer settled in her with a wave of calm. They hated the queen and her allies as much as her, maybe more so, especially after what happened today. They wouldn't turn her over. But still… "Don't tell them. Not yet."

He held her gaze, letting her see the sincerity in his eyes as he said, "I won't. No one will know."

With his promise between them, she left Will to his rest. Lingering would have been a dream. Her skin tingled every time she thought of their kiss, his words, or that look in his eyes that stole her breath. But he needed rest, and so did she.

Tomorrow they would get Mina to safety. Tomorrow they would figure out a plan. And tomorrow, just maybe, she'd get another kiss.

For the first time in a very long time, Anna went to sleep with a smile in her heart.

21

*W*ill's arm throbbed with every step down the rough road. Deep grooves had been rutted from wagons passing through day after day, bringing down gems and stone from the mines in the mountain, not to mention other goods. Those wagons had been wider than the small cart they pulled though. One wheel ran along a groove, smooth and easy. The other bumped along the coarse ground between the ruts, leaving the whole cart tipped at a precarious angle as they pulled it along without the aid of a work animal.

Another rock or something jolted the cart, and Will gritted his teeth.

"Son of a—" Brandt snapped his mouth shut and groaned as he adjusted the handle. He'd taken the high side, the harder side given the lack of the rutted groove. Brandt cut his gaze to Anna, color creeping above his beard and darkening his tanned skin. "Sorry 'bout that."

The younger brother had been flustered all morning, apologizing over and over for all the things he'd said and done when he'd thought Anna was a man.

"It's nothing I haven't heard before," Anna said.

Will hadn't told them her name. Nor anything about what transpired last night. Koen's occasional knowing looks between them said he'd seen enough. Whether he'd told his brother...who knew.

"Let me pull it for a bit," she offered.

"Can't let a—" Brandt cut himself off.

She'd dressed as a man again today. It was safer, she insisted, and she was probably right.

"I mean, I got it. You'n help that poor ba—ah hells," Brandt shook his head. "Help him." He jerked his head in Will's direction.

Will scowled. "I've got it." He could handle the pain. *I* will *handle it.*

Anna rolled her eyes and stalked around the cart. "You're not helping anyone if you rip those stitches open and bleed out everywhere."

He might have already done that by the feel of it. He had wrapped extra bandages around his arm just in case. His arm would heal, but Mina... His gaze drifted to the cart. His stomach knotted up every time he thought about the poor girl or caught sight of the thin blanket they'd stretched over her sleeping form. They'd done the best they could to keep her comfortable and safe on their journey—laid her on the softest blankets and stacked empty boxes around her. If anyone stopped them, they'd hopefully just think they carted supplies toward the mountains.

This was something new, whatever magic forced her into a deathlike sleep and held her there. It hadn't been used in the castle that he could remember, nor had he seen its like outside it. It was some new wicked concoction of the fairy godmother.

And that, they'd decided early this morning, was where they'd find the cure.

If Koen's potions didn't work, if the women of the convent had no solution, then they'd have to sneak into the fairy godmother's workhouse and find the cure. *There has to be one. There must be one.*

Brandt stopped, throwing his weight against the cart and forcing Will to halt his steps.

Anna stood just in front of him, brows raised. Hells, he'd been so wrapped up in his thoughts, he'd nearly run right into her. He let go of the cart. His hands groaned as he flexed, little calluses forming despite the gloves he wore.

They hadn't talked about last night, about her identity or their kiss. But as he held her gaze, he couldn't help remember the way her lips tasted, the press of her lithe body against his...or the terror when she'd realized what he knew. It had been worse than any doe that had spotted him in the moment before slaying her.

It could be a weapon, her identity—a tool to be wielded against the queen or to the benefit of anyone aiming to claim the reward. But he couldn't do that. Not to her, especially not now that he knew who she was and what she'd already suffered.

"If you get tired…" he began, stepping away.

"I've got this." Anna flashed a smile, but it didn't reach her eyes. Even so, a swell of pride rolled through him at her persistence.

"We should be getting close," Koen said from ahead.

The waiting mountains beckoned, their peaks stretching high above the tree line.

"Still don't see why they couldn't have built at the bottom of the mountain," Brandt grumbled.

Anna hefted her side. "Closer to the Mother here, it's said."

"Better be as grand as one of the high heavens," Brandt grumbled again.

"Never pulled the cart before?" Anna asked.

"Not up the bleeding mountain."

"I thought you were miners. Aren't the mines in the mountains?" she asked.

"Yes, but the route was mostly downhill," Koen said after a quick peek at Mina. "Toward the castle and the city."

"And we had a team of oxen." Brandt's shoulders hunched. "Miss those smelly brutes."

"What happened to them?" Anna asked, her focus on the road ahead.

His chest tightened at the silence that lingered between the brothers. Finally, Koen said, "Confiscated. When our brothers were taken. Couldn't afford new ones."

Will never thought he'd care so much about animals outside of a glorious kill, but he did. It was something the siblings had taught him without teaching, a side of himself he never would have known if not for all that had happened. It was one of the few things he was thankful for. If he'd been the man he was now, maybe Cinderella's reign would never have come to be. It was the only thing he clung to in order to keep the guilt from drowning him.

Evening was almost upon them by the time they reached the convent. Its square, white towers caught the setting sun, which painted them a bright array of colors.

The sight stopped him in his tracks. His lips parted, the hint of a gasp caught on his tongue around his heavy breathing.

Twilight already bathed the surrounding gardens and the small field where animals grazed. Cool wind slid down the nearby mountainside, bringing with it hints of pine and the tang of bold incense.

In one glance, he understood why the women of the convent had chosen this place. The difficult trek made the sight all that much more rewarding. Another thread of regret tugged at him. How many times had he been in these mountains hunting game, and yet he'd never bothered to come here? The old him probably wouldn't have appreciated it. He might have scoffed at these women living apart from the world.

Sometimes, he couldn't help but think it was a good thing the man he'd been was dead.

"Let me do the talking," Anna said as she drifted ahead of their cart.

Koen and Brandt pulled it now. He'd offered, but Koen had taken one look at his arm during their last stop, sworn, tossed more ointment at him, and refused to let him pull anymore. The man could be quite the mother hen at times.

He raced around the cart and slid into step beside Anna. "I'll come with you."

She skipped a step at his voice before blinking up at him in the dimming light. He could only imagine what thoughts raced through her mind, what worries caused her throat to bob and her lips to press thin. She'd stayed here for a brief time months ago, or so she'd said. They'd helped her.

The details of her stay and her departure, she'd not shared, and he had a strong feeling she wouldn't, not until she was ready.

They'd yet to reach the main entrance—two double doors made of pale birch—before one was drawn inward and a woman ventured out into the twilight.

She looked much the same as the priestesses who lingered around the capital city tending to the great cathedrals and shouting prayers to the Mother and her saints in the square on holy days. The old king had tolerated them, though he did little to earn their favor.

Robes of homely brown draped over her form, cloaking her tanned skin other than her wrinkled hands and face. Her brown hair—heavily strung through with silver—hung loose around her shoulders, straight as the tight press of her lips.

Her gaze probed him as they came to stand before her. The older woman searched him as if she could peel away his skin and see every secret hidden within him. Will shifted his weight from foot to foot, unwilling to break her hard stare no matter the way it made his skin crawl.

A sigh slipped through his lips when the woman finally shifted her focus to Anna, giving her the same hard appraisal.

"Sister Olga." Anna clasped her hands in front of herself and bowed her head. When she raised it, the hardness of the other woman's gaze shattered.

"My dear, welcome back." She crossed the space between them, taking Anna's clasped hands in hers. The smile Olga gave her brightened her features considerably. *Love.* It was pure sisterly love shining there.

So why had Anna left? Will's head cocked to the side, an odd ache swelling in his chest as he watched their reunion.

"We need your help," Anna said, freeing herself from the woman's embrace. "One of our friends is—" Her brows pinched. "Cursed?"

Olga gasped and stepped back, a weathered hand covering her mouth.

"Ill magic," Anna continued. "The fairy godmother's magic."

The older woman's lips pursed in distaste. "She is no god. No Mother." She drew a symbol with her hands and muttered something Will couldn't make out. "We will do what we can, but you know no men may enter here." She shot him a hard look before sliding her shrewd gaze to Koen and Brandt, where they advanced with the cart.

"It's not a man who is afflicted." Anna led Olga to the cart and pulled back the fabric draped over Mina.

The older woman gasped again, straightening before leaning over Mina and pressing a hand to her chest. "She breathes yet."

"But we cannot wake her."

Koen stepped in, listing off all the things they'd tried. The sister nodded along, absorbing his words as she laid her hands on Mina, feeling her head, her wrist, her cheeks.

"This I have never seen," she said at last. "But we shall try. We shall try all we can. It's a terrible thing for one so young to be afflicted so." Olga raised her fingers to her lips, and a piercing whistle split the air.

Will turned just as four other women, dressed similarly to the sister but varying in age and appearance, emerged from the open door.

"Help me bring her in." Olga gestured to the cart. To her visitors she said, "We'll return your cart once she is settled."

"Mina—" Brandt reached for her, but Anna stopped him with a hand on his outstretched arm.

"I'll go with them," she said. "Mina will be safe here. I promise it."

Brandt fumbled for words, his mouth opening and closing.

"Go," Will said at the same time as Koen.

Anna shot them each a glance and a nod before hustling after the women and into the light of the convent, now brighter than the gathering darkness around them. Seeing her disappear into that light, so comfortable with these women, something jagged prodded at Will, urging him to run after her lest she never come out again. The thought still lingered as the door swung shut.

Brandt blinked and shook his head. "We're just s'posed to wait here?"

"They don't allow men inside," Koen said simply.

"But Ansel—" Brandt gestured toward the door.

"They know who she is," Will said. Not just that she was a woman. He was certain they knew *exactly* who Anna was. Something in the look she'd shared with Olga spoke more than words.

Will surveyed the surrounding area from where he stood. Fields, flush with yellowing grass, covered much of the open space. Tidy garden rows near the main building bore an assortment of plants that he imagined were flush with ripe vegetables, ready for harvest. A few trees stood in orderly rows a little further away, probably bearing fruit on the limbs that draped heavily toward the ground. Even the barns appeared well-maintained with not a loose or missing board to be seen, though it was difficult to tell in the fading light. A few women carrying lanterns ushered the animals inside.

He pointed toward the large barn and the nearby outbuildings. "They might let us sleep there. We'll need somewhere to rest tonight, even if they're able to cure Mina right away." A fool's hope, but it felt wrong not to say it, especially to her brothers.

"Will's right. No men are allowed inside the main building, but a roof over our heads would be helpful." Koen glanced meaningfully toward the clouds that had blocked out the last of sunset.

Already the wet scent of earth perfumed the night. Rain would be upon them soon. It wouldn't be the first night he'd spent wet and miserable, but his arm—his whole body—could use a dry rest.

He glanced back at the towering main building. At least Anna would be dry, warm, and well-fed. After all she'd been through, she deserved at least that.

Brandt followed his gaze and crossed his arms over his chest. "Why *can't* men go in? Surely they don't think the Mother only cares for womenfolk."

Will scratched at his wild beard. *An excellent question.*

"This place is a sanctuary for them," Koen said. He pulled his pipe from where he'd stashed it on the side of his pack, a bundle of herbs already in his other hand and ready to be packed tight. He probably hoped for a quick smoke before the rain could ruin it.

"The women dedicate their lives to the Mother and caring for her children. Some choose that life out of joy. Others…" He packed the herbs tight, gritting his teeth as he pressed hard. "…choose to join the sisterhood to escape their lives. It offers them freedom. Safety." He cut his gaze to Brandt. "Usually from men."

Will swallowed the tightness in his throat. He hadn't known. He should have, but he didn't. "They were abused," he whispered.

Koen nodded as he dug around in his pack for his flint.

"Some of them. Abused…or worse."

Anna. Light flickering in some of the upper windows drew his eye. He could guess what ills she'd suffered at the hands of her stepsister, but had some man—some men—done even worse? His fists tightened until his arm roared in pain. He shook the thought away, unwilling to let it consume him.

One vengeance first, then he'd deal with anyone else who'd wronged her.

"You should use this," Koen said before tossing a jar of salve his way.

Immersed in his thoughts as he was, Will barely caught it before it could clatter to the ground. "How'd you know all that anyway?" he asked.

Koen struck the flint, the spark reflecting off his glasses as the pipe lit. He took a long drag before responding. "How do you not?"

Will's throat tightened. The way he said it, what he implied...

There was no way Koen could know. He held his friend's gaze, doing everything he could to keep his expression neutral, to reason out whatever knowledge lay behind his eyes.

"Well, I didn' know either," Brandt said.

The thread of tension snapped, and Koen glanced at his brother. "That's not surprising."

"Hey," Brandt fumed. "What's that supposed to mean?"

Noise at the convent doors silenced the squabble. Will blinked against the bright light that spilled forth, catching sight of shadowed figures as they slipped out into the falling night. A cluster of four women approached—slowly, warily—their arms laden.

"We thought to bring you some things," the woman at the head said. Her voice was strong, solid and unafraid. Her gentle countenance could have calmed the most startled man or beast. "A pot of fresh stew, bread, and blankets to ward off the chill. The snows are still a ways off, but the wind and rain can be cool up here."

Some of the others wouldn't look at them but simply held their gifts in arms outstretched as far as they could reach, wobbling with the weight of their burden.

"Thank you, sister," Koen replied on their behalf before taking a small step toward the women, his own arms outstretched.

The woman with the blankets passed them into his waiting arms. Will took the bundle of bread, still warm, and hefty pitchers of water and what looked to be wine, careful all the while to be respectful, to not accidentally touch the women or cause them discomfort.

Even so, he didn't miss the way one flinched at his nearness. The harm she must have suffered clawed at his chest. The man he had been could have helped these women—should have helped them. And yet he'd barely remembered they existed.

Brandt took the heavy pot of stew, holding it by the cloth-wrapped handle. "Thank you, sister." He flashed a blinding grin, his voice so loud and booming that the woman nearly dropped the thing in her hurry to turn and rush back to the convent.

"I didn't mean to," he sputtered, with a forlorn glance after her.

"We know," the lead woman said, a touch of sorrow in her tone. "I was surprised she volunteered to bring things out to you." She glanced back at the figure retreating into the light. "I think she wanted to test herself, and I know she'll be happy to have you try her stew. It's rabbit tonight." Her smile stretched wider. "A specialty of our house."

The savory scent swirling through the air already had Will's stomach rumbling. They were in for a generous feast. His gaze cut to the barn. "May we sleep there?" He nodded in its direction.

"Of course." The woman clasped her hands in front of her. "And any of the outbuildings that you find comfortable. They might be better than the barn this night." She gazed up at the clouds above, blocking out the rising moon. "Some of the animals get a little jumpy during storms."

As if on cue, lightning flashed in the distance. A stiff gust of wind followed, tugging at their hair and clothes.

"Thanks again, sister," Koen said. "Best get in before the rain."

With a last longing glance toward the convent, the men headed toward the barn.

22

*M*urmured prayers contrasted the roll of thunder. Half a dozen women swarmed around Mina's bed, some praying to the Mother and her saints, others performing more practical healing techniques. Though they'd worked tirelessly in the hours since they'd arrived, Mina had not stirred by even so much as a flutter of her eyelashes.

Guilt crushed her like a heavy weight, tethering Anna to the simple, wooden chair in which she sat. She should have insisted Mina not join them at the castle, despite her willingness. Anna knew the wickedness her stepsister could wreak when so inclined.

More than that, though, she should have found a way to stop this long ago, to put an end to Ella's wicked ways before she could rise to such heights—such power. How foolish she'd been that day when the prince sought Ella out after the ball and declared she would be his bride. Anna had been unable to think around her joy, around the pure elation that Ella would be leaving. She had what she wanted, her prince, her castle, the attention of everyone in the land. Surely she'd leave them be and let them live out their days in peace.

Anna scuffed her boot along the stone floor. She'd been so terribly foolish.

Maybe if she'd told the prince about her stepsister's true nature it would have made a difference. Though whether Nikolaus Kaiser would have believed her was another question. The arrogant man had barely looked her way and certainly wasn't interested in her or anything she had to say.

But she could have tried. She could have done *something*.

Brown robes fluttered across the stone in the corner of her vision. Anna glanced up to find Olga hovering at her side, a tightness about her face that stretched her lips in a thin line. The older woman crossed the room to the sisters near Mina, speaking to one of them in hushed whispers. Words tickled her ears, but she could barely make them out. The deepening frown on Olga's face spoke volumes on its own.

A minute later, Olga returned to her side and gave a silent gesture for Anna to follow. Her legs groaned in protest as she shoved to her feet. *Weak.* That was what she was, worn out in body and spirit. Her muscles protested as she forced herself to follow the sister into the hall. Her back and even her arms were sore and stiff.

They traversed the halls in silence, rain tinkling against the glass of the windows and the occasional boom of thunder shuddering through the stones. At length, they reached her sitting room, and Olga shut them inside. The space looked much as Anna remembered, with its simple wooden desk laden with books and papers. Wax formed a little mountain of cream on one corner where candles had simply been replaced after the last burned through, their wax left as a monument to their sacrifice.

Bookcases lined one wall, and a worn tapestry showing the Mother in her grace shared the other wall with a tall, pointed window. It was a peaceful, restful space, if a bit small.

Olga took the chair behind her desk, and Anna slid herself into the one at its front. The chair—simple, functional, yet comfortable—was made for long periods of sitting.

"You know what I'm going to say." Olga held her gaze, unflinching. She'd tell her true, even if it wasn't what Anna wanted to hear.

Anna nodded. She'd known before they ever arrived, but that didn't stop the little kernel of hope from taking root and blooming in her chest. Now it withered, her shoulders drooping with it.

"This affliction..." She shuddered. "...is unlike any we've encountered. Dark magic. Worse than what they taint the food with in the square these days. We haven't been able to put a stop to that. Or cure it. Only time away from those tainted *gifts* seems to ease their influence."

Time. The little sprig of hope fluttered. "Will she wake on her own? Once the magic has faded?"

Olga turned up her palms. "Only the Mother can say. The sisters were able to drizzle some honey water in her mouth. It can keep her alive."

Alive, but barely. Her delicate form would waste away into little but skin and bones without proper nourishment. There had to be a better solution, an answer. And if the sisters did not have a treatment for this ill magic, there'd be only one place to find a cure.

At the home of its creator, the fairy godmother.

"I know that look," Olga said. She leaned closer to the desk, her eyes squinting. "You plan to leave us again."

Anna stiffened. "About last time..." She reached for her hair on instinct, to rub it between her fingers, and met only air. *Oh, how long habits stayed.*

The older woman gave a tentative smile. "I'm not upset. You're free to come and go, as are all who reside here. Sometimes women come seeking a new home, others only a rest before they are ready to heal and move on. But I wish...I wish you'd said something."

"I'm sorry." She dropped her gaze, choking down her rising emotions. "I thought you might try to stop me, and I couldn't just stay here, not with my mother, my sister—" Tears threatened, choking off her words. Not only that, she couldn't risk Ella discovering her hiding place and taking it out on the sisters. They'd been kind to her, and she wouldn't have their charity rewarded with more pain and suffering.

Only Olga knew her full story—or at least, she was the only one she'd told. Some may have guessed. She hadn't used a fake name when she first fled here, hadn't thought of it in her panic, though she ought to have.

Olga reached her open palm across the table. Anna sniffed back her tears and extended her hand in answer to the other woman. There was something powerful and simple in the touch of her hand, the way it squeezed around her own, reassuring and comforting all at once.

"Do not get lost in your revenge. Don't let it make you into the monster she paints you to be."

Her throat tightened. What would Olga think if she'd seen Anna in the castle? She'd been ready to spring from that hidden passage, to draw her dagger, to use it. The thought bloomed in that darkness, ready and eager to end her sister's reign. It had taunted her since, over and over. *If only I'd been brave, I could have stopped her. I could have saved Mina from this fate.*

The older woman squeezed tighter. "None of this is your fault."

Anna forced herself to meet her gaze once more and managed the tiniest of smiles with her nod. But it was. It was her fault.

"I won't become a monster." She would stop one. If it took her life, she'd fix this.

"Good." Olga released her hand, sliding back into her seat. "Keep the Mother's light within you. May it keep you safe on your journey."

Anna's brows rose.

Olga only smiled. The old woman always saw too much.

"Can Mina stay here?"

"Of course. We would never turn away a woman in need. And we will do what we can for her for however long you are gone." Her eyes bored into Anna's. "However long," she said again.

Forever if they had to. If they didn't come back, Olga and the other sisters would protect her.

"The queen..." Anna couldn't use her name. It felt wrong somehow to speak it there. "She wants Mina. The fairy godmother too. Guards have been going door to door, searching for her. It may be a risk to—"

"Now don't you worry about that," Olga cut her off. "We're tougher than we look. We'll keep her hidden. Keep her safe."

As they'd done for many women over many, many years. Calm spread through Anna's limbs at the surety in her voice.

"You'll be taking your companions with you?" The implications of the question were clear enough. Mina they'd protect, but having strange men lingering about, the girl's family or not, wasn't something she'd be fond of.

"Yes, my friends are as eager for the cause as I am. They'll do whatever it takes to help Mina." Lightning flashed outside, and she jumped in her chair. "To help all of us," she amended.

"And you trust them?"

Thunder rumbled through the room.

Olga wasn't just asking questions for her benefit. She was leading her somewhere, giving little bread crumbs like she did in her teachings about the Mother. She was a guide more than an instructor. She pointed people down a path but left it up to them to choose, to follow if they would and make their own choices.

"You don't?" Anna asked.

"The girl's brothers are as easy to read as words on a page. Honest, true, and goodhearted, if a bit rough around the edges. The elder one has come here before."

Anna inhaled in surprise. *Koen?*

"He's brought us his potions and tonics in the past. They're as well-crafted as any of our own. He shared a few recipes over the years too and never asked a thing in return."

"I had no idea." Anna blinked. No wonder he made no argument when she suggested bringing his sister here. He'd had a twinkling in his eye like he should have thought of it himself. And he'd be content to let her stay here too—of that she was suddenly certain.

"The other one though." Olga's expression soured. There was something about him that made her unsure, and Olga, in Anna's limited experiences, was rarely wrong about such things.

"Will?" The chair beneath her grew uncomfortable, its back pushing against her. The barest whisper of his name made Anna's lips tingle, her cheeks heat. Every thought stole away from the moment as her mind drifted back to the night before. His lips against hers, the strong feel of his body, the way he made everything within her a warm, delightful mess—even now, in this stoic place.

"That's what he calls himself?" Olga said, almost as if she asked herself rather than Anna. Her lips wrinkled in distaste.

"Yes?" Anna replied, uncertain of the sudden change as damning as the claps of thunder outside.

"It may very well be his name, but that man carries secrets, Anna. I…" Her mouth worked, as if she tasted various words before choosing the right one. "I worry for you, my dear."

Her skin turned clammy. Olga worried about Will, about whatever secrets he carried. The fact that he lived was certainly a secret in some circles, not that she believed anyone in these walls would ever tell. "He knows. He knows who I am."

The older woman's lips parted. "You told him?"

Anna shook her head. "Not exactly. He figured it out, guessed. But he won't give me away. I know he won't."

"Perhaps…" She glanced toward the stormy night.

A sheet of hard rain pelted the window with another flash of lightning, as if the storm, too, tried warning her in echo of the sister's thoughts. Olga doubted him, but the way he'd looked at her, the way he'd kissed her… He wouldn't betray her. *Surely not.* What good could come of it, since the one who offered the reward for her capture wanted him dead too?

"Rest here tonight, my dear. Try not to let your worries trouble you, if just for this night. Stay a few if you wish." Her countenance was serene again, as if the last conversation had never occurred.

"I should check on them." She looked to the window, to the raging storm.

"The sisters already brought them blankets and refreshment. They've taken up in the barn. It's an old building but strong. It will keep them safe in this weather."

Anna's teeth bit into her bottom lip. Even so, it felt wrong to leave them out there while she was warm and comfortable within.

Olga rose from her chair, rolling her shoulders until her bones creaked audibly. "No sense in venturing out there and waking them if they already rest."

Anna glared at the window. *Like anyone could rest in this storm.*

A weathered hand touched Anna's forearm, and she turned toward the other woman. "Rest," she said. "Much looks different in the day than on nights like these. Besides…" Her face softened. "No one should start a journey with an empty belly and little sleep."

Anna nearly snorted. That had been exactly how she'd left the last time.

23

*A*nna didn't leave the convent until almost noon, striding across the open yard toward the barn where they still lingered. Sunlight caught in her short hair, and Will would swear he'd never seen a sight quite so lovely, especially with the mountains reaching skyward behind her.

Koen nudged his side with an elbow. "Stare like that and she might run back inside," he whispered.

Right. He shook himself. She probably hadn't seen them yet, not with the way she stared at the ground.

Will adjusted the pitchfork in his hand, at least pretending to look like he was still engaged in work. They'd stayed in the barn, keeping out of sight lest castle guards or anyone else should travel to the convent and report seeing men there. Such an odd sight wouldn't go unremarked upon.

But it had been Brandt who insisted they be put to work when a woman arrived just after dawn with fresh hot bread and porridge. He'd said it'd be a waste for his muscles to go unused and had flashed his bulging arms for good measure. The woman had blushed, remarking how it would be nice to have the help of a big, strong man.

Brandt nearly swooned like a maiden at that. The sight even brought a genuine grin to Will's face.

Though the brothers were undoubtedly tired from the trek the day before, they worked hard mucking out the stables, refreshing the hay, and fixing a few loose boards. They barely let Will help with his arm the way it was. Koen's tonics worked wonders on it, but the damn thing still throbbed with a bone-deep ache.

The hard work, though painful, would have been preferable to the minor tasks they doled his way. It'd have kept his mind from wandering. Too often he found himself staring like a dumbstruck boy toward the convent, searching for figures in the windows despite the glare of day hiding everything within. He'd been up half the night too. Will told himself it was thunder keeping him awake, the flashes of lightning and occasional hard pelting of rain. That was why he couldn't sleep, why he'd picked a spot with a clear view of the convent doors. It had absolutely nothing to do with their kiss, or how he longed to taste Anna's lips again, or about the way her lithe body had felt pressed up against his.

He was good at lying to himself, had done it pretty much all his life.

It wasn't until that morning, when he awoke with an empty longing in his chest, that he had to confront reality. He wanted Anna. He'd wanted her before he knew who she was or even that she was a woman.

It'd been months since he let himself feel anything other than his endless desire for revenge. It was the fire that consumed all, until another fire rose to beat it back and take up space within him that he didn't know existed anymore.

The last time he'd felt so strongly about something was around his father after one of his episodes, when he was sure he'd cast him off for being a failure. He never could live up to his expectations, to everything he'd wanted him to be. It wasn't that he didn't want to or didn't try, but nothing had been enough.

And now it was too late.

But not with Anna.

Brandt shoved past them, tossing his tools aside as he raced headlong into the sunlight. "Mina. How is she?"

Will's heart clenched anew at the dim expression on Anna's face. He knew what she'd say before she spoke.

"No change." Her head swayed back and forth, her gaze dropping back to the ground at her feet. "The sisters were with her all night, praying and trying their healing remedies." She barely stifled a yawn. If he had to guess, he'd say Anna had been there for much of it too.

She shook her head before meeting their eager stares once more. "Olga said she's never seen magic like this. They can keep her alive, protect her. And they will." She looked from one brother to the next before her gaze slid to him.

That look, that simple eye contact, had his breath catching in his throat. He dared hope it had the same effect on her as her lips parted and her gaze darted away.

"Then we go to the fairy godmother," Koen said.

Brandt smashed his fist against his palm. "We force that bitch to give us a cure and get our brothers back while we're at it."

Anna nodded.

A tingle of apprehension coiled around his throat, but they were right. It was the only solution. They couldn't leave Mina like this, and it'd be beyond difficult to get close to the chancellor or the queen after his scuffle in the throne room.

Time. It rushed away from them faster than ever, and soon they'd never be able to reverse the destruction it wrought. Waiting around for the opportunity to strike wasn't an option anymore.

The guards would be looking for the fairest in the land, checking every home and otherwise until they found her. Of that, he was sure. But he'd wager they had orders to search for someone else too—him.

Unless the chancellor was too scared to admit that he lived. Will rubbed at the back of his neck. *No, that bastard will come up with something, some way to tell the guards to be alert and bring me in without giving away exactly who I am.* His teeth ground together.

For years he'd had all the time in the world, and now, when he needed it, he had none.

Will exhaled a deep, steadying breath. "Then let's do it."

Anna met his gaze again, tentative but reassuring all the same. "Let's leave at dawn. It will give us time to plan and prepare," she said. "I'll see about getting some food for the journey. The sisters won't mind, I'm sure."

"Let's go now!" Brandt nearly fumed. "I'm ready to show that witch a thing or two and—"

Koen clapped a hand on his arm. "More rest won't hurt." He stared pointedly at Will's arm, then at Anna as she stifled a yawn, though Brandt seemed oblivious to both.

"Fine. Whatever." He shrugged off his brother and stalked away.

"He's always had a bit too much energy," Koen said, watching him go. "Surprised our parents had any more kids after the terror he put them through." A wry grin lit his features. "Never could keep their hands off each other though."

No wonder they had so many kids. Will had been one and only, though his father had often talked about his mother as if she were the most wondrous woman who'd ever lived—beautiful, happy, polite, graceful, but adventurous and wild at heart too. Will barely remembered. She'd died when he was still young, victim of an illness that took many that year.

His father had wanted him to find such a woman for himself, but he'd long ago deemed it impossible. Until he met Anna.

Something swelled in his heart as he watched her talk with Koen, discussing what supplies they'd need. She wasn't the kind of painted beauty he'd lusted after in his youth, nor so demure and willowy as Mina. She was polite...some of the time. But wild at heart? *Yes, that fits her perfectly.* In a different life, perhaps they could have been the perfect match, but he had little to offer now, and if she knew the full truth of all he'd done, well, she'd never want him anyway. He'd be lucky to ever see that fiery spirit that lived within her again.

"I'll let you know if there's any change," Anna said by way of farewell. She started to turn but stopped. "Will..."

His pulse kicked up. On instinct, he leaned toward her and reached out his hand.

"Never mind," she said with a shake of her head.

"What..." He blinked. *Wait.* There was so much to say, too many words and no time.

But she'd turned on her heel and took off out of the barn at a steady jog.

"Ever going to tell me exactly what happened between you two the other night?" Koen smirked at him.

Heat crept up the base of his neck. "Not a chance."

———

*W*ill almost wished for rain, for another thunderstorm to shake the roof over their heads. At least then he could pretend his distraction had something to do with the weather, not with the woman who'd yet to reappear since her brief visit to them earlier that day.

Probably asleep, he told himself. Why would she be out here with them when she could be warm and comfortable inside?

"Damn, man, just spit it out." Brandt slapped him on the arm—his bad arm.

Will hissed as pain flared out from his wound. "Fucking hells."

"Brandt, you idiot." Koen glared at his brother.

"I didn'—aw fuck, man, I'm sorry."

"Fine," Will grated. He'd had worse wounds than this. Like the one Brandt had saved him from when he'd pulled him from that hellish, icy river. He didn't remember floating down it or how he hadn't drowned. After he hit the cold water, everything went dark. *Dark, miserable, and awful.* Until he woke, brought back to life on the riverbank, his body a roaring, shivering beast of pain.

"But seriously, you're so hard up for Ansel. Does she know?" They still called her by her chosen name, and he wasn't about to spill her real one. "Did ya…" Brandt trailed off, making an obscene gesture with his hands.

Will nearly growled, his lips wrinkling in distaste. "Don't talk about her like that," he snapped.

"Woah, woah!" Brandt raised his hands in the air, his bloodshot eyes wide. "Just curious. I ain' going try anything with her."

"See that you don't." His fist clenched and unclenched at his side. *Damn.* He hadn't been this on edge around his friends in ages.

"Just wondering if you two were..."

Koen shoved his brother—hard. Brandt flailed and tumbled into the hay. It was a good thing Koen had the pipe hanging out of his mouth instead of his brother. Starting a fire would be poor repayment for all the sisters had done to help.

Koen smoked often, but tonight he indulged more than usual. Even Brandt joined in—and was that ever a mistake. Will had seen him drunk, but never high on the herbs like this. They did it to distract themselves, he'd no doubt of that. How many times had he done the same with strong whiskey? *Too many.* Both since he'd nearly died and before. Really, he couldn't blame them, not with Mina as she was and their brothers captive and in who knew what state.

"Unrequited love?" Koen raised his brows and offered him the pipe.

"No thanks." That would addle his senses even more, and he might just do something foolish like stalk right into that convent, scoop Anna up in his arms, and kiss her until dawn.

"Looks like it." Brandt gave a broad, toothy grin, his gaze dipping to Will's trousers.

Heavens and hells. He adjusted himself, fighting against the desire that'd flared deep within him and scowling at the brothers. He'd half a mind to knock some sense into them—not that they'd remember it. "You idiots going to keep this up all night?"

"Hells yes." Brandt pounded his hand on the ground. "Until you share all the good details."

It took more effort than it should not to lunge across the ground and strangle the man. Instead, Will pushed to his feet. "I'm sleeping in the shed."

"Sleeping?" Brandt called, sarcasm lacing his voice. "I'd say more like—"

He didn't need to turn to imagine the act Brandt imitated, especially as Koen's chuckle chased him toward the doors.

How he loved and hated those men. *And damn it all, they might be right.*

24

*I*n the quiet comfort of the shed, he could finally breathe. The herbal scents that wafted down from the drying bundles above were a pleasant change from the pungent pipe smoke. The herbs and leaves Koen favored might help ease his body and mind, but they sometimes smelled like a skunk's ass. Poor trade, in his opinion.

Better, though, was the lack of windows. He couldn't stare at the convent all night if he couldn't see it. The lantern he'd borrowed lit the space just enough for him to spread out his blanket and dig through his pack for more of Koen's salve. Will pulled off his shirt and set it aside, took a long swig of wine from the skein the sisters had brought them, and set about tending to his wound.

Not five minutes passed before there came a solid knock at the door. Will stiffened, his teeth grinding together. *Fucking idiots.* Didn't they know when someone wanted to be left alone? The hinges groaned, and he turned toward the door. "Can't I get—"

A moment alone.

That's what he'd planned to say. But every word, every thought fled as he beheld Anna standing in the doorway, bathed in lantern light, a bright spot against the dark night beyond.

He blinked at her, his lips slightly parted, the mirror of hers. It was all he could manage as a jumble of thoughts warred for dominance. *She's here. She came.*

Heavens and hells. Was that the hem of a nightgown peeking out from under the dark blanket wrapped around her shoulders? That little strip of creamy cloth nearly undid him.

Her feet were bare, toes wiggling in the thin grass just outside the threshold. It was as if she'd awoken in the night and run to him, sought him out without thought for her clothes or anything else.

A dream. My imagination. She had to be. There was no way she'd appear before him like this, like one of his greatest wishes come to life.

But then she spoke, and her voice alone nearly stripped him bare. "Will."

His name on her tongue had him hard in an instant.

"I—I just…" Her gaze trailed down his bare chest, back up. The tip of her tongue flicked out over her lips. "I just came to see about your arm," she said, not quite meeting his hungry stare.

He turned on the ground, just enough to show her that side. As he moved, he adjusted his crossed legs to hopefully hide his insistent erection.

"Could be worse," he said. Some of the redness had faded. It didn't appear to be infected. *Thank the Mother for that blessing.*

"Yes, well…" She reached toward her hair, as if it were long and she'd brush it away, but touched only air. "I see you have the salve. Good, that should help." She bounced a little on her toes. "Is there anything I can get you? Do you need anything?"

Yes. There was something he needed so badly he could barely breathe.

Will rose in one fluid motion, the salve forgotten on the floor.

A soft gasp tickled his ears as Anna's gaze dipped to his trousers, to the obvious bulge he didn't bother to hide. A deep flush colored her cheeks. Those pink lips parted wide. Her warm, brown eyes did the same as they leaped to his face.

"Will."

Time was running out, and he couldn't think of a better way to spend what he had left than wrapped up with her.

He closed the distance between them in one long step. Using his good arm, he encircled her frozen form and pulled her close. She all but stumbled into him. The soft skin of her palms slid against his chest as his lips claimed hers, stiff and uncertain. Her hesitance was enough to give him pause, to fear he'd made a horrible mistake, until she melted against him, passion blazing like a fire taking hold of dry timber.

The blanket fell from her shoulders in a heavy whoosh of cloth. Her palms slid up his chest, over his shoulders, and around his neck, as if she couldn't get close enough and wanted to weld them together. *By all the heavens, I want that too.*

His tongue flicked against her lips. He was a beggar for the temptation she offered, a man consumed by need. She parted for him, tentatively, like a flower just beginning to bloom. *Oh, her honey is the sweetest nectar— delightful, intoxicating.* The soft cloth of her nightgown pressed against his bare chest, but beneath it...*Fuck.* He sucked in a sharp breath at the feel of her taut nipples. He yearned to suckle them, to palm them in his calloused hands. But that meant releasing her and the hem of her nightgown he'd bunched in one fist.

He pulled it up, tugging it until he touched the softness of her upper thigh. He shuddered like a damn boy touching someone like this for the first time.

"Will," she gasped again, shivering under his touch. It was the only encouragement he needed to clutch that lovely thigh and drag her closer. Anna nearly stumbled. Will leaned into her, one step, then another, until her back bumped the wall and she twined those pale legs around him, clenching him tight.

His cock strained against his pants, aching for her, to delve into that soft, wondrous place that pressed against him as she held tight. She met his tongue with a flick of her own. She was so tentative but eager all the same as she gave into the dance, as her breath filled his lungs.

Groaning, he rocked against her, letting her feel the proof of his desire. His arm barked in pain as he held her aloft, trapped between him and the wall, but he barely felt it. The pain was worth it to taste the passion in her kiss and relish in the press of her body against his. It was a dream, a wonder. He'd take such pain any day if it meant he could hold her like this.

For the briefest moment he pulled back, just enough to glimpse the desire shimmering on her parted lips. Her eyes fluttered open, showing him just how much that kiss affected her. She was so raw and real.

So beautiful.

Anna's heartbeat pounded against his own. Heavy breaths filled the narrow space between their lips. Each one taunted him, teased him. And he leaned in for more.

But as he closed his eyes and dipped his head, his lips met her fingers instead.

He froze. His eyes flew wide.

A hint of something clouded her gaze. Sorrow? Regret?

Something heavy and miserable settled hard in his chest. *Why oh why did I stop kissing her? Fucking terrible decision.*

No words passed between them, but the signal to stop was clear enough. Her legs unwound from him, trembling as they settled on the ground, and he pulled his hands away.

Fuck all.

But he wouldn't ignore her request, her choice.

"I'm sorry," he said. Not for kissing her, he'd relish that forever, but for whatever made her ask him to stop. He backed away, gave her what space he could in the little shed. "If I made you uncomfortable. If I did something—"

"No." She reached for him, then pulled her hand back. "It's not like that. I just...I came here to talk to you, and if I didn't stop, if *we* didn't stop, well..." She bit her lip and looked away.

He ran his hands down his face. It did nothing to scrub away all the possibilities that leaped to mind, all the naughty things that flashed before his eyes as he saw those teeth nibble her kiss-flushed lips.

The nightgown, no doubt borrowed because he'd have remembered seeing that tempting garment, hung loosely about her frame, but he could still make out the soft swell of her small breasts and the pert nipples pebbled against the material. *Aw hells.* He reached over and jerked the door shut. They'd just given quite a show to anyone who cared to look.

"What did you want to talk about?" The hoarseness of his voice surprised him. So did his grip on the door handle, one he couldn't quite force himself to relinquish, not yet. It grounded him, centered him.

Anna seemed to realize her attire, or lack thereof, and grabbed her fallen blanket from the floor. Relief and regret warred within him as she pulled it around her shoulders, shielding herself from view.

"I—" she began, before stopping as she glanced around the shed. "Do you mind if I sit?"

"No." He had no chair or stool to offer her, but she didn't seem to mind as she settled herself on the blanket he'd spread across the floor. The one he'd planned to sleep on. And now it would smell like her. His cock twitched.

Damn.

One by one, he lifted his fingers from the handle and took a seat on the floor. Close, but not too close. The last thing he wanted was her to run away again, and he could see it, that hint of a need to flee like a spooked doe—a self-preservation instinct. And all at once he hated it, whatever caused her to fear so deeply. Her wicked stepsister perhaps? He already hated that bitch.

"You see, I was talking to Olga about Mina, about them keeping her safe here and that we planned to look for a cure for her."

His chest grew tight. This was it. This was the moment she asked to stay here. He wanted that for her, wanted her safe and out of trouble. But he'd miss her. He might never see her again, and that would be worse than any torture.

"And she talked about you all. She said, well—" She pursed her lips, glancing away again.

The fine hairs on his arms rose. "What is it, Anna? You can tell me."

"Olga has a way with people. She sees things sometimes that others don't, and she says you're shrouded in secrets."

Will stiffened. *Fucking hells.* "You don't trust me?" He couldn't blame her for that, but still, it stung.

"No, I do, but—" Her brows pinched together, and she shook her head. "I just can't stop thinking about it. I know your story, about how Brandt found you, about how everyone believes you're dead, or well, I guess they used to. But that's not so much a secret anymore, is it? So what does she sense? What aren't you telling me?" Her voice rose at the end, begging.

Anna had let her walls down. This was her, being vulnerable, asking him, not just trusting the words of the older woman. She was no longer Ansel in that moment, not the strong, tough person he'd met in the woods, but a damaged young woman looking for a reason to trust.

Still, he said, "What did she tell you?" His body tensed, ready for the damning words.

"Nothing more than that."

He let out a sigh. That's right, she'd kissed him back. She never would have if she'd known everything. He could tell her. He wanted to, ached to. But he'd lose her the moment he did—and Brandt, and Koen, and Mina, if she were ever to awaken.

Something dark and selfish in him couldn't sacrifice that, not yet. So he told her a truth, a dark and ugly one she likely didn't know, at least not about him, but it wasn't the darkest one, not nearly. "You know I was at the castle for a little while after Cinderella married the prince?"

She nodded. Though the blanket obscured much of her from view, he could sense the tension flowing through her, especially the stiff set of her shoulders as she waited for whatever he would say.

"And you've seen how she influences people, like those in the city."

Again she nodded.

"Some people she didn't just influence with the fairy godmother's magic potions, she controlled them. Some of the things I did..." He shuddered, shutting down the memories that tried to creep to the surface. He forced himself to look at Anna, to let her see the truth he wished could stay buried forever, if even just the surface of it. "The choices I made, that she forced on me..."

"What—"

"I can't, Anna." His voice cracked over her name. The violation was too deep, too personal, too awful. To be a marionette, helpless to control your own actions, only seeing them distantly, far away, screaming and being unable to break free from the cage of your own mind. It was too much. That man had died in the river, and he'd tried to live as a new person without that horror ever since. "You'd hate me," he said at last. "And you'd be right to."

Her curious expression broke, shattered into sorrow. "I'm sorry."

"You have nothing to be sorry for." He reached for her, took her hand in his and squeezed.

She didn't pull away. "I'm sorry you suffered because of her too. If I'd only…" She trailed off, shaking her head. "If I'd been braver, then maybe—"

"No." He squeezed her hand tighter. "You're not to blame for what she's done."

A sad smile touched her lips. "But if I'd stopped her…"

His chest shook with a humorless huff of laughter. He should have been the one to stop Cinderella—or better yet, never let her take power in the first place.

"You're not the type to have blood on your hands." It was all for the best that she didn't.

She squeezed his hand in return. "But I could have done more."

And so could he, but he hadn't. The guilt of it tried to drown him every day, just like that damn river. A rumble of fear quaked through him, not for him, but for her. "Did she…did she do that to you? Control you?"

"Not…not like that. Never like that. But I was a coward. I ran when I could have stood up to her."

"She'd have made you pay for that. Hurt you."

Anna nodded, her shoulders hunching in around herself. "But maybe she wouldn't have hurt Charlotte so much, my sister," she added with a weak smile. "Or you, or anyone else. Maybe she would have stopped."

Or she'd have only grown more terrible, with Anna a worse casualty in her trail of misdeeds. She sniffled, so quick he almost missed it, but there was no hiding the glassy sheen in her eyes. Will did the only thing he could think of. He scooted across the floor and pulled Anna into his arms. Her face pressed against his chest. The smallest splash of wetness touched his skin.

How many times had Cinderella hurt her? Made her cry? He stroked her hair as he held her close, savoring the feel of her against him, right where she belonged. Will tucked her closer until his cheek rested against the crown of her head. "I won't let her hurt you anymore."

Anna laughed, a soft, bitter note, before another drop of wetness rolled across his skin. "And how will you manage that?"

He drew back, cupped her face in his hands, and wiped away the last tear with his thumb. "I think we can find a way together."

"Together?" She snorted. "Oh yes, the handsome huntsman and the ugly stepsister. That makes so much sense."

No one could ever call her ugly, especially not once they got to know her. But he knew how deep some wounds went, how it was impossible to hear certain truths when one had their shield raised, so instead, he forced the smile her words conjured and said, "You think I'm handsome?"

She twisted away from him, her cheeks blazing. His chest swelled with desire. Will rubbed at his chin, at the horrid overgrown beard he was certain no one could appreciate, and yet she didn't mind. *Handsome, huh?*

He dared to slide closer, to wrap his arm around her and pull her tight to him. She stiffened but didn't pull away. Her pulse fluttered wildly in her chest, beating against his own. In that moment, he wanted nothing more than to hold her forever, to lose himself in that stolen beat of time and forget his revenge, forget their journey to come, forget every terrible wrong they hoped to undo. He fully understood then why Koen and Brandt had lost themselves to the pipe—a night of pleasure to keep the hard realities at bay.

They were all running out of time, and if the final grains of sand were to slip from the hourglass, he'd be damned if it happened before the woman in his arms knew just how lovely she was. Knew and believed it.

Will leaned in until his beard brushed her cheek. She shivered in response. "I think you're beautiful, Anna."

Her breath hitched. She stiffened and then twisted around with a look that echoed her words. "If you do, you're an idiot." She swatted at his good arm, light, almost playful.

"Maybe I am, but I'm entirely serious." A smirk drew up the corner of his lips as he dared to slip a hand along the bare length of her leg exposed between the folds of the blanket. "Would you like me to prove it to you?"

25

A tingle, sharp and bright as lightning, zipped through Anna at Will's touch. Her body quaked. Her thighs clenched tight around the desire strumming through her core.

The kiss had shattered her, obliterated her walls completely.

And though she'd tried to build them back up, to shield her heart as she'd shielded her body with the blanket, his confession tore her defenses down entirely. They stripped her bare. To be controlled as he'd been…she couldn't fathom it.

His daring fingers trailed further up her calf, rounding the bend of her knee. He toyed with the hem of her nightgown where it'd ridden up to the start of her thigh. She shivered at the mix of fire and ice—all that his touch ignited and his words that had chilled her to the bone.

Despite his pain, despite all that he'd suffered, he endured—survived. When Olga said he was shrouded in secrets, her heart had shivered in terror, imagining all the horrible things it could be. Some part of Anna was still certain he'd use her own secret against her and turn her over to her wicked stepsister in exchange for the reward.

Only an idiot wouldn't. But then, only an idiot would think her beautiful too.

And she did want him, this rough, half-wild idiot, more a man of the wilderness than any proper gentleman. But the proper gentlemen had never looked at her this way, had never made her feel so…wanted.

Will rubbed the hem of her nightgown between his fingers. The scruff of his overgrown beard scratched against her cheek as he placed a small kiss along her jaw, then moved higher, taking her earlobe between his teeth.

She pulled in a ragged breath at the unexpected contact, the gentle tug.

"Do you want me to stop?" His breath heated her skin.

Emotion raged within her, a stormy mess. She'd never wanted someone more but never been more frightened. Long ago, she'd learned to keep her walls up, to not let Ella's barbs or those of any of the people her stepsister influenced dig into her skin. If she let Will in, truly let him close to her, she'd never be able to fully rebuild that wall to keep him out.

He'd be a vulnerability.

At her pause, he drew away. His warmth left her, his smell. The intoxicating tingle of his touch vanished in a heartbeat, leaving her bereft. She whirled toward him, the blanket sliding down her shoulders. "No, I—"

He froze, maybe not even breathing as he watched her, waiting.

She held his gaze in return, not blinking. "I don't want you to stop."

"Anna." The way he said her name made her want to cry, not in sorrow but joy. His touch was featherlight as he cupped her cheek. "You're trembling."

His thumb stroked her skin, slowly, lightly, like he might calm a wounded animal. She was one, she supposed.

"I know you've endured horrors of your own, and you don't have to tell me," he continued quickly. "You never have to speak of them unless you want to. Unless it helps you."

She nodded, her throat suddenly tight. If she could erase them from her mind, she would, bury them far away.

"You may not believe my words, but maybe you'll trust my touch? Let me make you feel as desired as you are."

And she wanted that, wanted it so much she could scream. Even if her heart couldn't quite believe it, not yet. If this was a dream, a ruse, she didn't care. She just needed. It was need, desire, lust. And even if for one night, she wanted to give in to that, to feel…everything.

Will scooted closer across the blanket, his hand never leaving her cheek. He dropped his face level with hers, only a whisper away. "We'll take it slow. Tonight, just feel, just enjoy. If you want me to stop, say it and I will. Any time. Now. In the future. But I want to touch you, Anna. I want to taste you, to feel you, because to me, you're lovely. You're all I want."

All I want.

Her heart skipped a beat. Tears burned the corners of her eyes as Will closed the space between them and kissed her. His touch was gentle, the softest, slightest press of his lips to hers that nearly broke her with its tenderness. Before, he'd been a storm, raging like the night before— sudden, eager, and demanding as he'd drawn her to him and kissed her like his life depended on it.

Now, each press of his lips to hers was an unspoken prayer. His arms, as they encircled her, promised protection and safety. The blanket fell away, letting a whisper of cool night air race across her arms, but she didn't mind, especially not when his body filled that space, sharing his warmth with her, heating her up on the outside as every touch stoked the fire within her hotter and higher.

Will lowered her down onto the blankets and followed her. One leg slid between hers. His hips eased his weight between them until he rested on her abdomen, his good arm supporting his chest. The pressure alone had her core clenching tight despite the fabric between them. But beyond... *Heavens and hells.* She could feel the bulge of him against her thigh and never, *never* had such a simple touch made her so eager and wanton.

He wanted her. His body proved it.

Ella couldn't spin her lies around his head. She couldn't sway his desires toward herself. This was all for her.

"May I?" He slid back on his haunches to sit between her legs. Will's brows lifted as he grasped her nightgown.

Up? Off? She didn't care, could only bite her lip and nod.

He dropped the fabric, and Anna nearly groaned in displeasure.

But then his palm slid against her thigh and the world narrowed to that touch. So terribly slowly, he trailed it up her leg, taking the nightgown with it. Anna sucked in a breath, not daring to move as she watched him pull the garment up and over her hips. She lifted her backside just enough for it to pull free and pool about her stomach.

Will stared enraptured at the underwear she wore. It was threadbare. Some of the best she had left. The way he looked at her, though, one might have thought he'd dug up a precious gem from the mine. Her courage bolstered, Anna tented her legs and let them fall open, giving him a better view.

"Holy Mother." Will scrubbed a hand down his face. Another curse she couldn't quite make out followed.

Anna couldn't help it—she grinned. Having a man so enthralled was new, exciting. She slid her hand between her legs, letting her fingers trail over the fabric in slow waves. His rapt gaze made every stroke so much more intense than when she touched herself alone, as if it were his fingers pushing the cotton against her folds and teasing that sensitive bud of flesh.

"Do you like this?"

He shuddered, literally shuddered. "Fuck, Anna." He reached for his pants, adjusted that unmistakable bulge with a low groan. "Tonight is supposed to be about your pleasure, not mine."

"Not ours?" She stroked herself again. *Will he see how wet I am already?*

A flash of teeth greeted her amid his beard. "Seeing you like this is pleasure enough."

Disappointment hollowed her out. She couldn't stop the frown that tugged at her lips.

Will took her hand and pulled it away, easily enough since it'd gone limp at his pronouncement. Instead of moving it aside, however, he leaned in, making her heart skip a beat as he drew her fingers to his lips and licked—one long stroke from where her fingers met her palm to their tips. The same fingers she'd stroked herself with. Her core clenched tight as his eyes closed in ecstasy.

"You see," he said, settling between her spread legs once more, easing himself atop her. His fingers twined through hers, and she held her breath, her heart racing as his face nuzzled into the crook of her neck. "When I fuck you, Anna, I intend to do it properly."

She swore her heart stopped.

"In a bed." He kissed her neck.

"Where we can be alone all night." Another kissed graced the soft spot below her ear.

His beard tickled her, but she didn't dare move for fear of shattering this moment.

He whispered so quietly, she almost missed it. "Where I can fuck you 'til you scream in pleasure."

Anna moaned, a sound so guttural and wanton it took a moment to realize it'd come from her. Will chuckled low in his throat. Then, something moved between them.

Anna's stomach clenched tight as his fingers ventured over the mess of nightgown, across the exposed skin of her belly, and lower, to the hem of her underthings. On instinct, her thighs squeezed tight around him, and he stilled.

Breathe. Relax.

And she did, closing her eyes so she could just feel and enjoy as he'd wanted her to. Her legs fell wide. Will moved again, lower, delving into her secret forest, down until—

"Anna," he groaned, an echo of her moan as he found her sex. "Fuck, you're so wet."

She was. Saints help her, she was drenched and he'd barely touched her. His calloused hand delved between her folds, and she moaned his name, at least she thought she did. A moment later his lips claimed hers, and all words were lost. The glide of his tongue matched the stroke of his fingers, creating a rhythm of pure bliss. A knot deep within her pulled tighter with each glide and press. His thumb flicked her sensitive nub, and she bucked against his hand, literally writhed against him as one finger plunged into her. Her sex clenched around him.

And then he moved, curling that wicked finger inward until he stroked against something delightful and terrible and wonderful. Each stroke wound her tighter. Each curl of that finger threatened to undo her, to break a dam that was barely held in check.

All too soon, he withdrew. Will's lips left hers. A whimper escaped, pure wanton need laced with disappointment. She needed his touch. Just a bit more. "Will, please."

Light from the oil lamp glimmered in his lust-drenched eyes. "We're not done yet."

"Oh?"

His beard twitched at the pull of his lips into a heart-stopping grin. Then she felt his hands on her again. Those calloused fingers, still coated in her wetness, hooked into the waistband of her underthings and pulled. Anna arched her hips and let him tug the fabric away.

Something caught between a gasp and groan slipped from Will as his gaze fell to her sex bared before him. A shiver raced through her, but not from the chill air touching her most intimate parts. That look alone could set her aflame, warm her on the coldest of nights. Never had a man looked at her like that. Never had someone made her feel so desired.

Will blinked, and his hand trembled before it pulled her underthings the rest of the way down her legs. Her teeth dug into her bottom lip as she waited for him to touch her again, to climb back atop her and resume their passionate kiss. She nearly arched her hips toward him in impatience, yet he sat utterly still—transfixed.

But his lips didn't return to hers. Instead, he lifted her leg. The barest whisper of a kiss graced her ankle, her calf, then the crook of her knee.

"Will." Anna bucked toward him this time. She couldn't help it, not with every little touch sending her head spinning.

"I want your taste on my tongue, Anna." Another kiss, this one on her inner thigh.

"Taste?" The word spilled out, all reason and thought lost in the press of his lips further up her leg.

A chuckle teased her sensitive skin along with the scratch of his beard. "The sweetest honey." The tips of his fingers glided through her folds, one quick, teasing stroke, and Anna whimpered again.

"Please, just—" Her words broke off into a squeal as his tongue lapped at her core.

The room spun. Colors raced through her vision before the world returned. *Will. Between my legs. His tongue. Oh, holy Mother, his tongue! Hot. Warm. Wet.*

Anna thrashed on the ground, the feeling so intense, so wondrous. Her fingers dug into the blanket and scratched at the ground underneath.

Everything in her pulled tight, tense as a bowstring about to let an arrow fly.

His hands were on her again. Lifting her to him, holding her firm as he utterly devoured her. Will's lips found that bud amid her folds. One hard press of his hot tongue and she came apart, utterly shattered.

Her sight blurred. Her hips bucked and writhed. Anna's teeth rattled as she clamped them tight to keep from screaming into the night. Everything was a blend of pleasure, of feeling so intense it was like riding the waves of the sea near where she'd been born. It tossed her, dragged her under and turned her this way and that. She drowned, but it wasn't painful. Sand didn't abrade her skin. Her head didn't slam into any rocks, but she was lost all the same. When this wave brought her back, it was to Will staring down at her, panting as hard as she was.

Anna gasped, her chest shaking on the edge of hysteria, of bliss so total she'd lost herself.

"You...that..." It was all she could manage.

Will wiped at the wetness glimmering in his beard and around his lips —*her* wetness. Anna sucked her lip between her teeth. Wind whispered outside. A tendril escaped into the room and raced across her core, contrasting to the heat of her body.

She still couldn't move, her body limp and languid floating on the last of that wave, when Will crawled next to her and pulled her into his arms.

"Do you believe me now, dear Anna, when I tell you how lovely you are?"

Dear Anna. She nearly cried at that, almost sobbed at the overflow of emotion. Her voice still wouldn't obey, so she simply nodded, filling her eyes with all the things she couldn't say. He seemed to understand, especially as he pulled her closer and kissed her with such reverence it nearly broke her all over again.

He'd given her this, and yet...

She reached between them, desire fueling her bravery, and found him still hard within his trousers. "I'd like to...I want..." *You, I want you. I want to give you everything you've given me. To heal the wounds deep within.*

He hissed, his voice low in his throat as he said, "Another night."

Will pulled her hand away, slowly, carefully. Then he brushed her hair behind her ear, letting his fingers stir up a mess of feelings as they grazed her cheek.

"I'm yours, Anna. Don't doubt that, but…" He glanced meaningfully at the door. A hint of mirth danced in his eyes. "Wouldn't want anyone to come looking for you if they heard you cry out."

She'd…

Her cheeks flamed again. She'd been so lost in his touch she'd missed that. But he surely hadn't. Anna leaped away, righting her nightgown and scrambling for her underthings.

If any of the sisters came searching and saw them like this… Her neck burned. She'd never live it down. Never. Or if Koen and Brandt came looking. She hadn't even thought about them, and they had to be close. They probably heard *something*.

Anna searched for her boots, only belatedly remembering she hadn't worn any. *Hells.* And Will still lay on her blanket, stretched out like a king, his erection straining. She forced her gaze away and jerked the edge of the blanket out from under him, earning a low chuckle.

"In such a hurry to get away from me?"

She glared at him over one shoulder, and damn if his half-mast look didn't make her want to snuggle back beside him. "Your fault."

He smirked. "I suppose it is. Sweet dreams, Anna."

26

The days since they left the convent were a dream.

They shouldn't have been, not with Mina still slumbering, half the country probably searching for him, and the impossible task that lay ahead. But even so, Will couldn't remember being quite so content.

The days were hard, spent trekking through the foothills and keeping well away from the city. During them, Anna was Ansel again. Not the half-scared young man who he expected might sneak off at some point and never come back, but the confident, courageous one she'd bloomed into, never afraid of a little dirt, sweat, and hard work. She was easy company, tossing as many jabs as she took, and Brandt was full of them—tamer ones now that he knew she was a woman, but it couldn't turn off his nature altogether. Instead, he treated her like a sister. One blessing of that, he nor Koen never asked about that last night at the convent, though the looks Will caught in the morning told him they'd heard enough. They didn't question it either when he and Ansel snuck off at night for some privacy or woke snuggled up together in the mornings.

The nights. Damn, those are the best.

Anna had insisted on repaying him pleasure for pleasure. As long as he lived, he'd never forget the way her eyes widened when she'd first tugged his length out of his breeches, the way her lips had parted, or the feel of her fingers as she'd trailed him, base to tip. Though he'd love to forget how quickly he spilled in her hands—like a damn boy. At least she hadn't minded. Actually, she'd seemed more than pleased with herself about that—it was a compliment, she'd said. He supposed it was, in a way.

He'd lasted longer the next time. And the next. Each night was a study in each other, but he never took it further nor let her either, though it was hard, so damn hard not to sink his length into her inviting warmth when it was bared before him.

Last night tested his resolve more than ever. Feeling that strong woman come apart in his arms, crying her pleasure against his hand, her tight, wet core clenching around his other, he'd nearly caved. He'd have given her anything in that moment, carved out his own damn heart if she'd asked for it.

But she hadn't. Nor had she pushed or asked for more since that first night. Maybe it was best. When he finally took her just the way he wanted, he was damn determined it would be perfect. She deserved nothing less.

The rains had held off, and by some blessing of the Mother they'd only encountered a small number of travelers and no castle guards. They'd heard galloping horses a few times, but they were far enough from the main road to wait and hide until the thunder of hooves vanished from earshot.

Tonight they ventured a fire. It was the last chance they'd be able to before they were too close to the fairy godmother's workhouse to risk it. If they made good time, they might even be there tomorrow. Not that it'd do them any good if they couldn't come up with a solid plan.

Brandt had pulled a fish from the river by sticking his arm down in a hole. All the mocking taunts he'd tossed his friend's way in regard to his plan burned across the back of his neck when Brandt, dripping with water and cocky swagger, strutted into their little camp holding the monstrous thing by the gills.

He'd barely gotten it on the flames before Koen pulled out his pipe, packed it full, and lit a "celebratory smoke," as he'd called it.

"What if we smoke her out?" Brandt said, gesturing to the fire. "Build large bonfires all around and light 'em all at the same time."

"The four of us are going to do this?" Koen glanced at his brother sidelong. "It would take days, and her guards would certainly spot us."

"Not to mention the others inside," Anna said. "Can't risk them."

Her mother and sister.

"Hells," Brandt spat.

Their brothers.

All of them had people who needed saving.

"Still, I ain' heard any better ideas," he grumbled.

Every idea they'd spat out had been riddled with holes. Only one thing they could agree on—somehow, they had to get within the fairy godmother's stronghold and find a cure to whatever ailed Mina, maybe to the queen's persuasion magic too.

And if they were lucky, really lucky, maybe they could end the witch and save their families too.

Getting in was possible. Getting out...that was going to be the trick.

"We'll need to sneak in." Will's chest rose and fell in resignation. It was the only way.

"Didn't we agree that was too risky?" Koen asked.

"It was when we thought we had time. But Mina needs a cure, fast. We don't know what that magic will do to her long-term." He hated voicing the worry aloud. Koen flinched. Brandt looked away. But it was the truth. Would she wake? Or would she sleep forever? Worse, what if she ceased to breathe?

"The sisters will protect her, watch after her." Anna's confidence in that was unwavering. He just wished he could believe it too.

But Mina's condition wasn't the only reason to worry anymore. The guards would still be looking for the fairest in the land, checking every home and otherwise until they found her. But he'd wager they had orders to keep an eye for someone else too—for him. He knew too many of the queen and chancellor's dirty secrets to be allowed to live.

Will shoved a stick into the fire with more force than necessary, sending little embers dancing up into the darkness. That bastard would come up with something, some way to tell the guards to be alert and bring him in without giving away exactly who he was. His teeth ground together.

I am running out of damn time.

He gazed through the fire at Anna, who flashed him a little grin. Something twisted tight in his chest. For all the danger that lay before them, her courage never wavered. But she didn't know the worst of it. He still couldn't bring himself to tell her all his secrets—or the real reason the chancellor and the queen wanted him dead.

"We'll have to impersonate guards or something," Koen said, taking his idea and picking at it as they had all the others. "We'll need uniforms."

He'd thought of that too. "Robbing one of the wagons will be our best bet." Taking out a few guards near the fairy godmother's workhouse would be too obvious, too likely to be discovered before they could put their stolen clothes to use. Definitely before they could flee to safety.

Brandt scratched at his beard. "Thought you said they didn't carry extra uniforms? We didn' see any last time either."

"They don't."

Silence followed, turning heavy and dark as the feeling he'd carried since the idea formed itself in his head.

Anna's expression lost all its humor. The horror etched on her face was like a punch to the gut. "You can't!"

She clapped her hands over her mouth, scanning the surrounding forest.

Brandt cursed under his breath.

Anyone in a damn mile would have heard that shout. But the fire, small as it was, was the bigger risk. They'd have to douse it soon.

Each heartbeat was too long as they waited, listening for signs that anyone had heard them and was coming to pursue. Slowly, oh so slowly, the tension fled Will's shoulders, and his fingers drifted away from the hilt of his blade.

"You can't just kill them all," Anna said, much quieter this time, though her hands balled into tight fists at her sides. "We know not all the guards serve the queen of their own will. Some are coerced, just like the people in the city." *Just like you.* She didn't say it, but he read it in the frown of her lips and the creases between her brows.

"What choice do we have?" He ran his hand through his hair, some of it sticking from the sweat and dirt caked in it from days on the road.

Though near-death made him reflect on his old life, the way he'd lived, and all the errors of it, he did miss the regular baths—especially the soap. He could do with that again.

Anna's eyes darted. Her mouth opened and closed, and he yearned to kiss away her worries, tell her not to be afraid, that they wouldn't have to do anything terrible, but he couldn't. It would be a lie, and he wouldn't have any more of those between them.

"You just can't. I *can't*." The crack of her voice punched him with more force than if she'd used her fists.

"Then don't," he snapped—hard, far too hard.

She winced.

Regret slipped out as a sigh. He reached for her. "I—"

"What he means is we'll do it," Koen said, ever the level-headed one.

"Aye." Brandt lumbered next to her and threw an arm around Anna's shoulder, drawing her in close. "We won't let ya get your hands dirty."

It should be him. He should be the one comforting her. And yet he was the one responsible for the tears building in the corners of her eyes. *Fucking hells.*

"There has to be another way," she said, barely a whisper.

If there were, he'd take it. He didn't want blood on his hands any more than she did, but he might be able to make peace with it if they succeeded. Doing nothing, wasting more time where they could be captured and lose their chance to save everyone—that he couldn't live with. He'd have his revenge. The innocent would be freed from the fairy godmother's poisons of the mind and body. Or damn it to all the hells, he'd die trying.

"That smoke you created." Anna pulled away from Brandt with a pat of thanks on his arm, her hopeful gaze aimed at his brother. "We could knock them out. Steal their uniforms."

"That could work."

"But what would we do with the bodies?" Will asked. "The smoke only knocks them out a few minutes. We could get the uniforms, steal their horses, but what would stop them from following us or fleeing back to the castle to tell everyone what happened?"

For a few moments only an owl answered him, its hoots calm and comforting as the pine and autumn crispness perfuming the air.

"We tie 'em up." Brandt smashed a fist against his palm.

Anna glared at him sidelong. "And leave them to starve to death?"

"Er, well, we do it near a road, where they can call for help eventually."

Will rubbed at the back of his neck, a failed attempt to ease his growing frustration. "And then they still run back to the castle and give us away."

"If we move quick enough, we could get in and out before they have time to get back," Koen mused before taking a long draw on his pipe.

"Better than killing them all." Anna no longer looked at any of them as she toed at rocks on the ground. "And we still don't know that they'd even let us in, nor where we need to go. What excuse would we use?"

The brothers both looked to him. Will's teeth ground together. "I don't know yet."

Brandt grumbled but said nothing.

"If we're going after the guards, though, we'll need to change course, wait for their caravan to come through."

"They might have changed routes," Koen said. "After..." He waved a hand in the air.

After they'd robbed them. Little good it did.

"So tomorrow we watch the road. See what we can learn," he said.

Anna sent a little stone rolling into the fire with the toe of her boot. "And we what, just camp out for days hoping they show up and that nothing terrible happens?"

Will swallowed the tightness in his throat. She was right. It would take time—time they didn't have.

Heavy silence surrounded them, broken only by the crack of the burning wood and the chirping of insects in the woods around them. Anna picked up a stick and poked at the fire. Though she stared at the flames, her gaze was far away.

Will pinched the bridge of his nose. This wasn't how the night was supposed to go. All night he'd been looking forward to taking her in his arms again, perhaps the same way he had last night. She'd straddled his lap, her back to his chest. In that position, he'd had easy access to her sex. Even better, he'd felt every twitch of pleasure as she'd writhed in his lap, grinding her ass against his cock so that he nearly came in his trousers. If he closed his eyes, he could still feel her weight against him, the scent of her in his nose as her head thrashed on his shoulder.

He shuddered and forced the thoughts away. With the gloom hanging over her, he doubted she'd be in the mood for it, even if it might be their last night...for a while. He had to add that last part, had to promise himself they'd have a future.

"What if," Anna said, her voice rousing him from his thoughts, "we give the fairy godmother what she wants?" She raised her stick from the fire, turning it this way and that as a flame danced along the end.

A chill slid down his spine.

"What ya mean?" Brandt asked. He scooted forward on the log he occupied, arms braced on his knees.

Anna glanced at Will, a sad smile on her face. "She wants the fairest in the land, right?"

"But Mina—" Brandt began.

"No," Will snapped. "It's out of the question." His pulse slammed against his chest like a wild thing.

Koen lowered his pipe. "It could work."

Will glared at him, his fingers twitching on his knife hilt. "No."

"You know it's the only way," Anna said, resigned.

"Don't even—" Will half-rose to his feet. Too little, too late.

"We give her me, disguised as the fairest in the land."

"We are not giving you to her," Will all but snarled. He stood, unable to sit still and listen to this disastrous plan, especially not as Brandt sat straighter, looking thoughtful, like this horrible idea had merit.

"It would get us in front of her," Koen said.

"We wouldn't need uniforms either," Anna said. "We know the magic put Mina to sleep, so we pretend I'm asleep. You could be any citizens of the kingdom, hoping for a reward."

Will's hands slid through his hair, tugging at the roots. "No. I won't allow it."

Anna frowned up at him. "It's the best plan we have."

"We'll come up with a different one." He snapped into motion again, pacing back and forth. "We have time. We—"

The touch of a hand on his arm stilled him. He didn't even know when Anna had risen. "We don't have time. You know that."

Will took her face in his hands, not caring that Koen and Brandt looked on. "I am not risking you." He accented each word as if they could lock her up or get her to forget the terrible plan.

"No." A sad smile touched her lips. "You're not. I'm risking myself."

"Ansel." He all but shook her.

She pulled away from him. "People need me, need us. Mina, my family, theirs." She gestured to Koen and Brandt. "I'm not running anymore. I'm done running. And waiting."

"This is ludicrous!" He looked to Brandt, to Koen, for anyone who would listen to reason. "You'll get in, but how will you get out? How will you get the cure for Mina?"

Brandt cracked his knuckles and stared into the flame. "We hold her at knifepoint. That close, we should be able to. We demand the cure and our release."

Hysterical laughter crawled up his throat. "And when she laughs in your face? When her guards come to kill you?"

"We take her down first," Koen said as he pulled the fish off the fire, scowling at the charred edges. Who cared about a damn fish at a time like this?

"And you still die," Will snapped.

Brandt stood, flexing his muscles. "Gimme an ax. I'll take 'em all down. Hells, man, you fought a fucking castle full of guards." Brandt winced and glanced to Anna, but she might as well not have heard him. All her focus was given to staring Will down, her lips pressed thin.

"It was dumb luck and falling through the magic mirror that saved me."

"Lady Luck may be with us again," Koen said. "The fairy godmother does have a magic mirror of her own, or so they say."

Will nearly shook with rage, with fear, with myriad of emotions he had no name for. "You can't be serious. You can't risk yourselves like this. I won't allow it."

"Talking like he'd be king over us," Brandt grumbled.

Will snapped. A roar of frustration crawled up his throat, and he let it out, shouted it into the night until it rang back at him. Guilt coursed through him instantly.

Stupid, stupid, stupid.

If they were found out now it would be all his fault. But he hadn't been able to help it. All the frustration, the fear of losing people he'd come to care about—of losing Anna—had been too much to contain.

"Will." Anna reached for him, but he flinched away. His fists balled so tight, his hurt arm screamed in pain. He couldn't stand there anymore, couldn't listen to the people he cared about, who he loved, plan their deaths.

His chest ached, sliced up inside, as he turned away from Anna. Her voice, brittle as a leaf as she called out after him, cut him deep, but it was too late. His legs already carried him into the woods of their own accord.

27

*L*imbs tried to block his path. Will pushed them away.

Underbrush grabbed for him.

Roots tripped him.

None of that stopped him, not even the fading calls of Anna and his friends.

He needed space.

Time. He slammed his fist into a tree, savoring the burst of pain. *Damn it to all the heavens and hells, I need time.*

Will nearly collapsed against the abused tree—let his forehead thunk against it and bear his weight. The spicy tang of bark filled one deep breath after another as he forced himself to be still, to find that peaceful inner place he'd learned of long ago while hunting. It was a deep part of himself where the world could fade away and he could just be—still and silent for hours if needed. He needed that now—an escape, a way out, a moment of peace.

He stood there for long minutes, faded away into that place of solitude and stillness, until he felt a touch on his arm. It jolted him from his retreat of inner rest and thrust him into the world with a surge of panic. His fingers closed around the hilt of his dagger. Before he had the chance to think, he pulled it free and swung.

Anna gasped as the blade stopped an inch from her face.

Holy Mother. He'd almost ended the woman he loved.

The dagger shook in his hand.

"Will, it's me," she whispered, her hands raised before her.

I love.

Will's pulse beat wildly at his throat.

Anna touched the top of the blade, pushing it down, away. "It's me, Anna," she said again, but her words were distant, as if he heard them through water.

I love her.

"Anna." The dagger slipped from his fingers, falling to the ground, forgotten. He didn't give her time to respond, to react, before he pulled her into his arms and crushed her to his chest.

Alive. I didn't hurt her. He promised himself. One hand cupped the back of her head, sliding through her short hair, savoring the feel of it against his skin. He nuzzled the top of her head, inhaling her scent, letting it calm him. "I'm so sorry," he mumbled against her hair.

She shifted in his arms, pulling back ever so slightly to stare up at him. Moonlight filtered through a gap in the trees, painting her face in pale hues against shadows.

"I can't lose you. Not now."

Her body sagged against his, almost like a sigh. "I don't want to lose you either," she said. Anna stroked his cheek, and he closed his eyes, savoring the intimate touch. "But I, *we* have to do something. And you know this plan will work."

He forced his eyes open, letting all the worry filling him show. "The getting in will work. The getting out…"

"So we work on that, we—"

A branch snapped somewhere close by. Anna tensed in his arms even as he tugged her close, shielding her from whatever lay in the darkness.

Fuck all. He'd been so caught up in himself, his worry and fear, that he hadn't been listening. Only a fool let his guard down.

Anna barely breathed. Her heartbeat hammered as fast as his own.

A shadow moved out of the corner of his eye, drifting through the darkness of the forest. *Too big. Too fucking big.*

And too slow. A deer would have bolted by now.

My dagger. Hells. He'd dropped it somewhere at his feet. His bow lay back at camp, not that he could use it properly with his injured arm.

A grunt came from up the hill. An inaudible yell followed. His hair stood on end.

Anna tore from his arms, racing toward their friends, toward danger. She hadn't seen the movement. She didn't know.

"Wait!" he called in a hoarse whisper as he dropped to the ground, searching frantically for his dagger. His fingertips grabbed at dirt, at leaves. *A weapon, I need—*

Fuck. He pushed to his feet, sprinting after her. *No time. Never enough time.*

With his long-legged stride, he raced through the darkness, heedless of limbs, of roots, of anything but Anna racing ahead of him.

A shadow leaped from the trees. Her scream slew him worse than any blade. Someone grabbed at her arms as she thrashed like an enraged cat baring its claws.

"Don't touch he—"

Something hard and heavy barreled into him, knocking the wind from his lungs and sending him tumbling into the underbrush. Will roared in pain as he landed on his bad arm. Roots and stones stabbed and tore his skin as he rolled, unable to stop himself. A tree cracked against his back. Agony gripped him, but he shoved it away. He gritted his teeth, his fingers digging at the ground for purchase. He had to get to Anna. Had to—

The shadowed form was on him again, blocking out the moonlight and shoving him back onto the ground. "Stay down." A knee dug into his back. Weight pressed against his spine as dirt and leaves filled his nose and mouth. "Don't make me use this."

A blade? He couldn't see. *Doesn't matter.* Each wiggle earned more weight, more pressure, until his body screamed at him to lie still. "An—my friends. Don't hurt them. Please."

"Help me tie him up," the voice called into the darkness.

Leaves rustled. Sticks cracked. Whoever they were, they made no effort to be quiet anymore.

"Let go of me!" Anna's cry cut through all the rest.

"Don't hurt her," Will begged. Hysteria gave him strength, blocked out the pain. But another man was there now—no, two. "Please."

They hauled him up by his arms, wrenching his shoulders. Warm wetness slid down his arm.

"Who are you? What do you want?" Will bit out.

One of the men holding him stiffened. The stranger dropped his arm and stumbled away.

His mistake. Will jerked his elbow back, throwing his weight toward the other man. He collided with something too soft to be bone. Stomach? Groin? The man howled. His grip slipped. Will wrenched free, stumbling to his feet. He turned just in time to see the third man with his sword drawn, the clean blade glinting in a shaft of moonlight spilling through the canopy overhead.

Fuck.

They were outnumbered and unarmed.

In the thin, muted light, he could just make out hints of the man's attire—grey like the castle guards, but with a broad stripe of blue. The fairy godmother's men.

He had to get to Anna. Now.

Ignoring his years of training, Will turned away from the man with the blade and sprinted in the direction he'd heard the scream. In the shadows ahead, two figures squirmed against each other, still upright.

A male grunted. The slighter form twisted free.

"Will!" Anna cried, turning this way and that.

"Here!" He stumbled, going down hard, then pushed back up. *Have to save her. Get her free.*

She raced toward him. So close. Almost—

Another guard stepped from behind a tree and grabbed her arm, jerking her to a halt. Will's heart leaped into his throat as he glimpsed the dagger in his hand, pointed at Anna.

"Stop!" the guard roared. "Both of you!"

Will went utterly still, not just because of the threat to the woman he loved, but that voice…

A specter came back to haunt him. He'd heard it so many times, knew it almost as well as his own.

The guards caught up to him a second later. They grabbed his arms, forced him to his knees. He barely registered what happened, could only blink at the shadowed form he tried desperately to make out. *It can't be.* A shiver raced down his spine. *He was dead.*

"I see I'm not the only one surprised," the man said.

Anna stared at him, but he couldn't make out her expression or that of the man holding her. Will could only pray the man holding her was the same one he remembered.

"What happened to our friends?" Will asked. The forest had gone quiet again save for the snap and rustle of leaves as people he couldn't see moved in the darkness.

The man flicked his gaze to a companion. Will didn't turn his head, didn't look at whatever silent communication passed between them. He didn't dare do a thing other than pray to the Mother and every single one of her saints.

As if on cue, a guard shoved Koen into the narrow clearing with them, hands bound behind him. Something dark—blood?—trickled down the side of his face. But he walked, breathed, lived.

Another two grunted as they carried a large form through the underbrush. Will's heart plummeted into his stomach.

"No!" Anna lurched for Brandt, but the man held her firm, that knife still way too close to her face.

"Fought back," one guard said as he limped to join them.

"Alive?" the man holding Anna asked.

The other gave a jerking nod. "Had to knock him out."

Will sighed, sagging toward the ground. *Thank the Mother in the high heavens.*

"Any more friends in the woods?" the man asked, drawing closer with Anna in tow. He glanced at Will, at Koen.

Koen looked to him, and they answered almost at the same time, "No."

The man sheathed his dagger and shoved Anna toward another guard. She didn't try to fight, not this time.

"Now then." The leader of the group stalked toward Will across the clearing, coming into the moonlight.

Will sucked in a ragged breath. His old friend looked much the same as he always had, as Will did now, but changed. The planes of his face were sharper. The edges harder, worn down by life and misery. In some ways it was like looking into a mirror. But one thing was different, and it was that which made Will's teeth grind together. He wore traitor's colors, served the fairy godmother, and his eyes were far too clear for any potion to be controlling him or influencing his allegiance.

His friend knelt before him, an arm's width away, but a gorge might as well have been separating them. The man drew that dagger again, and Will felt the echo of a laugh stir in his chest. This close, he recognized it, a gift Will had given him three years ago after his friend had slain the buck nicknamed "the Forest King" for its impressive rack of antlers.

He brought the point up between him, making sure it caught the moonlight. He hadn't forgotten where it came from either. "You want to explain to me what you're doing out here? Alive?"

Will's body locked up. *Oh, he knows who I am all right.* But Anna—

His gaze snapped to her. *Fuck.* He strained against the men holding him, but their grip was firm. His eyes grew wide and pleading.

The huntsman tipped the blade to his cheek, forcing Will to meet his gaze once more. "Well, Nikolaus?"

28

*E*verything in Anna screamed at her to run. Will looked to her, wide-eyed and desperate as the man who must be their leader knelt before him and unsheathed his blade. He hadn't hurt her, hadn't been rough with his grip, though he'd had that horrible blade inches from her face, but that didn't mean he was kind. She knew far too well how someone could be polite one moment and horrid the next.

The man who gripped her arm had a loose hold. She could wrench free —maybe—take off at a run. Oh, how she wanted to. *Run, run, run,* her mind screamed. But how could she leave Will, or Koen or Brandt? And Brandt... Her throat closed up. He wasn't going anywhere in that state.

The man tipped Will's face up with the edge of the blade. Anna went tight and tense, a scream climbing up her throat.

"Well, Nikolaus?" he asked.

Nikolaus? She straightened.

Will roared. Her heart lurched, but the man hadn't cut him, not that she could see.

Koen cursed but didn't move, just stared at Will with an unreadable look on his face. The wrongness of it spoke volumes, but it was a language she couldn't read, couldn't discern.

"Come on now, can't tell your old friend?"

Friend? With someone who worked for the fairy godmother? Never. "You have the wrong person," Anna said. It was the only thing that made sense. They thought Will was someone else.

The man rose and turned toward her. Something that might have been a sad smile flickered across his face in the pale moonlight. "I don't think I do. See, I've known him most of my life. Since we were boys." He sighed. "And yet he doesn't acknowledge me. He can't stop looking at you, actually."

"Leave her alone!" Will cried.

The man glanced back over one shoulder. "Is it love at last?" He turned back to Anna with a smirk. "Though we thought it was before, too."

Before? Her chest grew tight. *He'd loved. Before...* Her thoughts spiraled. Down, down, down into the darkness inside of her. He said he lost family, a father—but more? A lover? A wife?

"Poor thing, she doesn't know, does she?"

What don't I know? She tried to ask, but the words stuck.

"Let her go. Let them all go." Will twisted against the men holding him. "You have me. You don't need them." His voice grew sharp, frantic.

The man stalked back to Will. "Of course, it must be hard to recognize your prince when he looks like this."

"Prince?" Her legs wobbled. A silent scream roared in the back of her head, but denial hit her lips first. "No. He's Will. The king's huntsman. Or he was, before..."

"I guess it would be king now, would it?" he amended. "You were coronated, or so we heard."

Murmurs from the guards tickled her ears, but she couldn't make them out, not over the rush of blood surging through her head. Anna swayed on her feet. The man at her side steadied her.

"Anna!" Will lunged for her. He'd used her name. Her real name. It hit her like a smack to the face, bringing her back and sharpening her senses. One of the others jerked him back, wrenching a near cry from his lips as he scrambled on his knees.

The stranger loomed just before her now. He stepped into her line of sight, blocking out Will in a silent demand for her attention. Only when she finally dared meet his moon-touched gaze did he say, "I'm William Jaeger, the king's huntsman. Or I was, when we had a king."

Will—the man she'd known as Will—roared something, but she couldn't make it out. Sound blurred, as did the world around her. Spots of color danced before her eyes as dawning horror wrapped around her throat and squeezed.

The real Will wrapped an arm around her shoulders, steadying her, holding her up as her knees failed. "That man there…" He pointed with his free hand. "…is King Nikolaus Kaiser."

The king. She stared at him, unable to look away, to run when she so desperately needed to.

He didn't shake his head, didn't deny it. His gaze broke from hers to drop to the forest floor, his shoulders hunching.

The painting she'd glimpsed at the castle flashed before her eyes. The cold-eyed prince, with his haughty gaze and upturned nose, the opposite of now. But finally, she could see the resemblance. Without the too-long hair and the overgrown beard, the one that had tickled her thighs when he'd—

Her legs gave out completely as she surrendered to a rush of panic-laden darkness.

The prince. No, the king. She'd given her heart to the king.

The same bastard who had married Cinderella.

29

*H*is second life charred to ashes. Everything he'd built, all his carefully crafted lies, the changes to his appearance... everything was for naught in the face of Will, his friend whose identity he'd stolen to survive.

Nik forced his gaze back to Anna to receive her yells, her tears. He braced for them, for the agony that they'd bring—that he deserved.

Infinite silence greeted him instead—no screams, no sobs. He tipped his head up just in time to see her body go slack and fall like a puppet with its strings cut. The huntsman cursed, nearly falling over himself in his effort to stop her awkward tumble toward the ground. Damn it all if a small part of him wasn't grateful to the bastard for that, even as he destroyed everything else.

The steady throbbing ache in his arm no longer mattered. It was nothing compared to the rending of his heart.

Anna would loathe him now. She'd have every right to. Worse was the brokenness in those moments before she'd fainted, as if everything between them had shattered like a dropped saucer of crystal.

A brief, flickering glance to Koen yielded another wash of pain. His captive friend had cursed once and hadn't spoken again, but the stiff set of his jaw and his averted gaze said as much as any words.

"Your friends," Will tasted the word and gave a nod, "didn't know who you were. And pretending to be me? Am I supposed to be flattered?"

Nik's teeth ground together as he stared down his former friend, half his attention lingering on the still form upon the ground behind him. He had no answer for him. An errant rock dug into his knee, sharp as the glint in Will's eyes. His friend turned traitor crouched before him, balanced on the balls of his feet, still lithe and limber as always. Will stabbed his dagger into the ground between his boots. Tantalizingly close but too far to reach, especially with the guards' fingers still digging into his upper arms.

"What? You thought you'd just try out the life of a commoner for a while? Leave us all to suffer?"

"Suffer?" Nik all but snarled. "You're in service to the fairy godmother! You're the ones causing the suffering!"

The other man's eyes narrowed, but his face gave away little. His words had been calm and even despite the threat simmering beneath.

"It's her potions controlling the people." All Nik's barely leashed rage spewed out like a dam finally burst. "They controlled me! Do you think I wanted this to happen? To lose my throne, my kingdom? The people all but enslaved to magic? Do you think I wished my father dead? Or yours?"

Will had the decency to flinch at that. Unlike Nik, Will had a father—Wilhelm—who was proud of him, who could never boast enough about his son, or Nik for that matter. He'd loved the old man too, had learned everything he knew about hunting and the forest from him. Nik's father thought it might make him a better man, toughen him up, maybe earn him some measure of acclaim.

In the wake of his wedding, which he barely remembered, many of his friends and supports had been sent away, Will included. Few were left who cared for him, and Wilhelm was the only one he could count as a true ally. The old hunter had been the one to eventually figure out that Cinderella had potions slipped into his meals to cloud his senses, his memories. He'd helped Nik avoid it and aided him in hiding the withdrawal symptoms that plagued him for weeks.

Nik's father had only gotten worse and worse. It wasn't just a potion she'd been slipping them, but a poison. She'd been subtle about it, little doses. Too late he'd figured it out, only when his father took to his bed and never left it. Acid burned the base of his throat, climbed higher. He hadn't been lucid at the end. Instead, he spent all his days talking to his mother as if she were still alive and hadn't died years ago. The king had no words for his son—he never had.

When bells rang to honor the end of the month of mourning following his father's death, he and Wilhelm stole horses and used that pious moment as a distraction to flee. They'd both been struck with arrows in hurried flight though the forest, the castle guards in pursuit, but Wilhelm took one to the heart.

On a day meant to be the end of mourning for one father, he lost another—the one of his heart, if not his blood.

Will snapped his fingers, pulling Nik from the bleak memory of when he'd pleaded with the Mother in the throes of his own death just before the river swallowed him up. "What are you doing out here, Nik? Tell me. Now."

What to tell him? The choice slipped away as Koen spoke. "We need a potion from the fairy godmother."

"Koen!" Nik snapped.

"To help my sister," Koen continued, voice strong and sure. "She's under an enchantment."

"Like half the country," someone said with a snort.

Will glared the man into silence. "And you just…what, plan to ask her for the cure?" He glanced between them, but this time Koen said nothing. Will's lips twitched. "I didn't think so." He pushed to his full height with a sigh. "You always were a cocksure fool," he said to Nik.

"You know…" Will picked at his nails with the point of his dagger. "…we heard about what happened at the castle. An attack on the chancellor, the queen searching high and low for the fairest in the land who fled in the chaos." He stopped abruptly and sheathed the dagger. "Our *dear* queen might be searching the city and countryside, but the fairy godmother had a different idea. She thought someone might just come looking for a cure. Told us to keep watch, and my crew here—" He gestured to the surrounding men. "—we wanted to be the ones to find them. Lucky for us, you seem to have forgotten everything we learned together."

A bitter laugh touched Nik's tongue but didn't leave it. *If only he knew.* He'd never thought about their lessons so much as he had the past few months. In fact, he'd done everything he could to truly be like Will, the king's best young huntsman, who wore the title like he'd been born to it. Which, being the son of a huntsman, he had.

But this man before him now wasn't the friend he knew. That man was gone, replaced with this doppelganger who knew all his most terrible secrets and lies and didn't mind spilling them out like the guts of a fish.

One thing was right though—they'd slipped up, made a fire. He thought they still had time before they neared the fairy godmother's workhouse, but time was never on his side these days. Worse, he'd given into his anger and yelled into the night. It was a foolish move made without thought on how it cost them.

"I'd wager," Will continued, a hint of cockiness slipping into his tone that teased him with memories of happier days, "that a potion isn't all you're after. Maybe you hope to stop a certain magical woman from helping a certain *wife*."

Nik bared his teeth. That title alone sent a shudder of disgust through his body.

Will's gaze slid to Anna. "Your tastes certainly have changed."

Nik snapped his teeth shut so hard they nearly cracked. "Leave her out of this," he grated.

"Moved on already, huh?" He winked, so at odds with their conversation.

"So, what now?" Nik asked, anything to get attention away from Anna and her defenseless form. "You're going to kill us? Turn us over?" *Not if I have anything to say about it.*

Will squatted in front of him again, close enough he could strangle the man if he could get his arms free. His stomach turned, years of memories and friendship sitting like a heavy weight within him, but he couldn't die. Nik couldn't let Anna or the others die either—or worse, be stuck in bondage to that witch. If Will had turned, a quick death was no better than he deserved.

"Nik." He tsked, shaking his head. "Don't you know me at all?"

The muscles in Nik's neck grew taut. He rocked on his toes, digging them into the dirt for a foothold to spring from.

Will clapped a hand on his good shoulder, and just as he was about to launch into action, he said something that stunned Nik to the core. "We're going to help you kill the witch."

30

*A*ll Nik could manage was a blink as his knees slid back down onto the rocky soil.

Will grinned, that broad, blinding smile that drew them together as boys. "Another report came from the castle. It said to be on the lookout for a ruffian whose description sounded a bit too familiar." The humor slipped from his features. "We know about the potions, what they do to people..." His gaze drifted far away. "What they did to us for a long time before we figured out how to fake it in front of the fairy godmother and those loyal to her." He shook his head, the shadows darker than the night taking flight. "I promised myself if it was you, if you were alive, I'd help you."

A surge of emotions Nik couldn't name prickled at the inside of his cheeks and sent a faint burning to the corners of his eyes.

"You always were a reckless fool." Will slapped his shoulder again. "But somewhere deep inside I knew—you couldn't be such an idiot as to marry that sneering blonde, no matter how nice a figure she cuts in a gown. Let the king up."

The guards holding him leaped away at the command. Apologies laced with "Majesty" had the back of his neck burning as Nik scrambled across the ground toward Anna. He hadn't heard that honorific in months, and he could do without it. He had been a cocksure fool—or worse, just a fool.

The men near Anna leaped back, bowing like he was someone worthy of it. He swept a hand through the hair across her brow. How could he feel any pride or encouragement when he'd broken the promise that mattered most? He vowed to protect her, yet he'd destroyed her. He'd seen it in her eyes before she fainted.

"Anna," he whispered. Nik sucked in a shaky breath and looked to Koen. His friend bent over his brother. Another guard unrolled bandages. "How is he?"

"He'll be in a mood when he wakes." Koen scowled at the surrounding guards. More than one flinched or looked away.

"Following orders," one mumbled.

Koen narrowed his eyes but didn't reply to that. To Nik he said, "He's had worse. Though you might be thankful he missed that little speech." He glared between Nik and Will. "When he finds out…" He shook his head.

Brandt would either be the proudest man alive for saving a king or Nik would wish Brandt had let him drowned in that damn river. The Mother only knew which reaction he'd get. He fought a sigh. *Probably both.*

"And you?" Nik asked.

Koen touched his head. Blood coated his fingers as he drew them away. He rubbed them together, staring in obvious surprise. "Guess I'll live." The hint of a smile twisted at the corner of his mouth.

A breathy whimper jerked his attention back to the woman on the ground. Her cheek tilted against his palm. That simple touch nearly broke him, so gentle and natural. His heart leaped into his throat.

Anna's eyes fluttered, barely visible in the night. "Will." The name—his old name—

struck him like a blade. "What…"

She stiffened. The accompanying sharp intake of breath had him doing the same.

Please… If she could only forget. *Give me time to explain…*

"Y-you." Her voice cracked. "You're…"

"Out of the way." Koen practically shoved him to the ground in his effort to get to Anna. "It's okay. You fainted. Don't move yet."

He bent over her slight form and encouraged her to remain still as she came back to the present. Anna hiccupped, the sound full of barely controlled tears. Koen adjusted his position until he became a wall between them.

For once, Nik was glad to have someone else at her side. An hour ago, minutes ago, things would have been completely different.

It took everything he had to push himself to his feet and move away, to give her the space she needed. Nik ran his hands through his hair, tugging the too-long strands until they hurt. Each of her soft sniffles, each of Koen's whispered words, bled him out little by little.

One step at a time, he forced himself away from them over to where one of the guards tended to Brandt. The guard stilled, dipping his head and muttering an honorific before continuing his work. Will joined them.

"What a pleasant welcome." Bitter sarcasm laced Nik's words as he turned to Will.

The other man shrugged. "Had to make sure who you were and what side you were on."

Nik bristled. "Did you really think I'd be aligned with that monster?"

Will cocked one brow in return. "You thought I was."

Hells, I had. Worn nails dug into his palms. He might have killed his best friend if he'd had the chance. Heaviness settled in his chest and clawed toward his spine. "These months have made monsters of us all."

The other man's throat bobbed in response. "Indeed. I'm sorry for your friend though." He glanced to Brandt. "You trust them?"

"With my life," he answered. They'd all saved him, one way or another.

"Yet you didn't tell them who you were?"

His teeth ground together. "It was best everyone believed me dead."

"Best for who?" Will scoffed. His voice held that dark edge again, the ring of command, sharp as iron, that hadn't belonged to him months ago. "Your people needed you, and you just disappeared."

"They tried to kill me." Nik drew himself up, his jaw set.

Others around them whispered, but he tuned them out as he held Will's gaze in the dappled moonlight.

His friend leaned in until they were nearly nose to nose. "And you let them!" Will snarled.

Even the bugs ceased their music as the accusation rang through the darkness. Will turned, stalking off into the night, but Nik couldn't let it go. He'd never been one to take a punch and back down. Not before, not now.

"I'm trying," he spat, pathetic as it sounded. "We're trying!" He gestured to his friends who were hurt—physically and emotionally. "It's better than you, following that witch's orders for months!"

Will went utterly still, a shadow against the surrounding trees. He twisted around faster than a snake about to strike. "We were controlled by her. All of us who were loyal to *you*." He stalked back to him with heavy steps. "It took months to figure it out, to get free of her power!"

"Me. Too." Nik grated between clenched teeth.

"Ah yes, but you've been dead for months now, reborn into a new life of freedom."

The verbal blow hit hard, but he wouldn't cower. Instead, he readied one of his own. "And working toward revenge. But what have *you* done? You want to kill the fairy godmother? Why haven't you?"

Will nearly shook with rage before he looked away. "To what end, Nik? So we could all die in the process? Or be killed when guards from the castle showed up after they learned what we'd done? It wouldn't stop Cinderella or the chancellor. They'd still reign. We've done more good working against her from within, limiting the potions that can be sent south, disrupting her plans in little ways. But you—" He stepped closer, prodding Nik's chest with an accusing finger. "With you alive, we have a chance, Nik. Don't you see?"

He swallowed. *Yes, I damn well see.* It'd been his goal for months, but he let this man, his friend, continue.

Passionate fervor drowned out the man's fury, sweeping over him like a wave. "Now, if we take out the fairy godmother, there won't be any more potions. Their effects will wear off, and then you can appear before the people, tell them your story, lead them in an uprising against Cinderella."

The air charged around them. Men scooted in closer, as if drawn by the eagerness in Will's voice. From the corner of his eye, he even caught Koen and Anna looking his way. All he wanted to do was go to them, but he held himself steady.

Will clasped him on the shoulder, drawing closer still. "We can get our country back."

Nik mirrored the other man's actions, creating an unbroken circle between their arms and bodies, a vow of trust. "We will then. Let's do together what we couldn't do alone."

A tingle of hope spread through his veins. They could do this. For the first time, he believed that. If they could shatter the alliance between the fairy godmother and Cinderella and stop one of them, it might let them stop the other too. Without the aid of the fairy godmother's potions and her magic, it would weaken Cinderella and the chancellor. They would lose some of their advantage.

A deep groan cracked through the moment. Nik broke away from Will, turning to where Brandt attempted to sit.

"Fucking hells." He held his head.

Koen raced toward him, probably for the benefit of others as much as for his brother.

Brandt shoved the man nearest him—hard. "Who are ya?" He scrambled on the ground, patting his side, searching for a blade no longer sheathed there.

"We're fine. It's okay." Koen held his hands up.

"Hells we are," Brandt boomed through the night.

"It's okay. They're allies," Nik said as he crouched on the ground near the man.

Brandt all but snarled. "Allies, huh?"

Koen stared at him across his brother. "You care to explain, or should I?"

Hells. Nik rolled his neck, rubbing the back of it as it cracked and popped. He sighed. "Might as well get it over with."

31

*M*ore than a day had passed since the revelation that nearly destroyed Anna's world. The remaining journey to the fairy godmother's compound gave her too much time to think, to stew in the revelation of Will—no, Nik's—true identity.

A king. The king. She bit her lip, nearly drawing blood.

They'd arrived in the forest outside the fairy godmother's workhouse the night before and finalized the plan they put into action earlier that morning.

She, along with Brandt, Koen, and *His Majesty*, took up shelter in the woods within view of the sprawling complex, out of sight but close, as they waited for William—the real Will—and his group to return from the fairy godmother's compound. Will and his men travelled there the previous evening, returning from patrol as expected, leaving only the four of them in the woods.

Will claimed all the guards in his group were loyal to him. Their eyes were free of the potion's influence, and they seemed nice enough, the few she'd spoken to anyway. Still, Anna couldn't shake the feeling that this might be one giant trap, a plot hatched by the godmother herself to draw them in like prey to the spider's web. That gnawing worry kept her awake much of the night, even when it wasn't her shift on watch.

No one came for them in the night—a small blessing. And for now, Anna was alone with the brothers and Nik. They could flee. But to what end? Everything they needed lay ahead. William and his crew would help them get in. Koen had shared their idea of using her as bait, much to Nik's dismay.

She hugged her arms closer around herself. Just thinking about him made her ache inside. His discomfort and anger fueled her to push for that plan, if only to cause him pain. A petty desire, but the thought of it appealed to some dark part of her. William and the others were hesitant to go against their *precious king* returned from the dead, but when he failed to produce a better idea, William had sided with her and the brothers.

Forest gave way to fields near the walled compound. Thus far, the only movement in the dew-laden fields below were the sheep, rousing from sleep and roaming in search of breakfast. From this distance, they looked like ants crawling across the landscape—muted figures in the dawn light.

There was no way to sneak up on the compound without being seen by sentries posted in one of the guard towers stationed around the corners of the walls. Within, various buildings dotted the space—one large and multi-storied, made of stone and seemingly held together by the plant life climbing its walls. The fairy godmother's workshop, they'd said. And where she lived. A few lights already glimmered in the windows. Smaller outbuildings surrounded it—prison houses for those sent to work in servitude to the fairy godmother, barracks for the guards, and other structures. Her sister and mother would be there somewhere —hopefully.

Small garden plots dotted what little of the inner yard she could see from the rise. William said that was where they grew some of the more precious plants the godmother required for her potions.

Brandt settled next to her on the tree stump, a warm and comforting presence against the chill still clinging to the air and her heart. He'd been as shaken as her once he'd woken from being knocked out. He was shocked, angry at the lies, and bellowed about it to half the forest.

But by morning, the revelation had settled differently. "Can't believe I really saved the king," he'd said more than once the day before. Each time had her nails gouging grooves in her palms.

If she and Nik's situations were reversed, if he'd married anyone other than her horrible stepsister, perhaps she'd have felt the same way.

Now, Brandt extended a crusty loaf of bread, a share of rations from William's crew, who were well-fed. She only hoped the prisoners fared as well. William had tried to assure her that they were. The fairy godmother needed them strong and healthy to tend her gardens and work in her factory, he'd said. It made sense, but she struggled to believe it.

"You should eat something," Brandt said, shoving the bread her way.

With a soft sigh, she took it, though even the bread's delightful smell turned sour in her nose. She'd managed nothing more than a few small bites the day before, and her body knew it. Her stomach chewed at itself, begging her to eat, but every bite tasted like sawdust and was hard as paste to swallow, no matter how well-baked the loaf or the delicious smokiness of the jerky they'd brought.

The bread called to her, but she just couldn't answer. It passed back and forth between her hands, uneaten. She nearly dropped it to the leaf-strewn ground when Brandt threw an arm around her shoulders and hauled her close as if she were Mina or one of his brothers. Her shoulders tensed at the sudden touch but quickly relaxed. She leaned into him, savoring the comfort she desperately needed.

"Ya know," he said, his voice a whisper, or as much a whisper as Brandt could ever muster. "Lying's a terrible thing, but he had his reasons."

Her stomach clenched. He had no idea. That lie she could handle, but what'd he done... She closed her eyes, forcing away the tears that wouldn't stop trying to break free.

Brandt leaned closer, a hint of the wild, acrid scent of Koen's preferred smoke blend clinging to his beard from the smoke they'd shared the night before. "He wasn't the only one who lied about their identity."

The accusation pulled her taut.

"Not that I blame ya for that," he hurried on with a pat to her arm. "I understand why ya did it too, but maybe don't be so hard on him? I saw..." A small cough slipped out as he shifted on the log. "I saw how the two of you were together. A lie shouldn't come between that."

"It—" The words caught in her throat. She had to tell him something, but they didn't know who she really was. Her name, yes, they finally knew that thanks to the king shouting it two nights ago when they were attacked. But they had no idea who her family was or her relation to the queen. She inhaled a ragged breath. "It's more than that."

Focused regard settled on her back. She didn't need the snap of twigs and rustle of leaves to know who stalked their way. He was being loud on purpose. For all his lies, he hadn't lied about his skills in the woods or on the hunt. He could have snuck up without a sound, but he wanted them to know he approached. It didn't help, only gave her pulse a chance to race, her muscles a chance to tense.

Brandt seemed not to notice as he focused on the valley below, on the dark specks leaving the gate and heading their way. "Right number of 'em."

Enemies at the front. Enemies behind...

Nik circled around their log, keeping a careful distance away.

"Here they come," Brandt said, oblivious to the heavy tension hanging around them.

"Right on time." Nik's words were hollow, spoken without thought. Anna nearly flinched as his focus shifted to her, lingering there a few heartbeats too long before he spoke. "Anna..." From the corner of her eye, she saw him rake a hand through his hair. "Can I speak with you?"

Her lips thinned. She couldn't talk to him, wouldn't. What could he possibly say to make things any better?

Not a damn thing, that's what.

Why couldn't he just leave her alone? She'd made it clear she didn't want to speak to him. She hadn't said a word to him since that horrible moment in the forest when she thought they were going to die and then almost wished she had.

If she could just get through this day, then she could leave him behind and forget anything ever existed between them. That'd be best. Either William was honest and he'd help them stop the fairy godmother before the sun set—their families freed, the potion to heal Mina in hand—or they'd be killed or imprisoned.

An ending either way.

The old Will, the one she'd loved, would be a shadow in the past or a memory in the afterlife. She'd take her mother and sister and flee like they should have done all those months ago. They could start over somewhere new. Besides, Nik and the others wouldn't need her to help stop Cinderella and reclaim the throne.

"I'm just gonna..." Brandt trailed off as he shoved to his feet faster than if a bee stung him.

Anna lunged for him, grabbing at his arm, his leg, whatever she could get her hands on. But he was too strong, too fast. Fabric slipped from her fingers. She half-tumbled onto the fallen log. Its rough bark scraped her palm as she steadied herself.

"Please, Anna," Nik's voice cracked over her name.

She froze, hands on the coarse pine bark. A silent scream of fury echoed in her head as Brandt hurried away, leaving her alone with Nikolaus.

"Don't you get it?" She whipped around, fury seeping from her like steam. A shard of ice slipped straight into her heart at the shadows under his eyes, his averted gaze, and the hair that looked even more wild than she remembered, hanging free to nearly brush his shoulders. "I have nothing to say to you."

She had nothing to say when she stalked away from him every time he got close.

Nothing when she slept as far from him as possible.

Nothing when she woke with his cloak over her and tossed it away like a snake that could poison her.

"I didn't love her, Anna. I didn't choose to marry her," he whispered, his voice soft and controlled.

She snorted air through her nose. "I was there, you idiot. At the ball?"

He flinched.

"I stood a step behind her. You only had eyes for her. I saw it, damn you!" She thrust an accusing finger at him. "Can you really tell me you were under the influence of potion then?"

He looked Anna in the eye and swallowed. "No. I was a fool."

Half a scream poured out before she could choke it down. She dropped her head into her hands, unable to look at him.

The scrape of bark had her fists closing around hunks of hair. How dare he sit so close? When she raised her head, his position matched hers at the far end of the too-short log.

"It was my fault at the ball. I fell for her charm," he said to the dirt, each word a little dagger inside her. "But after that..." He drew in a ragged breath. "It wasn't of my own will. I didn't love her. I didn't choose to marry her. The king—my father—and the chancellor, they chose for me. I protested once. My father...he struck me." He rubbed at his face, as if remembering the wound. "And then..." He dared a glance over at her.

Anna didn't move. Barely breathed.

"It must have been the chancellor. I saw myself announce her as my future bride. I saw the wedding through my own eyes. But that wasn't me, Anna. I told you I was under the influence of the fairy godmother's potions."

The way he said it grated against her, as if he'd told her the truth when he'd barely scratched the surface of it. The words, the accusations, splintered and shattered the last of her control. She shoved to her feet, fists balled at her side.

"You dare to act like you told me everything, to make me feel—" She cut herself off. "How dare you when you fucked my stepsister!"

A whistle slipped through the air behind her accompanied by a muffled, "Oh damn."

Everything burned, as if she could suddenly burst into flame. *So the brothers heard. Fine.* Maybe they'd finally understand her fury.

"I-I never fucked her, Anna."

Air hung in her lungs, unable to move. She blinked at him, waiting for the excuse and explanation. "You married her." She gaped, and fury washed into that void. "I know you were married. For months!"

Nikolaus stepped forward and reached for her, but then stopped and swallowed. His gaze cut away as a hint of color touched his cheeks. "I... couldn't. On our wedding night, I couldn't—" He gestured between his legs. "—rise for her. Not like I could for you, Anna." The hint of a broken smile played amid his beard. "Apparently, not even her potion could influence that."

Damn her traitorous heart and the way it thumped. She looked away first, staring at a clump of leaves on the ground. "That was just one night," she muttered.

He edged closer. "And she never tried again."

At that, she glanced at him sidelong. *Who wouldn't want to sleep with a gorgeous prince?*

"I think, now, looking back on it, she already had someone else in mind. Someone who wouldn't want to…share."

She blinked at him. "The chancellor."

Nikolaus nodded slowly. They'd seen them together, leaning into one another, their closeness of actions and words. They were a couple now, clear for anyone to see, but perhaps it had started long ago. Though what her stepsister saw in that man was beyond her. He was handsome, yes, if old enough to be her father. One look in his eyes and Anna had known him for a cruel, ruthless man, one who'd no doubt helped her stepsister seize the throne. "The throne," she echoed almost numbly.

"She wanted my crown, as had most every woman I met until then."

Not me. She said in silence behind lips pressed tightly closed. Anna would have given anything for him to be anyone else. A prince, a *king*, was the very worst person he could be.

"I was a fool. Seduced by a pretty face. But I wasn't enough of an idiot to marry her or fuck her. If almost dying taught me anything, it's the error of who I was. I'm not that man anymore, Anna. I chose to be Will, a better man than me. I vowed never to be swayed by a pretty face and honeyed words. Never again. I lost everything because of that. I'd change what happened to others, but not to me. I—"

The crack in his voice begged her to look at him, so she did.

"I deserved what happened to me," he hung his head in defeat. "I'd choose it again."

She reared back. "You wanted to die?"

"No." His attention snapped back to her. "But the lessons I've learned about who I was, I wouldn't have learned any other way. I was the stupid boy my father thought I was. I see that now. But I can be different this time. I want to be." He'd drawn near as he spoke, only an arm's length away now. She hadn't realized, so enraptured at his words, until he said, "And I wasn't lying about you, Anna."

Her heart leaped into her throat, squeezing out the denial that she yearned to throw at him.

"Everything I said was true." He reached for her, his fingertips a hair's width from her arm. "Everything I—we did, that was honest. Truth." His shaking fingers dared to graze her upper arm, and she let them, holding stiff as a board, barely breathing.

"I was drawn to you before I knew who you were, Anna. Before I even knew you were a woman."

A soft gasp caught in her throat as he drew closer still, until she could almost feel the heat of his body, a sharp contrast to the cool, misty morning.

"I fell for you—not your name or your identity or who you were before. And I wish..." He drew his hand away, clenching it into a tight fist at his side. But his touch lingered, tingling through her like crackling frost. "I wish you could see me the same way."

I want to.

The words lingered unsaid, caught in the middle of their locked gazes. His chest rose and fell in deep, intentional breaths. Perhaps his heart raced as fast as hers, the only thing that moved in that frozen moment of time.

I want to.

Nikolaus's eyes widened—hopeful, intent. He dared a half-step closer.

I want to, but...

He halted, reading that lingering doubt she dared not utter.

Part of her longed for nothing more than to leap into his arms, to press her lips to his and forget who he was before and what he'd done.

Another part stung—the wound his identity, his past, left on her still open and bleeding. Maybe he hadn't slept with her stepsister. Maybe he truly hadn't wanted to marry her. But he was still the prince from that ball, the one who'd seen her sister and no one else, the one who wouldn't even look her way. She couldn't scrub away the memory of that cold, haughty gaze from the portrait, the only one she'd ever seen the prince wear.

And they wanted him to be that man again.

That was William's plan, one that Brandt and Koen embraced too. They relished it, cheered for it.

There was no place for her in that future. He'd be the king once more. Back to his old life.

Her huntsman was gone.

That loss echoed through her like a dark, hollow thing, leaving an emptiness in her chest.

Anna turned away as the tears burned at the corners of her eyes. One moment longer and she'd have rushed to him, thrown her arms around his neck, and tried everything she could to block out the horrible truth.

The silence that clung around them was absolute. Even the birds couldn't bother to interrupt. Koen and Brandt busied themselves with their packs, a poorly performed act to disguise the fact that they'd been listening. Heat raced up her neck as she jolted into motion, striding into the dense pines.

No footsteps followed, and she'd be damned if she'd give him the satisfaction of seeing her look back, no matter how bad she wanted to. Everything was jagged, wrong, and maybe she was making it worse, but she couldn't ignore the way his truths cut her open and bled her out.

William and his crew would be back soon—for good or ill. She wouldn't let them see her cry. Anna would hold herself together with the few narrow threads of hope she had left. She wouldn't fall apart in front of them no matter how terribly she frayed apart at the seams.

32

*I*t hadn't been enough. He'd laid his truths bare, embarrassing and difficult as they were to confess, and she'd still turned away. The tiny spark of hope he'd kept buried inside gutted to ash the moment he saw her features shift, saw the hint of yearning in her eyes fade to despair.

Something in him cracked and died. He loved her. Maybe he should have said that too, but if she'd turned her back on him after that confession, it would have slain him fully. He couldn't fall, not yet, not when his revenge was finally in reach.

Nik tucked that brittle, broken side of him deep down within. By the time Will and his men returned, his features had smoothed out, he could breathe again, and the brothers treated him like normal.

Anna though… Two days earlier, he'd have run after her. But if she'd truly fled this time, who could blame her? He'd free her mother and sister, everyone held captive by the fairy godmother. He owed her—everyone— that. Her goal would be complete. Why should she stay with him any longer?

Because maybe she loved you too, a traitorous voice whispered in the back of his head.

He shoved that thought back into the depths of his soul. If she did, he'd broken it—shattered her trust and her heart by withholding the damning truth. He'd feared losing her by telling it.

He'd lost her anyway.

Once Will's men had returned, she'd reappeared at the edge of their little camp. For a moment, he thought he caught her gaze on him, just a glimpse out of the corner of his eye. But by the time he turned his head, she looked elsewhere.

It was a fool's hope, and he had no time for that.

They spent much of the day perfecting their plan and making preparations.

"Care to test it out?" Will said, gesturing to the litter they'd crafted.

Koen told them of Mina's condition, the sleep from which nothing would wake her. If they were going to pull off this plan, much as he hated the method of it, they'd need a way to carry Anna into the compound as if she too were trapped in sleep.

"Think your skills have gotten rusty?" Nik asked, faking a half-smile. He ached, not from his wound, which Koen's salve had taken the sting out of, but from a soul-deep ache at the loss he'd suffered. There'd be time for mourning later—if they were successful.

Nik laid on a swath of material they'd lashed between thick branches. Will, Brandt, and a few others hoisted him up. He sagged, as expected, but it held.

"Excellent," Will said, admiring his handiwork. "We'll rub some dirt on it, make it look a little more worn. Should do fine."

It would be fine as long as no one noticed the fresh-cut ends of the skinny trunks. Hopefully, there wouldn't be time for that. *Get in, get in front of the fairy godmother, take her out, secure the compound, free the prisoners.*

He huffed air through his nose. *What could go wrong?*

"Now there's a sight," one of Will's men said. His eager eyes and wide grin focused on the trees behind Will.

Nik's stomach bottomed out. It could only be Anna. He hadn't seen her yet, not in the dress Will had smuggled from the compound, but he knew the sight would destroy him. And the way this man looked at her... Nik worked his jaw, letting the tension pop and crack. He had half a mind to snap at him, but he swallowed down the urge.

She wasn't his, no matter what he wanted.

Will half-turned. A blinding grin lit his features, that easy, friendly smile he'd missed. But this one wasn't for him, but for Anna. He stepped to the side, just enough to see her perform a mock curtsy with the skirts of the pale blue dress. The hint of a blush colored her cheeks as she regarded his friend.

He'd be perfect for her. The thought hit him out of nowhere, punched so hard he flinched and stepped back.

"A perfect fit," Will said in admiration.

Her blush deepened. "This dress..." Anna ran her fingers along the delicate flowers stitched into the bodice. "Where did you get it?"

Will's grin stretched wider, his gaze almost wistful. "A lovely lady with quite a sharp tongue. One of our allies inside."

Anna's eyes turned glassy, and Nik had to hold himself back from going to her. "Charlotte," she whispered.

Conversation around them died. Will's smile faltered as he blinked at her. "Yes. How did you know?"

The mix of joy and sorrow that crossed Anna's features could have been a painting on the walls of his castle. "My sister."

He'd known the answer before she said it, yet something about the love behind those words filled him with a bittersweet ache.

His friend relaxed. He took Anna's hands in his. "Anna. I should have known it was you." Nik could only see the profile of his face as he spoke, but the tone of his words, the softness of his jaw said even more than words. He embraced Anna like a lost sister, not a potential suitor. "She's told me quite a lot about you. Worried endlessly. To be able to tell her you're safe, you're here, will be the greatest gift for her." He shook his head in disbelief.

Safe. Not hardly.

Nik turned away, doubt clawing at him. She shouldn't go in there. Not when he couldn't guarantee her safety. He opened his mouth, ready to suggest they abandon this whole stupid plan, when Brandt stumbled forward and boomed, "Wait, you're Anna Schneider? The queen's stepsister?"

Anna flinched, retreating into Will's protection.

Nik all but bared his teeth at his friends—Will, Brandt, all of them.

"You just now figured that out?" Koen gaped at his brother.

"It's not like the rumors say..." She looked around frantically, a deer about to bolt.

Will clapped a hand on her shoulder. "We know." Anna stilled under his touch. "Charlotte told us everything."

Brandt charged toward her. That sprung Nik into action. He leaped between them. Brandt shoved him to the side, but he refused to budge. "Move ya dolt." Something in his tone had Nik stumbling, just enough that Brandt edged past him and knelt before Anna.

"Should be Princess Anna then, shouldn' it?" He gazed up at her in wonder that shook Nik to his core.

"I'm not—" She fumbled for words. "I never—"

Princess Anna. Yes. Something swelled in his heart as she flicked her gaze to him. *Or maybe a queen.* The look she gave him was brief, but he'd take it, even as she focused back on the ruffian kneeling before her.

"Ya suffered at her hand, and still you ventured to the castle with us and faced her."

Koen jerked his brother up by his shirt. "Excuse him. He doesn't know how to handle himself."

A tentative smile spread across Anna's face. "I know."

"But she's—" Brandt pointed to Anna. "This whole time we've—" He shoved his brother. "And you knew?"

Koen adjusted his glasses. "Only recently."

Anna giggled, and the sight warmed his heart.

"Some friends." Will shook his head. "Any more secrets between you all that you care to share?"

Without thinking, Nik looked at Anna, and she shocked him by looking straight at him.

Well, fuck me. The blush on her cheeks and slightly parted lips knocked him speechless. She'd almost slayed him earlier in the day, and now she offered this, whatever it was.

"That was already obvious," Will said with a smirk.

Nik looked away first, conscious of the heat blazing up the back of his neck.

Anna mumbled something.

Will laughed before turning serious. "Well, it's almost time. Should we be on with it?"

Nik looked to Anna and she to him, something unspoken in her gaze. *Worry?* "You don't have to do this," he said. "You can stay here, hidden and safe."

A fragile smile twitched at her lips. "The dress won't fit anyone else here." She turned to Will, her features resolute. "Let's do it."

33

*T*he walls of the compound, grey stones fitted with mortar, rose up before them as they advanced on the main gates. The last of sunset glared off the top stones, soon to fade into bleak, gloaming twilight —the perfect time of day to wear shadows as an extra cloak of protection, when the guards wouldn't feel the need to wield their lanterns to see.

Nik rolled his shoulders, already stiff from having his wrists bound behind him. Koen and Brandt were bound similarly with loose, false knots they could pull free at the opportune moment but that looked real enough to get them inside.

"Whatcha got there?" A man called down from the tower near gates. The iron still had a shine to it. The wood showed little sign of age or wear. It'd been constructed recently. Nothing like this had existed while he'd been prince—at least, not while he'd been in full control of himself.

"They thought to pay the fairy godmother a visit," Will yelled back, gesturing to the brothers and him. Guards flanked tightly to their sides. Another four carried the litter at the front just behind Will. Anna played her part well, stiff and still as Mina had been the last time they'd seen her.

"Thought we'd give them an escort in." The cold, dark edge of his friend's voice sent a fleeting chill across his skin.

"Is that—" The man leaned out, a torch in hand.

"Indeed, it is," Will replied, sweeping a hand toward Anna's still form.

The man snapped back into the tower, flame fluttering. A moment later, chains rattled and the door groaned open. A tingle of doubt tickled Nik's spine. Once they went in, there was no turning back. He scanned the walls, the towers, and swallowed. The time to retreat had already fled. The only way out was further in.

Various figures moved through the yard inside the gates. The guards were easy to identify in their clean uniforms. Others, men and women in worn and faded clothes, filtered toward the outbuildings—their cells, even if they lacked the bars and gloom of the ones under the castle.

His shoulders loosened a fraction as he took them in. None of the people he saw were too skinny, nor did they bear awkward limps or strained movements that spoke to torture or physical abuse. No putrid scents of death and decay burned his nose. Instead, an odd sweetness permeated the air, mixing with the tang of dirt and smoke billowing from the chimneys of the main building.

But no one deserved enslavement, physical or of the mind.

"Where is she?" Will asked a nearby guard, a little too loudly.

Nik cut his eyes to the windows nearly concealed by the ivy growing up the building. Thought it was closed, old glass like that often let sound in. This building had existed for some time, though he couldn't recall what it may have been. His jaw shifted as he wracked his brain, trying to remember the lessons of his childhood. He'd never been the best student, especially not when it came to the more mundane elements of his reign such as the history of the territory and which prominent families lived where—now or in the past. *By the Mother, I hated those days of study.*

"Believe she's still in the workroom, sir," the man responded.

Will had authority here, respect. He'd seen it from the men with him, but even the ones here yielded their regard to him.

At his side, Koen coughed, drawing Nik's attention. His raised brows and flickered glance showed his friend's thoughts mirrored his own. Will had always been good at putting on a show and drawing people to his side. He would have made a great actor if he'd had the desire. He was putting on a great performance for someone now, and if it was them, they were fucked. Nik shrugged in return, a much more casual gesture than he felt.

The central building stood in sharp contrast to the new outer wall and gate. It was old, barely patched together with new mortar. A musty scent swarmed him as they entered. Even the swept, polished floors and dust-free walls couldn't disguise its age and wear. A family crest, a lion clutching an arrow, had been engraved on the far wall between the spiral staircases sweeping upward. An old memory crept to the surface: a book spread before him, his tutor harping about the great families that had fallen to ruin due to the lack of an heir—as his would if he didn't marry and sire children. The constant reminders from his father and others about family and duty still dug under his skin like thorns. Perhaps if they hadn't badgered him so much he'd have tried harder toward that end. Maybe he'd have met Anna before all this mess.

She lay still as death, and he constantly had to remind himself it was an act. *She is fine, and by all the hells and heavens, I will keep her safe.*

The further they filed into the massive entryway, the more odd scents teased him. Some pleasant: flowers, pine, a whiff of fresh-baked bread. Others were decidedly out of place. Something peppery forced him to choke down a sneeze and had Brandt failing terrifically at that. The loamy scent of rotting leaves followed, mixing with something else sharp and bright. The scents chased each other through the room like fallen leaves on an errant breeze.

Some of Will's men broke off from their group, waiting in the main room as the rest of them filed past the stairs and through the double doors beyond.

The cavernous room and its arched ceiling held a sight that drew him to a sudden halt. Large cauldrons roasted on roaring fires nestled in hearths on either side of the room. Worktables spread out in between, covered with assorted bowls, pots, dried herbs, and other things he couldn't decipher. A few people milled about, one at each pot, a few working at the tables. None raised their head. No whispers of acknowledgement or surprise reached him.

Something heavy settled in his chest as he shifted his gaze between the two men tending the concoctions bubbling over the fire, ones whose sharp scent burned the hairs of his nose, even from this distance. Blank stares focused on the pots they stirred. Clearly, they were under the control of strong magic. Had he been that bad?

Why oh why did no one say anything or try to stop it?

"Move along." One of the guards pushed him roughly forward.

The few people standing around tables were no better, mindless bodies carrying out a task over and over. What might have once been a great feasting hall had been reduced to a workroom for mindless slaves, a reflection of what the country might become if they failed.

"Hans!" Brandt shouted. He jerked against his ropes, nearly splitting the false knot and knocking into one of the guards.

Oh no! One of his brothers. Nik swallowed against the dryness in his throat as he took in the man Brandt stretched toward. His hair and skin were mostly clean and washed, his clothing the same. But if there was any bit of his brother in there behind the potion clouding his eyes, he was well and truly trapped by the magic. He never turned from stirring the pot. Not even his dark hair shifted to show a twitch of his ears or turn of his head.

The guards pulled Brandt into line—physically, and with scathing reminders that he was a prisoner. They couldn't say the truth, not even here, but the veiled words got through enough for Brandt to step back into line even as his face reddened in fury.

Koen, on the other hand, had paled and hung his head as if he might spill his stomach across the stone floor.

"This is what happens to those who don't follow orders," Will bit out.

Will advanced on the far door and the two guards standing on either side. Unlike the others, they dressed in all black, and their gazes were just as vacant as the others in the room. The rumored Shadow Guard.

At a signal from Will, they opened the door wide. Much of the sight through the threshold was blocked by the guards.

"What is this, Captain?" a woman demanded, her voice like crackling ice in the high mountains.

He didn't need to see her to know who the voice belonged to. It was the same voice he'd heard through the mirror, so eerie and awful it'd haunt his dreams forever after.

"Godmother." Will bent at the waist, still half in the doorway. "Apologies for the interruption, but I thought you'd like to see her straight away."

"Who—" Her question broke off as the guards carrying Anna—making themselves as thin as possible—squeezed through the doorway with the litter between them. Beyond them, Nik caught a glimpse of the room. Shelves lined the walls from floor to ceiling filled with all colors and shapes of vials and jars.

"*That* can't be her." The disdain dripping from her voice set his blood boiling. How dare she talk about Anna that way?

"She's asleep, just like you said to look for," Will replied, calm and even. "We brought those who were with her."

At Will's gesture, they were nudged forward to the looming door. Inch by inch, the horrible woman came into view. She stood in front of a heavy wooden desk covered in papers and potions. The walls were lined with hundreds more books and bottles.

The fairy godmother was shorter than he guessed—she'd barely reach his shoulder. Weathered and gnarled hands were planted on either wide hip as she stared toward them, a deep scowl across her aged features. A few wisps of grey hair slipped down around her face, no more substantial than spider webbing. The rest of her body was hidden under the grey, hooded cloak that ended just above her pale blue eyes on the front and pooled on the floor around the hem of her sapphire dress.

This is the fairy godmother? The woman everyone fears? He nearly scoffed. A strong gust of wind could break her. Her glittering gaze landed on him. His breath caught until she moved on to the next of his companions.

"The girl's brothers." The hint of a smirk twitched on Will's face, the expression so real it made him queasy. "Said they were coming to you for a cure." He chuckled, a dark sound so unlike his friend. A few others echoed it.

She snorted, her lips curling in distaste. "They look nothing alike."

The back of his neck burned. *Hells, they really didn't.*

"Different dads," Brandt snapped. "Or ain't you ever heard of that?"

The godmother's nose twitched. "Quite a mouth on you."

Brandt gave a wide grin, showing his teeth amid his beard. "One of my finest features."

Her frown deepened, eyes narrowing. "You'll learn to keep it shut in my presence."

The two shadow guards entered, closing the door behind them and sealing them all in the room.

"Or ye'll do what?"

"Brandt," Koen warned.

The fairy godmother pulled a stick from somewhere within her cloak. The dark wood was nearly as gnarled and twisted as her fingers but long as her forearm. "One more word, and you'll lose that mouth." The end flared a cold, eerie blue.

Magic.

Not the stuff of potions and powders, but pure power like Nik had never seen. It shook him to the core.

Nik looked to Will, waiting for a signal. She had only her two guards. They could take them. What did Will wait for?

34

*L*aying still had never been so hard. Anna had the easiest task, supposedly—don't move, pretend to be asleep no matter what happens. But all she wanted to do was run.

She didn't dare crack her eyes to view the fairy godmother or her workshop. That small movement could give them away, and she wouldn't risk it.

But heavens and hells, I want to.

She'd nearly sneezed in the first room, some horrid scent tickling her nose before being replaced by something less repulsive. It'd been an agonizing fight against her instincts to hold it in, but somehow this was worse.

The voice from her nightmares was right in front of her. It was just as awful as when she'd first heard it in Ella's room at their old house. A voice she wasn't meant to hear and wished to the Mother she'd done something about then and there instead of running away and pretending it hadn't happened.

After Ella lost her father, after she found that horrible mirror and began communing with the fairy godmother, everything got so much worse.

"Fairest in the land," the godmother scoffed, her voice closer now, the second jab at her appearance in as many minutes. It shouldn't hurt anymore, but it still did. Worse, it made it so much harder to hold still.

She'd heard Brandt and Koen, their presence a small comfort. But Nik? He was there too. He had to be. Part of her wished him far away. But another part wanted him close. She'd been horrible to him after his confession. The hurt was so raw, deep, and fresh that she couldn't stand to be around him.

But time, those precious minutes alone in the woods, had been as soothing as the moss under her fingertips. He didn't love Ella, never had. And even if he was the very prince she'd spent so many months hating and cursing for being a blind idiot and getting them all into this mess, he was Will too, and she loved him. Just thinking about it was enough to make her eyes water, and she couldn't afford that, not now.

She couldn't explain it to him before. There hadn't been any time. Once she realized her heart's truth, they had to leave, and what she had to say wasn't for the ears of everyone else—just him.

But they had to survive this first, had to make it. And she had to be still.

So when the scent of smoke and bitter herbs floated across her face, she didn't cough. When the fairy godmother touched her hair, she didn't scream.

"I suppose she'll do." Fabric swished as the fairy godmother moved away.

Anna dared let out a breath.

"Leave her over there," she said, as if Anna were a sack of grain.

"How do we wake her?" Koen asked, the spew of words so fast they nearly blended together.

Another swish and glide of fabric sounded across stone.

"How? Please!" He begged for Mina, she knew, and it nearly crushed her.

The sound stopped.

"Take them away," the godmother ordered, an edge to her voice.

"No!" Koen cried to deaf ears. Anna heard the scuffle of boots.

"Now?" This from Will, his voice raised over the commotion.

"Of course, now," the fairy godmother all but yelled. "Put the girl over there and leave."

"You heard her," Will said.

Her muscles clenched as her litter rocked and movement resumed. *Please, holy Mother.* They couldn't leave her here. Will hadn't betrayed them, surely not. She ached to leap to her feet and dash for the door.

"No! Anna!"

Nik's pained cry wrenched her heart.

"Anna?" the godmother asked, an edge to her tone. "That's not the name the queen gave me."

Oh, hells.

The men carrying her stopped. Heavy silence hung in the room, and she dared not breathe for fear it might be heard.

"Well," Will drawled, a hint of humor in his tone. "About that..."

Metal sang through the silence—blades pulled from sheaths.

"Guards!" the godmother called. "Traitors!"

The world fell out beneath her as the guards dropped the litter none too gently. Her back slammed against the stone floor, knocking the breath from her lungs. The fall sent her rolling to the side, and on instinct, Anna opened her eyes. Her palm slammed against the floor to steady herself. She gasped in a breath, wincing at the ache from the tumble.

Spots danced before her eyes as she adjusted to light after so long behind closed lids. The sight beyond was no better. A flurry of booted feet raced across the stone floor. Swords clanged. Wood groaned and splintered as it was forced open, sending men stumbling back amid the chaos. The black-clad Shadow Guards moved as if possessed—silent and lethal.

Light flashed against steel as Will tossed a blade to Nik. He turned to block the strike of a man who'd barreled in from the room beyond. Anna fought back a scream.

She had to do something, but what? Anna had never been skilled with a blade. Nor did she have one to wield.

Droplets of blood splattered on the stones near her hand. Nausea crept up her throat. She bit it back, refusing to consider the source.

Off to the side stood the fairy godmother, an old crone of a woman dressed in a hooded robe. Bits of shimmering blue fabric peeked out between the sides of the cloak that obscured much of her form. She used her desk as a shield—crouched between it and the massive shelves clinging to the wall. All sorts of colorful bottles and jars lined them, but the Mother only knew what those contained.

Anna shoved to her feet. Resolve stilled the slight tremor running through her. She could get to the fairy godmother and take her captive. Someone had to.

One of Will's men dueled a Shadow Guard. The fury of the guard's blows sent the man stumbling between her and the godmother.

Anna leaped back, avoiding an errant swing of a blade. The edge of something hard bit against her spine. She whirled, coming face-to-face with a large window, its hinged panes closed. The walled inner yard spread out below. A few figures still walked through the gloaming, oblivious to the chaos within. One had long hair in a braid down their back, their form and gait all too familiar. Anna's breath hitched. For the briefest moment, the world froze and the battle behind her silenced.

Charlotte. It has to be.

Anna flew into action as the din of the struggle returned, louder than before. Cries and groans of pain sent a spike of dread through her middle. *No time to look. No time for fear.* She fumbled with the metal clasp holding the panes together, then shoved them apart.

"Charlotte!"

The figure stopped and turned her way. The basket in the woman's arms tumbled to the ground.

If what Will had said was true, they had more allies outside this room, and Charlotte would find a way to help.

Please. Please be right.

A muted squeal teased Anna's ears before the woman took off at a run. Guards rushed along a far wall. Anna slammed the windows shut. *Damn.* Allies or enemies, she didn't know, but they certainly had some idea something wasn't right.

The hard, wet sound of a blade stabbing deep made her twist around fast.

Anna gasped at the sight of a sword plunged into the Shadow Guard's stomach. Will's man twisted the blade, dropping the guard to his knees.

Beyond, the fairy godmother worked in earnest. She no longer hid but grasped one potion after another, dumping them together into the heavy cauldron dominating one side of the desk. She turned to sneer at the dying guard. Her lips curled back, showing yellowed teeth—more missing than not.

Faster than an ancient crone should be able to move, the godmother snatched a bottle from the shelf and hurled it at Will's man. He barely flinched as the glass shattered against his leg and spilled its contents. A fly might have bothered him more. All his focus remained on the dying man in front of him.

But then his eyes widened. He screamed, losing his hold on the blade.

Anna watched in horror as a wave of grey rushed from where the potion had landed on him, racing across his skin and clothes alike until all was solid and still.

She clasped her shaking hands over her mouth.

Stone. The potion turned the man to stone.

The dying guard grabbed the blade, pulled it from his gut, and swung the hilt toward Will's man. One touch, and he crumbled into a pile of rocks. The Shadow Guard went down with him, falling atop his own blood and spilled entrails.

One splatter of potion and the man had turned to stone. Now he was dead—shattered.

Any of them could share his fate if the fairy godmother had another such potion in her arsenal.

Frantically, she scanned the crowd for Nik, but it was Brandt who caught her attention as he dodged blows from a man with a blank expression and even more vacant eyes.

"Hans!" he roared after blocking another blow. "Snap out of it!"

A sick certainty settled into her stomach. He fought his brother, or rather, tried to keep his brother from killing him.

In her periphery, the fairy godmother stretched for another potion off a high shelf.

She had to stop her, couldn't let anymore of her friends suffer or die.

Anna rushed forward, crouching to pick up a fist-sized stone that once had been part of a man. Perhaps he'd have some measure of vengeance in this. She hurled it with all her might at the fairy godmother. The stone struck her arm, causing the old woman to cry out and drop the last of the vial she poured into her cauldron.

"You bitch!" she screeched, holding her wounded arm.

Smoke rose from the iron pot, though there was no fire Anna could see. Bubbles followed, deceptively beautiful as they floated upward before popping.

Anna grabbed another stone and threw it. It missed, smashing into the shelves and spilling substances everywhere. The fairy godmother hissed and jumped back, the mess a narrow moat between them.

The fairy godmother grabbed something from the shelves and tossed it at Anna as she reached for another stone. Anna froze, a stone in her palm, as the jar swished by, narrowly missing her face. It crashed behind her.

Shaken but undeterred, Anna rose. "Stop her!" Anna begged anyone who would listen. She hurled another stone. This one bounced off the rim of the cauldron.

The godmother tossed something in it, and a green mist rose. She narrowed her eyes at Anna as she lifted a worn stick from the table. "I've waited too long for this. Too long!" She jabbed the stick into the cauldron, swirling it faster and faster.

Anna tossed her last rock. The godmother cried out but didn't break her focus on the task. A terrible chill slid down Anna's spine. Whatever magic steamed and bubbled in that cauldron was awful, evil. She couldn't let the fairy godmother use it.

Gritting her teeth, she clambered over the pile of stones.

The fairy godmother pulled her stick from the cauldron and aimed it at Anna. Every muscle in her body locked up as Anna stared it down. The point shimmered and glowed like flame but didn't burn.

The witch cackled. "Farewell, dearie."

35

S weat slid down Nik's back as he slammed the pommel of his borrowed blade into the side of the man's head, knocking him unconscious. The older man fought with all the strength and fury of one in his prime, and by the glazed expression frozen on his face, none of it was his choice.

He'd never seen control so strong, so absolute, and he sure as all the heavens and hells wasn't about to punish the old man for it. But he'd had to stop him. Whatever compulsion pushed the workers to attack them lacked mercy and care for those it wielded as mindless weapons.

"I've got him." Koen rolled the man over and set about binding his arms. A thin cut marred one cheek, but otherwise his friend was unharmed.

"Room clear!" one of Will's men shouted from the far side as he tightened the knot binding an unconscious woman's legs. "We'll get the hall."

Will's men. The oddity struck him even amid the chaos. His friend had held true, as had his men. A lucky thing, since the fairy godmother had set not only her Shadow Guard but also the workers upon them. "Watch them," Nik ordered with a gesture to the unconscious man.

He didn't wait for Koen's response before rushing back toward the scuffle ongoing in the room laden with potions. The sharp tang of blood filled the air, overriding the pungent herbs and other foul maladies that had permeated it on their arrival.

Will filled the space just beyond the door, his blade thrust through the chest of a Shadow Guard struggling and fighting through the throes of death. Nik's jaw tightened, his teeth grinding together. There'd be no sparing that one.

The guard—silent to the last—gave one last twitch and went still. Will jerked his blade free.

But it wasn't his friend he worried for. Will could take care of himself. Anna, on the other hand...

"Stop her!"

The familiar voice cut through the din of battle straight to his heart. Nik's head snapped toward it in time to see Anna hurl a stone at the fairy godmother. He lunged toward her, only to have his path blocked by Brandt, who wrestled with another man—his brother, by the looks of it.

The witch shouted something. Anna hurled another stone.

Have to get to her. Have to.

Fear took control of him, forcing his movements as the old crone pulled something from the steaming cauldron and pointed it at Anna. "No!"

He pushed through the fighting, heedless of the danger to himself.

The tip of the object glowed with eerie light. Anna stood frozen, her eyes wide.

"Move!" he shouted.

Nik's heart hammered against his ribs. Rage boiled his blood.

I can't lose her. Not now.

Never.

An inhuman cackle cracked through the room. Light blared.

Nik leaped the last few feet to Anna.

Her gasping scream echoed in his ears as he wrapped her in his arms and they slammed to the floor together.

Sharp pain raced under his skin, but not from the impact of the fall. That was a dull thrum compared to the cold needles stabbing into him everywhere, inside and out.

He released Anna to claw at his skin. His back bowed, seeming to crack and twist on itself. Spots clouded his vision. Air became scarce.

"Nik! Nik!" Anna's pained cry slipped through the haze of suffering, a torment all its own.

He was helpless to go to her, to do anything but thrash in agony on the floor as the life seeped from him.

Cold. So fucking cold.

A furious screech echoed through the room, so loud it could have been right in his ears.

He shivered hard enough to make his teeth rattle.

"No! No! It can't be!" the witch screamed.

Will's voice followed, the words there and gone like water in the stream. Something soft and warm touched his arms, the only comfort in all the world.

"Nik," Anna sobbed.

Suddenly, the cold receded. It burned away like morning frost, taking the stabbing pain with it. The soreness in his limbs remained—aches from the battle and the fall. But that pain was familiar, an old friend who visited often. The rest of it was new, wrong, crippling.

He tried to move then, but everything took more effort than it should have, as if his body were a blade gone to rust and ruin. Even his sight was blurred and refused to fully clear as he gazed at Anna where she knelt at his side and wrapped her arms around him. Fat tears plopped against his cheek.

"You're hurt." The words cracked from his lips, all frail and wrong.

She shook her head. "I'm fine, really. But you—" Her words choked off in a barely leashed sob.

"Let go of me, you ingrates!"

The sounds of battle had ceased, replaced by the fairy godmother's fury, a groan of pain, and Will's commanding voice. "Go! Secure the compound!"

Boots thumped away in the wake of his words as Nik pushed into a sitting position.

"Anna." He reached for her, aimed to brush the tears from her cheek, and froze.

The hand that moved to touch her wasn't his. It couldn't be. It belonged to some old man, all withered and wrinkled like spoiled fruit. Age spots marred skin too pale to be his.

A shiver of uncertainty wound through the confusion. His hand shook. Teeth too frail and chipped chattered together. "Anna?"

"Oh, Nik." She threw her arms around him, pulling him tight against her in a hug far too strong for her lithe form.

A deep well of fear opened within him and sent his stomach bottoming out.

"You shouldn't have. Why?" Her voice cracked over the words. "She wanted me."

"That's right, you little bitch!" The godmother's voice was deeper, stronger.

"Shut it, witch!" Will snarled, then sucked in a sharp breath. "Nik..."

Nik closed his eyes and leaned against Anna, savoring her warmth and strength. All at once, he knew what happened and why the fairy godmother had wanted the fairest in the land.

One rattling deep breath after another steadied his nerves as he carefully pulled himself from Anna's embrace and twisted around.

The fairy godmother was a far cry from the old crone she'd been. A spotty beard coated her face. The cloak she'd hidden beneath had been shed. Muscled limbs had ripped the seams of her sleeves, mere threads keeping them in place. She'd grown taller, leaving her hem to fall just past her knees. Though most shocking of all were the gossamer things twitching where they rose just above her back.

"Wings?" He gaped at the sight.

He assumed she played at being a fairy creature, used it to bolster her reputation. And yet here they were, shimmering thin and frail as a spider's web, and they surely hadn't come from him.

"A pixie," Will spat. "And not the friendly sort."

Nik blinked at the woman, even as she sneered at him wearing his stolen youth and strength.

People talked of them, especially in islands and the lands bordering the Cerulean Sea. But here? He'd never met one in all his years. Traders from afar told stories sometimes: dust that could let a man fly off to pleasant dreams, the tonics some brewed, fortunes rare ones could tell, how they healed the land after storms. But magic like this? Never. Mostly pixies kept to themselves. Or so it was said.

When he first heard of her, he'd wagered the fairy godmother was a wizard from far east, past the mountains. Some humans were born with magic there, rare as it may be. Or possibly he thought she might even be an exiled noble from the north where their goddess was said to have blessed some of their nobility with skills beyond normal man. But she was a fairy creature after all, a pixie turned to evil, one who corrupted her nature.

One of Will's men, a head taller than him, held the pixie firm, arms bound behind her. Will slid his dagger free and pointed it at the godmother's throat. "What'd you do to him?"

She snorted air through her nose and raised her chin, defiant.

Koen joined them in the room. He froze halfway through wiping his brow, his wide-eyed gaze locked on Nik as he paled. "Mother above. Nik?"

Brandt stilled a half-step behind him. "Fucking hells."

Some of the weight fell from his shoulders. His friends lived, even if he now had one foot in the grave.

"You've lost, witch." Will adjusted his grip, undeterred. "I've far more men loyal to me than you." His gaze slid to Nik. "Loyal to our rightful king."

Nik stiffened. Potentially revealing his identity was a foolish risk.

Will seemed to catch his mistake. A brief wince flitted across his features.

"Heal him," Anna pleaded with the fairy godmother. She crouched beside him, an arm around his shoulders. Anyone but her, and he'd have shrugged her away for fear of looking as weak as he felt. "Undo this spell."

"And become an old crone once more?" A bitter smile accented her features as she glanced up at Will. "As you said, I've lost. Why give up my youth?"

"That's why you wanted our sister," Koen said. "You wanted her youth. Her beauty."

The fairy godmother's smile grew. "Magic can't stop the flow of time, but the best can steal it from another. Why settle for less than the best?"

The cackle that followed had his nails digging into his palm, drawing blood. Koen lunged for her like a cat gone rabid, and Brandt—Brandt of all people—had to hold him back.

"How do we wake our sister?" Koen demanded as he struggled against his brother. "You worked your spell. You have your youth. Let us wake her."

Nik's jaw stiffened, and he fought the urge to grind his teeth. The bitch would never tell. He could see it in her smug look.

"Tell us." Will angled the blade at her neck. A bead of crimson spilled down the edge. Even an evil pixie could bleed.

"The most complex spells sometimes have the simplest cures." She notched her chin higher, as if proud of herself even in the face of defeat. Her nose twitched once. "True love's kiss."

A knot of tension uncoiled in a rush. *So simple?* There had to be a trick to it.

"True love?" Koen's shoulders dropped, all the strength gone out of him. Brandt barely kept him on his feet.

"She's just a girl. Unwed," Brandt stammered.

"If you lie, witch—" Nik said, rising to his feet with Anna's help.

She looked between them all, a sneer curling her lips. "What's the problem? No true love?" A dark cackle spilled from her.

Mina's true love? But she'd never... Realization dawned, and he looked down at Anna, sorrow etched across her features.

Mina had been enamored with Ansel, of the young man he thought Anna was.

"Ansel." Hope sparked across Brandt's normally gruff features, lighting him up. "She was more than a little sweet on ya, er, him."

Anna dropped her gaze and shook her head slowly from side to side. At length, she raised it and looked to each of them with tear-glazed eyes. "She knew."

Anna sucked in a deep breath and scooted closer to him. Nik's arms wrapped around her on instinct. He'd longed to hold her again, and now she finally came to him—when it was too late.

"Mina knew I wasn't Ansel," she said to the brothers.

"But—" Brandt sputtered.

"I told her before we went to the castle, when we were changing." Anna looked away again.

No wonder Mina had seemed so off that morning. It wasn't just the ruse they'd planned, the risk they took. She'd had her heart broken in a way.

Crushing emptiness hollowed him out. The girl had no true love, no one to free her except the evil witch before them.

Nik saw it a moment too late. The fairy godmother jumped back from the blade, using the distraction of their heartbreak to smash her head against the man holding her and sweep Will's legs out from under him with her newfound strength. His friend hit the stone floor with a heavy thump and deep groan. The other man held his face, blood pouring down from his broken nose.

Fuck.

He had to stop her before she hurt anyone else. Nik summoned what strength he had to pull away from Anna. Her protests fell on deaf ears as he raced across the space between them.

The fairy godmother grabbed a bloodied sword from the ground. "Fool," she spat. She heaved the blade, swinging a wide arc just as he came between her and the wall of shelves laden with potions. Nik ducked, or rather fell, with creaking knees to dodge the blade. He hit the floor with a cry. The fairy godmother teetered and stumbled forward. The stolen strength had unbalanced her as she swung, just as he'd expected. She may have taken his body, in a way, but not his mind. The fairy godmother failed to catch herself, crashing into the wall of potions.

Glass shattered. Pungent scents nearly choked him. Colorful powder and smoke plumed around the fairy godmother as she gave an unearthly wail, scratching and clawing at herself where the spilled contents touched.

Nik scurried further away as she thrashed and shattered more jars. Will had regained his footing and stared wide-eyed. Anna, Brandt, and Koen did the same. Even the man with the broken nose watched on in horror.

He'd thought the potions might distract her, or at least enrage her enough for them to gain the advantage. But as he watched her fall to the floor, steaming and convulsing, absolute dread crept up his back with clawed fingers to tighten around his throat and draw him tight as a bowstring.

The fairy godmother gave one last eerie cry and stretched a burned and welted arm toward Nik. The last of her wail still hung in the air as her body burst into glittering dust.

Now they were well and truly doomed.

36

*R*evenge gave no absolution, only deepened the endless ache in Anna's soul.

She turned away from the pile of dust and clothes that had been the fairy godmother. Anna covered her mouth with her hand and prayed to the Mother and all her saints to keep the contents of her stomach from spewing across the floor.

Tears stung her eyes anew, and she let them fall.

How could they possibly wake Mina now? Or heal Nik? A silent scream roared through her head. Nik, who had taken the blast aimed at her, the spell meant to steal her youth and what little beauty she could claim as her own.

She'd been so angry with him, hurt. And yet he'd still risked his life for hers. *No, not risked, given.*

"What the fuck do we do now?" Brandt bellowed into the quiet room.

Unchecked emotion forced its way up her throat, ending in a scream as she tore at her short hair.

"Anna?" A voice called from outside the room.

She drew in a sharp breath. Her eyes fluttered against the tears. "Charlotte?"

Anna was on her feet and halfway across the room before she could think. Men spilled in through the doorway, causing her to draw up quick.

"Manor secure," the one in the lead said.

Will's men. Allies, some rational part of her mind whispered.

And then Charlotte was there, pushing past the men and forcing her way into the room. She froze for the briefest moment, her gaze locking with Anna's before they raced toward each other and met in a crushing embrace.

"Charlotte." Anna couldn't conjure up more than her sister's name. She was there. *Here. Alive!*

Tears streamed down her face as she buried it in the crook of her sister's neck, inhaling the familiar hint of lavender that clung to her even here. Charlotte pulled her close, stroking her hair and muttering words too laden with unchecked emotion to understand. After all this time, they were finally reunited, finally free. But Charlotte wasn't the only family member who'd been captured.

Anna released her sister and pulled back just enough to see her face. "Mama?"

Charlotte nodded, smiling amid her own tears. "She's here."

Another sob tore free, this one filled with relief. Anna's shaking knees gave way. Charlotte followed her, taking her in her arms again as they held each other on the stone floor smattered with the signs of struggle and death.

The others gave them space, carrying on their own conversations, which buzzed in the background. Anna ignored them. Charlotte was here. Their mother was still alive too. For one brief and fleeting moment, joy filled her heart.

Then *his* voice joined this distant conversation. Nik. Her reckless huntsman turned lost king. Anna's throat tightened, and she clung to Charlotte harder, grieving for all she'd gained and lost—all he'd given for her even after she'd shunned him.

When the sisters finally broke apart, Charlotte wiped at her eyes, ever the strong one trying to erase her tears. She'd lost weight these months. It accented her cheekbones and made her whole face sharper.

"I knew you'd save us." Charlotte cupped Anna's cheek, her once soft palm now calloused and coarse.

A huff of humorless laughter flew from her lips. Anna had been far less sure. But in the end, she'd had little to do with her sister's rescue other than play a young woman cursed to sleep. *Mina.* Her heart clenched tight once more.

"I prayed to the Mother every night to help you."

Anna raised her brows at that. Her older sister had never been particularly pious.

"Well." Charlotte slanted her gaze away and shrugged. "Some nights. But I wanted to be ready for when you came. I thought maybe I could help weaken them from within. Luckily, I wasn't the only one." Her attention flicked to Will and back, the lightest touch of color rising to her cheeks.

"Thank you." What else could she say? There weren't enough words for it. "How did you manage it? Figuring out how to avoid the potion, gathering allies?"

Now it was Charlotte's turn to lift one brow. "How did you? I'd wager there's a story there."

Anna forced a smile. Even Charlotte's tone had changed, gone back to the more casual tongue from their youth by the sea. The formal airs they'd tried to don after their mother's second marriage had vanished surely as the sun below the horizon.

"Too long a one to tell right now."

Charlotte merely nodded and helped her rise. No doubt her sister's story was as well. Anna glanced at Nik where he stood among a cluster of men. Their eyes caught and held. His once brown hair, rich as the forest trees, had turned fully grey, his beard too. Deep wrinkles lined his face. He hunched slightly, rather than standing tall and steady as he always had. But his eyes, those brown eyes she'd once loathed in the face of the haughty prince, hadn't changed.

"Where's the fairy godmother?" Charlotte asked. "She escape?"

Anna shivered. "Not exactly."

"Dead." Will turned their way. A bitter hardness edged his features.

Yes, they'd taken the manor, but at what cost? To what end? With Nik as he was, older than even the former king had been, it'd be impossible to present him as their not-so-dead king. Who would believe that?

"Pity." Charlotte wrinkled her nose. "I'd liked to have killed that bitch myself if I'd ever had the chance."

At that, Will grinned.

Nearby, Brandt and Koen knelt over a bound, prone form—their brother, by the bits of conversation she caught.

"What can we do for them? Those who were under the godmother's compulsion?" Anna glanced between Will and Charlotte. They'd overcome it, at least Will had.

His lips thinned once more. "Time."

It was a luxury they might not have, especially not once Ella learned of the fairy godmother's demise. Anna grimaced.

"Unless we can find something in this wreck." He gestured around him. "Though after what happened to that witch, I don't want anyone near the stuff on that wall."

She shuddered at the memories that tried to overtake her, of both the godmother and their fallen ally. Did Will even know about his friend who lay as rubble mere feet away? A tang of bile burned her throat. The evil pixie's death hadn't reversed her spells.

"Let's look through her books, her records." Koen rose, dusting off his pants. "Where's her room?"

Smart. Anything of true value she'd keep close at hand.

"Upstairs," Will said. "Some books here too, but who can make sense of that stuff?"

Koen swallowed. "I might."

Will looked at him askance. Charlotte took a step back.

"He's right." Anna left her sister's side to stand with Koen. "He knows herbal medicine." She took his hand and gave it a squeeze. "Some of it may be the same. Worth a try."

"Be good if all your puttering came to something," Brandt grumbled at their backs. "Smellin' up the house all the time."

Koen rolled his eyes. "Let me try, at least." He kept his voice calm, stoic as his demeanor, but Anna could feel the tremor running under his skin, the barely contained fear for his siblings still trapped under spells.

"Done." Will gave a jerking nod and held out his hand to Koen, who took it. "Better yet, some of us can help you search."

Koen nodded in return. "But first, we find our other brothers."

There were three more. Anna's chest drew tight. Hopefully, the rest were in better shape.

The men went to their task, and Anna once again searched for Nik. The moment she spotted him, still where he'd been, Charlotte slipped her arm around her. "We can help in a bit, but we need to check on Mama. She's been so worried for you these months."

Mama. Her heart leaped with joy once more. "Where is she?"

"She was tending to some of the wounded. This way." Charlotte practically dragged her from the room, but Anna dug her heels in. She caught Nik's attention again and mouthed "Mama."

He nodded once, his look filled with more than she could comprehend. She returned it. "I'll be back," she promised. That was all she had time for before Charlotte pulled her away.

37

The pages of the book were all a blur. At first, Nik had been able to squint to make them out, straining his eyes in the dim light from the dripping candles smattered over the table. This manor was built before gas lamps, and it hadn't been updated since they came into use like the castle had been. More the pity, since his aged sight was poor at best and more light could only help.

He shoved the book away with a heavy sigh.

"Nothing useful?" Will asked as he emerged through the open door. He'd spent most of the evening seeing to the security of the compound and mourning his lost comrades. Men died in battle, even small ones such as this. Nik had known death would follow them today, theirs or their enemies. It still didn't make it any easier. The knowledge of it turned his stomach, and he'd never even met some of the fallen. At least they had moved quick, stopped those loyal to the fairy godmother and the queen from fleeing to the castle with news of their conquest. It would give them time to plan and protect those here.

Tomorrow they would burn the bodies of the fallen, send them back to the Mother's waiting embrace.

After that...

He glanced out the window at the dark night beyond. Clouds obscured the moon, blocking even that bit of light—dim as the little hope they had left. Nik saw the accusation in Will's eyes, felt the weight of the words his friend had yet to utter.

He was the key to their victory. The piece that would turn the tide.

Or I had been. No one would believe he was their lost king now, aged well beyond his father's years.

They'd ransacked the fairy godmother's private rooms searching for a cure. For him, for those lingering under her influence—now tied and bound in makeshift cells until they were themselves again—and for Mina.

Will insisted Nik stay inside. For his safety, of course. Though Nik guessed his friend held some kernel of hope that they could fix this, that their grand plan hadn't gone up in smoke with the fairy godmother. Once the men saw him like this, they might lose hope. So he'd stayed out of sight, searching the manor with a few others.

Books and tomes they'd found aplenty, all manner of potions too. And then there'd been the mirror. A shudder gripped him, and he wrapped his frail arms around himself. It was a smaller version of the one in the throne room, but just as odd and eerie. Mist swirled beyond the glass. It had to be the one the old witch used to communicate with Cinderella, they'd found no other. Nik ordered it covered with a sheet and the room locked until they figured out what to do with it.

"Nik?" Will asked again. Chair legs scraped on the stone floor as he took a seat across the table.

Nik shook the cobwebs from his thoughts. "Can't read the damn thing." It hurt to admit it, almost as bad as the way his joints ached every time he moved. He had a feeling it would only get worse as the night dragged on.

"Ah." Will clucked his tongue. "We should you get you to bed, old man."

The attempted humor did nothing to soften his mood. It only deepened the frown pulling at his lips. Age wasn't the only thing wearing on him. He thought Anna would return. He could have sworn she said she'd be back. Besides, the way she'd held him, cried for him, planted a seed of hope. Saints alive, the look in her eyes alone nearly ripped him to bits. There was so much to tell her.

But her sister had taken her away, and she hadn't come back.

Why would she? His mind taunted him. She had what she wanted, her sister and mother safe. They could leave, flee somewhere far away from all this. After all, their plan was a ruin, and he truly had nothing left to give her, not even himself—aged as he was.

Nik was happy for her, truly he was, despite the deep ache that he couldn't rub out of his chest. Anna was happy, safe—for now. She had her family. But he wanted more. It ate at him constantly and consumed his thoughts. That desire nearly drove him to ignore Will's request to remain indoors, to ignore reason and seek her out.

That was the trouble with wanting. It bred all sorts of ill-advised ideas.

"Come on, let's get you up." Will rose from his chair with fluid ease and rounded the table.

Nik waved him off. "I can stand on my own." But as he did, spots colored his eyes, his back popped, and he nearly stumbled to the ground.

"Woah there." Will wrapped an arm around him.

"Damn." Reluctantly, Nik leaned against his friend. "This is awful." No wonder the fairy godmother wanted his strength and youth. Well, not his, but better him suffering like this than Anna.

"That's why you need rest."

Nik snorted air through his nose. *As if that will help.*

"Got a room all set up for you. How long since you had a bed?"

Too long. And his body knew it. He wouldn't be getting any rest on the ground, not with what the witch had done to him.

"Besides." Will clapped him on the shoulder as he helped him down the hall. "Can't have you dying on us."

"Right. Can't mess up our plans any further, huh?"

Will briefly stiffened, almost missing a step. "Yeah, well..." He drawled. "We'll figure it out. Just get some rest, huh?" They stopped in front of a door. "If you can anyway." Will winked at him.

Nik's brows drew together, but Will sauntered away with a backward wave before he could ask more.

Somehow, Will always managed to find the bright side of a situation, even when all the world was going to shit. He'd envied him that for years —among other things. He may have been born to royalty, but Will would have been a far better ruler. His friend had all the smarts, skills, and talents Nik's father would have admired—if he'd bothered to notice anyone other than his own reflection and the chancellor. Most importantly, Will would never have fallen for Cinderella's false charms.

With a sigh toward his friend's retreating form, Nik pushed open the door.

The sight inside stole the breath from his lungs.

He had to be dreaming, must have fallen while standing up and hit his head.

The room was ordinary enough—simple, plain, and small. But the woman sitting on the narrow mattress was a wonder.

Anna rose, a tentative smile breaking across her features before her cheeks flushed and she looked at her feet. She still wore the borrowed dress. It fit her as well as one of her own might, but she'd be radiant in anything. Nothing could dim the beauty of her spirit that outshone any physical beauty.

His throat grew tight. His body refused to move.

She pulled her bottom lip between her teeth as she glanced back up at him. "Would you come in?" She bunched the fabric of her skirts in her hands.

"Your mother?" he croaked out, easing inside the threshold.

All at once, her face lit with joy. *Good.* He'd asked the right thing.

"She's well." Anna pushed at her hair, tucking the short strands behind one ear. "A little thin, tired." She sucked in a breath. "But well. So much better than I even hoped for."

Heady warmth stretched out to his limbs. He'd never had great love for his father, not the way he ought to have. But he'd cared deeply for Will and his father, Wilhelm. He hadn't realized it before, had been too consumed with himself, but he loved them. They weren't the only ones either. Koen, Brandt, Mina, and now Anna. He loved more than he ever believed possible.

"I'm glad." It was the most honest thing he'd said that evening. Nik closed the door behind him. The moment it shut, the air grew thick. Perhaps that was a mistake, but it was too late now.

They both began at once.

"Did you—"

"Are you—"

Nik rubbed at the back of his neck and looked away. "Ladies first."

Anna crossed the space between them, stopping just short. Nik drank her in, memorizing the sparkle of her eyes, the little bow of her lips, the way her short hair framed her face. If this was the last time he saw her, if this was goodbye, he'd etch this memory into his soul to treasure for all time. Or whatever time was left to him.

"Thank you." The words flew out in a rush. "It was supposed to be me. You—" A sheen of tears filled her eyes, and she blinked rapidly. "You could have died." Her voice cracked.

Nik reached for her, but the flood of words continued. "They need you. What were you thinking?" She stomped her foot. "They can't take the kingdom back without you."

A tear streaked down her face. Nik wiped it away with his thumb and the next as it fell. His weathered hand lingered on her cheek, savoring the feel of her soft, smooth skin beneath his palm.

"I wasn't," he admitted, throat thick. "But if I had been thinking, if there'd been time, I'd have made the same decision."

Anna's lips wobbled. "Nik, I—"

Something heavy and terrible tumbled in his stomach. This was it, where she tried to tell him goodbye. Or worse, she decided to stay and fight their hopeless battle. They couldn't win. Not with him stuck like this. "You're safe now," he rushed on. "Free. You have your family. I'm sure there's gold here or something of value you can sell or trade. Take your mother and your sister. Get away from here. Start a new life."

Anna flinched as if he'd struck her. "You really think I'd leave you?"

Words clung to the tip of his tongue, unsaid. *You should.*

Her lips pressed thin. Determination shone in her eyes as she closed the short distance between them and reached for his face.

Nik stiffened, leaning away. "Anna, what are you—"

Anna clasped his cheeks between her palms. "Kiss me, you idiot."

"But I'm—" *Old. Decrepit. Unworthy.*

Her deep sigh teased his lips. "I don't care what you look like." She caressed his cheek, and he shuddered. The touch, so soft, warm, and gentle, nearly had his heart leaping out of his chest. "Didn't you tell me that once? That it didn't matter what others thought of me? What I looked like? That I was beautiful to you?"

"Yes." He trembled at the fierceness in her gaze. "I did. You are."

Another tear slipped down her cheek, curling over his skin before he thought to brush it away. "Then how could you doubt me? You're still Nik. And I love you. How could I ever leave you now?"

"You—" The word echoed through him. "You love me?" he asked in disbelief. Even knowing he was the king, that he'd married her wicked stepsister, that he'd doomed them all. And now he was an old man, one foot in the grave.

A sad smile lifted the corners of her lips. "I love you, Nik."

She leaned in. He didn't fight it, only pulled her closer, his fingers gently sliding into her hair as her lips touched his.

His heart pounded so hard he might die—literally. But Nik didn't care. There'd be no better way to go than with Anna in his arms, her breath in his lungs, her sweet scent sending his head spinning. He tugged her closer, savoring the moan that slipped from her as she leaned into his chest.

The kiss was soft, tentative, full of love so tender it nearly broke him. Heat flushed his face. His chest burned up from within. Every bit of his skin tingled with a mix of pain and pleasure that he couldn't get enough of.

No kiss had ever been like this. Not their pretend one in the castle, nor their first real one in the cabin, and certainly none of the kisses he'd shared with others before then. This was life, water in the desert, air trapped below the surface. And he couldn't get enough, never enough.

His body trashed in the throes of passion from her simple, careful embrace, like his heart might leap from his chest or his bones powder to dust. It had to be age, the surge of emotion too strong for this old body to handle. *It's worth it, so damn worth it.*

Anna pulled back, her teeth tugging at his bottom lip with the sweetest bite before she released him. Nik cracked his eyes open to be greeted by her blinding smile and tear-streaked face. Her chest heaved with what could be sobs mixing with laughter for the sounds that bubbled out between them.

"Oh, Nik…"

He grinned at her in return, feeling as strong as he had that evening—maybe ever. His brows drew together. Her touch was so intoxicating, so precious, his body forgot for a moment it was wasting away. His hand flexed on her back, and for one wild moment, he pictured lifting her in his arms and carrying her to the bed.

The act would break him, he knew. And she couldn't want him *that way*, not as he was now, even if she loved him. Still, the fantasy sent his head spinning, his body thrumming with joy.

Nik froze as he glimpsed a mirror sitting across the room on the dressing table. No, not a mirror, it had to be a window because Will held a woman in his arms, but she—

He sucked in a sharp breath. "Anna?"

He pulled his hands between them and stared in wonder. *Tan, calloused skin, no wrinkles, no age spots.*

Anna nodded. "Sometimes," she said with a sniffle, "the most complicated magic has the simplest cure. Isn't that what the fairy godmother said?"

"True love's kiss." He touched his cheeks in wonder. Gone were the signs of age. His body ached, sore from battle and use, but not in the bone-deep way it had only moments ago. "I'm back."

Anna leaped for him. He caught her, pulling her against him as she buried her face in his shirt and let out a cry.

A tingling feeling rushed under his skin. He was back, his youth and strength returned. He blinked, holding her tight, grasping at the impossibility of it all. Radiant joy welled up within him, pushing away everything else and sending his chest shaking in heaves of relief and wonder.

"Y-you saved me." His fingers slid through Anna's hair.

She glanced up at him, her head cradled in his palm. "You saved me first. It's the least I could do."

"True love's kiss," he said again, still unable to fully believe it. "I do love you, Anna. So much."

She sniffled once more and blinked away her tears. "I love you too, Nik, and I won't leave you, no matter what."

"Never ever." It was as much an answer as a promise.

Then Nik kissed her, sharing all his love, all his passion, all his praise.

She was the perfect woman he never knew he wanted, and more than he ever deserved.

38

*I*t worked. *It actually, really worked.*

     Anna clung to Nik as if he might vanish, might slide through her fingers like smoke and be gone forever. She loved reconnecting with Charlotte and her mother. They were safe. Together again. It was the one thing she'd worked toward and dreamed about all these long months. But somewhere along the way, she'd found something she'd long ago given up searching for—true love.

She deepened their kiss, twining her arms around his neck as Nik lifted her from the floor and into his arms.

She hadn't lied to him. Anna would have loved him old and withered as he was, but young again, they had time—a future.

A tremor of anticipation coiled through her center as Nik laid her atop the narrow bed and followed her down. His weight pressed against her, warm and all-consuming. But then his tongue flicked out to tangle with hers, and everything vanished into the feeling of his kiss. He lapped at her like a man starved, taking everything she had to give and begging for more. Anna gave it willingly, meeting him in a joining of passion.

Delicious warmth spiraled out from her center. Her pulse thrummed between her legs, her core already slick and needy. Anna's fingers wound through his hair, savoring its silken feel, so different from moments ago.

She pressed him to her as if somehow she could get him even closer, could merge their spirits so nothing could separate them no matter what was to come.

She whimpered as he pulled back, Nik's heated breaths on her cheek. His lips planted a quick kiss there. Then he trailed to the lobe of her ear, the crook of her neck. Anna ground her hips against him, impatient, but he only chuckled and licked at the pulse hammering in her throat.

"I promised you a bed, but I hoped for more than this," he said, voice thick.

A heady laugh slipped from her throat. "I'd have you anywhere." *This bed. The floor. Under the stars.* She'd wanted him that night in the shed and would have had him if not for his desire to do things properly...or the wall of secrets she couldn't manage to climb over.

She understood now, somewhat, why he'd kept his identity a secret. Truly, she'd have done the same if he hadn't figured her out—at least for a little while longer, until she was certain of him. But wanting him? That'd she'd been sure of far longer.

Nik nipped at her, grazing his teeth along her sensitive skin, a tease, the slightest hint of pleasurable pain. "My Anna." Her heart swelled at the desire laced in his words. Nik's calloused hand ventured under her bunched dress, sliding up her leg. "I got us to bed too soon."

"Too soon?" She arched against him, feeling the bulge of his desire through his pants.

He chuckled deep in his throat. "It may not be the place I'd have chosen, but I'd still like you naked. Nothing between us." He raised up on his knees and pulled off his shirt. "I want to see you, Anna. All of you." He reached for his belt.

Desire bloomed brighter in her core, and her thighs pressed together of their own accord, trapping his knees. Suddenly the dress was too tight, the air too thin. She needed it off. Now.

She scooted back and slid off the bed, turning the laces on the back of the dress in his direction. "Perhaps you'd—"

But he was already tugging at them, eager intent etched on his features. She had the sudden urge to rip the dress free—might have if it hadn't been borrowed. Moments later, the dress slid to the floor, leaving her in only her thin chemise and simple underwear. Cool air tickled her skin, failing to calm her racing heart or tame the perspiration attempting to form across her skin. Behind her, she heard Nik shucking the last of his clothes—the thump of boots cast aside, the slide of breeches down his legs.

Suddenly, all her insecurities came rushing back, trying to spoil the moment. Ella's old taunts about her appearance echoed through her head. Memories of men's sneers or disregarding glances, usually in Ella's presence, flashed before her eyes. And that had been with her clothes on, her assets shown to the best she could muster. Even the few she'd lured closer barely looked or touched other than taking what they desired and never looking back.

Yes, Nik had seen her before. He'd made her feel things no one else had ever come close to. But Anna knew she was no great beauty, no beauty at all really. She was too skinny now, no real curves to speak of and plain features. Even the hair she'd once treasured was gone. Dirt marred her skin, tanned in places and pale in others. She was a mess at best—certainly not the lady her mother had once hoped she'd be.

And Nik was a king again, at least in the eyes of these people, and soon to be the whole kingdom if they had their way. She would be a joke at his side. Anna hugged her arms around herself. Her shoulders hunched as if she could hide from the man behind her, though her feet refused to move.

"Anna?" Doubt curled around her name like a lover.

"I—" *What to say?*

"You don't have to hide from me."

Her eyes squeezed closed. *Breathe. In and out.*

"If you don't want me—"

"I do!" It burst from her in a jolt.

"Then—"

She flinched from the movement in her periphery and spoke on. "You're sure you want me? You're a king. Young again. And I'm…" *I'm me. Just me.*

Anna gasped as his fingers toyed with the shoulder strap of her chemise. She couldn't manage a single rational thought as he caressed her skin, trailing his fingertips down her shoulder, her arm, and carrying the strap with them.

Nik's warmth crept to her from behind, though he'd yet to touch but one arm. His breath tickled the back of her neck, her ear. He kissed the curve of her neck, and she shuddered in pleasure, the cool night air stirring up gooseflesh on her heated skin.

"You loved me when I was older than my father." He pressed a kiss at the tip of her spine. "When I was the villain in your story." His beard scraped softly along her shoulder. "And perhaps even when I was no one but a wanted man with nothing to give." Another kiss teased her skin as he pulled the second strap free. The garment fell to the floor. "Do you really think my love so fickle?"

He reached around to splay his palm across her bare stomach. Every inch of her drew taut as he pressed against her from behind. *So warm. So firm.* And there was no mistaking the stiff prod of his erection at her lower back.

Slowly, oh so slowly, she relaxed against him, as much as she was able with desire clouding her thoughts.

"I love you, Anna," he whispered at her ear, his beard tickling her sensitive skin. "As you, as Ansel, as whoever you wish to be. If you won't believe my words, then believe my actions."

Gathering her courage, Anna turned in his arms. He held her tight against him, feeling *all* of him, his palm making little circles on her lower back. The hair on his chest teased her pert, small nipples.

Nik lowered his face to hers until their foreheads pressed together. "I want you, Anna. If you'll have me."

She laid her palm against his chest, feeling the heavy, racing thud of his heartbeat. "Yes. Yes, Nik. I want you." For however long she could have him, could live this dream, she wanted him.

Her acceptance still lingered in the air when Nik laid her upon the bed once more and covered her body with his. His knee urged her legs apart, and she opened for him, letting him settle against her underthings—thin and worn as they were.

Anna wound her arms around his neck as Nik's lips claimed hers once more, gentler this time, a slow savor compared to the earlier feast. They broke only for a moment, time for Nik to hook his fingers under the hem of her underthings, and at Anna's bashful nod, to tug them off. The night barely had time to caress her sex before Nik settled back between her legs, the hard length of him prodding at her entrance.

"I love you, Anna," he panted against her, their lips a breath apart.

"I love you too, Nik." She arched up, stealing his lips and pulling him back to her.

Pressure built at her entrance where the tip of his cock slid in her wetness, hot and eager. She widened her legs and flexed her hips against him. He eased inside. The edge of pain at his girth faded to bliss as he filled her, sinking deep into her wetness in a sure and solid thrust.

"Oh fuck," he groaned against her lips.

She had no words. There was nothing but the feel of him inside her. *So right.* So perfect, like he was the missing piece she'd finally found. He moved, sliding out and back in, sending a rush of pleasure rolling through her core. Tightness built low in her stomach, that wondrous feeling he crafted days before with his fingers and his tongue. But this—this was beyond that, a joining of souls as much as bodies, a winding and twisting that wouldn't end in a burst of release but remain tangled up within her.

They found their rhythm with ease, coming together until all thought fled and stars danced behind her eyes. She no longer knew where they were, couldn't remember her own name. All she knew was Nik, and it was his name she cried out as he brought her over an edge of pleasure so high and all-consuming that even that vanished in a cry of pleasure.

When she came back down, he was there, cradling her body, panting her name in his own pleasure. Sweat beaded on his skin and dampened his hair where she wound her fingers through it.

Neither slept that night, but as dawn broke over the world, Anna welcomed the day without fear and curled against Nik's chest in pure contentment.

39

*C*onversation died away to silence as Nik entered the room. Those gathered in the fairy godmother's old sitting room dipped into bows and curtseys. Nik pulled at the collar of his shirt. He had asked them *not* to do that, but some old habits died hard.

The morning after his first night with Anna, he'd met with Will. His friend had been overjoyed, Brandt, Koen, and their brothers too. Hope spread through the compound like a massive wave of joy, bringing bright smiles and laughter. Less than an hour later, everyone knew their king had returned. By that evening, thanks to Koen's skills in understanding the fairy godmother's ramblings, they had the basis of a plan. By noon the next day, they were ready to put it into motion.

Thank the Mother for that. Sooner rather than later, Cinderella and the chancellor were bound to realize something was wrong.

Charlotte hopped down from the table she'd been sitting on and broke the silence. "Damn. What a difference a shave can make."

Anna's mother shook her head at Charlotte's choice of words, a common occurrence it seemed. Imprisonment in the fairy godmother's compound had been hard on many. Only today had Brandt and Koen's brother Hans started to come back to himself. It wasn't the same for Charlotte though. The hardship let her break free of the expectations of society, to be who she wanted—sharp tongue, foul mouth, and all—rather than the lady everyone expected. She'd even taken to breeches as Anna had, much to her mother's dismay and Will's delight.

His friend had departed with Brandt and a number of others two days ago, headed for the castle. The first step in their plan moved into action, and now it was time for the next.

Nik rubbed at his chin, free of whiskers for the first time in months. He'd been loath to get rid of the last vestige of his stolen identity. Besides, Anna liked it. He grinned at her where she stood next to her sister. But for this plan to work, he needed to look as much like his old self as he could.

"At least the outfit works. You look radiant, Majesty." Anna's mother dipped into a low curtsy, the portrait of a fine lady.

"Thank you." A touch of heat crept up the back of his neck. If they did take back the kingdom, he'd have to do something about that honorific. It didn't sit right with him anymore. To think he'd once flown into a fit in his younger days when a new maid failed to use it.

"Quite handsome," Anna said, stalking his way, a small vial peeking out over the top of her fist.

It was the best they could manage in a few days. Anna's mother had learned much from her first husband, the tailor, and her skill with decorative needlework would make any lady jealous. She'd fashioned a guard outfit into attire fit for a king, even managed to make the coat stiff as the ones he used to wear and still secretly loathed. Though he wouldn't tell her that, not with all the effort she'd put in.

Koen snatched up a few more vials from the table with care and brought them over. "You're sure about this?"

"Too late to back out now." Will and Brandt would be in the city by now, along with many of the guards who were loyal and able to ride.

Dark smudges loomed under Koen's bloodshot eyes. He'd barely slept these past days, determined to comb through as many of the fairy godmother's books, notes, and ingredients as possible. He still searched for a cure for Mina. Nik's throat dried at the thought of the girl trapped in slumber. Without a true love she was doomed, unless they found something else—for who could fall in love with her now, even pretty as she was?

Koen would be back at his search the moment they left. He'd be staying here, along with Charlotte, Anna's mother, and a number of others who were injured or unable to fight, while Nik and Anna passed through the mirror to enact the rest of their plan.

"If you don't hear from us in two days…" Nik's gaze flicked to the women.

Koen nodded. Thick emotion colored his whispered voice when he said, "I'll get them to safety."

If they didn't come back through the mirror and no one returned from the capital with good news, they were to flee. Cinderella would know the fairy godmother's compound had fallen, if not the old pixie's fate, and he wouldn't risk more innocent lives destroyed by his failures.

"Good luck, brother." Koen clapped him on the shoulder and passed him the vials.

Nik fought against the tightness in his throat as he replied, "You too, brother."

They were brothers, he realized. In trust and love, if not in blood. Of all he'd learned since his fall, that might have been the most important lesson.

"Now remember," Koen began, sliding back into his serious tone as Anna joined them, "drink the blue vial first and make sure to think of exactly how you want to look while you swallow. It should alter your appearance to whomever you think of. The green is for after. To change you back."

"And this—" He walked back to the table and grabbed a small jar. "—is the sleeping powder. Don't breathe it in yourself or we'll all be in a world of trouble."

"We won't." Anna took the jar, wrapped it in a cloth, and tucked it into the pocket of her dress. The blue gown swished around her feet in a wide hoop. She had fashioned much of it herself, working on it just about every moment they were locked together away from the world. It might have been hard to wait the days after Will left to enact this next step in their plan, but with Anna at his side, he savored that time they had together, moments of peace and bliss before the storm.

There was nothing better than waking up with her curled against his chest.

"Anna," her mother called. "You don't have to do this. Someone else can go."

The pain in her voice nearly broke his heart. The love there...no one could doubt it.

Anna crossed the room and gathered her mother in an embrace. They were about the same height, and their hair could be the same color except for the streaks of grey that twined through the rich brown waves gathered up into a bun behind her mother's head.

"I'll come back, Mama," Anna said. "I promise."

He'd asked her to stay too. Though he'd known she'd reject the idea before he ever proposed it, he couldn't help but want her out of harm's way. Anna had a point in her rebuttal though. No one knew Ella quite like she did, except perhaps her mother and Charlotte, but she wouldn't hear of either of them going in her stead.

If anyone was going to pretend to be the queen and present him to the world, Anna would do it best, and they needed every advantage.

"Let her go, Mama," Charlotte said as she gently pried her mother away. "Anna can do this."

The sisters shared a silent look that spoke volumes, and he found himself glancing away, unwilling to intrude.

A minute later, Anna brushed against his side and twined her fingers through his.

With a last farewell to their friends and family, Nik and Anna entered the fairy godmother's private study hand in hand. The night the fairy godmother died, Will and his men scoured the compound, rooting out any loyal to the queen and creating a safe place for their allies. Among the fairy godmother's possessions, they'd found a magic mirror, smaller than the one in the throne room, but with the same odd fog swirling near the edges. Nik had ordered it covered with a sheet, unwilling to risk the queen or someone else catching a glimpse of them and ruining their plot. The mirror loomed like a specter across the room, higher than even his tall form.

The time had come to uncover it.

Anna shivered and gripped his hand tighter. "Will you be doing the honors?" She cocked a brow and gestured toward the mirror.

He flexed his fingers, savoring their connection. With her at his side, he could do anything. Reluctantly, he let her go and crossed the room. The cloth felt cold to the touch, much more than it should have been given the closed-off room. It chilled Nik's skin as he grabbed a handful of it and jerked the sheet away.

His breath caught in his throat. The sheet fluttered to a heap, forgotten. Mist swirled within the gilded frame like a thing alive. No one could ever mistake this mirror for anything ordinary.

"It's still...what did Koen call it? Active?" Anna stepped to his side, threading her arm through his.

"Looks like it." *Hells, it gives me the creeps.* They probably should have stopped the magic using the instructions Koen found scribbled in a notebook, or at least tried, but he was too afraid to mess with it. The other side undoubtedly led into the castle, likely to the queen's bedroom based on the conversation they'd overheard while hiding in the old servant's corridors. None of them knew what would happen on the other side if they tried to adjust the magic, and giving away their ruse too early could ruin it all.

"Better make sure though," he said, stepping away from her. With a quick prayer to the Mother, he touched the gilded frame, following the pattern he'd memorized from the pixie's notes. At the last touch, a shimmer passed across the surface, rolling out like a rock tossed in a still pond.

Nik slipped the blue vial from his pocket. Time to become someone else, someone he hated. His teeth ground together. *A necessary step. Temporary.* He'd only wear that bastard's face a few minutes—nothing more.

"You're doing it now?" Anna asked.

"Might as well."

Anna had said she hoped to at least catch a glimpse of Ella before drinking hers, which she would if they arrived in her bedroom—hopefully, with the queen still asleep, early as it was. It would be easier to perfect her look that way, and she needed to be precise for their plot to work. He, on the other hand, just needed to get through the halls without questions. A memory would do. It would have to.

Nik pulled the stopper and downed the contents of the vial. The thick liquid clung to his tongue, bitter and sharp all at once. It took effort to choke it down. As it slid down his throat, a sharp tingling seized him, rushing up and down from the tips of his toes to the top of his head. His nails dug into his palms as he held himself still, eyes closed, remembering the face of the man he hated—Chancellor Stephan Friedrich.

He'd seen the horrible man nearly every day he'd been at the castle, from youth until his flight from the castle. Nik had always found him off-putting for a reason he couldn't quite place. He was haughty, arrogant, always at Nik's father's side. He'd poisoned the king against him all his life, pointing out every fault he had to prevent his father favoring him too much. It hadn't been hard. He'd never been good enough in his father's eyes, no matter how he tried. Nik certainly had his faults. He saw that now more than ever, but Stephan made sure his father took note of each and every one in excruciating detail.

Awful as the man was, Nik never realized the chancellor coveted the crown for himself. It made sense—now. What an idiot he'd been. Stephan poisoned his father against him and had probably literally poisoned his father to death too.

The sensation of needles prickling his skin faded, then vanished completely. Nik opened his eyes and looked at Anna. She blinked at him, wide-eyed.

"It worked?" He snapped his mouth shut, teeth rattling. *Hells.* Even his voice had changed.

Anna visibly shivered. "Good enough."

He shifted his jaw, feeling it pop, and extended a hand to Anna. "Let's hope that stepsister of yours is a sound sleeper."

40

*W*alking through the mirror felt like falling into a pool of honey. Not that Anna ever had, but there was no other comparison for the thickness of the air or the way it stripped away all sound and tugged them in. The mirror swallowed them up. They couldn't stop it if they wanted to. If not for Nik's solid hand in hers, panic would have taken hold. Even so, it clawed at the edges of her mind, crept up her spine, and urged her to rush back toward the room they'd left, impossible as that was.

When it seemed like they might be trapped forever, the mirror spat them out, sending them stumbling into a dim room.

A low-burning oil lamp sat on a table near the four-poster bed, providing the only illumination. The curtains were still drawn tight, blocking out whatever first rays of dawn might be creeping over the horizon. A quick glance around the room proved they landed exactly where they expected—the queen's bedroom. Thick rugs spread out under their feet. An assortment of jewelry was displayed on the far vanity, diamonds managing to sparkle even in the darkness. Heavy wardrobes clung to a wall, to say nothing of the richly cushioned chairs and sofa with its sweeping, curved back.

But of all the finery, there was one important thing missing.

Ella.

The bed curtains had been left tied up to the posts. The sheets and coverings were wrinkled on one side and tossed back, as if someone had slept there but already risen for the day and left the bedding askew to be straightened by a maid.

Nik tightened his grip, drawing her focus to him. *Privy?* he mouthed, echoing her thoughts.

Anna shrugged. She was never an early riser, or she hadn't been when they lived under the same roof.

If Ella had crept out to a hall privy rather than using her chamber pot, she'd be back likely any moment. "We need to hide," she whispered.

They had to at least give it a few minutes to see if Ella returned. If she was already up for the day, their plan could crumble.

Nik nodded, not daring to speak.

There were few places to hide. Anna hurried across the room and threw open a wardrobe. A flood of colorful ball gowns spilled out. *Hells.* She sucked in a breath.

Then Nik was at her side, shoving the heavy silks back into the wardrobe as she tried to force the door shut. What a horrible idea. They'd never fit with all those clothes in there, nor could they just leave them in a heap on the floor. Finally, it closed, but Anna wouldn't dare try the others.

She scanned the room, a question on her lips, when Nik placed his finger over them, silencing her. He jerked his head toward the wall and the door occupying it. Then she heard it, a whisper of sound beyond. A soft scream slipped through the door. The fine hairs on her arms rose. Other sounds followed—deep groans, another cry, a word that might have been "yes."

Color raced to her cheeks as the noise died away.

"That door," Anna whispered.

She could barely make out Nik's reply of, "King's room."

Her face burned. That had to be where Ella was. It was her stepsister's cry of pleasure she'd heard. But with... She looked at Nik, at the face he'd donned. Anna stiffened, her lips curling with distaste. "The chancellor?"

Nik's hand tightened on hers, almost painfully. The hard set of his jaw spoke volumes, but whether it was about Ella being with that man or the room he occupied, she couldn't say.

Conversation rose up again, muffled at first, then a feminine voice grew in volume. Anna's heart leaped into her throat. Ella was coming back. Her gaze darted. There was only one place that might work to hide. Anna tugged Nik with her and dropped to her knees before sliding under the bed. Nik followed without question.

No sooner had they squeezed beneath the frame holding the mattress aloft—for no queen could sleep on the ground—than the door adjoining the rooms swung open. Anna chanced a peek out the gap between the bed sham and the floor. Ella entered, barefoot, a long, pale nightgown swishing about her legs, and all but slammed the door behind her.

"Bastard," she muttered.

Anna's eyes widened in surprise, as did Nik's where he lay beside her, still and silent. Whatever tryst Ella had been up to hadn't ended well.

The queen huffed, stomping her feet into the thick carpets as she crossed to her vanity and slammed down into the chair. Anna's heart skipped a beat. If Ella looked too closely, she might catch sight of them under her bed. Thankfully, her sister hung her head in her hands, staring at nothing on the table before her.

Carefully, Anna felt in her pocket, checking for the sleeping powder. A soft sigh heaved her chest as her fingers slid around the cloth she'd wrapped it in. Unless Ella returned to a natural sleep, though, it'd be hard to use it. She'd planned to sprinkle a little over her sleeping form and keep her asleep while they worked the rest of their plan. After all, if Anna were to take the potion to make herself look like Ella, it wouldn't do to have the real queen out and about in the castle.

A soft sob carried through the air, forming an unexpected heaviness that settled on Anna's chest.

"Wouldn't even let me stay," Ella said to her reflection as she wiped at her face. "Again."

Sorrow ate at Anna. Ella had done such horrible things, and yet her misery was easy to see in her tears, the hollows of her cheeks, even the way her shoulders hunched around her. She might appear a queen in the light of day to the people, but all Anna saw was a broken woman. It'd been years since she'd seen Ella like this—since the days after her father passed so unexpectedly, his heart given out in one horrible moment in their family sitting room.

Ella grabbed a vial of something from the table and tipped it back. An herbal remedy to prevent a child, perhaps? Anna's cheeks burned. She probably should have been taking something herself, but that was a worry for another time.

The queen rose from her chair and wandered toward the windows. Anna held her breath, praying to the Mother she wouldn't open them. The morning light could too easily spill across the bed and give them away.

Instead, Ella shook her head, sniffed once more, and retreated to the bed. Her stepsister tore at the ropes holding the bed curtains, scrambling across the mattress in haste to shut herself in—or the world out. Dust and who knew what else floated down from the mattress. It tickled her nose, and Anna clasped her hand over it, praying not to sneeze and give them away.

The sobs returned the moment the curtains stilled.

Anna's chest ached like someone tried to pry it open. Ella had everything she'd wanted it seemed, yet she sobbed like the world might be ending.

Nik took her hand and squeezed. His support gave her strength enough to lay still, to listen to her stepsister cry out her pain as minutes dragged on.

They needed to move, but she doubted even those sobs would fully conceal their exit. Not to mention she still needed to take the potion. She could do it now, go by memory, but every time she closed her eyes, she saw Ella as she'd been when her father passed. Younger, on the cusp of womanhood, eyes red and swollen from tears, hair tangled and matted around her face.

That would never do for their plans.

A few minutes later, the crying stopped. The mattress no longer moved.

It would be a risk to slip out from under the bed, but they couldn't stay there forever. Brandt and Will were probably already in the square, urging citizens to wait for the queen's urgent announcement. Doubt curled itself around her neck and tightened. It may have been safer for them to do this in the square themselves than through the throne room's mirror. But the queen never went to the square. In fact, some said Ella hadn't left the castle at all since arriving.

Anna made to move, but Nik stilled her with a touch on the shoulder. Instead, he crept out first. It made a certain sense with the disguise. Ella might not want to see the chancellor, not after...whatever had happened, but he'd be a more believable sight than her.

He made impressively little noise slipping from under the bed. The curtains were barely a whisper as he parted them. Anna tensed, prepared for the worst.

But no one screamed. No one spoke.

Nik knelt and waved her over. Anna let out a soft sigh and scrambled from her hiding place. Ella lay sprawled face-down upon the bed, her hair a golden sheet splayed down her back. She'd pulled a large pillow over her head, covering her face thoroughly so that Anna could only make out the curve of her neck.

Heavens and hells. Her shoulders drooped. How were they supposed to use the sleeping powder now? Worse, how was she supposed to copy her stepsister's image?

Should we move it? She mouthed to Nik.

He gave one jerk of his head. *Too risky.*

He was right, much as she loathed it. There was only one thing to do now. Anna pulled the blue vial from her pocket, flipped the stopper, and drank deep. She nearly choked on the vile stuff. With a hand clapped over her mouth, she shut her eyes and did her best to block out the horrible tickling and needling sensation racing across her skin.

Think of Ella, she reminded herself, *how radiant she looked at the ball, how happy she was before the wedding, all her dreams come true.*

The feeling slipped away with a last, tingling shudder. When she dared a look at Nik, he swallowed hard, then gave a short nod. Whatever she'd done, hopefully it was enough. Heavy weight settled down her back, and she reached for her hair, marveling at the sudden length and light color. What a wonder the potion was. But she had no time to gawk at herself.

With Ella asleep the way she was, it would be impossible to use the sleeping powder without first waking her, and that was a risk they couldn't afford. One scream and they'd be done for. Leaving her in a natural sleep wasn't ideal, but there was nothing else to be done.

Anna smoothed out her dress, straightened her shoulders, and notched her chin higher. All she had to do was be her sister, either of them really. Confident, arrogant, and in charge. She pasted what she hoped was a cunning smile on her face. Nik raised his brows and smiled in return, though seeing that look with the chancellor's features turned her stomach more than made it flutter.

Without a moment to lose, she exited the main door of the suite. A guard jumped to attention in the hall. Her heart skipped a beat before thundering against her ribs.

"Your M-Majesty." He bowed. "I'll call your maids at once—"

Anna flicked her hand in dismissal. "No need. Carry on."

She started at the voice—Ella's voice. Now *that* was magic, more than any wig or make-up could ever do. Luckily, the guard averted his eyes as he was no doubt trained to do. "Yes, Majesty." His gaze flicked up, taking in Nik for a brief second. "Chancellor Friedrich." He bowed again. "Sorry, sir."

"Keep the maids out until luncheon. I'd prefer my rooms undisturbed when I return," he said. "Her Majesty as well."

"Indeed," she echoed, folding her hands in front of her stomach as she'd seen Ella do many times.

Two more guards greeted them at the end of the hall, and Anna couldn't help but hold her head even higher. It was a dizzying feeling, the respect, the awed regard. Or perhaps that was just some side effect of the potion.

No one stopped them as they strode through the halls. No one questioned why they were up, dressed, and about so early—it wasn't their place to. The guards and servants they passed may have whispered about it later, but respectful greetings, bows, and averted gazes were the only things aimed their way. *Thank the Mother and all her saints for that.* If her transformation was imperfect, no one looked close enough to know.

Nik guided them through the halls, his arm woven through hers as they'd seen the queen and the chancellor do on the day Mina fell into slumber. Keeping in step with him, it gave the appearance that she knew where she went, though truly she had no idea. She barely recognized the doors to the throne room as they approached. Only Nik drawing them to a halt and his subtle cough confirmed the slight suspicion.

The guard at the door rushed to open it, probably thinking Nik's cough a command directed at him. *Poor kid.* For that's all he was, not quite an adult and no doubt given the morning watch that no one else wanted.

"We wish to be alone within," Anna said, her tone sharp and firm. "We're not to be disturbed, no matter what. Do you understand?"

She almost felt bad for her tone when the boy replied with a stuttering, "Y-yes, Majesty."

"Good." She flicked her hand in dismissal as they passed by, not bothering with a backward glance. Ella wouldn't. And as she expected, the boy obeyed, closing the heavy doors behind them and leaving them alone in the throne room.

Morning light spilled in through the large windows, shimmering off the marble floors. And there, to the right, stood the massive mirror, the one Nik said he'd fallen through in his flight from the throne room days before. Its twin—or other half, as Koen described it after reading the fairy godmother's ramblings—stood in the central square.

Anna turned to Nik, freeing her arm from his. "So far, so good."

"Ah, but now the fun begins." He pulled the green vial from his pocket. "Let's hope this works."

41

The liquid in the green vial to return him to his true self tasted smooth, sweet, and went down easy. A quick shudder and shiver took him before the magic washed down his form, almost as if he'd stepped into a river and let the water flow across his skin.

"Nice to have you back, my love."

Nik shuddered. He couldn't help it. *That* voice still haunted his nightmares, but he forced a smile for Anna's benefit. "Tell me that again after this is over."

"Of course." She beamed at him.

He had to blink and remind himself that she was Anna, not her stepsister who they'd left asleep upstairs.

Hells. Had it been this hard for her when he changed? Either time? *Damn.* It was nice to be in his own skin again. Helpful or not, he'd be thankful never to use a potion again.

"My queen," he said with a flourish of his hand toward the mirror.

Anna rolled her eyes, and for the briefest moment, he could see *her* beyond her altered appearance. She approached the mirror and placed her hands on it in the pattern that, should the fairy godmother's notes be correct, let them speak to the people in the square. A shimmer passed over its surface as Anna stepped back, hands clasped in front of her once more.

Nik wandered to the far windows, their great panes stretching high above him. If it worked, if they could see, Will had promised some kind of sign. He tugged at his collar, the stiff thing suddenly itchy and irritable.

A glance over his shoulder showed Anna waiting patiently, a forced smiled stretching her features. His chest tightened, and he fought the urge to rub at it. Maybe he should have waited before taking the second potion.

Movement in the city below caught his attention. Nik leaned toward the glass. A large, blue flag waved back and forth above a far building that he estimated to be near the square. The signal.

A rush of warmth raced through him. It worked.

So far.

He twisted toward Anna and gave her a single sharp nod. Her smile faltered and then smoothed out into one genuine and blinding.

"Good people," she began, head held high and regal as any queen. "Thank you for your attention this morning. I have important news to share with you all, and I beg you to listen. I—" Anna looked at him, a flash of uncertainty crossing her features.

They'd discussed the point of the message but not the details of it. Anna assured him she knew what to say, and he believed her, but in that moment, he sensed a change, some decision made.

"I'm afraid I was untruthful with you all. You see, King Nikolaus Kaiser, my h-husband…" Color rose to her cheeks. "…is alive."

She paused, and in that silence he could imagine the gasps of disbelief from the crowd. If they were still under the influence of the fairy godmother's potion, they should believe the words of their queen or be coerced to believe them. He only hoped the transformation potion would be enough that the words didn't have to come from the queen herself. However, even if that didn't work, the sight of him should.

Nik crossed the room to stand beside Anna and smiled at the crowd he envisioned on the other side of the mirror. "Good people. It is nice to see you all once more."

Anna slid her arm through his. "He was gravely ill, and we feared him lost forever." Her other hand came to graze his chest, and he forced himself to see Anna, not the woman she pretended to be, as he smiled at her with love. "And so," she glanced back to the mirror, "I lied to you all.

To spare you the long suffering and uncertainty of his future. I believed it better if you knew the kingdom was in safe hands. And now I can return power to where it truly belongs." She beamed up at him. "To our rightful king."

She'd spared the details of her sister's treachery, gave the lies a shine of silver and gold her stepsister didn't deserve. But he believed in Anna and her reasons—whatever they were. Though there was one detail the people must have.

"There are some within the castle, however, who dissent my...renewed health," Nik began. "Chancellor Stephan Friedrich would see me cast aside or dead and take my place himself. He almost did." He pulled Anna tighter. "If not for the help of the woman I love, I would surely be resting in the tomb beside my father."

His voice cracked a bit over the last word, emotion creeping over the loss when he'd have sworn there was none left—not for the father who never seemed to care for him the way one should. Nik's throat tightened, the words he planned to say turned hazy in his mind, but thankfully, Anna stood strong at his side.

"I implore you to support your rightful king," Anna said. "Come to the castle today, right now. Let us celebrate and hear your voices ring out for your king."

Nik swallowed and whispered a silent prayer to the Mother. *Don't let it come to bloodshed. Let the guards see me, believe me. Let the chancellor surrender and the queen as well.*

What they'd do with them, how he'd explain Anna at his side instead of Ella, was a trial for another day. First they had to have the people's support.

A commotion outside the throne room drew his attention. Anna stiffened. His smile dropped as his teeth ground together. They were out of time. His free hand trailed to his side, to the pommel of the sword strapped there.

"Please, as your queen, I beg you to listen to what I've said," her voice rose, a quaver of uncertainty coloring her words. "Tell everyone you see, your king is alive!"

The doors crashed open. "Sir, please—"

Nik shoved Anna behind him and turned to face the intrusion. Dark fury reared its head as the chancellor barged into the room, a small retinue of guards on his tail.

"How dare you," Anna began, but she couldn't hide the wobble in her voice anymore.

"Now, this is an interesting sight." Stephan's voice rang through the room as he crossed his arms.

Nik all but snarled. "You're a traitor to the crown. You killed the former king and tried to kill me too." *Let the people hear. Let the chancellor damn himself in his arrogance.*

"Did I?" He raised one greying brow. "Or was that your dear wife?"

A laugh caught in his throat, and he choked it down.

"Though…" The chancellor broke his stance and stalked closer. "I don't recall that dress." The way his gaze raked over Anna set his teeth on edge. "Funny how the guards said it was nice to see me *again* this morning, yet I'd just left my rooms. Come, my queen, don't let this man fool you further with his many faces."

Fuck. A pit opened in his stomach as Stephan's lips quirked into a smirk. He wasn't so oblivious after all.

"He is Nikolaus Kaiser," Anna said. "Our rightful king." She stepped out from behind him, keeping one trembling hand on his arm. "My husband."

"The king is dead, Your Majesty." He held his hand out to her. "You attended the funeral yourself. Now come away."

Guards spread out around the edge of the room, circling them.

Anna turned to Nik, uncertainty in her wide-eyed gaze. His chest rose and fell with heavy breaths. He had to save her, protect her. "Go to him."

"Nik." She clung to him tighter.

"It seems our queen is not herself this morning," the chancellor said, projecting his voice loud for all to hear. "You two." He pointed to two of the guards who accompanied him. "Check the queen's rooms. Now. She may have been bespelled."

Fuck all.

"You shall not enter my rooms without my permission." Anna stomped her foot, drawing attention.

The guards halted, indecision written on their faces.

"Now!" the chancellor ordered.

The men ran off.

There was no longer any doubt who truly ruled the castle.

"Guards, protect your queen from this man."

A few edged closer. Others held their ground. "But he—" a brave one started.

"Is a clever charlatan," Stephan interrupted, his lips curling in distaste. "If the king were alive, wouldn't you, a guard of the queen, know it?"

In a few words, he shredded their ploy to ruins.

The men began to advance. Nik called some of them out by name. The ones he named stopped, wide-eyed. A few others as well. "I am your king. You've known me for years," he implored. "I know things only your king would know. Ask me. Ask me anything."

"A clever ploy," the chancellor said. "You think he couldn't easily learn your names?"

Anna tore herself from his arm. "Wait!" He reached for her, but she'd already stomped toward Stephan.

"That's enough!" She planted her hands on her hips. "Am I queen here or not?"

Warning raised the hair on his neck a moment too late. The chancellor grabbed Anna, pulling her tight against him with a blade to her throat.

"Don't touch her!" Nik roared. "How dare you draw a blade on your queen!"

The chancellor leaned in, his lips a hair's width from Anna's neck. Fear held her still, her eyes pleading. The look alone gutted him.

"Is she?" the chancellor said against her skin. "Cinderella never smelled quite so...sweet. She was never so tense in my arms either. Quite the opposite," he chuckled.

"Stop this at once," Anna said, an edge of hysteria in her voice. "Or—or I'll have you arrested."

"What's going on here?" The high, lilting voice shattered his world. Nik closed his eyes in anguish as Cinderella raced into the ballroom.

When he pried them open a moment later, the queen stood frozen just inside the doorway, staring wide-eyed at the scene within the room. In that moment she looked nothing like a queen. Even from a distance, he could tell her eyes were bloodshot and puffy. Her long hair lay in a torrent down her back, and nothing but a simple dressing robe was wrapped around her nightgown. The guards may very well have pulled her straight from bed and dragged her there.

"There's our queen."

Nik's fist tightened painfully around the hilt of his sword. He'd give anything to wipe the smirk off Stephan's face in that moment, anything.

But Cinderella wasn't looking at the chancellor. Her wide-eyed gaze locked on him. "Nik?" A dainty hand covered her mouth as she stumbled back a step.

The chancellor never saw her horror as he said, "And if there can be a false queen—"

Anna cried out as Stephan tightened his hold, snagging Nik's full attention once more.

"Let her go!" Nik cried.

"There can be a false king." The chancellor shoved Anna—hard—sending her tumbling to the ground. "Arrest them!"

Blood rushed in his ears as the guards closed in on Anna. Nik drew his sword and raced toward her, but too late. Heart hammering in his chest, panic gripping him, he could only think of one way to possibly save them.

Nik pointed his blade at the chancellor. "I challenge you to a duel."

The older man laughed. "A duel? Don't be ridiculous."

The guards helped Anna from the floor but didn't take her away. They were uncertain, cautious. He'd use it.

"A duel," Nik said again. "If you win, arrest me. But if I win, you confess your lies, how you killed my father and tried to kill me too. You tell the people the truth. Here and now."

"Nik, no!" Anna cried, but he ignored her. He had to do something, for her sake if nothing else.

Stephan sneered, his nose turning up.

"Look around you, Chancellor. Not even your guards believe you." Maybe that wasn't fully true, but there was hesitancy, doubt, and he'd fuel it any way he could. "To say nothing of the people." He pointed to the mirror. "They've heard the truth. They've seen me. They recognize their king." His own lips curled into a smirk. "And so does your queen."

Cinderella hadn't moved. The woman stood as frozen as a statue, her face drained of its color like she'd seen a ghost. From her perspective, he probably was.

The cocky sneer dropped into a feral frown. "Fine, *boy*." Stephan stared at the surrounding guards. "No one interferes."

The chancellor drew his blade. A strange peace settled over Nik as he adjusted his stance. Vengeance or death, he'd end this today.

42

*A*nna shook with barely leashed fear. Everything in her told her to run, to flee while the chancellor and his guards were distracted by Nik's proclamation of a duel, but she couldn't leave him. *Never.* While there was breath in his lungs, and hers, she'd stay by his side.

The two men sized each other up, flashing their swords and readying for the opening blow. *Please, Mother, keep him safe. Let him win.*

She wouldn't flee, but she couldn't possibly just stand there either. She *had* to do something. Interrupting the duel would invalidate it. Their friends were far away in the square. Saints only knew what was happening there with all that the people had witnessed. Anna turned, catching sight of her stepsister. Ella stood alone, still appearing to be in shock. Whatever had happened, she'd genuinely believed Nik to be dead. It was as clear on her face as if someone had written it there.

The chancellor may think he ruled, but Cinderella was still the queen.

"Ella," Anna said in a harsh whisper as she rushed to her stepsister. The clang of steel behind her gripped her like a vise, but she shook off the feeling.

The queen snapped out of her stupor. Her pale brows pinched together. "Who *are* you?"

"Anna," she replied, just loud enough for her and no one else.

"Anna?" Ella wiped at her swollen face, not that it helped.

"Your sister. Stepsister."

She blinked rapidly. "Anna," she gasped in recognition. "But you, you don't—" She gestured to Anna's appearance.

"It's a potion, a spell."

Ella stiffened. "But only the fairy godmother can do such things."

"I know. I got it from her." She left out the rest. No point trying to explain it all now.

"I don't—"

"Ella." Anna grasped her sister's hands, wringing a soft gasp from her lips. "There's no time for this. That's Nik, it truly is, I vow it to the Mother."

She risked a glance over one shoulder to see Nik barely dodge another swipe from the chancellor. Acid crept up her throat, fighting with the scream aching to break free. She swallowed it down—she wouldn't distract him, couldn't.

"But he..." Her sister shook her head.

"You have to do something. Stop this. You're the queen."

At that, she huffed a hollow laugh. "Am I?" Something flashed across her features, and her face fell. "Once I...I thought that was all I wanted— queen, beloved." Her head drooped.

Of all the times for Ella to have a crisis of confidence, this was the worst. "Snap out of it."

Her stepsister met her gaze just as a sharp cry rang out behind her.

"Nik!" This time, she couldn't hold in the scream, not as she saw the streak of red marring his arm—his already injured arm. The bastard went right for the wound he'd given him before.

"Care to yield?" the chancellor taunted.

Nik bared his teeth and fixed his grip on the sword hilt. "Never."

Anna whirled on Ella. "He's your husband." The word burned her tongue. "Save him!"

"Only in name. He never...he didn't *want* me." The all-too-familiar disgust that Ella wore like a second skin bloomed on her face. "Stephan, however, wanted me plenty. He loves me." Her nose wrinkled, and Anna knew it for the lie it was. *Lie or denial.*

Less than an hour ago she'd been sobbing over him, and not the kind of tears of a woman in love. She'd know.

"Nikolaus is dead," Ella snapped. "The king is dead. It's only us now. Stephan and I." She drew herself up, wearing her title like an outfit all its own, and Anna had to admit she wore it well. Not even at her best could she imitate that kind of confidence.

"Your lover will die if he loses."

At that, Ella flinched.

Metal clanged. Ella lurched forward, her hand outstretched.

Anna whirled to look. The chancellor stepped back, touching a thin line of red on his cheek. She sucked in a breath. A narrow miss. *Too bad.*

Ella grabbed her arm. "Why are you here, Anna? Why do you look like me?"

Damn. She picked the wrong time to ask the right questions—or the wrong ones for Anna.

"You plan to steal my crown." Ella dropped her arm like it burned. "My kingdom."

"It was never yours," Anna replied.

Ella scoffed. "Wasn't it? I married the prince. I was his wife, his heir." Her eyes narrowed. "Do you love him? Is that why you tried to be me?"

Her face blazed. *As if I need to look like Ella to win a man.* Though... doubt clutched at her throat, squeezing tight. Something sharp burned at the corners of her eyes. That was what she believed for so long. It was what Ella made her believe.

"Yes. I love him. And he loves me."

Her stepsister snorted. "Only because he thinks you're me."

Fury burned under her skin. Anna snatched the vial from her pocket, yanked out the stopper, and chugged it down. Sweetness flowed across her tongue. A wave of something cool washed across her, like a wave on the seas of her youth.

Ella's smile faltered, no doubt taking in Anna's true form.

"No," Anna notched her chin higher. "He loves me for who I am..." She gestured to herself. "...as Anna. And I love him as Nik. Not the king, but *him.*"

Her stepsister's mouth opened and closed. Her nose twitched. Finally, it settled in a thin line before she said, "Guards, arrest her!"

But no one moved. All their eyes were trained on the duel as the chancellor knocked Nik's sword from his hand and sent it clattering across the floor.

43

*S*weat beaded on his brow, his lip, and slid down the back of his neck. Nik had given the duel his all, and now he was truly fucked.

He'd known Stephan was a good fighter. Their earlier scuffle proved that, but he'd expected him to still be hampered by his injury. The chancellor had used Nik's old wounds against him, much to his detriment.

"Expected less of a fight?" the man taunted. Nik gritted his teeth. Of course, Stephan couldn't just finish it.

"The fairy godmother can be quite...helpful in certain matters." He smirked.

Fuck. He hadn't thought to look for a potion to grant him strength or stamina. Deviousness had never been a strength of his. And now it cost him.

Nik's gaze met Anna's. She was back to herself again. A last gift from the Mother—an image he'd take to the grave.

Run, he mouthed. He screamed it in silence, begged her to understand, to take this chance and flee. He had to save her even if he couldn't save himself. It wasn't supposed to be like this.

More guards ran into the throne room before coming to a halt and gaping at them. They waited for something, but Nik could only guess at what. He'd lost. The chancellor would make sure he died this time.

A window shattered, sending glass tinkling across the floor.

"What's this?" Stephan roared in outrage.

Noise flooded in from outside—chants, calls. A shiver raced across his skin. People called his name.

"The people, sir!" one of the new guards answered, voice quaking.

A surge of hope burned away the darkness threatening to swallow him. The people were rising. They'd seen. They'd heard. Best of all, they still believed in him. He didn't deserve it, but he'd take it.

And he'd take the opportunity fate spread before him too.

Nik dropped to a crouch and pulled the small dagger hidden in his boot. Before the chancellor noticed—too distracted by the interruption—Nik sprang at him.

"Stephan!" Cinderella screamed.

The man reacted too slowly, barely raising his sword arm before Nik plunged his dagger into the back of his hand. Nik jerked it free as the chancellor cried out in pain and dropped his sword. Pulse hammering in his chest, he swung his leg wide and low, connecting with Stephan's shins and sending him tumbling to the ground.

Movement blurred in his periphery. Voices and screams echoed around him, nothing but a blur against the blood rushing in his ears. The old man barely had time to recover the breath knocked from his lungs before Nik had him pinned to the ground, his blade at the chancellor's throat.

"Yield!" Nik commanded, as much for those around as the man whose body went still beneath him.

"Dishonorable ingrate!"

A splatter of spittle landed on Nik's cheek as he leaned in closer, teeth bared. "Says the man who murdered his king!" Nik pressed the knifepoint to his throat, forcing him to go still again. "Who tried to murder his new king and failed."

"Murdered?" Cinderella's gasped cry tickled his senses. Real or fake, who knew? He couldn't turn his head to check her face, nor to see her expression. All his focus rested on the man before him.

Nik's fingers twitched around the blade. A voice in the back of his head screamed to slice it across the chancellor's neck and be done with it. "Do you deny it?" he yelled.

"Guards, seize this traitor!" Stephan's pupils widened in fear.

Now he chanced a glance at the surrounding guards. A few had the cloudy-eyed look of those under the fairy godmother's influence, but it was weak at best. Even they didn't advance, stuck in a muddle of questioning glances between one another.

"I am your king. Nikolaus Kaiser." He wouldn't beg, wouldn't plead. Instead, he stared them down—strong and confident. An old lesson from his youth whispered like a cooling spring through the back of his mind. *A king looks down to no one. He is brave and courageous. He does not bow or weep.*

All the while, the chancellor shouted his lies. He begged. He threatened.

Nik said nothing. His fingers flexed around Stephan's throat, holding him firm, tight, the blade close. One by one he met the eyes of the guards nearby and savored a glimpse of Anna at her stepsister's side.

A chorus of noise rose outside the broken window. Cinderella flitted around, nervous as a bird, the urge to run plain as day on her features.

Then the first guard knelt. "King Nikolaus."

Another followed.

His shoulders sagged. Pure joy washed through him in a surging rush as if his very blood danced in his veins.

A wave of them took a knee, the points of their blades pressed into the marble as they knelt before him.

Anna was safe. She would be safe. Already he could breathe easier.

"You're traitors. All of you!" The chancellor thrashed, nearly ending himself.

All the joy of the moment turned foul as he glanced down at the man he'd known all his life. He never cared for him, but the foolish prince he'd been would never have believed him capable of such treason. Worst of all, his father had loved the man like a brother, trusted him like a confidant, and often favored him over his own son. He'd never said that, of course, but Nik knew. Deep in his heart, he could never quite forget the many times his father admonished him, telling him to act more like Stephan.

Bitterness crept up his throat. If only his father knew the truth. Maybe he had in the end, somewhere beyond the fairy godmother's magic potions that clouded his father's mind as much as his. Maybe even more.

"What should I do with you?" Nik asked, his voice entirely too calm for the raging emotions he felt.

"Spare him!" Cinderella raced toward them, blonde hair flying behind her.

Anna caught up with her just as a pair of guards blocked her path. Their swords remained low, but it was clear they'd let no one pass, not even their queen. Anna grabbed Ella's arm, tugging her back and saying something too quiet for him to make out.

"You were never fit to rule," the chancellor snarled. "Too soft and spoiled, head in the clouds. I would have led this country to prosperity, but you'll lead it to ruin!"

Nik's teeth ground together. There was truth there, but that was before he'd nearly died. Before he'd lost everything he'd ever known. Before he lived a new life and learned so much. "Then I should thank you, Chancellor. Without you, I wouldn't have become the man I am. I've learned. I've grown. And I won't use magic to bend the people to my will."

"You dare—"

"This kingdom was never yours to rule." His gaze flicked to Cinderella, wide-eyed and still in Anna's arms.

Stephan turned his head just enough to see the queen.

"Please!" she cried again, begging like the poor, broken woman he'd seen that morning. Whatever confidence and grace she'd worn at the ball all those months ago, the chancellor, the crown, or perhaps the weight of both had shattered it.

Stephan huffed. "I would have been king. Once the year of mourning passed." A smirk curled his lips. "Did you know I fucked her on your wedding night?"

Nik waited for the jab to sting. But it never came.

"Before then too, after. So many times after. Even this morning."

Nik almost laughed, the start of it building in his throat. Once he might have cared. But Ella had never been his true wife, his love match.

That title had yet to be claimed, and there was only one woman he'd give it to.

"The dungeons for now, I think," Nik said, ignoring the man. "You'll have plenty of rats to spin your insults to."

"Halt!"

Nik's attention snapped toward the women as Cinderella shoved past the guards, Anna on her heels.

"Stop!" Nik commanded, an echo of the guards. He angled the blade for emphasis.

Cinderella drew up short with a sharp gasp. Anna grasped onto her once more as the guards closed in around them. "Please." She jerked free from Anna and dropped to her knees. "I didn't know, I didn't—" She shook her head. Tears welled and dripped down her face.

Something in his chest twisted. She'd seduced him with her pretty looks and magic. Cinderella claimed his father's approval and won her place at his side, and she was fair enough he didn't fight the arrangement as hard as he might—and too drugged with magic later to complain. Maybe she hadn't known of the plot to kill his father and him, but she'd brought the fairy godmother into his court. She'd allowed the chancellor his freedom and aided his plans. Worst of all, she'd been horrible to the woman he loved for years.

He should never pity her, and yet he did.

"I'll cede the crown, just let him go. Let us go." The words spilled out in a sobbing rush.

"Ella..." Anna began, blinking at her stepsister in what could only be shock.

But the queen ignored her. "Send us somewhere far away, across the sea. We won't bother you anymore. I promise."

"It's done, Ella," Stephan said, finally quiet and solemn. "The fairy godmother?"

"Dead," Anna supplied.

The chancellor's body went slack under him, his eyes closing in defeat.

"What?" Cinderella whirled on her stepsister. "She—she—" Another sob cut off the rest.

Nik's jaw stiffened as he chewed over Cinderella's words. Perhaps they could share a cell. He had no interest in beginning his reign with bloodshed, and even with all the horror she'd wrought upon her stepmother and stepsisters, the look in Anna's eyes said she wished no harm on her Ella. Not anymore anyway.

She was a better person than him, stronger. He met her gaze, reading the silent plea there as she held the other woman who fell to pieces.

She'd make a fine queen.

"Exile together," Nik mused aloud.

The chancellor's eyes snapped open. "You expect me to live like a beggar in a foreign land?" he snarled.

"Please, Stephan," Ella begged. "We'll be together, like you wanted."

"You'd prefer a cell?" Nik asked, ignoring her pleas.

"Never. I'll be no one's prisoner."

Before Nik realized what was happening, Stephan jerked upward and impaled himself on Nik's blade.

Cinderella screamed, as did Anna.

Blood splattered onto his hands and flooded onto the marble.

Noise and movement blurred around him as he blinked at the dying man, his whole body gone suddenly numb. There was a flash of white as the queen fainted.

Guards closed in, but he couldn't make himself move.

The man he loathed was dead, and he felt nothing, no joy, no sorrow, no satisfaction. Stephan had always been a prideful man, bent on perfection and having nothing but the best. Even so, Nik had never foreseen such an end for him.

Questions were tossed his way, but none of them stuck. Nor did anyone dare to touch him.

At last, a voice pierced through the haze. "See to the queen. Take her to her room."

Anna.

Nik shook himself and finally rose to his feet. The blade fell from his trembling fingers to clatter on the floor in the puddle of blood. Feeling returned to his limbs. He hastily wiped his bloody hands on his pants— anything to rid that feeling from his skin.

Then she was there, stepping around a guard, head held high, already giving orders to the stunned guards. "Tell the people their king lives. Hurry! Go!"

Anna turned to Nik, and her confident expression broke. Tears sparkled in her eyes as she stared at him, chest rising and falling in heavy breaths.

That look finally snapped him out of his stupor. "Anna!"

He rushed to her, uncaring if the whole damn kingdom saw. Nik pulled her into his arms, crushing her against him as she buried her face against his chest and let out a sob. *Alive. Safe.* He ran his fingers through her hair, savoring every touch, inhaling her scent.

By some miracle, they'd won.

44

*E*lla sat on the cushioned stool in her room, staring at the mirror on her vanity table. She'd been there for the better part of an hour, entirely still except for the occasional blink.

Anna sat on the edge of her stepsister's bed, a careful distance away. Someone needed to keep an eye on her after the shock of the day, and her stepsister allowed no one else near, sending them away with a flick of her hand. She hadn't spoken a word since the chancellor's suicide—not to Anna nor anyone else.

She hadn't even protested when Nik ordered the guards to move the fairy godmother's mirror out of the room. By rights she should be in a dungeon for her part in the treason, but Nik showed leniency in having her locked in her former room—for now.

Nik.

Anna suppressed a smile at the thought of her love. Nothing had quite gone as they'd planned, and yet he was safe and alive. Acknowledged as the king once more. Her heart fluttered awkwardly at the thought, myriad feelings dancing around like crickets in the field.

But she'd almost lost him. Her stomach bottomed out as a memory surged to the front—her turning to find Nik defenseless against the chancellor, expecting to see the man she loved cut through in mere heartbeats. That moment of horror would forever be etched in the back of her mind.

Her stepsister must be reliving an even worse torment now, seeing the chancellor's death over and over as she stared at nothing in the mirror. Anna's chest tightened. Somehow Ella had loved that horrible man. And love, however strange or unexpected, could breed such incredible joy or terrible pain.

"He chose to die rather than live with me." Ella's words were so soft, Anna nearly missed them.

She sucked in a sharp breath, unsure what to say or if the words were even directed at her.

"Death was better than me." Ella still didn't turn, didn't so much as move.

"Ella." Anna rose from the edge of the bed.

Her stepsister twisted around in her chair fast as a viper, and Anna flinched back, prepared for the worst. But the expression Ella wore now was far from any Anna remembered from the years they spent together. Her eyes were red and puffy, her face pale and drawn. Even her hair hung straight and spindly around her face like dry stalks of wheat.

"I..." Her shoulders hunched further in on themselves. "I thought he loved me. It's all I wanted. I just..." She finally looked up, meeting Anna's gaze across the space between them. "I just wanted to be loved."

It was the most honest thing Ella had ever said.

The words lingered in the heavy silence that spread between them, sinking into Anna's soul like the prickle of frosty morning dew on the grass. The truth was she ached for her, for her horrible stepsister who she'd vowed never to feel a moment's sorrow for.

"That's why you used the fairy godmother's potions and spells? To force people to love you?"

Ella flinched, her lips drawing thin.

Anna almost felt sorry for the question. Almost.

"It didn't work, did it?" Ella's gaze traveled to the carpets and stayed. "The people...they loved their queen, but never me. Stephan—" She shuddered, fists tightening in her lap. "Nikolaus..." She shook her head.

"He married me, but he never loved me. I saw that the night of our wedding. He couldn't even...we never..."

The tang of bile burned the base of Anna's throat. Ella confirmed what Nik had told her, but hearing about it still made her queasy. That Ella thought she could somehow win his love that way made it all the worse.

Ella drew her gaze from the carpet back to Anna. "But he loves you, doesn't he?" Anna opened her mouth to respond, but Ella hurried on. "I could see it. The way he looked at you in the throne room. He'd have died to protect you."

Achy warmth clenched her chest. She'd have died for him too.

"After father died, I just hurt so much. I was alone. Unloved."

"No." Anna rose to her feet.

Ella's brows drew together. "Yes, I was."

A sad smile touched her lips. "You were never alone, Ella. You were never unloved. We loved you. Charlotte. Mama. Me."

A twitching and wrinkling took hold of Ella's face as her emotions fought a visible war. "It's not the same," she said, her voice creeping above a bare whisper for the first time. "You were family. Your mother doted on you. You all had each other."

"We were all family." Anna reached a hand for Ella but let it drop. "We tried to be there for you. Then you ran off." It was two weeks after Ella's father died. She'd disappeared in the night. The whole house had been in a furious panic the next morning. Mama, Charlotte, the servants and gardeners—everyone searched for Ella the day through until nightfall, then the next day too. It hadn't been until the second evening when Anna finally saw her stepsister crossing the fields. She'd run to her then, calling her name, thanking the Mother for her safe return.

But Ella had barely reacted to her crushing hug, all but pushing her away and cradling the small, weathered hand mirror she'd acquired in her absence.

The fairy godmother's mirror, she knew now. Whatever had happened to that one, though, she had no idea. At least it was too small for a person to fit through, unlike the one they'd had removed from the queen's chambers.

Nothing had been the same after that day.

"Little good it all did me," Ella said. "The fairy godmother promised so much, and for a while, I thought I had it. I thought...I thought I had everything I ever wanted."

Perhaps that was the worst spell of them all, one the fairy godmother didn't even need magic to weave.

Anna swallowed down her apprehension and crossed to her stepsister. Ella barely flinched when Anna touched her shoulder. She didn't turn nor speak.

"You still have a family, Ella. This is not the end of your story." However painful it may be, she was her stepsister. They were family.

Ella huffed, her shoulder shaking under Anna's touch. "Yes, and I'm sure you all love me so much after all I've done."

Love? Something twisted tight in her chest. With pain came awareness. Anna hurt for her. She'd stayed in this room with her because somewhere deep down, beyond all the pain of the last few years, below the scars carved into her heart that never fully healed, there was a kernel of something that still burned for her stepsister. In that dim fire, she saw Ella the way she'd first met her when her mother moved them to the manor to marry Ella's father. How grand Anna thought her new sister, a bright ray of light whose smile could rival the sun. Her laughter was infectious, her glowing presence even more so.

That young woman had been lost along the way, carried off by a wave of grief when she was on the edge of womanhood, then molded by cruel hands into the bully she'd become.

But if she could be that girl once, perhaps Ella could find herself again. Perhaps there was room for love to grow once more.

Love. The idea struck her like a bolt of lightning, leaving behind the burning glow of a plan.

"Suppose it won't matter in the dungeons, will it?" Ella said, perhaps as much to herself as Anna.

"It doesn't have to be the dungeons for you."

"What?" Ella jolted, no doubt assuming the worst.

"Not like that." Anna shook her head. "But I have an idea."

45

*T*he carriage rolled along the bumpy, dirt road, the chill morning air slipping through the open window. But Nik wasn't cold, not with Anna nestled against his side and a bundle of nerves and anticipation twisting tight in his chest. He rubbed at it with the palm of his hand, taking in the lightening sky above the tree line.

Anna let out a wide yawn as she roused. How she managed to doze during the ride, he had no idea. Tired or not, he'd found rest impossible.

Of course, that hadn't stopped him from insisting they wait until morning for this venture. Brandt and Koen had argued for setting out the night before, once Anna shared her idea, but travel in the dark of night had risks, and the brothers *really* needed rest. He'd wager Koen had been up for days scouring the fairy godmother's books. Apparently, the old woman had been obsessed with creating a magic mirror that wouldn't just be a doorway to somewhere nearby but to another world altogether. She wished to go to someplace called Wonderland, though he couldn't recall such a land from any of his studies. Brandt had ridden hard with Will and the others to make it to the square in time. Yesterday they'd carried out their part of the plan without error. Ushering people to the square, confirming his story, and adding their own tales to his words. They'd had the people on his side before the chancellor's untimely arrival and had managed to keep most of the people out of a panic, even when doubts briefly set in.

Nik heaved a relieved sigh as Anna rubbed the lingering sleep from her eyes. His friends were safe. They'd stayed true to him. Even now, Will was probably waking up somewhere in the castle and keeping a watch over things for him while they were away. His lips quirked up. Charlotte would be somewhere nearby, having come through the mirror with Koen, Anna's mother, and several others after they'd taken the castle. The fiery woman was probably already ordering Cinderella's horrible fashion taste stripped from the castle. He'd been more than happy to oblige her request to redecorate for him. Well, him and Anna. He'd never been more shocked in his life than when Anna asked him to go to Cinderella's room the night before. Will and Charlotte came as witnesses too. The queen gave him two things—a signed letter confessing their marriage a sham and declaring it invalid. The other? Her advocation and confession to treason.

Actually, she'd given him three things, the last so intangible and unexpected he still could hardly believe it. An apology.

It couldn't compensate for all the ill she'd wrought, intentionally or not—the death, the pain, the suffering. His hand closed into a fist at his side. Nothing could erase that completely.

But the apology was a step, perhaps the hardest one of all.

Without it, he couldn't say if he'd have gone along with Anna's request —well, the part of it concerning her stepsister anyway. Even for her, the woman he loved. But then, that was one of the things he adored about her. She saw the good in everyone, even Ella.

"Are we there yet?" Anna asked.

"Soon."

They'd left before dawn, heading toward the convent with their fastest carriages. Truly, he'd forgotten how uncomfortable they were, especially at these speeds, but there was no time to spare.

Mina still slept on, unaware of her brothers' rescue or the changes in the kingdom. It was time for her to wake, and he only prayed Anna's hunch might work. No victory could be complete until she was saved. His friend...his sister of a sort.

Dawn turned to day by the time they arrived, and he helped Anna out of the carriage and into the light. Sisters hurried from the doors of the convent, Olga at their front.

A twinge of guilt assailed him in the wake of their wide-eyed glances and hurried questions. They probably should have sent word ahead.

The brothers were loud as ever as they jostled one another, each trying to be the first out of the two carriages they'd occupied on the ride from the castle. Brandt, of course, won. Even Koen brimmed with barely contained excitement. Only Hans emerged in hesitant silence. The effects of the fairy godmother's potion still had their tendrils wrapped around him. He'd always been the happiest brother, or so the others said, prone to bouts of booming laughter and always good for a joke. He'd be that man again. Deep inside, Nik was sure of that. It just took time to heal. He, of all people, knew that.

All six brothers drew quiet as another carriage opened and a blonde woman stepped out into the light. Her braided hair hung down her back. She wore a simple dress with little adornment, her eyes downcast.

Anna broke from him and went to her stepsister. Nik followed, a heavy lump lodged in his throat.

"You're sure?" Ella asked her sister as he approached. "They'll...accept me?"

Anna smiled, such a tender look it wrenched even his hardened heart. "Everyone deserves a second chance. And the Mother, well, the Mother welcomes all, as do those who love her."

Olga drew up to their group, her robes swishing through the grass. "Dear Anna." She reached out her hands, and Anna took them. The women shared a smile. Then, the older woman looked at him and gave a shallow bow of her head. "My king. We're glad of your presence once more."

Nik blinked at her, taken aback. The woman's smile grew, her gaze knowing.

Heavens and hells. She'd known who he was. Even when no one else had, this woman knew—and told him to sleep in the barn. A huff of laughter caught in his throat. It was no more than he deserved.

"Sister Olga." He nodded in return.

"And who do we have here?" She released Anna's hands and turned to Ella.

If she'd recognized him, he was certain she knew who stood before her. Yet she asked. She waited, the portrait of innocence and grace—a true representative of the Mother herself.

Anna slid a glance at her stepsister, who shifted on her feet. Her throat bobbed, and her gaze fell before she answered. "Ella. Just Ella."

"Well, Ella." The sister took her hands as she'd done Anna's. "Will you be staying with us?"

Finally, she looked up, meeting the other woman's curious look. Ella's eyes held a sheen of tears. "If you'll have me."

"All are welcome here." The older woman called to a few others waiting in the yard and beckoned them over. "This is our new sister, please see her settled while I attend the others. Did you bring anything with you?" she asked the fallen queen.

Ella shook her head.

The older woman gave a knowing nod. "Many come with nothing. Don't worry, we have all you'll need."

The other women led Ella away. She looked back once, sharing a look with Anna that he couldn't quite decipher.

"We'll take good care of her," Olga promised.

"I know," Anna said. She sniffed, blinking away unshed tears. Nik put an arm around her, drawing her close. If Nik had it his way, those would be the last tears she shed over her stepsister.

Even so, something like relief settled in as he watched the former queen be led across the yard. There would be no more bloodshed, no more magic. If they were lucky, the last remnants of her reign would burn away with the afternoon sun and she would be simply who she claimed —Ella.

Nik savored the feel of Anna at his side, her strength, her grace. She was regal today, chin raised, eyes bright, strong in the face of so much change and trial. He's never seen a more beautiful woman. No one could know her heart and ever find her ugly as her stepsister had claimed. And —his other hand drifted into his pocket, finding the cool metal of the ring lingering there—if the Mother was truly watching, perhaps, by the end of the day, the people would have the promise of a new queen.

"I'd wager you didn't all come just for that." Olga glanced at the brothers who'd settled into an edgy quiet.

He sucked in a breath, letting it calm his nerves. "No," he confessed. "We—Anna," he amended, "believes she may have found a cure for Mina."

She nodded. "Good. Come with me, all of you. I believe we can let some men inside just this once."

46

*M*ina lay on a bed in an antechamber off the central atrium where the sisters sang their daily prayers. Her hands were clasped over her chest, her dress spread out like a fan around her legs and draping over the edges of the simple bed. Bundles of flowers lay around her, tributes to the sleeping girl.

The brothers spilled around the bed, silent sorrow overcoming their eagerness as they took in their sister.

"We've kept watch on her night and day," Olga said. "She hasn't moved. Her breaths are so shallow you can almost miss them, but they're there."

Koen took one of Mina's hands in his, squeezing tight. "Yes," he said after a moment. "I feel her pulse. Faint, but there."

"We've given her honey water to try and keep her strength up."

"But if she's sleeping—" Brandt started.

"A few trickles in the mouth, several times a day. It's not much, but it's the best we could do in her state. All our medicines and prayers have been ineffective." Olga turned to her, and something swelled in Anna's chest, almost like a bubble of air lodged deep in her throat. "You believe you have a cure?"

Anna fought against her nerves and nodded. It had to work. It *had* to.

"The fairy godmother said the cure was true love's kiss." Nik took her hand in his, squeezing tight. His presence gave her strength, confidence. They *would* save Mina. She glanced up at him, savoring the love shining in his eyes.

It was love Mina needed. They'd all thought the fairy godmother meant romantic love, the soul-deep connection she and Nik shared. But being around Ella had reminded her that love had many forms. And true love—she glanced around at the gathered siblings—wasn't just for lovers.

"Ah." Olga clasped her hands in front of her and smiled at the brothers.

"But we already—" Koen cut Brandt off, a knowing look crossing his face.

"There is no truer love than those who risk themselves for one another." Olga panned her gaze around the siblings, hope lighting in their eyes, brightening their faces. She continued, looking over to Nik, then Anna.

A soft gasp caught in her throat as Anna saw the truth shining out from the older woman.

"So simple," Koen said. He knelt beside the bed, Mina's hand still clasped in his. "We had the cure this whole time."

I hope so. Anna couldn't say it out loud. She wouldn't let the tingle of doubt spoil their hope and whatever power that could give them over the magic.

The brothers clustered around the head of the bed, leaning in toward their sister.

"You two as well," the sister said to Anna and Nik.

"Us..." Nik's hand flexed on hers as he shared a look with Olga, then her.

"You love her too, do you not?"

Anna looked at Nik, seeing the understanding spill through him as it warmed deep in her chest. *Yes, I love Mina.* And so did he. He nodded once, and they split, squeezing in around the sleeping girl.

One of the brothers shifted down. Anna took Mina's hand, opposite Koen. "Now," he said, barely a whisper. The brothers leaned in to kiss their sleeping sister.

Anna closed her eyes and brought Mina's soft, warm hand to her lips. *Please. Please.*

A gasp split the silence.

The hand against her lips twitched.

Anna's eyes flew open as Brandt let out a choked sob.

Mina's eyes fluttered. Her chest rose and fell with heavy breaths.

A gasping sob tore from Anna as a rush of tears blurred her vision. *It worked. Thank the Mother and all her Saints, it actually worked.*

"Where are..." Mina's soft voice slipped into the tidepool of emotion. "Hans? Conrad. Edmund. Gunther!" Mina called out to each of her brothers in turn, wonder widening her gaze as she attempted to sit. Her dark hair shone in the light of the room, but not so brightly as the smile that broke across her face. The brothers crammed in closer, each trying to be the first to embrace their sister. Brandt literally leaped onto the edge of the bed, sending the whole thing creaking as he pulled a smiling—and now sobbing—Mina into his arms.

Nik touched Anna's shoulder, and she started. "Let's give them a moment," he whispered. Yes, she loved Mina and knew Mina loved her, even if she wasn't the boy the girl had fancied when they'd first met, but her brothers could have her first. There'd be time later, time for all of them. Anna wiped away her tears, pure joy radiating through her as she followed Nik into the main hall.

"You were right," he said when they were alone.

"I'm just so glad," she admitted. "I wasn't sure, but it struck me that the fairy godmother said true love, not romantic love, not passionate love. Simply true love, and what love could be more true than what they all share?" She gestured back toward the tearful reunion.

Nik took her hands in his. "What *we* all share."

"Yes." That was true. "Love binds us all, doesn't it?"

"It does." Staring into his eyes, no one could question the sincerity there, or the deep love that nearly made her head spin with its passion. "And I know that love will help us all build a better kingdom, together."

That's right. He was king once more. And she—

Nik knelt on the ground before her.

"What are you..." She trailed off, her lips parting in surprise as he pulled a small silver ring from his pocket.

"It was my mother's." His voice was thick, full of emotion, as he held up the ring for her inspection. A little dimple formed at the side of his mouth as he gave her a quivering smile. She hadn't noticed it before, not with the thick beard he'd always worn. The man was full of mysteries, but these little treasures, they were ones she enjoyed discovering.

"I found it last night, tucked away in my old room. I'd planned to give it to my future bride, but I never gave it to Cinderella. It never felt...right. Even in the thrall of the potion, I knew that much. Before the queen abdicated, she had my marriage declared fraudulent. I'm free, Anna, free to give this to the woman I love."

Free. And she could hear it in his voice—the relief, the lightness, the thread of hope that sparkled in his eyes like the light from the high windows.

She bit the inside of her lip, staring at him in disbelief.

"There's no one else I'd rather have at my side for whatever is to come. I love you, Anna. Only you."

Blinding joy sent her head spinning. She knew he loved her, believed it with her whole heart. But to see him like this, a king on his knees professing his love, overwhelmed her completely. Pressure built through her chest, sending a tingling along her limbs. But it wasn't worry or fear, or any of the other things that'd threatened to crush her over the past months. This was joy. Undimmed, pure, bright joy.

And love, plenty of love.

"Nik." His name was all she could manage.

"Marry me, Anna. Be the queen this country deserves."

She couldn't manage words just then, could only shake her head and lunge at him, throwing her arms around him and burying her face in the crook of his neck.

Nik caught her, and they tipped backward, nearly spilling onto the floor before he steadied them.

"Is that a yes?" he asked, near breathless.

Anna savored his warmth, the feel of his breath on her skin, before she tugged in her emotions and pulled back enough to look at him. "Yes, Nik. I love you. I'll marry you."

Whoops and hollers filled the hall behind them.

Heat raced to her cheeks as Anna twisted around, catching sight of

Mina standing in front of the gaggle of her brothers. They beamed at them, some slapping each other on the back or punching at the sky. Koen's smile was bright as she'd ever seen. Brandt gave them an exaggerated wink that had Nik chuckling.

"I suppose we had to tell them sometime." His lips quirked up in the corner as he glanced down at her.

"What a happy ending to wake up to." Mina giggled.

Anna laughed, a wide smile stuck on her face. A happy ending indeed.

In that moment, everything was perfect, and with Nik at her side, she knew they had a bright future ahead, together.

Thank you for reading! Did you enjoy? Please add your review because nothing helps an author more and encourages readers to take a chance on a book than a review.

And don't miss more Reimagined Fairy Tales coming soon, and find more from Megan Van Dyke at www.authormeganvandyke.com

Until then, discover THE NIGHT'S CHOSEN, by City Owl Author, E. E. Hornburg. Turn the page for a sneak peek!

You can also sign up for the City Owl Press newsletter to receive notice of all book releases!

SNEAK PEEK OF THE NIGHT'S CHOSEN
BY E. E. HORNBURG

Eira never dreaded sunset. Or the Moon Festival. Or returning home. Or seeing the Oxarian royal family. She had always looked forward to those things. But not today. If only she could stop time.

No, not stop time, exactly. If she stopped time, Eira would never become queen.

She'd spent her life, all twenty-odd years of it, preparing to reign. She wanted to stop the *wedding*, something she should have been as prepared for as ruling Cresin.

Eira twirled the betrothal band around her wrist. The wedding was going to happen, regardless of what she wanted. With a deep exhale, she closed her eyes and sang, hoping to ease the storm brewing inside and instead focus on the peaceful magic bestowed on her by Luana's priestesses.

The song ignited the crescent moon tattoo on her chest, and as it glowed, stars formed and sparkled around her head. Swirls of darkness poured out of her fingers and mingled with the betrothal band. The tune and words were meant to sooth and calm the soul, make the singer become one with Luana and be as peaceful as the night sky. Yet it did little to ease the darkness, ice, and stars warring underneath Eira's skin.

Luana grant me peace...grant me grace...

The wedding was this week. Tonight, she and Alvis were going to perform the opening ceremony for the Moon Festival, ushering in Luana's season, where the nights became longer than the day. This year, it would also signify the start of the wedding celebrations. As the Chosens of Luana and Ray, it was believed pieces of the souls of the god and goddess resided inside both she and Alvis, making them the closest to the deities their people would ever have. The two had been betrothed her entire life. Yet now the week arrived and she still wasn't ready.

A knock came at the door, breaking Eira's trance. With a wave of her arms, the stars and darkness vanished, and her tattoo faded. Taking a deep breath, she closed her robe and moved to the door, where the knocking was becoming incessant.

"Eira! Will you quit all your praying and let me in?" Rose's voice drifted from the other side of the door.

Her younger sister almost clubbed Eira in the eye with the velvet box she held as Eira pulled the door open.

"I'd imagine after a year of visiting temples, you'd have had enough of praying by now." Rose barreled into the room, leaning on her crutch, and dropped the box on the vanity with a thud.

"It was more necessary than usual today." Eira shut the door behind them and exhaled, pressing her lips together before placing her hands on her hips. "And maybe if I hadn't received dozens of letters from you and Father begging me to come home from those temples, I wouldn't need to pray so long this morning."

Rose waved Eira off. "It wasn't as though you hadn't planned on being home in time for the Moon Festival. We were simply reminding you."

She dropped her crutch and it clattered to the ground as she flopped onto the plush, deep blue bed, pale freckled arms outstretched. Her copper hair splayed out on the quilt like fiery waves.

Eira had only been home for a few days since her yearlong pilgrimage, and had a curious new fascination with Rose. In so many ways she was the same, but in spite of sending letters all year and seeing one another for the holy days, there was still something different Eira couldn't put her finger on. Rose had always been as fiery as her red hair and ready to speak her mind at any given chance. She never sat still for more than a moment. Yet now there was an air of unease and distance about her Eira didn't recognize. This was one of the reasons she was glad to be home, in spite of everything. She wanted to get to know her sister again.

"And it wasn't *dozens* of letters," Rose replied. "It's been a difficult year."

Eira crossed the room and sat on the bed next to Rose.

"I'm aware. It's not as though I was only sitting in temples praying the whole time. I went and visited as many of the villages that needed help as I could. They're recovering from the fires, but it's going to take a long time."

"I'm not only talking about the fire recovery." Rose propped herself on her elbows. "People have been…talking."

Eira shifted in her seat. "People talk often Rose, whether I'm here or not."

"Last night after supper, Father and I overheard the Oxarian king and queen talking. It appears they have been concerned about your dedication to the betrothal."

"Oh?" Eira rubbed the band on her wrist again, as though it were squeezing her tighter with each moment.

"It's been five years since your original wedding date. While Father and Alvis have been more than happy to let you go off to university and travel the kingdoms, and your pilgrimage came at the perfect time after the forest fires so you could help the people while you traveled, King Rahim and Queen Shideh and other nobles from Oxare don't see it the same way."

They were smart. Of course they were. They'd raised Alvis, after all, and he was one of the most intelligent people she knew. Eira had been running for so long, and now there was nowhere else to go.

She straightened her shoulders and smiled. "Well, I'll have to prove them wrong, won't I? The whole opening ceremony for the Moon Festival is the commencement of the wedding celebrations. Once they see me there, they'll know I haven't changed my mind about the wedding."

Rose groaned and pushed into a sitting position. "It's not only them. There're other people, too. They're wondering why you haven't been around."

"That's ridiculous," Eira said, through a clenched jaw. "Royals travel through their kingdoms all the time. Father did before he became king, and still does. Besides, after I get married, I'm going to be in Oxare with Alvis for half the year anyway."

"I know."

Rose's touch on her arm sent a wave of warm comfort through her, and Eira felt her shoulders relax. A hint at the closeness they once had.

"But you know how people are. Normally I wouldn't worry about it, and I've been defending you, especially with the guard, and you have so many who are loyal to you..."

Of course Rose defended her. It's what she'd been doing for her their entire lives. What they both had done for each other. No matter how many months Eira was away, she knew she never had to doubt Rose. Even when Eira doubted herself, if Rose was there, she knew all would be fine.

"But?" Eira prodded.

The hesitation in Rose's voice was enough to make Eira's concerns heighten.

"But it's not only gossip. Some members of the council eventually listened, and talked too. So did Queen Amelia." Rose grimaced at the idea of their stepmother. "You know how she is, though. I don't suspect any of the priestesses have gossiped, but you know how close High Priestess Nyx is to some of the council members. I don't want to concern you, but I'd be lying if I said I wasn't relieved you were coming home. This ceremony could be the start of your gaining back their trust."

The new complication brought more to consider, and Eira rubbed her temples to ease the faint throbbing that had started, and slid off the bed. While she respected High Priestess Nyx as the leader of Luana's temple, the two of them often disagreed in matters of theology and politics.

With Nyx having the ears of many councilmen, planting seeds of doubt, Eira was sure all eyes would be on her even more so during the ceremony and wedding celebrations. Regardless, whatever doubts Eira had about herself or this marriage, she couldn't—and shouldn't—let it interfere with ascending the throne someday. Her people needed to have complete confidence in her.

She may not have been ready to be married to Alvis, but her desire to be queen never faltered.

The remnants of an afternoon snack sat on the vanity next to the velvet box, and Eira took a piece of apple, popped it into her mouth, and gobbled it. When she opened the box to reveal a silver and blue diadem, the stardust sprinkled on the metal twisting around diamonds made it sparkle on its own without needing any light from the room. Eira lifted it out and perched it onto her long dark hair.

It was one of Cresin's oldest antiques and had been worn by Luana's Chosen for hundreds of years. Eira didn't wear it often, but when she did, she found herself sitting straighter, with her shoulders back and head held high. When she wore it, she could imagine herself being a woman worthy to have it on her head and to live up to the legacy she'd been born into.

She could do this.

She had to do this.

People always said she looked like Queen Isadore—the first Chosen of Luana—and Luana herself. Not as though she ever had anything to compare herself to, other than paintings that followers of Goddess Efare created of what they supposed Luana and Isadore looked like. Legend said all of Luana's Chosen through the generations looked like Luana, and all Eira's life people claimed she had the closest likeness since Isadore, with pale—almost translucent—skin, blood-red lips, dark hair, and sky-blue eyes.

Each of the firstborn heiresses of the Cresin throne were the daughters and Chosen of Luana, as the firstborn heirs of Oxare are the sons and Chosen of Ray.

Rose grabbed her crutch and limped over to Eira. They stood side by side in front of the mirror, opposites at first glance, with Eira's gentleness and Rose's wild nature. On further inspection, the two sisters were perfect compliments to one another.

Rose groaned. "You're not even dressed yet and you already look perfect. It's not fair."

"Perhaps it would help if you changed out of your training leathers."

Rose had a unique and free beauty about her, but usually she was too busy beating the other members of the guard on the training grounds for many to notice.

Or at least, not for Rose to notice others noticing her.

Another knock came at the door. The familiar melodic voice of Priestess Cynth came from behind it.

"Your Highness? The opening ceremony is supposed to start soon. We need to prepare you."

Eira's heart sank. Once Priestess Cynth and the ladies-in-waiting came into her chamber, it would be nonstop preparations, celebrations, and being surrounded by people until she was at the altar and at Alvis's side for their wedding at the end of the week. She'd have no peace. No personal space. No chance of stopping the wedding.

Outside her window, past the white rose tree which bloomed and grew up the wall no matter what the season, the songs of Luana's priestesses floated in the air. Part of Eira wished to join them. They didn't know how lucky they were. Free to worship, to make friends, and even to take whoever they wanted to bed whenever they liked.

She could do it. Be one of the priestesses. She'd been bestowed with the same powers, and studied Luana's ways the way they had been—even more so as the Chosen. She'd trained and studied longer than most priestesses, and was given more power at her dedication ceremony as a young woman than the others. Traveling to all of Luana's temples over the past year had shown her this, especially when she'd been in the oldest temple in the Paravian Mountains and her magic awoke there.

Cynth's own mother, who was a priestess there, welcomed Eira with open arms, and when she'd left, promised there would always be a place for Eira.

The town was small, and the mountains dangerous, with strange winged creatures terrorizing them. But she'd still go back in a heartbeat.

And priestesses weren't required to marry.

Eira turned and glanced at herself in the vanity mirror, with the stardust circled around her hair, looking like the midnight sky. She was a queen. Or at least, was going to be.

Queen. This was what she should be focused on. Becoming queen was what was important here.

"Are you all right?"

Her sister's touch on her shoulder brought Eira back to reality.

She blinked and forced a bright smile. "Of course. Why wouldn't I be?"

Rose cocked her head, with a raised brow. "It's a big week, and we've barely talked for months. It's not an odd question."

Priestess Cynth knocked again. "I'm sorry to disturb, Your Highness, but we do need to prepare. Sunset will not wait for us."

No. It would not.

Luana bless it.

Eira took a couple deep breaths, touching her thumb to each of her fingertips to calm herself.

Her pulse slowed to normal, and her muscles relaxed.

"Yes, please come in."

A flurry of women entered the chamber with dresses and cosmetics overflowing in their arms and excited chatter pouring out of their mouths like a waterfall, drowning out the priestess's songs from outside. Lady Evony at the back of the group held glasses in one hand and a bottle of wine in the other. As the women went to work at removing Eira's robe, Evony, court's unofficial patron of festivities, passed out the glasses and poured the wine with extravagant flourishes and twirls, without spilling a single drop.

Whatever calmness had resided in Eira vanished. Her nerves fired off, her senses overloaded at the ruckus surrounding her. She barely registered the weight of the drink in her hand.

The ladies cheered when Evony raised a glass over her curly head of hair, and they all followed suit.

"To our royal highness, Princess Eira," Evony said, "her betrothed Prince Alvis, and the coming of Luana's season. Gods know all the fun happens in the night, after all."

The stardust in the ceremony gown Priestess Cynth held glimmered in her eyes as she looked over her shoulder at Evony.

"I wasn't aware you had the patience to wait for night for your type of fun," Cynth said.

Rose chuckled when Evony placed a hand over her heart and dropped her jaw.

"It's not my fault people beg for my company, no matter the time of day," Evony said.

Rose cleared her throat. "Less drinking, more helping." She stretched her permanently twisted ankle in front of Evony, and wiggled it in a circle. "I can never get my straps tight enough."

Evony sighed before she finished off her wine, then set the glass on the table with a thud, and cocked her voluptuous hip.

"Out of all my talents," she said, "this is the one I'm asked to do. Whoever said coming to Farren Castle was going to be glamorous, never mentioned this."

"Yes, I'm sure the fish in Slania are much more glamorous," Rose said.

"It took months to get the smell out of my clothes." Evony took the straps from the pile of Rose's ceremony clothes, and winked.

Within minutes, the white leather-like straps were wrapped around Rose's ankle, straightening and smoothing the limb. It had been a gift from their grandmother, who served Kutlaous, the god of nature, in Eral Forest. The straps were enchanted with fae magic to give Rose the strength she needed to walk without a crutch for short periods. Such as evening ceremonies and balls.

Or as Rose preferred, on the training grounds and while patrolling the castle.

The white of the straps faded until they were invisible, showing off Rose's tattoo, dedicated to Aros, the god of war and hunting. When unbound by the straps, the tattoo appeared to be thorny rose vines etched into Rose's warped and twisted skin. When straightened by the straps, it was the sword of Aros, with white and red roses wrapped around the blade, like the roses outside each of their bedchamber windows, planted after their mother died. A symbol of Rose's dedication not only to her god, but to their bond as sisters and princesses.

Something stirred inside Eira each time she saw it.

The time spent preparing went by in a blur of cloth and perfumes and stardust. The sparkling gown clung to Eira like a second skin once it was pulled over her head and down her body. The skirt swirled around her legs and ankles in a silver river. The neckline, like all of her ceremonial gowns, dipped low and wide to expose her tattoo. A symbol to be showed off and admired, proving she belonged to Luana. It was a fashion Eira had grown used to after she'd received her tattoo.

When she was younger and first growing into her body, she'd felt exposed and shy. Now she was proud to show her dedication to Luana and kingdom. She enjoyed the power mixed with sensuality in her costumes.

Where there wasn't fabric, there were crystals and stardust stuck and painted to her arms, legs, and bosom. This day, it was a gown she could hide in. In this gown, she not only belonged to Luana, but *was* Luana. Goddess of the night, darkness, and winter. In this gown, she was supposed to welcome the changing of the seasons, where the daytime was shortened to make way for longer nights.

She was also supposed to greet her lover, Ray, god of the sun.

Eira could only imagine what Alvis's ceremony attire would look like.

Perhaps Eira could at least pretend to be Luana if she was dressed for the part, and be separate from herself.

Time moved too quickly, and before she knew it she was being escorted by Priestess Cynth out of her bedchamber and toward the great hall. All the attendees were waiting for them there. Her father, stepmother, Alvis and his family, and all of the lords and ladies of the kingdom. Her kingdom. The one she'd spent months helping to regain their bearings after flash forest fires burned through the villages, leaving only ashes in their wake. The one she'd been born in, and who believed in her through every step of her life.

Until she'd started running away five years ago.

Now she returned, and people were talking. Eira's cheeks burned as shame washed over her. She'd been foolish and immature all this time. So many others had it far worse than she did, and Alvis was a good man. One of the best she'd ever known. He was the perfect person to bring the kingdoms of Cresin and Oxare together the way Isadore and Sanson did all those centuries ago, when they were at war with one another.

Rose was at her side when they approached the great hall's door, and squeezed Eira's hand. She was out of her training leathers and wore a simple silver gown which resembled a long jacket with short sleeves. It was shorter in the front, revealing tight leggings, and billowed out in the back like a cloak. If it weren't for Rose's usual playful smile, she'd look regal.

"You'll be wonderful," Rose said.

She gave her sister a warm hug, then walked away and into the great hall, leaving Eira and Priestess Cynth alone. Eira pushed her shoulders back and straightened her diadem, despite that her heart sank as it begged her to turn and run.

No, it was time she behaved like the future queen and Chosen they all pictured her to be.

———

Don't stop now. Keep reading with your copy of THE NIGHT'S CHOSEN, by City Owl Author, E. E. Hornburg.

Don't miss more Reimagined Fairy Tales coming soon, and find more from Megan Van Dyke at www.authormeganvandyke.com

Until then, discover THE NIGHT'S CHOSEN, by City Owl Author, E. E. Hornburg!

≫━━━◦━━━≪

Chosen of the Moon Goddess. Destined to rule. Fated to marry.

A quest to save her family, kingdom, and heart.

For the past five years Princess Eira has run from her impending wedding. As much as she loves her goddess and kingdom, she's searched the kingdoms for another way to rule as queen someday while also choosing her own husband.

Yet, Eira's claim to the crown falls into jeopardy when her father, King Brennus, is poisoned and fated to a sleep of living death and Eira is next on the assassin's hit list – who happens to be her stepmother, Queen Amelia.

After Eira escapes Queen Amelia's clutches she journeys to the northern Paravian mountains in search of an enchanted cup to save her father.

Her quest is more than she anticipated with evading Queen Amelia's guards, traveling with the one man she shouldn't be with, and having to bargain with the ancient dragon guarding the enchanted cup.

She'll have to decide how to save her family and kingdom, even if it means sacrificing her heart and all she's wanted her whole life.

≫━━━◦━━━≪

Please sign up for the City Owl Press newsletter for chances to win special subscriber-only contests and giveaways as well as receiving information on upcoming releases and special excerpts.

All reviews are **welcome** and **appreciated**. Please consider leaving one on your favorite social media and book buying sites.

Escape Your World. Get Lost in Ours! City Owl Press at www.cityowlpress.com.

ACKNOWLEDGMENTS

This book is dedicated to my husband and the love that he's shown me throughout our time together. However, it's also a love letter to everyone who has struggled with bullying and/or being made to feel less than they are. Unfortunately, it's something that many of us have experienced, myself included. I wish I could say it was limited to my youth, and honestly, that's probably when it was the worst, but it's something I've endured as an adult too. It can happen when you least expect it and from people who you think are there to lift you up and support you. I was bullied in school, in the workplace, and even while trying to find my place in the writing community. It's from the latter that the idea for this book sprung to life.

Some people are willing to do terrible things in secret and then play the victim before the masses, turning others against the very person they've wronged. I'd like to think most people aren't inherently bad or evil. Maybe something in their life causes them to lash out. Maybe tearing others down makes them feel better about themselves. After all, if other people like them, they can't be terrible all the time, right? Bad behavior, especially at the expense of others, is never okay, though. It shouldn't be okay. It shouldn't be normalized or accepted. And, I firmly believe that a person's bad deeds will come to light eventually.

Those beliefs sparked an idea: What if Cinderella just pretended to be mistreated to gain sympathy? What if she was truly the terrible one? Would anyone ever know?

The entire novel sprang from those questions during a moment of personal pain and hardship.

I hope that reading this book gives others strength. You're not alone.

No matter how dark things get, they can get better. You will find people in your life who see you for who you truly are and love you for your true self. Good will win out in the end. And if you're the bully? Maybe there's a reason why you hurt others. Maybe this book will help you understand that wound and choose a different path in the future. No matter where this story finds you, I hope it leads you to your own happy ending.

To all my family and friends who show me so much love and support day after day, I am so thankful for you. I literally would not be here without you, and I am so blessed to have you in my life. To my Oceans11 CP group, y'all are the best. Seriously. You pick me up and patch up my wounds more than you know, and you never fail to help me through the hard times, especially when the bullies come out to play. To all my writing friends, especially my fellow Owls, thank you for always being such a source of encouragement, knowledge, help, and support. I couldn't do this without you. My Street Team, you all are such a wonder, and I'm so honored to be on this journey with you. Finally, to my readers, thank you for letting me live this dream by sharing my stories with you. Writing this book was therapeutic for me in a way I didn't know I needed, and I truly hope you take something good from it as well.

ABOUT THE AUTHOR

MEGAN VAN DYKE is a fantasy romance author with a love for all things magical and romantic, especially fairytales and anything with a happily ever after. Many of her stories include themes of family (whether born into or found) and a sense of home and belonging, which are important aspects of her life as well. When not writing, Megan loves to spend time with her family, cook, play video games, and explore the great outdoors. Megan currently lives with her family in Florida. Be sure to sign up for her newsletter so you never miss a minute!

www.authormeganvandyke.com

instagram.com/authormeganvandyke
facebook.com/AuthorMeganVanDyke
twitter.com/AuthorMeganVD
tiktok.com/@authormeganvandyke
bookbub.com/authors/megan-van-dyke

ABOUT THE PUBLISHER

City Owl Press is a cutting edge indie publishing company, bringing the world of romance and speculative fiction to discerning readers.

Escape Your World. Get Lost in Ours!

www.cityowlpress.com

facebook.com/CityOwlPress
twitter.com/cityowlpress
instagram.com/cityowlbooks
pinterest.com/cityowlpress
tiktok.com/@cityowlpress

www.ingramcontent.com/pod-product-compliance
Lightning Source LLC
Chambersburg PA
CBHW022209010726
47493CB00002B/489